Granville Moody

A life's retrospect

Autobiography of Rev. Granville Moody

Granville Moody

A life's retrospect
Autobiography of Rev. Granville Moody

ISBN/EAN: 9783337112899

Printed in Europe, USA, Canada, Australia, Japan

Cover: Foto ©Raphael Reischuk / pixelio.de

More available books at **www.hansebooks.com**

Granville Moody

A LIFE'S RETROSPECT

AUTOBIOGRAPHY

OF

REV. GRANVILLE MOODY, D. D.

(BRIGADIER GENERAL BY BREVET)

EDITED BY

REV. SYLVESTER WEEKS, A. M., D. D.

CINCINNATI:
CRANSTON AND STOWE
NEW YORK:
HUNT AND EATON
1890.

PREFACE.

THIS book is strictly an autobiography so far as the writing and collecting of previously printed matter is concerned. The name "Retrospect" is Dr. Moody's own selection for a title. He quotes: "The retrospect of a life well spent affords peace of mind in old age."

I have endeavored to arrange the subjects and events in chronological order, but found some difficulty, and possibly did not in every case succeed. Many of the newspaper clippings were without date. Dr. Moody, like Paul, was in the habit of "going off at a word;" that is, the association of ideas suggested something kindred to the subject in hand, and he turned aside from the direct narrative to notice that, and, in some instances, the two circumstances were far apart in point of time. I have grouped together facts and incidents of a similar nature, arranging them chronologically, as nearly as the data enabled me so to do. The reports from charges, dreams, advocacy of reforms, and prayers, illustrate this grouping of kindred events. In the material furnished by Dr. Moody there were a number of sermons and addresses, lectures and essays, which it was impossible to embody in the limits of a single volume. Enough, however, has been furnished to allow the autobiographer to reveal his distinct personality, and to demonstrate his interest in every religious, moral, philanthropic, educational, and patriotic subject before the people in the half century of his active life; and also to show his mode of thought, manner of treatment, and his rhetorical setting of his subjects.

He was verbose, without reduncancy. The length of his literary productions, whether written or spoken, was owing to the abundance of matter, and was not a mere superfluity of words. He was descended from generations of scholarly ancestors, graduates of Harvard, Dartmouth, and other New England colleges. His father graduated from Dartmouth in 1798, and became one of the best educators of the period. Dr. Moody's reading was classical, historical, solid; his trained memory was capacious, ready, and retentive. His splendid physique gave him the physical qualifications as to presence and power of endurance for an orator, while his well-modulated voice enabled him to pass from the stentorian tone of command to the depth of tender pathos, and the play of his expressive features, lighting up his countenance till it was all aglow with emotion, intensified the impression, and fixed it indelibly in the mind and heart of the hearer. He was six feet four inches tall, with development in proportion that was massive, without being adipose. I have in my mind a picture like this. I asked him to offer the closing prayer at an early Christmas morning prayer-meeting in Ripley, in 1873. He kneeled on his right knee, the left being at a right angle, his hands resting on the top of his heavy black cane with massive silver head, his body erect, with the cape of his military overcoat draping his shoulders; his head, covered with luxuriant white hair, was a dome of vigorous thought, while his speaking face was turned heavenward. The pose was one for an artist. His prayer was the language of one at ease with God, culminating in thanks for "the unutterable gift."

One familiar with the Miami Valley could trace his itinerary by the doctrines he combated—Calvinism at Oxford, Universalism at Montgomery and West Chester, Socinianism at Franklin, Radicalism at Lebanon, and intemperance, Catholicism, and disloyalty in Dayton, Springfield, Cincinnati, and Piqua. And yet some of his dearest friends were his antipodes in doctrine; showing that his antagonisms were not against persons, but against systems of belief. Then, too, the subjects of his communications to the Church papers indicate the depth of his interest in the polity of the Church. He wrote and spoke on the division of the Book Concern, episcopacy, pewed churches, the presiding eldership, and various phases of slavery.

His religious experience was deep, founded in the Word of God; the one word that impressed me as I searched and classified his memoirs of himself, was "authority." To duly constituted authority—divine, ecclesiastical, or civil—he bowed with unquestioning loyalty. His early training in a pious house established him in the principles of morality; his prayerful and careful examination in his youth of the doctrines of religion, with the Bible as the ultimate appeal, settled him immovably in matters of faith; his conversion, in which he was Scripturally, thoroughly, and consciously saved, was a genuine experience, affirming his morality, confirming his doctrine, and eminently qualifying him to deliver his gospel message with no reservations as to its adaptation to save. His was a growing experience. At the close of his itinerant ministry he wrote:

"From the memorable November 25, 1831, a divine energy has been forming me, amid many conflicts and various experiences, into a growing conformity to God's perfect will; and, upon the whole review, I find that I have been putting off the old man of covetousness, self-will, pride, and self-indulgence, and have been putting on the new character of humility, submission to God, and love to God and to men,—to good men because of their goodness, and commiseration, and pitying love to the naturally degenerate portion of society, who remain in the bonds of iniquity and in the gall of bitterness, and strangers still to the covenant of grace—recognized as those having no hope, because without God in the world.

" I can also attest that the bud of regeneration, the divine beginning of the new life, has blossomed and progressed and ripened into the fruit unto holiness, with the assured prospect of everlasting life. . . .

"I can also attest that a life of devotional, self-

denying, and active piety has become more habitual
and delightful, and sin in any and every form, as
viewed in myself and in others, has become more
and more hateful and painful, deformed and horrible, and vile and detestable and detested. . . .
My contemplations of the heavenly state are becoming more realizing; my aspirations for it are
more fervent, and my desires for earthly things are
more moderate. I live, yet not I, but Christ liveth
in me; and the life I now live in the flesh is a life
of faith in the Son of God, who loved me and gave
himself for me, and to me as well. Thus, by faith
in Christ, my life has been a progressive life, has
been a life of religious decision, of care for my
own personal salvation, of devotional piety; a life
of assurance of acceptance with God in Christ; a
life of communion with the Holy Trinity, of upward and onward tendencies, of cheerful submission to providential allotments, of laborious usefulness in persuading men to reformation that flows
from gospel salvation; a life of patriotic devotion
to our country; a life of active opposition to intemperance and Sabbath desecration; and my
closing prayer for all my family is, that our sons
and daughters may walk by all these rules, and
mind the same things, and meet wife and self in
heaven."

He was a connecting link between the pioneer
and the present ministry in Ohio. He diligently
instructed the children in every pastoral charge;
he observed and enjoined the quarterly fast; he
urged and insisted upon attendance upon the

means of grace, of which he considered class-meetings not the least.

At the session of his Conference in 1886—I quote from the Minutes—"a committee was appointed to examine and report upon the manuscript autobiography of brother G. Moody, as requested by the Conference, and the following brethren were so appointed: R. S. Rust, A. Lowrey, C. H. Payne, William Herr, S. D. Clayton, A. B. Leonard, and J. F. Marlay." Appointed on the first day of the session, they reported on the fifth day as follows:

"The Committee, to whom was referred the manuscript autobiography of our venerable and beloved brother, Rev. Granville Moody, D. D., would respectfully report:

"1. We greatly rejoice in the presence of Dr. Moody with us at this session of our conference, and that we have been permitted to hear once more on the floor of the Conference, and in the devotional exercises of the session, the familiar tones of a voice which we have been so long accustomed to follow as that of a born, tried, and trusted leader. As a man evidently called of God to take a leading part in public and ecclesiastical affairs, and richly endowed by high qualities of physical, intellectual, and spiritual manhood, Dr. Moody has been a conspicuous and honored figure in the most eventful period of our country's history; a man distinguished above his fellows for labors abundant in Church and State, whose praise is not only in all the Churches, but which also occupies a large place in the history of the great Rebellion, in which he bore so noble a part in defense of the Union.

"2. We rejoice that in his enforced retirement from active service, on account of impaired physical health, Dr. Moody has found time to collect the facts and incidents of his long and useful life in the form of an autobiography, which we have examined as fully as our time would allow, and which we take great pleasure in recommending for publication by the Western Book Concern, as a contribution of rare interest and value to our denominational and biographical literature."

This report was signed by all the committee, and was adopted by the Cincinnati Conference by a rising vote.

On Sunday morning, May 29, 1887, Dr. Moody, in company with his son, Charles P. Moody, was going from his country residence to Jefferson, Iowa, to preach a memorial sermon before the George H. Thomas Post, No. 23, G. A. R. In turning a corner a trace became detached; this allowed the breast-yoke to move forward, so that, the carriage-pole falling, both occupants of the carriage were hurled violently out. On the third day pneumonia of a type defying medical skill developed, and the end drew near. His life-long familiarity with the Scriptures was manifested during his closing days of life in his frequent repetitions of the "exceeding great and precious promises," which were as manna to his soul. He looked forward to the goodly company awaiting him—bishops, ministers, and from the laity. He alluded to the more than eight thousand who, through his ministry, had been led to God; many of them would meet him. "Best of all who have been with me on earth, Lizzie will meet me there." A little later he uttered his last connected sentence, repeatedly exclaiming: "On the tree! on the tree!" At five minutes before six o'clock, on Saturday, June 4, 1887, his spirit departed, passing out of the Saturday night of earth into the unending Sabbath of a blessed eternity. The funeral services in the church at Mount Vernon were participated by Revs. Dr. Heald, pastor; Luke Fish, A. K. Baird; President W. F. King, of Cornell College; C. M. Sessions, I. W. Joyce, D. D. (now bishop), Chaplain J. H. Lozier, and Captain C. W. Kepler, of the G. A. R. Post.

Awaiting the resurrection of the just, his mortal remains rest in the soil of the State he chose for the home of his declining days, while his ransomed spirit sings with deeper fervor than earth could know, his favorite:

> "Thou art my soul's bright morning star,
> And thou my rising sun."

We trust this Autobiography may be full of pleasant reminiscences to the older readers, and an inspiration and guide to the younger.

SYLVESTER WEEKS.

CINCINNATI, September 3, 1889.

CONTENTS.

11

Chapter XX.

ADVOCACY OF REFORM AND LIBERTY.

Chapter XXI.

COMBATING ERROR.

Chapter XXII.

FRAGMENTS OF CLERICAL LIFE.

Chapter XXIII.

AS COLONEL OF A REGIMENT.

Chrpter XXIV.

IN CIVIL LIFE.

CHAPTER XXV.

MORE FRAGMENTS OF CLERICAL LIFE.

CHAPTER XXVI.

SUPERANNUATION.

INTRODUCTION.

A N Introduction to any book written by Rev. Granville Moody would seem a superfluous task, and
it would be such were the work designed only for
the Methodists of Ohio, and especially for those now
well advanced in life. The same is true of the work
which sets forth his personal experiences, labors, and
observations. He was too well known to need introduction, and the Methodist people who knew him
require no inducement to read what he has written
concerning himself, or with reference to the times in
which he lived.

It is difficult to realize that one so conspicuous and
impressive in his personality is gone from our midst,
and that only a volume remains to perpetuate his
memory, and in some degree to continue his influence
in the Church he served so long and so well. For
half a century and more he was a prominent partici-
pant in the affairs of Methodism, working with all
the energies of his enthusiastic nature for the up-
building of the kingdom of righteousness, and no one
who knew him will even suspect that he lacked a
single element of loyalty to God, to his Church, or to
his native land. What he believed, he believed, with
all his heart, and what he did, he did with his might.

He entered the ministry at a time when it was

necessary for Methodists to "contend for the faith"
they professed, and to do it with an aggressiveness
that would, at the present day, seem intolerant and
offensive.   Mr. Moody was not a man to be a spectator
in the presence of an emergency demanding positive
exertion to maintain what he believed to be the truth
of God.   Hence, in early life, he prepared himself
thoroughly to defend the doctrines of his Church ; and
his preaching, without lacking elements of spiritual
power, was rich in theological thought and forceful
in polemic learning.   He championed the cause he
espoused, and stood ready to measure swords with any
who crossed his path in the advocacy of Calvinism,
Unitarianism, or Universalism.   It was not merely
the impulsiveness of his nature that made Mr. Moody
active and prominent in the controversies of his day.
He possessed an intellect of wonderful activity and
force, an industry which was untiring, a heart that
burned with zeal for the truth and the right; and, possibly, no one excelled him in pure dislike to all that
seemed dishonoring to God or the Church.   It was not
in him to remain uninformed in the current thought of
his time, or to lack any knowledge available for the
defense of the positions his conscience approved.

It sometimes occurs that men of marked peculiarities, or of extraordinary strength in given lines of
action, come to be so well known in those things
which distinguish them from others, that their general
ability to do the ordinary work of their calling is
scarcely appreciated.   Mr. Moody was a man of
striking peculiarities, yet he was also well rounded

and thoroughly capable, and eminently efficient in every department of duty as a Christian minister and pastor. While he became proficient as a speaker and writer in the controversies which belonged to his times, he developed large capacity for all the services required at his hands, and neither the social nor spiritual interests of his charges suffered from neglect or inattention. He sought to understand Methodism in her inner life as well as in her doctrinal principles; and his allegiance to her ecclesiastical methods was far from being a blind devotion to unappreciated traditions. With a generous love for all evangelical denominations, and with a catholicity unknown to smaller minds, he grasped the connectional system of Methodism, made himself familiar with its forms and usages, and gave to these an intelligent approval which carried with it the warmth of his great soul. He was, therefore, an ardent Methodist, while he despised bigotry.

The following chapters will give a better idea of the characteristics hinted at in the foregoing periods, than could be given by further descriptive phrases in the brief space allowed for this Introduction. He was a man of great mind, great heart, great impulses, and great intelligence; and whatever may be said of his peculiarities, it is not probable that any one will ever think of him as other than a man of high purpose, lofty aim, noble sentiment, pure thought, and honorable life. The record he has made, and the portraiture here given, will be read and cherished by thousands who admired him in life, and who will associate him in memory with the heroes of Methodism, as well as with the heroes of the Nation.

The literature of the country and of the Church is enriched by such a volume as this. Its perusal by the young will enlarge the horizon of their thought, and stimulate their desire to be loyal to God and to every good work. It presents the thoughts and experiences of one whose life was a success, and whose example in study and zeal and work and sacrifice, as well as in devotion and patriotism, may be imitated with profit.

S. M. MERRILL.

CHICAGO, 1890.

AUTOBIOGRAPHY

OF

GRANVILLE MOODY.

CHAPTER I.

INFANCY AND CHILDHOOD.

AN autobiography is the life of a person written by himself. It is a delicate and difficult task to write one's own history. It lays one open to the charge of egotism or self-glorification. It were better far if "every Johnson had his Boswell." But, then, every Boswell might be too friendly to his Johnson, and, knowing his subject but in part, and disposed to lionize his friend, he might be suspected of partiality.

The subject of this autobiography was born in Portland, Me., on January 2, 1812. His parents were William and Harriet Brooks Moody. A family legend is that his birth was accompanied with the most violent storm that had broken on that ocean-girt land within the memory of the oldest inhabitant. Whether "the prince of the power of the air" had any agency in this tempest at this epoch is not for me to determine. But as this juncture marked also the beginning of the War of 1812, I came, and amid a rejoicing circle waked "maternal love, the word that sums all bliss." Family

history speaks lovingly of my infancy, and of my
baptism when six weeks old—presented at God's
holy altar in the old frame church where the Rev.
Edward Payson, D. D., faithfully preached the
gospel of the Son of God to crowded audiences,
and solemnly administered the ordinances of baptism and the Lord's Supper. There stood my
parents, and presented me to God, taking upon
themselves the parental obligations to "bring me
up in the nurture and admonition of the Lord."
And doubly sure I am that never into holier hands
was infant form committed than when, from my
mother's bosom, my father's hands conveyed me to
the fond arms of him who stood in Jesus' place
and name and welcomed me to his kind and warm
embrace. Giving me back to my parents' arms
and hearts, he said: "This child is now the Lord's
by your act of consecration; take it as his property, and bring it up for God and, 'he will give you
your wages.'" He closed the service with a prayer
for parents and the child then baptized, and for
the children all, that they might make an unbroken
family in heaven. This is the authentic record
of that great hour in my early life when Pastor
Payson prayed for me and for the family in his
saintly style, with fullness of faith that God would
be my parents' God and the God of their children
after them.

My parents were of good New England stock,
pure Christians, believing in the Bible as a book
divinely inspired, containing the mind and will of
God in our salvation from sin and from its results,

revealing Jesus Christ as the great object of faith
and hope and love. To them were born seven
sons and four daughters, to wit: Harriet Peaslee,
John Brooks, William Henry, Louisa Brooks, Granville, Ellen, George V., Nathaniel Peaslee, Edward
Payson, Samuel Stillman, and Sarah Hudson. My
father was the sixth son of Humphrey Moody,
whose farm adjoined Haverhill on the Merrimac,
eighteen miles from the Atlantic Ocean, and
twenty-seven miles north of Boston. Six of my
father's brothers served as volunteers in the Revolutionary War. My grandfather's house was
burned by the British in 1776, and the family
scattered. After peace was declared, the sons
gathered at the old homestead to rebuild. In
clearing away the rubbish, some one with his mat-
tock knocked off the neck of a cider-bottle, and
lifting it out of its sandy bed, imbibed the ancient
beverage, and gave notice of his luck. His fellow-
laborers found that the whole cellar floor was occupied by such bottles, the interstices and six
inches over the tops of the corks being covered
with sand. The *débris* of the dwelling falling
into the cellar had formed a seven years' covering.
It is also part of the story that within an hour
there could not be found a sober man on the
premises. The treasure was all exhumed and
distributed in quantities of a dozen or half-dozen
bottles to the veteran officers of the Revolutionary
War, Governor John Hancock sharing in the results of the discovery.

In 1632, twelve years after the Pilgrims landed,

my great-great-grandfather, William Moody, wife,
and three sons, named Caleb, Joshua, and Samuel,
immigrated into Plymouth Colony from Scotland.
Humphrey Moody, my grandfather, was a large
land-holder in East Haverhill, and was much respected as one of its best citizens. He married
Abigail, daughter of General Nathaniel Peaslee,
of Haverhill, who gave each of his children a
valuable farm. His word was law and gospel in
State and Church. Born and raised a Quaker, his
house was their home. He lived to be ninety
years old. He was known as a "Commoner," as
he held large bodies of land by public authority.
He represented his district in the Legislature.
He was a consistent and devout Christian, a member of the Congregational Church for over sixty
years. His daughter was remarkable for her pre-
eminent mental powers, her extensive education,
and her great range of reading. Having read the
public library of Haverhill thoroughly, she then
undertook the same of the library of Boston. She
was regarded as the encyclopedia of her day.
She was a woman of great firmness of mind and
decision of character, and withal a real statesman,
her society being sought and her opinion highly
regarded by persons of the greatest distinction in
State affairs. She lived to the age of eighty-two
years in almost uninterrupted health and vigor,
erect and active as when in youth. After living
in widowhood for twenty-five years she married
General James Brickett, M. D. He was eminently
useful in the Revolutionary army as a physician,

and commanded a regiment at the battle of Bunker Hill.

My father graduated at Dartmouth College with all its honors. After graduation, he was employed as principal of the seminary in Portland, Me. He was very successful as a teacher of navigation, being especially expert in lunar calculations. In 1805 he engaged in the fur-trade; but great depreciation in prices made his venture a failure, and he returned to the principalship of the seminary, in which he continued till 1816, when he removed to Baltimore, Md., having been elected president of the first female seminary in that place.

My mother's maiden name was Harriet Brooks, daughter of Captain John Brooks, a native of South Carolina, holding the office of captain in the Continental army during the Revolutionary War. He was ordered to the military station in Salem, Mass., where he made his home after peace was declared. His ancestors came to South Carolina with other Huguenots. My mother was one of three children. She was born June 1, 1787, in Boston, at the "Boston Stone" residence in the then "South End." This stone was a landmark in the original survey of town-lots. It was imported from England as a paint-mill. It was a large, square stone, having an excavated center about two feet in diameter, into which a ball of stone, of slightly smaller diameter, was placed. A mortise six by six inches received an upright post, and a sweep-pole was fitted to the top of this. A horse, moving around in a circle, turned the stone,

which was used for grinding paints in oil. While
I was attending the General Conference in Boston
as a delegate of the Cincinnati Conference I appropriated an afternoon in hunting up this relic.
I found it built into the rear wall of a warehouse
on an oblique street, within one square of the
celebrated Cockerill church. The stone ball was
so built into the wall as to expose a projecting
disk, oblong in shape and standing six inches out
from the surface of the wall. On this disk an
eagle with outspread wings is depicted in gold-
leaf. My mother resided in the house then on
this spot till her marriage, March 28, 1803.

My maternal grandmother was Sarah Hathorn.
She was born after the death of her father, and
was brought up by her grandfather, Mr. Eustis,
of Salem, an eminently pious man, a member of
the Congregational Church. He fasted at regular
intervals, abstaining from even a cup of water
and the use of his pipe from sundown to sundown. He died at the age of ninety years, very
happy, saying: "All is peace and joy and hope."

My uncle Benjamin Moody was very tall, being six feet four and one-half inches high; and
withal remarkably muscular and active. He re-
tained his faculties when ninety years old. When
eighty-five he walked thirty-five miles in a day.
In the Revolutionary War, in a repulse of his company, he stood his ground, and went for the red-
coats with his clenched fists, knocking down fifteen men before he yielded. A platoon charged
on him with fixed bayonets; but a British officer

spurred in between the charging platoon and
Uncle Ben, and shouted: "Halt! Halt! So true a
man shall not be killed." For fifty years after,
when a man showed great valor, it was said: "He
fights like Ben Moody." He died at Landaff,
N. H., in 1850, aged ninety-six years.

In my father's valuable papers I find an item
of family antiquity. It is a transcript from the
Court of Heraldry in London. It purports to be
"The Coat of Arms of Baron Moody." It is a warrior, armed with a shield portraying the Holy
Cross, showing that he had been a Crusader. On
his head is a helmet, with the visor down; on the
summit of the helmet is a badger, couchant; beneath this a festooned roll of honor or scarf of
valor. Baron Moody was one of England's sturdy
men who combined to extort Magna Charta from
King John in 1215. The badger denotes persistency. Natural history asserts that he can not be
conquered; he may be killed, but never cowed.

This reminds me of an incident which occurred in May, 1873. I happened to meet Jesse
Grant, the venerable father of General Ulysses S.
Grant. After salutations, the aged man said to
me: "Do you know that you and my son Ulysses
are blood relations?" I replied that I was aware
that our families were related, but did not know
how the kinship came about. He added: "Well,
my father, Noah Grant, married Margaret Moody,
of New Hampshire, and I am one of that family
of children. I named one of my daughters Margaret Moody, to keep the maiden name of my

mother in the family.   Ulysses gets his persistence
from his grandmother.   I never knew two persons
more alike than this grandmother and grandson.
Whatever he undertook to do, he did with all his
might; he always held on with great determination till it was finished.   I have often thought
that I would tell you about this relationship when
I should meet you."   I thanked him for the information, and told him of the "badger" and
its heraldic significance of persistency.

In a book published in Boston in 1847 by
Charles C. P. Moody, entitled "Biographical Sketch
of the Moody Family," a succinct account of eighteen families named Moody is given, of whom ten
were clergymen.   An interview which I had with
Daniel Webster shows the estimate he placed
upon the family.   Being on my way to Boston in
1852 to attend the General Conference, having
some pending business in Washington, I called
on Ohio's favorite son, Hon. Thomas Corwin, then
Secretary of the Treasury.   He suggested that we
call on the peerless Webster, Secretary of State.
Away we sped, and on entering the office, there
sat the grand man at his desk, a grand presence,—
sallow countenance; magnificent mouth; broad and
massive and finely chiseled chin; more than human eyes, at great width from each other, and
deeply set and of lustrous beaming; an ample and
full bearing chest, agile limbs, and courtly feet.
All combined to make and mark a manly form,
befitting tabernacle of the mighty spiritual force
which inhabited that magnificent presence.   His

dress was in rigid taste,—a mazarine-blue coat with gold buttons, a buff vest, pantaloons of snowy whiteness, white silk stockings, and well-fitting shoes. I felt that I was in the presence of a great man, may be the greatest in the United States.

Mr. Corwin advancing, said: "Good morning, Mr. Secretary! Allow me the pleasure of introducing my special friend and former pastor, Rev. Granville Moody, of Springfield, Ohio." Mr. Webster rose to his feet, erect, firm, self-poised, and with extended hand and benignant smile, responded: "I am pleased, sir, to make your acquaintance; but tell me whence you derive that old New England name. That name does not belong to Ohio." "No, sir," I replied, "I am from New England, name and all. I was born in Portland, Me., though my mother was a Boston lady." "Then, sir," he said, "I claim you as one of our Old Bay State men; and let me congratulate you on bearing one of New England's most ancient and honored names—a name without which New England's history, in Church and State, can not be written."

CHAPTER II.

BOYISH YEARS.

MY memory dates back to about the first two years of my age. I can distinctly recollect my mother in her large easy-chair, seated with her children arranged in a semicircle for cate-chisation on the afternoon of Sabbath. As she closed with devout and weeping prayer, I would look up with wondering sympathy and listen to her melting prayer, and cry myself because my mother cried in prayer. Later a year, or when I was three and a half years old, I distinctly re-member this petition: "O, may I never raise a babe or rear a child that shall be lost, but may we make a family in heaven!" That form of words holds precedence in my memory.

When four years of age I remember my father addressing me whilst I was worrying myself trun-dling the family wheelbarrow, saying: "Well, Granville, how would you like to go with me out on the wide ocean, and go by ship to Baltimore?" My heart leaped for joy as the new idea pos-sessed my mind, and I said: "O pa, let us go; it will be so nice!" I remember how my father stood and looked as we held this colloquy. I remember the busy preparation and the family talks and prayers connected with this enterprise.

How clearly does Dr. Payson stand out before my retrospective view! In his frequent pastoral visits he had always some cheering word suited to my tender years; and his visits were received by my parents with devout gladness and gratitude, and seemly reverence for the reverend man, as though his business were somehow divine. My parents' regard for this holy man of God, with seeming deference to his will, diffused a veneration which environed and enthroned him in our estimation. He was familiarly known and styled as "Payson, the pastor." My father and mother would often remind me and say: "My dear child, that is the holy man by whom you were baptized when we gave you to be the Lord's."

My memory is filled with the preparations for our removal—the packing of furniture and boxes and bales of carpeting. The day we left, Dr. Payson was present, and engaged in prayer for the family, with that particular unction which made each one feel that he was committed to the gracious care of the great Father, "without whom not a sparrow falleth on the ground." At about one o'clock we left the house together, Dr. Payson with us, conducting me by the hand down to the wharf of the finest ocean harbor on the whole Atlantic coast. We went on board the *Brutus*, a large and well-built brig, fit to battle with warring winds and surging waves. This was in the early spring of 1816. We had another season of brief prayer in the cabin of the brig; then all went up the companion-way but myself.

While the passengers were waving their "adieus" with white handkerchiefs to the friends they left behind, the brig cast off her hawsers and swung out on Casco Bay, beautiful with its numerous islands—some say three hundred and sixty-five in all. I found a door open into the bread-room, and, climbing up to a small, open window, was amused with the rushing waves made by the brig, which was now under strong headway, east by south, under a stiff breeze. The hissing, boiling waves, with thousands of little water-flowers gleaming in the billowy current, amused me with the entire novelty for awhile; then looking around, I espied a barrel of ship-bread, each biscuit about the size of a large dinner-plate, and about the same thickness. These I commenced throwing out of the little window, one after another, till I could see a straight line of them a mile long, rising and falling on the intervening waves, to my great wonder and delight. Meanwhile all on deck were surprised at this appearance on the ocean wave, probably concluding that the brig was pursued by circular fishes, unknown before. While all were in wonderment, the mate leaned over the stern of the vessel to ascertain more accurately the nature of the phenomenon, when his eye saw that they were ship-biscuit thrown out of the bread-room by some agency. He ran down the companion-way and came upon me with fury beaming in his eyes and countenance. He seized me with his brawny hands and uttered a most profane oath, the first I had ever heard, and said: "You little rascal, if I catch you at this again, I'll pitch you right out of that window." Locking the door, he rushed up-stairs and reported progress, leaving me to my reflections. The horrible profanity of the mate made me shudder with affright, and left such an alarming impression upon my mind as was profitable to me during all my after life.

After a stormy trip, we gladly entered Chesapeake Bay, and beat our way two hundred miles amid scenes of beauty on either shore till we were safely landed at our journey's end. Our house was on Gay Street, corner of Orange Alley. Here, too, we found the holy Sabbath-day. Dr. Inglis's church, on the corner of Lexington and Broadway, had two steeples, galleries around three sides, and in the end opposite the pulpit was a massive pipe-organ. The back of the pulpit was hung with heavy maroon drapery in dark folds, for twenty-five or thirty feet. The pulpit was reached by two long flights of stairs. Our pew was No. 61, immediately in the rear of the one occupied by William Wirt, the great lawyer of Baltimore. Mother sat next the wall, then sister Harriet, then brothers Brooks and William, sister Louisa, myself—my father next the aisle. Worship was very exact and formal,

"While through the long-drawn aisle and fretted vault
    The pealing anthem swelled the notes of praise."

I can furnish but a slight description of Dr. Inglis. His sermons were far above, out of the range of my thought, but his general bearing was impressive, his appearance dignified, his mannerism clerical; and yet I have no clear recollections of him or of·his services. Once a quarter the long communion-tables, about fifteen inches wide, and covered with snow-white linen, were extended in the wide aisles, and across in front of the pulpit, and the Lord's Supper was observed. Mother sat on that Sabbath next to father, so as to be able to accompany him to the table easily. These services were very solemn and affecting to my mind. The nature of the holy communion was explained to us in our regular catechisation at home by father and mother on Sabbath afternoons.

My father's school was the first female seminary ever established in Baltimore. He presided over it for sixteen years. It was his lot to furnish the means of education to the first families in this growing city. He was very methodical, giving the weekly reports of presence, conduct, and lessons in a neatly printed book, furnished by him, signed "William Moody," and to be countersigned by the parents. It was issued every Friday afternoon, to be returned every Monday morning. The school was opened every morning with Bible-reading and extempore prayer. Every Monday morning each scholar was required to state whom she had heard preach, the text used, and the impressions left by the services. This was followed by appropriate exhortation. My sister Harriet taught French, Algebra, and Belles-lettres. The tuition was twelve dollars and fifty cents and fifteen dollars a quarter.

My father was a large and comely man, perfectly healthy, of a social and lively turn of mind and manners, scholarly and sedate, apt to teach, and with the art of good government. Much was said of his Friday afternoon exercises, in which the entire week's work was briefly reviewed, and a parting admonition in an address from five to seven minutes long was given. At the dismissal, father, standing at the door, gave each student her book, to be returned on Monday.

During my attendance as delegate from the Cincinnati Conference to the General Conference, held in Baltimore in 1876, numerous ladies, who had received their education from my father, sought my acquaintance. They accosted me joyously, and I was greeted with remarks like these: "Why, Granville, is this you? I went to seminary to your father. What a great, noble man he was! How like my own father he seemed to me! I am so much indebted to your father, and so glad to meet you. But few of the clergy of this city exerted a wider influence than your honored father, and an influence is still spreading in this community through heads of families, who from him learned the value of true religion. He regarded it as of paramount and permanent importance. Surely he was a public blessing to the highest good of this city during the years that he was our preceptor." My own education was obtained partly from my father. I spent a year in "The

Lancasterian School." I attended a school for boys taught by Mr. Johnson. I was for a time a pupil in the Classical School of Rev. Dr. Gibson, pastor of a Scotch Presbyterian Church of "the most straitest sect." He believed and taught that the Psalms of the Bible alone should be used in social and public worship; though surely neither Sternhold's nor Rouse's version could claim inspiration in its ill-joined couplets. I studied Latin under Dr. Gibson; his Scotch dialect gave dead Latin a queer living utterance.

I attended Sabbath-school in our church regularly, and had the good fortune to belong to a class taught by Mr. John Chambers. His sole object seemed to be to produce such a change of mind in us as would lead us to choose Christ as our Savior as he is presented in the Bible, having the wisdom of a prophet, the sanctity of a priest, offering himself as a sacrifice for our sins, and the authority of a king to rule all within us to his glory and our good. Single-minded man! How much am I indebted to him for his assiduous toil in my behalf! He became a distinguished clergyman, located in Philadelphia, where the name of John Chambers became a tower of strength.

My school-boy days were very interesting times. In autumn I spent my Saturdays in the country, nutting, roaming through fruit-laden orchards, drinking cider as it gushed from the press, hunting rabbits and squirrels, playing in the vicinity of Fort McHenry. In winter I coasted down the high hill where the court-house stood, debouching into

Monument Square, in the center of which stood
the monument in memory of the heroic dead who
fell in the battle of North Point. Their names
environ, diagonally, the shaft. In summer we
boys would run from school, on its dismission at
four P. M., to the rafts in the Patapsco River, and
by scores and hundreds would bathe, diving from
rafts and from spring-boards into water from
twelve to eighteen feet deep, going to the bottom,
and bringing up a handful of gravel as proof that
we had reached the bottom. At five o'clock the
large steamboat would cast off from Bowley's
wharf. By the time it reached us, the boat would
be under full headway, with the waves running
high on the larboard and starboard sides. We
boys, in rows just outside the steamer's run, would
swim into the billowy flood abaft the ponderous,
thundering wheels, be caught to the summit of
the tossing waves, and whirled into their depths,
and thus luxuriously would ride to the wonder
and delight of the passengers.

One day my mother sent me to Bowley's wharf
to my oldest brother John, requesting him to buy
and send home by me six chickens. While he was
out after the chickens, I walked about the wholesale commission-house in which he was book-
keeper. Twenty or more dealers in cigars, collected by an advertisement of the arrival of a
large invoice of cigars direct from Cuba, were examining the lot, and all were smoking. I asked
the proprietor if I might have a cigar. He
promptly and smilingly said, "Yes," and handed

me five. I lighted one, and commenced puffing away. My brother returned, and started me home with three chickens in each hand. As I went smoking along, the cigar did its work, and I was intoxicated as with rum; my brain reeled, the pavement came up into my face, my legs twisted, I staggered to and fro, and at last fell to the left upon three chickens, which screeched and cackled, while the people laughed, and I got up and staggered on. I fell to the right on the other three chickens, which in their turn screeched and cackled. Thus annoyed, I worried along, smoking incessantly, till I reached home; when, giving the terrified fowls to our colored woman, I crept between the rose-bushes and the fence, and vomited most immoderately. The colored woman reported me to mother, who came out and said: "Granville! come out of there immediately." She and the woman took me up-stairs, and laid me on the bed, and mother questioned me very closely. "Where have you been? What have you eaten? Have you drunk any liquor?" To all of which I said, "No, ma'am." "Have you fallen down? How did you muddy your clothes so? Has anybody hit you?" "No, ma'am." "Well, what is the cause of all this sickness?" I replied: "Mr. Read gave me some Cuba cigars, and I smoked one, and it made me sick!" This solution of my difficulty relieved my mother's mind, and she went to the medicine-chest and returned with a table-spoonful of ground mustard and a tea-spoonful of salt dissolved in warm water. This administered, my nausea was temporarily increased, but ultimately removed.

I was so effectually cured of the use of tobacco by this illness and mortification that the cure lasted a life-time. I recollect a tobacconist's sign in Baltimore:

> "We all agree the weed to use;
> One smokes, one snuffs, another chews."

But since that homeward reeling I have never smoked, nor snuffed, nor chewed the nerve-destroying weed.

CHAPTER III.

YOUTH.

AFTER my school-boy days, my parents put me into the employ of Howard & Jackson, commission merchants, 225 Main Street, Baltimore. I was the youngest clerk in the house. The business was in dry-goods and wool. The firm were agents of numerous cotton and woolen mills of New England. A large wholesale trade was carried on with Maryland, Pennsylvania, Virginia, Ohio, and Tennessee, by means of six-horse wagons. I served in the store and counting-room—copied all business letters into the letter-book; attended to all post-office business; carried hundreds of thousands of dollars to and from three banks; received and aided in packing hundreds of thousands of pounds of assorted wools, under the direction of Mr. Whitmarsh, an old Englishman, who could close his eyes, grasp a fleece of wool, and tell you its strain.

One morning by six o'clock I had opened the store and swept it. While sweeping the pavement I was accosted by Mr. Thomas Tenant, a merchant, who kept six ships and brigs afloat, and with whom I was acquainted through collecting my father's seminary bills for the tuition of his daughter. "Granville," said he, "when will Shaw, Tiffany & Co. open for business?" Their house

was directly opposite ours; their business was large
and well-established. "I am disappointed," he
said, "in getting flour of a desired brand, and I
want to get three-quarter shirtings and one and one-
quarter and one-yard muslins to finish the lading
of one of my ships for a South American port, to
sail at twelve o'clock noon to-day. I wish they
were open." I replied: "O, they have made their
pile, and won't be open before nine o'clock. You
had better deal with this house. We are commission agents of many New England factories.
Just step in, Mr. Tenant, and look at our stock;
please do." He came in, and I turned and locked
the front door, saying: "Our baled goods are in
the rear warehouse. This way, please."

I showed him hundreds of bales of just such
goods as he had called for, piled up to the ceiling
in lengthened rows. He was delighted, and the
more so as I opened a bale of each kind for him .
to examine. "Granville," he said, "your firm is
absent just as Shaw, Tiffany & Co. are." "What
of that?" said I. "I can sell you these goods as
cheap as they could or would if they were present." "O no." "Yes," I replied, "I can. You
see they do not own a bale themselves; they are
commission merchants; they get so much per
cent for selling, and are limited as to price. The
owners write, 'Get so much for three-quarter goods
or hold,' and so of all the rest. I am invoice clerk,
and I will show you the invoices and the limitations, and will sell you all you need on manu-
facturers' limits; and that, sir, is all the firm

could do were they here. If they sell for less, they must make good the difference." "Let me see your invoices," he said. We went into the counting-room, and he found as I had said. "Now," said he, "if I take all you have, for cash, will you agree to deliver them at my wharf at Fell's Point, three miles from here, by half-past eleven o'clock A. M., without fail?" "Yes, sir." "Agreed," said Mr. Tenant; "you deliver them, get my captain's receipt for them as in good order and well-conditioned for shipping, bring the bill and receipt to my office in the custom-house, and I will pay you the cash."

I hired four colored men, and had them pile the goods four and five bales high along the front doors. I hired drays in numbers sufficient to transport them, and had the bales checked off as loaded. The book-keeper and the partners in succession came to the store and questioned as to the meaning of that array of goods on the sidewalk. They were pleased with the transaction. I told them that if they did not get around sooner, I would sell them clean out some day. At the wharf I suggested to the captain that, as the goods had been classified and loaded accordingly, he could examine them on the drays before bulk was broken. He accepted the suggestion, and asked me on board to get my clearance. I carried the papers to Mr. Tenant, and received his check on the United States Bank for $14.730. This operation took place when I was sixteen years old. About a fortnight thereafter, Mr. Jackson, the junior member of the firm, said to me: "Granville, what color would you prefer for a suit of clothes? We intend it as a present for that clever transaction of yours." I left the question of color to his judgment. He selected blue, and gave me an order to a first-class tailor for the making. The next Sabbath I wore my suit, the first long-tailed coat I had ever worn, till then having worn only roundabouts.

About this time my father, who was still plodding along as Preceptor Moody, educating and supporting his family of seven sons and four daughters, sold the interest which my mother still held in the Boston Stone house, and invested the proceeds in a farm, which was located four miles from Baltimore, and adjoining the village of Hookstown. This country-seat my father called "Haverhill Park," in memory of his native place. The farm was well equipped. The house was approached by a carriage-way lined with cedar and cherry trees, planted alternately. The fencing was cedar posts and chestnut rails, which material, a man said, "would last forever, for his grandfather tried it twice." There were seventy pear-trees on the place. Many of them the former owner, a Frenchman, had imported from France. Shortly after the purchase, I left the commission-house and began farm-life. My father went daily to the seminary, leaving the farm to me and Josiah Chew, a slave belonging to Mrs. Chew. My father hired him at fifteen dollars a month, and Josiah at the end of each month claimed his

wages, and taking one of the horses, Saturday
afternoon, carried his silver to his mistress, and returned Monday morning with her receipt. He
was an extraordinary man, about forty years old,
and well skilled in practical farming; and, as I
knew nothing about it, I deferred to his superior
knowledge, and he taught me. I have often felt
duly thankful that God in his providence gave me
my education in farming under Josiah Chew. I
am indebted to him for much wise counsel and
many sage utterances. He was honorable and
temperate, with habits of patient industry, enterprise, and reliability. His Christian character and
example were profitable to me. He was a member of the Methodist Episcopal Church.

Intemperance, if not universal, was the general
habit in those days. Hard cider was legal tender.
Monongahela whisky was the one thing needful.
Jamaica rum, Holland gin, and Port, Madeira, and
Malaga wines were common as household words.
Ale and beer were used freely. My father bought
whisky for his hands by the barrel, and each hand
had his pint-flask, with a spread-eagle on one side
and the star-spangled banner on the other. I as
regularly filled up three such flasks out of our store-
room as the morning came, and put them out on
the window-sill. I also filled my own flask with
cherry-bounce, sweetened with sugar. The drinking customs of society were terrible. The abnor-
mal appetite became imperative, and the nation
was given up to this social pot-vice. Cause will
have its effects, and the usual effects were almost

omnipresent. It was so in my own case, and, though my father was an abstemious man, and I never saw him affected with liquor, yet he took three small wine-glasses a day from his liquor-case, which sat on the center of the sideboard. He carried its key on his bunch of keys, and when visitors were in the house he would invite them to the sideboard for the social glass. But I was not thus abstemious; and when Josiah would perceive that I had imbibed too freely he would propose extra exertion, and so sweat it out of me before the dinner or supper hour would call me into the presence of my parents and my band of sisters.

About this time Dr. Lyman Beecher preached and published his "six sermons" on Intemperance, which sounded an alarm in God's holy mountain, and attention was called to the alarming fact that we were indeed a nation of drunkards. The Methodist Episcopal Church, through her ubiquitous ministry, sounded the alarm. Word was spread through our neighborhood that Rev. Henry Slicer would preach against dram-drinking in the Methodist church in Hookstown, next Sabbath, at half-past two P. M. I resolved to hear him. I had made many objections to going into Baltimore to church for many months before this epoch; but this Sabbath I directed Clem to saddle "Rock," and have him at the persimmon-tree in the back yard at two o'clock. I wended my way to the "Stone Church." A crowd was in attendance. I got a sitting two seats from the door, and waited developments. A young man arose in the pulpit, dressed in the Methodist garb of the period. He was a splendid specimen of a man—about five feet ten or eleven inches high, about one hundred and ninety pounds weight, fine, florid complexion, flaxen hair, his body round and well shaped as could be, with ample breast. He was straight and erect as an Indian chief. He had gentlemanly manners, amenity of address, and a fairly modulated voice. He announced as his text: "And as he reasoned of righteousness, temperance, and judgment to come, Felix trembled, and answered, Go thy way for this time; when I have a convenient season I will call for thee." (Acts xxiv, 25.) After appropriate unfolding of the text, he said: "Temperance was one-third of Paul's preaching before Felix; but had he lived in our times he would have made it the warp and woof of his discourse." He then showed up the drinking habits of the then present times, the statistics of the subject, the shameless practices which prevailed, the dire results, the desolations of heart and hope and home; the ruinous effects to the body, the mind, and the estate; the ruin rum had wrought in all classes, in Church, and in the world; the abuse of the social feeling, the desolations in married life; the degraded husband, the disappointed wife, the hapless and to-be-pitied children; the utterances of the Bible on this sin of sins, and the thousands in haggard plight and form that make the procession which is filled up at this end as rapidly as the advancing column

passes into perdition, while God says: "No drunkard hath any inheritance in the kingdom of God."

I became isolated from the crowd, engrossed
with the potency of the subject, convinced of the
truth of every word he said; and when he painted
the progressiveness of the vice and its association
with other vices, his words had confirmation in
my own experience. As he went forward and
pointed out the outcome, I was convinced that it
would be also true to the culmination of its horrible sequences. When he said these could all be
obviated by the understanding and use of one
word of seven letters—namely, "Abstain; who
will say, 'I pledge myself totally to abstain?' who
will say, 'I will?'"—my quivering soul said, "I
will!" Not waiting for the conclusion of the sermon, I left the house and chose the woods route
home, meditating on the burning words I had just
heard. I thought to a conclusion, and resolved
to clinch my resolution, and called Clem into the
family-room, and told him what I had just heard.
I said: "Now, Clem, I am going to quit; you
may do as you please. I will fill your flask if you
wish it; but, as for myself, I have quit." Taking
up my father's Bible that lay on the stand, I said:
"Clem, you see this book, which I believe to be
the Book of God, and filled with promises for the
obedient and curses for the disobedient. And
now, Clem," turning the leaves from Genesis to
Revelation, "bear me witness that I here vow
to give up all of God's promises, and incur the
evil of God's curse upon me, if I let one drop of

any kind of intoxicating liquors pass my lips for three months; and, then, if I find that I get along as well without liquor as with it, in view of the appetite it creates and the habits it forms, I pledge myself to abstain all the days of my life. So help me God. Amen." I closed the Bible and struck the book again, and said: "So help me God. Amen!"

The negro's eyes popped open like dogwood blossoms, and in piteous tones he said: "My Lor', Massa Granville, dat is awful! Never heard a man swear hisse'f away dat a-way before. My God! I would not see you take one drop after that ar' swearing off, not for all this world!" As he went back to the kitchen, he kept on with similar expressions: "Massa Granville done gone now forever if he touch a single drop! My Lor', dat's the hardest swearing I ever heard! No hope for him on that platform, sure." I listened to Clem's remarks, and they rolled in on my soul to an unexpected degree, and made me feel that I had passed "the Rubicon," and that naught remained but liberty or "the perdition of ungodly men."

I went to the barn, on the gable end of which swung the large gate that opened out to the central road. I wheeled a double-sided cart up to the barn, and, mounting to the top of the side-board, with a big nail I inscribed on the whitewashed barn, in characters twenty inches long, "24th of April." That was to me the token of the covenant I had made with God, and was to be the memorial of that engagement.

O, what a trial I endured for about six weeks! My total abstinence left me to wrestle with the thirst for the ruinous draught. My remedy was to go into the milk-house and drink a pint of sweet cream or morning's milk from three to six times a day. But I conquered the intrenched foe by the force of my awful oath. I should have relapsed from a mere promise a score of times. How much better I felt as I kept the pledge for three months—May, June, July 24th, the three hardest farming months; but I got through, and ratified the covenant for life; yes, for my life to the end. Total abstinence from all intoxicating drinks as a beverage—a Rechabite unto the Lord! Amen and amen.

In making and keeping this pledge I "built better than I knew;" for, as it was followed by my blessed conversion and self-consecration to God, it marked an epoch in my whole history and life.

5

CHAPTER IV.

WESTWARD HO!

IN the summer of 1829 my mother, putting her hand on my right shoulder as I sat on the porch, discovered there a tumor about the size of an acorn. In the fall I noticed that it was enlarging with great rapidity. We called in a physician, who pronounced it "osteo-sarcoma;" and Dr. Smith, professor of surgery in the University of Maryland, advised a surgical operation, to which I was very averse. Treatment, internal and local, failed to arrest its development, and in two months it doubled in size. The doctor advised me to call on a gentleman of Baltimore similarly affected, and be governed by what he said in the case. He had consulted surgeons in Philadelphia, New York, Boston, London, Paris, and Berlin, all of whom had advised the knife; but he, disregarding their advice, was now beyond that help. Failing to see him, I consented to follow the advice of his wife, who had, with motherly tenderness and delicacy, examined my shoulder and pronounced the trouble the same as that of her husband. In his case surgery was hopeless, and he was undergoing sleepless nights and agonies inexpressible. The surgeon was pleased with my decision, and appointed the following

Thursday as the time for the operation. He
brought with him several physicians and the senior
class from the university. I saw the preparation;
an old carpet spread above the center of the room,
a tub of warm water, a roll of towels, lint, ban-
dages, and the polished instruments. There were
no anæsthetics in use at that time; so that, as I
was seated on a chair, naked to my waist, a doctor knelt on each side of me, with one arm about
my waist and the other holding one of my arms.
The cutting was as if the surgeon was using a
red-hot instrument, and the sawing of the bone
was torture, indeed. When the wound was dressed
Dr. Smith showed me what he had removed, and
congratulated me on being a sound man. In two
months I was well, and I have had no trouble
with that shoulder since.

About this time I began to feel a deeper
interest in family devotions, which were observed
with regularity by my father. His precision of
expression, devout manner and spirit, and his
spotless life, gave emphasis to the worship, at
which I was always present. Father's table devotions were very impressive and instructive, well
calculated to keep alive a sense of God and religious obligation. His bland and courteous manners, and all the sweet civilities of life, tended to
make religion appear attractive and to be a
reasonable service.

On Sabbath afternoons he seemed to enjoy the
sacred rest of God's holy day, calling "the Sabbath a delight," and practically honoring it by

turning his feet away from the paths of those who desecrated the hours of this day of the Lord. I think no one ever came nearer fulfilling the description of acceptable worshipers, as described in Isaiah lviii, 13, 14, than my honored parents. My father had a melodious voice, and I often hear echoes of his Sabbath afternoon soliloquies, uttered in intoned and measured notes, the originals of which I can not find. He was a Puritan of the Puritans by constitution and by education, in manner and in habits. In 1834, in autumn's somber hours, he passed away peacefully and expectantly, responding to mother's query when he neared his mortal hour: "Mr. Moody, what are your feelings and prospects now?" "O Harriet, it is all well with me now. I have trusted Christ; I must trust Christ; I can trust Christ; and I do trust Christ; and I know whom I have believed, and am persuaded that he is able to keep that which I have committed unto him against that day. But O, Harriet, what will you do? I leave you and your fatherless children to God. A Judge of the widow and a Father to the fatherless is God in his holy habitation."

Some fifty rods south-west from my father's house, in a very humble cabin, situated on a portion of land of fifteen acres, belonging to Ned Griffen, there lived two superannuated negro slaves, named Uncle Jim and Aunt Violet, whom we all visited in leisure hours. Uncle Jim was a "tooth-ache doctor," a burly, cranky old man. He used to interest us children with stories of slavery and slaveholders, and how he suffered; and he accounted for the loss of his front teeth, above and below, by saying that they were knocked out by his master's blows with his heavy hickory cane. "He would have his plantation-bell rung before sunrise," thus he went on, "and then come out on his porch, and clear his throat three times; then woe to the man or woman who was not up and at work. 'Come here,' he would say; and he followed his words with blows right in your face or mouth, and the teeth would fly or go down your throat. O, he was a bad man! He would work his slaves on Sunday. One time, on turning the mule-teams out of a wheat-field which he had sown on Sunday, he said, with oaths, that he would have the best yield off that field of any in the county; and, sure enough, he had the biggest crop I ever saw—thirty-five bushels to the acre. Was n't that strange?" Jim was a good farmer. He made every edge cut. He would buy a horse for five to ten dollars, work him hard, feed him nine ears of corn a day, and when he died, as he soon did, Jim made his complaint to his neighbors, who would make up a similar sum for him, and he would reinvest.

His wife, Aunt Violet, was a jewel. She was seventy or seventy-five years old. She had been the body-servant of Madame Hollingsworth, of whom she had no complaints to make, and of whom she was proud to speak in the highest terms of commendation. The mistress died, and the younger members of the family, who were wild and careless, "quit-claimed" their interests

in her, and she married Uncle Jim, and Ned Griffen gave the old couple those fifteen acres during
their life-time. Aunt Violet always washed for my
mother on Monday. She was a Methodist, and at
her work sang Methodist hymns with a charming
voice. Her conduct was such that everybody
said she was a Christian. I heard her say one
Monday morning, on looking at the big basket of
clothes: "Massa Jesus and I has got a big job before us, but we 'll be good for it;" and she sang:

> "'Jesus all the day long
> Is my joy and my song.'

Blessed Jesus! He is here. He makes me
happy now. Jesus and I can get through it, sure.
Glory! Hallelujah!"

She would stand in the center of the gallery
in Hookstown church, at love-feast, and narrate
her experience; profess that she had had her
heart cleansed and perfected in love, and then she
would sing:

> "Arise, my soul, arise!
> Shake off thy guilty fears."

My mother believed in Aunt Violet's deep and
consistent piety, and being a member of the Bible
Society, and charged with seeing that every house
that would receive it should have a copy of the
Bible, she procured a large Bible and presented it
to Aunt Violet. She kept it wrapped in a snowy
towel, and deposited in her ample chest. When
young or old would visit her she would take out
the Bible, and, with a sweet smile, say: "My Heavenly Father has sent Aunt Violet a big letter, but

she can not read a word of all this letter; now won't you read a portion for me, that I may hear what Great Master says to me?" Who could refuse a request so uttered by the holy woman? She was as polite as she was pious. Every time I visited her, she would bring out her Bible. While I was reading she would sit and pray and praise the Lord. She would draw in her breath, hearing as if by inspiration. I would feel strangely affected, so that I dreaded this ordeal. My lips would quiver and my tears flow. I would be so filled with emotion that I would have to stop reading. I would then select some historical or genealogical portion; but before I knew it I would feel the strange emotions again, produced by the sacred Word. By the fervent prayers of Aunt Violet, the Holy Spirit would take of the things of Christ, and show them unto me.

Now came the crucial test. My brother John had married and moved to Norwich, Muskingum County, Ohio, and entered into merchandising. He wrote to me and my parents, inviting me to spend a year in his store; that he would start a good store in the country at an eligible site, make me a partner, and we would both do well.

It was so arranged, and I was to start on Monday, August 31, 1831. The morning came; breakfast was over; family prayers followed, in which my father led, and asked God's blessing upon the enterprise, and implored his blessing upon me in particular, praying that God would say unto me: "Wilt thou not say unto me at this time, My

Father, thou art the guide of my youth?" Then, pronouncing his blessing upon me, we all arose. Mother kissed me good-bye, and my sisters, Harriet, Louisa, Ellen, and Sarah, gave me the sweet parting kiss. Josiah Chew and all the servants bade me good-bye, whilst "Kitty," a smart gray mare, stood chewing her bit and stamping her feet, anxious to be released. I went out and adjusted my saddle-bags, and was about to mount, when I remembered Uncle Jim and Aunt Violet. I said: "I must not forget them; I'll run up and say good-bye."

I found them at the table, eating their breakfast. Everything was in perfect neatness and order. I broke in, saying: "Well, Uncle Jim and Aunt Violet, I am just starting to go to Ohio, and I came up to bid you good-bye." "Good-bye, young Massa Granville," said Uncle Jim. Aunt Violet rose from the table, and I extended my hand and said: "Good-bye, Aunt Violet; good-bye." She took my hand in hers, and held it. I backed out of the cabin door, and she followed me into the yard, and we stopped. Holding on to my hand, she said: "Young Master, I must speak to you. I hope you will kindly receive what I am going to say to you now. You is going far, far away, and this may be the last chance to speak to you. You has been well raised. Your father and mother are good Christian people. They have set you a good example; have prayed for and with you every night and morning; have taken you to Church and Sabbath-school, and taught

you the catechism of your people's Church; and
yet, notwithstanding all this, you has steadily gone
on in your wicked ways; and now I fear you is
worse and further from God and salvation and
hope than ever you was before. And now you is
going to leave all these good influences, and going
away out to de West, 'way beyond de mountains,
and among a people that do n't care for God nor
for your soul. O, what will become of you, young
master? Besides all this, God's Holy Spirit has
done his office on your heart powerfully, I know.
When I used to ask you to read my Bible, which
your precious mother gave me for my own, while
you read I prayed that it might do you good as
well as me, and I often saw how the truth of Jesus
would affect you, and your voice would fail you,
and your lips would tremble, and your eyes over-
flow with tears. I was praying that God would
use his own word by his present Spirit to convince
you of sin, and to give you conviction in order to
your conversion. But you resisted de Holy Spirit;
and oftentimes, when you was swearing at the
hands or the horses, I has drapped right down upon
my knees wherever I mought have been, and
prayed for you, dat de Lord would not lay these
things to your charge, but give you repentance
unto life not to be repented of. But you have
grown worse and worse, and now you are further
off from God than ever you was before, and are
going away, like the prodigal son, into a far-off
country. O yes, young master; the Holy Spirit
has done his duty with you, and called you to re-

pentance, and I have felt his presence with the Word you so often read for me. I did hope it might do you good, and cause you to turn to de Lord and seek salvation from de reigning power of sin to newness of a holy life."

All this time she held me by my right hand, and became wonderfully earnest. She swayed her person up and down, right and left, while streams of tears attested her holy agony for my welfare. Her arm was bare to her shoulder, and a neat little white band, an inch wide, contrasted strangely with the jet-black skin of her sinewy arms with large veins, which seemed leaping with the excitement she felt and showed, as she pleaded with me to submit myself to God and begin a new life. At length she let go of my hand, and raised her long black arm toward the skies, and said: "Young master, I has done my duty for the last time. And now," she said, standing with that long black arm extended, "and now let me charge you, Master Granville, do n't you meet me at the judgment-seat of Christ in an unconverted state; for if you do, Aunt Violet must there appear as a swift witness against you. The Holy Ghost has done his work on your heart a many a time; and now I say to you, Do n't, O do n't go on in sin. Do n't live and die in your sins; for if you do, you will make it necessary for Aunt Violet to come out against you there as a witness in that great day. De Lord lead you to repentance and salvation, and no one will be more glad than Old Aunt Violet will be to hear of your choosing the good part, which shall not be taken away from you. Farewell, young master, farewell."

There I stood like a culprit before this Nemesis, this voice of God. As sentence followed sentence, and appeal followed appeal, and my conscience attested the truth of every charge, my mouth was stopped. I was appalled, and shrank from her earnestness. Her most eloquent appeal convinced me that God was speaking through her to me. How I got away from the breezy shade of the peach-tree, beneath which we both stood, while sunlight struggled through the leaves, I can never tell; but I was most powerfully convinced of sin, of righteousness, and of judgment to come; and, like Felix, I trembled with dismay, and went along that string of fencing with far different feelings than when I went up half an hour before. I said nothing to my parents of what had occurred, but mounted my horse and left, with my parents' benison and my sisters' weeping faces and utterances of good-bye. As I rode along the pike to Hookstown, I cast weary, longing, lingering looks behind. The arrows of the Almighty were sticking fast within me, and tall, gaunt, gesturing, warning Aunt Violet stood before my vision. Her closing words, "Do n't meet me at the judgment-seat of Christ, or Aunt Violet will be compelled to appear as a swift witness against you there," rung like the knell of destiny in my ears. I tried to reason away the spell that rested upon me; but that tall, gaunt, figure, and that lifted and extended black arm pointing upward "would not

down." Aunt Violet was a Christian; her character was her own, and her reputation was coin-
cident with it. There was a gentleness and gen-
tility in her mien, and a pathos, a power of
persuasion and eloquence and point in her, that was
admirable and potent; and, withal, there was the
presence of the same Spirit that aided Paul in
preaching to Lydia and the jailer and Felix and
Agrippa. My conscience echoing her words of
truth and soberness, I could not reason away the
feelings that swayed my bosom.

I arrived at my destination on my ninth day
from home, September 8th. My trip across the
Alleghany Mountains was delightful. What alti-
tudes! What ranges of vision, mountain slopes,
gurgling rills, rivulets, and rivers! The National
Road has been superseded by the railroads, the
great wagons and stage-coaches as well. The
taverns, with their six-foot long grates; rooms
filled with wagoners and travelers; their vast table
comforts of mountain-mutton, corn-bread, hominy,
venison, bear-meat, pheasants, partridges, and wild
turkeys; stables brimming with mountain-oats,—
these are all of the past.

Norwich, O., was the Mecca of my hopes. It
was a town of less than a thousand inhabitants.
My brother welcomed me, and I set to work at
once with a will to learn the business. The first
Sabbath came, and I went to the Presbyterian
Church. A great crowd of people was there, and
the regular pastor conducted services in an aus-
tere, dogmatic, and self-sufficient manner. He

preached a rigid Calvinistic sermon. Intermission
for an hour was announced, and then followed
another sermon. The membership partook of the
austerity of their pastor; and, stranger though I
was, no one spoke to me. I felt like a stranger
among strangers, and fastening to them seemed
like anchoring to the north side of an iceberg,
where gloom and shadow abide.

In my awakened state of alarm and concern I
had, before coming to Norwich, settled down upon
a purpose to forsake a sinful life, and "cease to do
evil and learn to do well." Under all my previous training, and especially under the close
personal exhortation of Aunt Violet, I was among
the class of persons who are said to be "prepared
for the Lord." My morality was unexceptionable
to the people of Norwich, and I was looking for
the open door.

The next Sabbath was the regular preaching-
day in the Methodist Episcopal Church. Rev.
John W. Gilbert was preacher in charge, and
Rev. Levi P. Miller junior preacher. The junior
preacher was to officiate, and I went to hear him.
He was as "one that hath a pleasant voice, and
can play well upon an instrument." His preaching was evangelical, instructive, and consoling.
He was a Barnabas, a son of consolation, very
amiable in spirit and winning in address. At
the close of the meeting the people shook hands
with me, gave me kind looks, and said, "Come
again." The superintendent of the Sunday-school
invited me to attend his school at two P. M., which

I did, having been used to Sunday-school from my early childhood. I was assigned to teach a vacant class, and thus was harnessed and put to work at once. A few weeks passed, crowded with business six days and Church-work nearly all day Sunday; yet my heart was burdened and longing for the pardoning voice of a forgiving God—longing for a deliverance of my soul from the burden of condemnation and the bondage of my corruption into the glorious liberty of the sons of the Lord God Almighty.

There was one member for whom I conceived the highest regard. I reverenced his godly character. This was Isaiah Brown. When he spoke in meeting, it was in the demonstration of the Spirit and with power. When he prayed, it seemed to me that he was talking with God. When he sang, he seemed to be making melody in his heart to the Lord, whilst he spoke to the people in psalms and hymns and spiritual songs. He always became unspeakably happy in singing the hymn beginning,

> "My God, the spring of all my joys."

He was an illiterate man, a cooper by trade, yet he wore Jehovah's seal upon his brow. With tearful eyes and uplifted countenance, all illuminated by the Holy Spirit, he would close the hymn in ecstasies.

About the first week in October my brother's wife, who was a Baltimore Methodist, invited the junior preacher to take tea with her family. After supper was over, my brother attended the store, leaving us three together. Conversation followed about Methodism, to which I was a stranger, having been raised after the straitest sect of New England Congregationalism, with the very highest regard for and deference to the "Saybrook Platform," a rigid Calvinistic body of divinity. We both soon had our hands full. Feeling an obligation to the faith of my ancestors, I set my squadrons on the field in the five points of Calvinism,—unconditional election, particular redemption, total depravity, grace irresistible, and perseverance of the saints. I had the answers of the catechism at my tongue's end. I had also in memory the Confession of Faith, with its formulated doctrines and supposed proofs, cited by the Westminster divines; so that I had the advantage of the preacher, who had not been trained Calvinistically or polemically. The disputation lasted till two o'clock in the morning. On his leaving for his lodgings, sister Mary said: "Well, Brother Granville, you need not think to get Brother Miller to adopt your notions, for he has been brought up a Methodist, and has been received into the conference." "Now, sister Mary," said I, "just change the terms and your remarks will apply to me as well, except the conference. I do not think he answered one of my arguments; do you?"

The latter part of the week Brother Miller, with smiling countenance, calling me "Bub," said: "Will you read a book on the subjects we talked

about nearly all night, without reaching any conclusions?" "Certainly I will. What is the name
of the book?" "'Fletcher's Checks.' They are
checks to the system of doctrine you defended so
zealously," he replied. Said I: "I should like to
see any one attempt to check the faith once delivered to the saints. I will read carefully, and write
you a reply." In the evening he handed me a
large book marked Vol. I, of four volumes. I
thought that "Fletcher's Checks" was a two-
penny pamphlet, and I was not prepared to face
so formidable a work. The books I had had access to were in favor of Calvinism. I had never
heard of Fletcher or any of the representative
men of Methodism. I took the book, and read and
read, and pondered much, and reasoned as well as
I could. I borrowed the remaining volumes, and
compared the several teachings with the Bible.
I recollect my mental processes as one morning I
sat sideways to the counter and closed my eyes,
comparing the truth of God with "the hoary faith
of my ancestors." Taking up "Fletcher's Checks,"
I said: "This man is right in his views on all
the five points of Calvinism, and I now believe
with him in conditional election of believers in
Christ to salvation; universal atonement in Christ
for every child of man; a graciously alleviated
depravity; grace resistible, but not resisted by
the saved; the amissibility of grace." Thus was
I brought out of Calvinism by being placed in
contact with the master mind of Methodism.

I bless God that I ever read Fletcher's works,

so clear, cogent, and conclusive. Rev. Levi P. Miller was always afterwards my warm personal friend. He labored till old age arrested him, when he had to retire from the conference. Plowing corn on his little farm, he ran a broken bone into his foot; lockjaw developed, then death. We shall meet in heaven.

6

CHAPTER V.

CONVERSION.

THE reception of this new mode of thought of God, of man, of morals, of immortality, was the means of bringing me into the spirit of bondage to fear. The logic of Calvinism had its effect upon my mind and heart, my hopes and fears as well. I reasoned thus: "I am one of the elect, or I am one of the reprobates. If I am one of the elect, in God's time and in due time I shall have that effectual calling of which I have learned in the Catechism, even that work of God on and in my heart by which I shall be persuaded and enabled to accept Christ as offered to me in the Gospel. I shall, under a sight and sense of my sins, have Christ revealed to me as my Savior; for thus all the elect are brought in. Neither are any others redeemed, called, justified, or regenerated, but the elect only. When God wants me converted, he will visit me with his effectual calling. If I am one of the reprobate, I shall be lost, do what I may; for none but the elect shall be visited with effectual calling. All others are passed by, and ordained to wrath for their sins, to the praise of God's glorious justice. So, elect or reprobate, my case is fixed by the universal divine agency of God and his all-embracing decrees."

Thus, tempest-tossed and not comforted, I was

driven from reef to rock. The five points of
Calvinism seemed now to be reduced, by the irref-
ragable logic of John Fletcher, into a quintet of
endless jargon, confusion worse confounded. I
was led into the faith of the Arminian Remon-
strants. The counterpart of the five points of
Calvinism now appeared to me to be the common
salvation. These doctrines, new to me, had the
effect of answering my every objection. They
laid my guilt and ill-desert at my own door;
placed God on the throne in his own glorious per-
fections, all complete; placed me at the footstool
of his mercy, commanding me to "behold the
Lamb of God which taketh away the sin of the
world." Eternal life is communicable to all on
the same terms. These wondrous and harmonious
truths were the burden of the gospel messages
which greeted my willing ears from Sabbath to
Sabbath. They were made prominent in the
Sunday-school. These exceeding great and precious promises were reduced to the test of experience in the lively members of the Methodist
Episcopal Church in Norwich, and in all the
region round about. They were the themes of
thought spread on the truth-illumined pages of
the newspapers of the Church, the "Advocates"
of Christianity.

One night I had attended a called meeting of
the officers and teachers of the Sunday-school.
The subject for consideration was: "By what
means may we lead our scholars to Christ, and
secure their salvation?" Much was said that was

good and wise. At the close, I walked homeward
with Isaiah Brown. He said to me: "Brother
Moody, we ought indeed to labor with our pupils
so that their conversion may be secured." I
thought, Now is my opportunity to secure the
sympathy of this good man, and I promptly said:
"Mr. Brown, I more need such instruction and
influence to secure my own conversion; for I am
myself in the gall of bitterness and in the bonds
of iniquity, and my heart is not right in the sight
of God, and therefore I have neither part nor lot
in this matter. Will you not pray to the Lord that
he will take away my heart of stone, and give me
a heart of flesh?" He raised both hands and
said: "Why, Brother Moody, I thought that indeed you were already a Christian. Be sure I
will pray for you at least three times a day—at
six A. M., and one and six P. M. You may be
assured I will be in my closet and upon my knees
in prayer to God for you by name; be sure I will,
and you do the same for yourself." I requested
him to keep this secret, and said if I found the
Lord I would confess him before men.

Business was very brisk; but never did the
pressure of my sin-burdened soul cease. My language was: "O that I knew where I might find
God! I would order my cause before him; I
would fill my mouth with arguments; I would
wait for my sentence from my Judge." I felt
the guilt of my sin, my desert of punishment for
my iniquities, which were great. I bewailed my
depravity, and mourned over my prevalent dispo-

sition to sin against God, which mastered my mind
and ruled in my evil heart of unbelief in departing
from the living God. I daily found a warfare, such
as that described in Romans vii. "O wretched man
that I am, who shall deliver me from the body of this
death?" was my anxious cry, my utmost and all-
engrossing solicitude, and almost despairing outcry.
Sometimes hope inspired my soul, and then I almost feared that peradventure I had passed the
limits of God's grace, and my sins had justly
separated between me and my God. Truly this
was the spirit of bondage to fear, and such bondage and such fear of a God who is to the un-
pardoned and unaccepted only as a consuming
fire. Thus did it please the Lord to bruise me, to
put me to grief. Truly all his waves passed over
me. I found trouble and sorrow; then called I
upon the Lord: O Lord, I beseech thee deliver my
soul from this burden of condemnation, and from
this bondage of corruption, and enable me to flee
from this damnation of hell. But God saw it best
for this agony of sorrow to continue for about three
weeks ere the joy of his salvation came into my
soul. Fast bound with the bonds of iniquity, my
heart not right in the sight of God, and not right
in my own sight, how I watched for the light of
the morning of salvation! O, how I sighed for the
coming Deliverer and the deliverance! Frequent,
vivid recollections of my parting interview with
Aunt Violet came up,—her entirely unexpected
meeting with me; her kind solicitude for my spiritual welfare; her calling my sins to our mutual

remembrance; her allusion to my pious parents and their care for my spiritual interests; the morning and evening family worship; her reference to the effect of the reading of her own Bible by me to her, in answer to her concurrent prayer for my welfare; her assigning the convictions I had felt to the Holy Spirit; and her final charge: "Young master, do n't meet me at the judgment-seat of Christ in an unconverted state; if you do, Aunt Violet must appear a swift witness against you there." Hers was a message from God, performed not perfunctorily, but as if immediately moved of the Spirit to speak to me, and it proved the power of God to my salvation.

Thus week by week sped on, I visiting Brother Brown in his shop. Busily engaged, I can see him now, with stalwart form, sinewy arm, placid countenance, beaming eye, and ready tongue to speak a word to a weary one, as I sat beside him and listened to his instructive voice showing me the way of salvation. Thanksgiving-day came on November 25th, in 1831. The Methodists, according to their custom, held their prayer-meeting on Thursday evening. I attended. There was a goodly number present, and the services were devout and cheery to the Church; but my spirit was in dissonance with theirs. Fierce trials were upon me. Doubts and fear prevailed, and I was in a perplexed state of mind, and far from God. It seemed to me to be the hour of darkness and the power of the evil one. I had sought the Lord for nearly three months; I had ceased to do evil,

and had tried to do well; but no peace, rather
waning hope and distraction of mind. A broken
law, with its soul-withering curse; a reproving
conscience, which would not rest; bondage through
fear of death; an apprehension of fiery indignation beyond the grave,—these, like dreadful cata-
racts, poured wrath and misery upon me; while
divine knowledge, heavenly peace, gospel purity,
the love of God shed abroad in their hearts, and
blooming hopes, like celestial fountains, communicated streams of joy and gladness to the souls
of the peaceful worshipers that evening. Strange
contrast between them and my poor desolate,
agitated soul!

The assembly was dismissed, but I lingered in
one of the back seats of the church. Six brethren
tarried, and gathered around the stove in cheerful conversation. I left my seat, and walked up
to the group, composed of Isaiah Brown, Israel
and Enos Jennings, Lewis Virden, Israel Putnam,
and Rev. E. D. Roe. They each shook hands
with me, and one of them said: "We had a good
meeting this evening, Brother Moody." I replied:
"I am glad you enjoyed it; but it has been a most
unhappy time for me." Brother Brown then told
them that I had been seeking religion for a number of months. O, how it shocked me, that this
man, whom I thought to be the best man I
had ever known, to whom I had committed my
secret, which he promised to keep, should now
tell it to these brethren without my consent!
Satan took advantage of me, and I turned upon

my heel and went toward the door, thinking, with Jonah, that I did well to be angry. A sudden and strong impression came upon me to return and ask the brethren to pray for me. I obeyed the impulse, and, extending my hand to Mr. Brown, asked him to pray for me, bursting into tears as I spoke. He assured me that he had been praying for me since the evening I had disclosed to him my state of mind. But I said: "I want you to pray for me here and now." He prayed, and such a prayer I have seldom heard before or since. The darkness darker seemed, and I asked Brother Israel Jennings to pray. While he and the other brethren, whom I called on in succession, prayed, I agonized in prayer; but the distance between God and me seemed to increase. Then I called on them in rotation again, till twelve prayers were offered, while the heavens became as iron above me. Then Brother Brown said: "Brother Moody, the fire has gone out, and all the candles but one, and it will soon expire; let us go home." I looked, and lo! there was one faint candle, with blackened wick two inches long; the unplastered walls absorbed the glimmering rays, and the ceiling, dark with coal-smoke, reflected no ray of light; and I was but the deeper impressed with the gloominess of my situation. I then prayed myself, telling the Lord all my heart-rending woe, my anguish and distress, and pleaded the all-availing name of Jesus as my only plea, and as my exclusive trust and hope: "Lord, I believe in Jesus Christ. O, help my unbelief! O, look upon the face of thine

Anointed, and then look upon me with eyes of love, and give me the smile of acceptance, which shall seal thy salvation to my soul. O, reach down thy powerful hand, and take me from this horrible pit in which I am, and from the miry clay, and set my feet upon the rock, and put the new song into my mouth. For Jesus' sake I ask."

Joy and peace now pervaded my soul. I felt I had experienced a great change, being translated from the kingdom and power of darkness into the kingdom of God's dear Son. The brethren were glad, and, grasping my hand, they said: "You are through now, glory to God! You are through now." I said: "Yes, I hope so." One of them said: "You hope so! Why, brother, you may *know* your sins forgiven, and that your name is written in the Lamb's book of life." "Yes," said Israel Jennings, "for thirty years I have had the Spirit of God's Son bearing witness with my spirit that I am born of God, and therefore I cry, 'Abba, Father!'" As we walked homeward over the crisp snow, the moon shining from a cloudless sky into our faces, I asked each of the others the momentous question answered by Mr. Jennings, and received substantially the same reply. One said: "When you get home, look at Romans viii, 14, 16; and Galatians iv, 6." I read the passages, and found: "For as many as are led by the Spirit of God, they are the sons of God. The Spirit itself beareth witness with our spirit that we are the children of God;" "And because ye are sons, God hath sent forth the Spirit of his Son into your hearts, crying, Abba, Father." "Wonderful! wonderful! wonderful!" I exclaimed. "I 'll seek this blessing for myself." Then, kneeling at my bedside, I prayed as I never prayed before. Extinguishing the candle, I retired to my pillow. The bright moonlight stole a glance into the room as I thought upon the texts, which spread forth like vast prairie scenes, and rose up like mountain ranges; and, feeling an undefinable spirit of peace and reconciliation, I fell asleep in Jesus—safe.

The next morning I was up before sunrise, and knelt and prayed without sensible emotion. I went to the barn to feed three horses we were fattening to send to the Baltimore market. I stepped into the oat-bin, six feet wide by eight feet long, containing at the time about eighty bushels of oats, about two feet deep at the front and sloping up to eight or nine feet deep at the back. I filled the half-bushel and turned to go, when I felt inclined to kneel and ask for the blessing of assurance of which the six brethren spoke, and which I found portrayed in Romans and Galatians as the new birthright of the sons of God. I threw down the half-bushel and knelt in the oats to pray for the promised blessing of the Holy Spirit's attestation that I was also a child of God by "the washing of regeneration and renewing of the Holy Spirit shed upon me abundantly through Jesus Christ, my Savior; that being justified by his grace I should be made an heir according to the hope of eternal life." Kneeling down in the yielding oats, before I stopped sinking I stretched out both my hands, and lifted my face towards heaven; but before my thoughts could form themselves into prayer, the blessing came down upon me, and within and through and around me, like a cataract of light and love and power and joy and peace and brightness and glory. It seemed to me as if the sun had shed forth an effluence of grace and glory, and that the Word made flesh, full of grace and truth, was near; and that, of his fullness, I received grace for grace. It came like rolling billows from above, and swept me with lightning-like rapidity, shedding abroad the love of God in my heart, till I comprehended with all saints what is the breadth and length and depth and height, and was made to know the love of Christ which passeth knowledge, and was filled with all the fullness of God. Then the eyes of my understanding were enlightened to know what is the hope of this calling, and what the riches of Christ's inheritance in the saints, and what is the exceeding greatness of his power to usward who believe—the fullness of him that filleth all in all. Being renewed unto repentance unto life, that quickening Spirit was poured out upon me from on high, and I was made partaker of the Holy Ghost, and tasted the good Word of God and the powers of the world to come, and received the blessing from God, good measure, pressed down, and shaken together and running over.

"Of my Savior possessed,
I was perfectly blessed."

My soul dilated itself beyond its ordinary capacity, and expanded to receive this tide of joy which filled and overwhelmed it.

Nor was this illapse of grace a merely momentary glare. It was not

"Like lightning o'er the midnight sky,
Which makes the darkness darker seem;"

but rather, "His going forth was prepared as the morning; and he came unto me as the rain, as the latter and former rain unto the earth." This heavenly visitation lasted from six to ten A. M., in one effulgent outpouring of the Holy Ghost. Breakfast hour came and passed unnoted. The store was obliterated from my mind. Several times my unconverted brother John came down to the stable, as I was afterwards informed, and found me in my rapturous amaze, or pleading with God to awaken him also, and make him partaker of like precious grace. At about ten o'clock my wise and compassionate Father, in very great condescension to my weakness, graciously drew a veil over glories too dazzling for mortal eyes long to sustain, and left me in the enjoyment of the peace that passeth all understanding. "Glory be to the Father and to the Son and to the Holy Ghost! as it was in the beginning, is now, and ever shall be, world without end. Amen."

The next week I wrote to my parents, telling them what I had experienced, and asking their approval of my choice of membership in the Methodist Episcopal Church. They responded, grateful to God for his rich mercy to me, saying,

in their joint letter, that whilst they much pre-
ferred that I should unite with the Presbyterian
Church, as doctrinally the Church of my ancestors
for centuries, and the Church in which I was consecrated to God in holy baptism, yet still, if I
felt it would suit me better to be a Methodist,
they could and would not interpose any serious
objections, as they believed that "Christ had
many of his beloved and saved ones, who were
his true followers, though not following Christ
with us; and that this was specially true of the
Methodist Church, in which communion many of
the Lord's elect were doubtless found."

In my mother's letter a singular case was recorded. She wrote that on Thanksgiving-day she
sat up quite late alone in the family-room, all
having retired. As she sat knitting by the dying
embers of the fire, musing, meditating, and praying, she felt mysteriously that one of her children
was just saved; it was strangely revealed to her
at that hour, and she rejoiced with exceeding
gladness.

CHAPTER VI.

LICENSED TO PREACH.

SHORTLY after my conversion I was invited to the residence of the gentlemanly proprietor of the tavern to spend an evening with a party of young people. I accepted the invitation, and spent a pleasant evening, socially. At nine o'clock a sumptuous supper was enjoyed, and at ten a fiddler appeared and began to twang his strings in dancing strains, and the young men chose partners for the giddy dance. I quietly went out of the room and left the house, reminded by Scripture to "flee youthful lusts." I thus escaped a well-circumstanced sin. Self-denial must come to the front in the Christian life. When we will as God wills, and do as God admonishes, we are safe. The golden-mouthed Chrysostom, when asked, "What is the first element in Christianity?" responded, "Self-denial." "What is the second?" "Self-denial." "What is the third?" he still answered, "Self-denial."

On Christmas, 1831, the second quarterly meeting for Norwich Circuit was held in Norwich. At the close of the love-feast on Sabbath morning I united with the Church, securing the aid of Isaiah Brown to go forward with me; but when I had taken two or three steps, all trepidation left me, and I walked firmly and joyously forward, and gave my name to Rev. John W. Gilbert. The brethren rushed up around me with congratulations and rejoicings, and welcomed me into the communion of saints. I was now publicly committed to my course as a member of the Church.

In the assemblage of all spiritual blessings I lived, and in the prompt discharge of every duty I delighted. My walk was close with God. I was filled with all joy and peace in believing, and abounded in hope by the power of the Holy Spirit. I had then no thought of preaching the gospel. I was prompt at Sabbath-school as a teacher, steady in my attendance at class, always present in prayer-meeting—praying when called on. I delighted in public worship, and found supreme delight in attending upon the Lord's Supper.

I had told my brother, in whose store I was employed, that I could not sell whisky to any one; that part of the business I must decline doing, though all the stores in the town sold it and treated their customers freely. He made no objections to releasing me from that part of the business.

I studied about forty pages a day. I read Wesley's sermons and works, Watson's "Institutes," Fletcher's works, Dr. Adam Clarke, Burder's "Village Sermons," and the lives of Hester Ann Rogers and Jesse Lee. My plan was to rise early—say, five o'clock in the winter and four the rest of the year. As business did not begin till nine o'clock, I had several of the best hours of the day for careful reading. Some time in January, 1832, as I closed the reading of the last page of the "Life of Jesse Lee," a seemingly audible voice said, in mandatory and emphatic tones, to my inner consciousness: "Go and do thou likewise." I was so impressed that I looked up and around reverently, when the utterance was repeated with words of thrilling and encouraging, persuasive, impelling power, conveying their divinity in tones and emphasis, though not through verbal or audible characters, yet with a convincing influence, impelling the conviction that God himself had spoken to me with authority and force. I paused in wondrous amazement and consternation, thinking intensely of saying: "Send by whom thou wilt send, but send not me, O Lord." But these thoughts and emotions were evanescent, and sat silent on my tongue. The sober second thought prevailed, and I responded: "Be it unto me even as thou hast said. Behold the servant of the Lord." Instantly a gracious and glorious illapse of the Holy Spirit came upon me like a heavenly baptism. I was alone in the store. There I made a covenant with the Lord, and consecrated to him all that I was and had.

That divine vocation was my commencement-day. I found my place at once. I vowed to make everything subservient to this one great business of my new nature. This secret of the Lord I sacredly kept, believing that in due season the Church would issue a corresponding call, and

these two calls would be my warrant for entering
and remaining in the ministry. My walk was
closer with God from that blessed hour. I looked
forward to my work in the ministry. O, how
carefully I watched over myself! I daily renewed my consecration to the Lord, who seemed
to me as the God who maketh his mind known
to those who walk with him. How precious did
his Word become to my inquiring mind! I had
been brought up in the nurture and admonition
of the Lord. I had my memory stored with Holy
Writ at home, and by the plan in vogue in Sabbath-schools, of giving one blue ticket for committing ten verses of the Bible to memory, a
white ticket for each hundred verses, and a red
ticket for every thousand verses. In my ministry
I found great aid from my early trained memory
and familiarity with the Word of Christ, which
dwelt in me mightily. In those blessed days I
fasted every Friday. I found this practice very
strengthening to my soul, and I advanced steadily
in the divine life.

As spring advanced, my brother and I were on
the lookout for a proper position for a country
store. We found such a site at Wade's farm,
eight miles from Norwich. I boarded at the farm.
The domestic circle was made up of Mr. and Mrs.
Wade and their daughter, with her husband and
flaxen-haired little girl. They were members of
the Lutheran Church. They were plain, honest,
Christian people, in a log-cabin home. Here I
prosecuted my theological studies. My happiest

days were the rainy days of winter, when customers were fewest and I had time to study. I
had made it a rule to say the Lord's Prayer at
my bedside; then, as soon as dressed, to go over
and start a fire at the store; sweep out, and sit
down to read till breakfast. I studied divinity
without temptations to evil, or trials to cross me,
or diversions to distract my mind from the constantly widening circle of religious thought. I
now studied from sixty to eighty pages a day.
Ever and anon I would meditate on what I had
studied, and try to restate it in my own language.
I would walk my store-room, classifying what I
had learned as facts, doctrines, precepts, prohibi-
tions, sanctions, rewards, punishments. Thus I
trained my memory to tenacity, committing to it
as to a store-house.

Sitting one afternoon (Thursday, February 28,
1832,) at the front of my store, reading Fletcher's
"Checks," I noticed a stalwart man riding up the
road on horseback. He was seated on top of a
two-bushel bag of wheat. He was dressed in
homespun, with overcoat and cape, and wore a
broad-brim hat. Riding up to where I sat, he
said, as one having authority: "Young man, the
Master has need of you for other work than store-
keeping. I have an appointment next Sabbath at
Spry's meeting-house, nine miles south-east of
here, and I wish you to meet me there at ten
o'clock in the morning and exhort after I have
preached a little while. My name is Samuel
Steadman, a local preacher in the Methodist

Church, and a farmer in this township. The Lord of the harvest has work for you to do. I am on my way to mill. Now you go into your store, close the door, and get down on your knees, and lay what I have said to you before the Lord in prayer; see what he will say to you, and I will stop on my way home and get your decision." I asked him for his authority for such a salutation, as he was an entire stranger to me. He made the laconic reply: "I know all about you, young man. Now mark my word, and let me know what is your mind after praying for divine direction." Without further conversation, he rode away, and I did as he told me. My soul was stirred within me, and God's baptism came upon me wonderfully, accompanied with the impression: "Go with him, nothing doubting; for I am with you alway, even to the end." O, how my soul did rejoice and magnify the Lord! Yet I rejoiced with trembling. I made up my mind to go with the man. I could at least relate my experience, and tell to sinners what a dear Savior I had found. Mr. Steadman returning, I told him that I would meet him at the time and place.

I started, but, having gone a short distance, I turned into the woods, and prayed to God that if he had indeed called me to the work of the ministry he would give me knowledge of his will by a baptism of the Holy Spirit. Immediately the baptism came upon me, and I arose refreshed in spirit. I rode rapidly about a mile, when temptation came again, about running before I was called, and I was again on my knees, apologizing to the Lord for my temerity in presuming that the Head of the Church would call one so recently converted, who knew so little and needed to know so much, and whose opportunities in preparation had been so small. At the next mile something said: "How can you dare stand up as a minister of the mysteries of the Gospel, when other men find it needful to spend years in college and a theological seminary ere they venture to stand up for Jesus before his wily foes?" I prayed, and received such a copious baptism of the Holy Ghost, descending from on high, that my heart was wonderfully enlarged and filled with God. Eight or ten times I stopped and communed with God about entering upon the work of the ministry. Within a mile or less of the Church I prayed the last time; it was a sweet communion with the Father of my spirit, and was accompanied by a full surrender of my soul and body and being to Father, Son, and Holy Spirit, the Triune God, for his work and will. This was followed by a fuller communion.

I reached the church twenty minutes after ten, and found that Mr. Steadman, usually punctual, had not arrived. When he came we entered the pulpit, and as we knelt for silent prayer, I made an entire surrender of myself to God, to walk before him while I lived and to bless him when I died. The covenant was confirmed in an instant, and when I arose to my seat the anointing of the Holy Spirit sweetly assured me of acceptance, assistance, and success. After the introductory services by Mr. Steadman, I spoke about twenty-five minutes, and gave out a hymn.

A fair opening had been made on my life work. A divine voice seemed whispering: "Fear not, for I am with thee; be not dismayed, for I am thy God. I will help thee; yea, I will uphold thee. I will make crooked places straight, and rough places smooth. I will be with thee in trouble. When thou passest through the fires, they shall not kindle upon thee." I went home that afternoon, wondering at the love that crowned me with loving-kindness and tender mercy.

I heard that my service was very acceptable; and months afterward, when my name was presented to the quarterly conference for a license to preach, Mr. Spry said: "I heard this young man preach his first sermon at our meeting-house, and I shall vote with both hands for his license as a local preacher. I hope I shall have the privilege of voting in the affirmative for his recommendation to the annual conference as a suitable person to be received on trial into the traveling connection." I received the license; and was at the same time recommended to the Ohio Annual Conference, to be held in Cincinnati, August 21, 1833.

I had found my place. I rejoiced in my calling, and with a new zest set about giving all diligence to get a readiness for my great vocation. I had three appointments—twelve, eight, and six miles away. I wrote a sermon every week, committed it to memory, and then prepared a brief of about four pages, the size of my Testament, to which I pinned it. I always wound up with an off-hand exhortation to attention, to repentance, to prayer, to confession to God, to faith in Christ, and profession before many witnesses.

At this time I was engaged in packing butter for the city market. My cooper was a jovial man. One week he came with his wares, and I did not see a fifty-pound keg that I stood in pressing need of. Accosting him earnestly about it, he said quietly: "Judge nothing before the time." Starting the hoops of a barrel and taking out the head revealed the smaller vessel. I took occasion to exhort him to be in like manner "in Christ;" that if found savingly united to Christ by faith, and so remaining to the end, he should be saved. Some years after this I attended a quarterly meeting on Norwich Circuit, and this man arose and said: "Hearing that Rev. Granville Moody was to be at this meeting, I came to tell him that his fidelity to me, and especially his remarks about being in Christ as the little firkin was in the larger vessel, resulted in my spiritual regeneration. As a believer I entered into Christ, and, abiding in him by faith, I am saved with the power of an endless life."

In the spring of 1832, Mr. and Miss Ridgely, brother and sister of Mrs. John B. Moody, visited her. They came in their own carriage, drawn by two large, well-broken horses. They visited Cincinnati by stage. During their absence I went to

Norwich, and my horse took sick. It was necessary for me to return to the country store with seven or eight hundred pounds of freight. I took one of Mr. Ridgely's team, and started. At the first hill the horse refused to work, and acted quite ugly. I was alone. I used all my skill in vain to get the horse to pull a pound. He was very restive; he made a clean balk, and I was getting restive too. All at once I tried a new plan with him. I knelt down and told the Lord my dilemma, what I feared if the horse still proved obstinate ; that I knew what I could do with the horse, but it might prove hazardous if I was compelled to enforce discipline. I might succeed, but at the loss of my religion. "Now, Lord, please interfere and make this horse obedient, and save me from the necessity of compelling him. Help me in this emergency, for Jesus' sake. Amen." I arose from my knees, took hold of the lines, and started the horse with a word. He went up the hill wilingly, and I gave him a good rest on the summit. For the eight miles he went up hill and down. Prayer is mighty, and does prevail. I believe this was the prayer of faith which God ever delights to honor. This horse had never worked alone before.

Late in August I attended a camp-meeting held for Norwich Circuit, I heard L. L. Hamline, Leroy Swormstedt, and other noted men of the period preach. A collection was taken up to pay deficiencies in the allowance of the preachers. I gave two or three times, in all about three dollars and fifty cents, all the money I had with me. In consequence I and my horse fasted for the day, but the preaching was of a high order, and I presume it did me all the more good for my enforced fasting.

CHAPTER VII.

ADMITTED INTO CONFERENCE.

THE sympathy and approval of my parents, in reference to the work to which I was called, are shown by this joint letter:

BALTIMORE, November 6, 1832.

DEAR SON GRANVILLE,—We received your affectionate letter of the 28th ult., and were all pleased to see your ardor and zeal in this best of all occupations—this striving to do good. We believe that our good Lord has, in his abundant grace, given you a desire to become his faithful servant. And now, my son, take a word or two of parental advice; and may our great and good Parent help us to give a word in season to you! You must surely feel, and others must see, your absolute want of more mature and better digested human learning; and we have talked and thought the matter through, and come to the conclusion that you had better spend one year at least in some pious and respectable college before you take your riding habiliments and assume that sacred office. Now, if you determine to keep on in your present business till August — reading and studying and exhorting, and thus strengthening both talents and memory, confidence and piety—you will then be prepared to enter college, and there to make the most of your privileges. And we, by that time, most probably, shall receive another payment from our purchaser, and be thus enabled to give you that assistance you will need. . . .

Now, my son, be assured of my prayers, and of the increasing interest and affections of your father,

WILLIAM MOODY.

BALTIMORE, November 7th.

MY DEAR CHILD,—It was with no ordinary feelings of joy and happiness that I received your last letter, but with feelings overwhelmed with thankfulness, humility, and praise to our covenant-keeping God for what he has done for you. I trust it is He that has led your mind to the choice of your future course in life. It is a great and glorious work to which you essay to put your hands; and O, that your whole heart, soul, and mind may be engaged in it, and that the great Head of the Church may set you apart entirely for himself and his cause in the world, is the hearty prayer of your mother; that you may ever have such a strong desire for the glory of God and love of souls as will lead you to be willing to make every sacrifice and be willing to spend and be spent in the service of so good a master as the Lord Jesus, who saith he requireth none to go a warfare at his own charges!

My dear son, for more than twenty years, at times, I have been praying that God would condescend, unworthy as I am of such a blessing, to take one of my sons, if no more, to proclaim his glorious gospel to a dying world. But for the last two or three years before your sister's conversion I had become so discouraged I could but seldom pray with fervency for your conversion; but whenever I saw a youth standing up as an ambassador for Jesus, my mind always led me to beseech God to remember my boys for good, and take one of them to serve him in his Church; and now it seems the Lord is answering my petitions. O that I may feel humble under a sense of his great goodness, and remember what God saith, "Not for your sake do I this, saith the Lord God, be it known unto you, but for my great name's sake and for my oath's sake!" for God hath said there shall be a fulfillment of the desires of those that put their trust in the Lord. "To trust in the Lord is better than to put confidence in princes." It is the believer's privilege and duty to trust in God at all times.

You speak of dark seasons; hard strugglings. Well you may, when you have three great enemies to contend with; but, thanks be to God, more are they that are for you than they that are against you. Resist Satan, and he will flee from you; live near to God. Very much is lost of real happiness by loving this world and the things of it too much. Pray for your mother, that she may be weaned more and more from this dying world, and set her affections on things above. . . . Write as soon as you have made up your mind about spending a year at some theological seminary. I advise you to do it by all means. Do n't think about the expense. I shall look upon it as money well laid out. . . .

Your brothers and sisters all desire to be kindly remembered to you all. Your ever affectionate mother,
HARRIET MOODY.

Through 1832 I remained in the store, studying religious books belonging to Rev. E. D. Roe, then keeping store in Norwich, with whom and wife and her daughter, Miss Davenport, I formed an interesting and improving acquaintance. He was especially a valuable friend to me, taking charge of my theological studies, loaning me the standard Methodist books. I owe much to his wise care. The daughter subsequently became the wife of Cyrus Brooks, of the Ohio Conference, later of Minnesota.

My brother William, of New York, was invited by brother John to take my place in the store, and about the middle of August, 1833, my share was transferred. I settled up all accounts; and, free from debt, owning a horse, saddle, and bridle, trunk, clothing, and books, I was prepared for the approaching conference, which met in Cincinnati, August 21st. I was received on trial as an itinerant preacher, etc. The first week in September official notice was sent to me of my appointment as junior preacher on Springfield Circuit, with Joshua Boucher as preacher in charge. Leaving Norwich on Tuesday, I reached Columbus, took lodging at the tavern, and, after supper, found my way to the Methodist Episcopal Church, in charge of Russel Bigelow. Without making myself known to him, I was all eye and ear and memory for the occasion. He looked inquisitively at me; but, as we had never met, I was relieved from any service, much to my gratification. He began the service by reading about ten verses of Scripture, and then gave out a hymn. This wry-mouthed, one-sided man, with every physical disadvantage, was wondrously talented and accomplished. He impressed me as a man of rare abilities. I wonder not at the unsophisticated boy who listened to his entrancing eloquence and fervent appeals, and said to his mother: "What would be the effect if Brother Bigelow could talk out of both sides of his mouth as other preachers do?"

The next day I reached Springfield, and was

hospitably entertained by Brother Bretney. Saturday afternoon I started to South Charleston, where I made my commencement as a traveling preacher. My first text was: "For if, when we were enemies, we were reconciled to God by the death of his Son; much more being reconciled, we shall be saved by his life. And not only so, but we also joy in God through our Lord Jesus Christ, by whom we have now received the atonement." William H. Raper was my presiding elder, and in him I found an abiding friend. I had a year of great happiness.

On Monday of the conference session, held the next year (1834), I received a letter from my mother announcing the death of my father, and requesting my return temporarily. I was released and went by stage to Baltimore, and found my widowed mother bowed down with this pressure of grief. My father was ill but three days, but the sudden attack found him in a state of habitual readiness. He was graciously prepared for an exchange of worlds.

Returning to Springfield, I finished out the year on London Circuit, so that for six months there were three preachers; but there was territory and work for all three.

My third annual appointment, in 1835, was to McKendree Chapel, in the town of Fulton, now a part of Cincinnati. I went from Columbus by stage-coach, reaching my appointment September 14, 1835. I was domiciled at the residence of Brother Joseph Herron, a principal in the public schools; eminent as a teacher, a friend, and as an official member of the Church. He was an Israelite indeed, in whom there was no guile. He was afterward principal of Herron's Seminary, in Cincinnati, and to the day of his death was a noble educator of youth. His wife, a Christian lady, his son James, and daughter Lucy, made up the family. I boarded with them the first of the year; and, as my allowance was small, Mr. Herron and I opened a night-school, four evenings in the week, in the basement of the church. We had a full and flourishing school, and the financial results were very satisfactory, and helped me much in getting ready for housekeeping the first Monday in May, 1836.

On January 19th of that year I married Miss Lucretia Elizabeth, daughter of William H. and Elizabeth Harris, at their home, four miles east of Springfield, O. The marriage ceremony was performed by Joshua Boucher. She was a holy woman of God. Her first appointment as a minister's wife was to Fulton.

Shortly after our wedding, my wife, having entered upon her duties in the Church, found and felt her need of more grace to fit her for the holy services of a minister's wife. She sought, found, and professed the blessing of holiness of heart so freely promised to believers in Christ. She meekly, confidently, and joyfully confessed what grace had done for her, and ever afterward made the good confession of purity of heart by faith in our all-sufficient Savior.

This year in Fulton is redolent in our memories, having the odor of salvation to ourselves and more than a hundred others, who pressed into the kingdom. The names of Hazen, Morris, Smith, Gordon, Lithebury, Ready, Weeks, Sacker, Lehmanowsky, and hundreds of others, rise from the mists of memory. During this year I became acquainted with William Nast, who labored as German missionary in Cincinnati, under much obloquy and the bitter persecution of the Roman Church. As he patiently wended his way from house to house, preaching Christ and him crucified, the vilest epithets were heaped upon him. After about a year he gathered the nucleus of a Church. I transferred to him Brother and Sister Sacker, Brother Lehmanowsky and wife, and others, who became members of the first class of German Methodists. At the house of Amos Wheeler, in Fulton, I performed the marriage ceremony between Dr. Nast and his bride, Miss Eliza McDowell. She studied German after their marriage, and took her children to Germany for their education when they became old enough for training.

My fourth appointment (1836) was Wesley Chapel and New Street, Cincinnati—W. H. Raper, preacher in charge, and William B. Christie, presiding elder. Wesley Chapel was the parent Church in the city, and had the largest building in Ohio Methodism. I trembled at my appointment in view of my incompetency, but rejoiced in God as my support and aid, and confided in

Brother Raper as an eminent pastor and divine. We shared a large brick house with L. L. Hamline and wife, with whom we formed pleasant and profitable acquaintance. We had a laborious year, but a glorious revival of religion, and many scores were added to the Church. I recall the names of Josiah Lawrence, Christopher Smith, Robert Richardson, Sacker Nelson, N. W. Thomas, William Neff, James Ewan, Benjamin Urner, Benjamin Stewart, Morris Sharp, and William Wood.

The General Conference was held in Wesley Chapel, in May, 1836. One of the delegates, Orange Scott, had attended an Abolition meeting during the session of that conference. I can see him walk out into the central aisle in response to allegations made against him and others for attending such a meeting at such a time. His defense made a deep impression on me in favor of Abolitionism, and the speeches of Southern men, such as William Capers and William Winans, affected me most unfavorably against the peculiar institution of slaveholding, as an obligarchy founded in wrong.

CHAPTER VIII.

CINCINNATI AND ELSEWHERE.

"NO foot of land do I possess." On an autumn evening of 1837 my wife and self happened to be the guests of William Neff and wife. Mr. and Mrs. Neff were of the excellent of the earth. Her name was Clifford, and she was a daughter of General Wayne, of South Carolina. They were among the wealthiest of the families in Cincinnati. We enjoyed their acquaintance, friendship, and society, and received many substantial tokens of their regard.

On the evening referred to, at about half-past eight o'clock, the door-bell rang out merrily, and the servant announced "Mr. Urner." He was dusty and soiled, as he had just arrived by public stage from Illinois, where he had spent two or three months as the head clerk of Mr. Neff, entering government lands for his employer in Champaign, Piatt, and Sangamon Counties. The entry amounted to hundreds of thousands of acres of the best land, prairie and timber, in Illinois. After a conference of two hours in the back parlor, Mr. Urner excused himself, and Mr. Neff, entering the front parlor, smiling, said: "I suppose you have been amused at our interest in our recently entered lands; and now, Brother Moody, I will atone for my absence this evening by the following proposition : I will sell you a section—that is, six hundred and forty acres—of my recent purchase at precisely what they cost me—that is, one dollar and twenty-five cents an acre—not adding anything for costs of entry; and you can take whatever time you please to pay it; say, three, six, nine, or twelve years, with interest at six per cent. I will take your mortgage on the section you choose; or, if you please, we will let Mr. Urner make the best selection for you that he can. You can pay in any sums, from five dollars, upward. I will indorse the payment on the mortgage and send you a receipt. In the course of seven to ten years you can pay the price of the whole section, and have an inheritance for your old age which will be very valuable."

I thanked him heartily for his considerate and generous offer, and told him that we would consider it, and report to him in three days. "Well, well," said he, "you are welcome to the section, and I will instruct Mr. Urner to make you a good selection." Three days afterward I saw Mr. Neff, and reported our determination not to embarrass ourselves with such an indebtedness, though appreciating his kind and liberal intentions. He was much surprised, but we were afraid of pecuniary embarrassment. We thought, "out of debt out of danger ;" and a Methodist preacher's allowance in those days was very limited, and we dreaded any hindrance to our ministerial vocation. Those lands are now worth from forty to sixty dollars an

acre; but I negatived the proposition in the fear
of the Lord, lest I should be embarrassed in the
work of the ministry. I gratefully remembered
Brother and Sister Neff by naming our daughter
Clifford Neff Moody.

In 1838 I was traveling Troy Circuit, with
Joshua Boucher as preacher in charge, and resided
in Troy. My wife was on a visit to her father,
near Springfield. The month was May. On Monday, after dinner, I was in the saddle to visit the
Harrises on Buck Creek, and my widowed mother,
then living in Springfield. Just a little way from
a turn of the road I saw a group of two men, one
woman, and three or four girls and boys, and a
mare and her colt. The halter was in the hand
of one of the men; and as I approached I heard
loud talk from the man who held the mare by the
halter, and earnest talk from the other man. As
I came nearer I saw the woman, babe in arms,
wiping her tears, and heard her say: "What can
we do with our corn-crop if you take away the
mare? Why can't you take the colt?" "Why,"
said the man, still holding the halter, "I can't
get twenty-three dollars for that colt, with its
crippled shoulder. I am compelled officially to
take what I can make twenty-three dollars out
of; I could not get ten dollars for that colt." The
woman and children were weeping; and the man,
declaring his inability to make his crop without
the animal, had tears flow adown his manly
cheek. I rode up and halted in the ring of the
assembly, and said: "Why, what is the matter

here?" The sheriff, still holding on to the halter, said: "In due process of law, sir, I have seized this mare in legal action for debt against this man, and he and his wife want me to leave her and take this scrawny, shoulder-crippled colt for the debt. This would trammel me, in giving up good property which I have found to be his. Out of the sale of the colt I could not realize ten dollars at the utmost; and so, you see, I would not be doing my duty as an officer, and it would make me liable for the deficit. I can't do business in that way."

I saw the force of his reasoning, and pulling out my pocket-book, I handed the officer twenty-three dollars, and said to him: "Here's your money; take that rope off the mare and return her to her owner, and put the halter on the colt, and give it to me, and that will settle all this trouble, if you are all agreed." The sheriff was pleased, the farmer and his wife were delighted, the children were glad, and, unknown by any of them, I rode off leading my colt, which limped along vivaciously, and in an hour I reached Springfield, where I sojourned for the night; and the next day I went on to my father-in-law's residence, which I reached about noon. Father Harris and his seven sons were at the house, and came out to see my new purchase. They agreed that I had given twice the value of him; and Father Harris remarked that as a charitable operation it might do very well, and told me to turn him into the west pasture. My wife was glad for the poor woman's sake, that her family were helped along so well in securing the season's crop.

The colt was turned into good pasture, through which Buck Creek flowed; and, as we frequently visited home during the next three years, we were pleased to see him develop into a large, strong horse. Some three years after I was appointed to Oxford, the seat of Miami university. Rev. George Junkin, president of the university, arrived on the same day, a Thursday in 1840; and we both began services the same Sabbath. I first hitched the colt up to an old-fashioned gig, for which I had traded L. L. Hamline a modern-built sulky. The young horse worked right along to the gig, in which wife and I and baby Clifford made our debut into Oxford. We were hospitaably entertained by that prince of hospitality, Mr. Townsend Payton, whose hospitable home and wife and sons and daughters were the representatives of old Virginia manners and of old Virginia hospitality, which I never afterward saw excelled in all my varied experience.

That year and the next were replete with revival interest. Scores and hundreds were added to the Church. Two young men, sons of an elderly farmer, were added to the Church in the winter of 1840. They gave satisfactory evidence of their being born of the Spirit. The following spring they both took sick, and the elder died in the triumphs of faith in Jesus Christ. The younger lingered long, but recovered. I visited them in their sickness regularly, and preached the funeral sermon of the one that died. One day in May I visited the family during the convalescence of the surviving son, and after dinner and prayer with the family, the gentleman said: "Brother Moody, let us go to visit a sick man in the neighborhood, who will die, I fear, without religion." I bade the family "good-bye;" and on the way to the stable the brother said: "Brother Moody, I and my family feel greatly indebted to you for your labors with our sons and with ourselves, and especially for your influence over our deceased son. I wish to give you a token of our gratitude for your faithfulness with our sons, resulting in their happy conversion— and one of them is in heaven now. I have noticed that you are ill mounted; the horse you ride is not a good saddle-horse at all. He is a rough farm-horse, and rides clumsily. I have, I suppose, the best horse in this county, five years old, a dappled gray of high blood, splendid action, as good under the saddle as he is superior in harness, and high spirited. I sold him to my son-in-law for one hundred and fifty dollars, and the next day I took his money back to him and told him I could not part with Black Hawk for money, and must have him back. The horse-buyers have been after me many times to get him, but I have refused them. And now I want you to have this horse. I will put your saddle on my horse, and you take him and welcome, as a free gift. I will keep your horse, and you need not tell anybody how we traded; and, if you should ever want to trade back, just bring Black Hawk and take yours away."

I could hardly believe my eyes or ears. I said to myself: "This is the Lord's doing; it is marvelous in our eyes. Here God has returned the twenty-three dollars I gave for the colt more than seven-fold; yes, more than ten times over has the Lord reimbursed me for the relief I gave that poor family the day that I bought their colt. Amen! Ebenezer! hallelujah! *Dominus providebit!*" I went to see the sick man with my friend, and rode to Oxford delightfully, hitched the new horse to my gig, and drove down the street. Many who knew the horse and horseman, too, came out and asked me: "Where did you get that horse? That is the best horse in Butler County."

While I was pastor of the Church in Oxford, I learned that a debate on "Universalism" was to take place in Cincinnati between Rev. Dr. Rice, of the Presbyterian Church, and Rev. Mr. Pingree, editor of the Universalist paper, the *Star in the West*. I started on Monday morning with my wife and Clifford, who was then about ten months old. We went seven miles over a dirt road, on which there had been heavy rains. My horse and gig were very muddy, and so I concluded to ford the Miami River instead of going over on the bridge. I met a man, who assured me that the river was perfectly fordable, and directed me to go straight across above the bridge.

I entered the swollen stream and, within three

rods from the shore, the water was over the horse's neck, and he swimming; the gig was submerged up to my waistcoat pockets; my wife was holding the baby above the water. The wild flood of waters was proudly sweeping downward; our trunk of clothing was in the water. "Steady, Black Hawk! steady! steady!" so my voice cheered the noble horse as he rolled in the surging flood, snorting defiance to its current. "Steady, Black Hawk! steady, my boy!" Circling up stream he breasted the turn, passed the critical point, and safely landed us at the place where we entered. He struggled like a modern Bucephalus; all I could see of him while in the wrathful current was his head and half of his stretched-out neck. As he came out on dry land I jumped out of the gig, and hugged and caressed the noble animal that had just saved us from a watery grave. There sat my wife, pale as death. She was clasping little Clifford, who, with her, had lately escaped such imminent danger. I thanked God for his help in this emergency. I thanked Black Hawk for his gallant conduct in this unexpected struggle where life or death was the stake. As he stood wave-washed, I gazed on his every muscle, so lately strained to their utmost to save me and my family from the overwhelming flood. I gloried in his strength and sagacity and suasibility and quickened sense in the presence of danger. I afterward sold him to Rev. William Simmons, and thus four years were added to his "ministerial life," under a presiding elder.

While I was stationed at McKendree Chapel I became acquainted with a noble Methodist man named Vanaken Wunder. He was a butcher by trade, and a worthy and influential member of Wesley Chapel. I received from him many tokens of kindly regard. This good-will had its continued growth for forty years and was perpetuated in his family in their generations. During my pastorate in York Street, Cincinnati, in 1872–3, I became acquainted with the sister-in-law of Mr. Vanaken Wunder, Jr. She was an invalid. I visited her during a protracted illness, and led her to Christ, in whom she believed to the saving of her soul. She finally died in peace, and hope, and Christian joy. I preached her funeral sermon, and attended her burial.

At the close of this pastorate in 1873, I was appointed presiding elder of Ripley District. Peculiar circumstances made me impecunious at this time, and I found it difficult to furnish myself with the equipments necessary for a presiding elder. I had procured a nearly new buggy and harness; but was as yet destitute of a suitable horse. Whilst ruminating lugubriously, and perchance saying, "A horse, a horse! my kingdom for a horse!" we unexpectedly received an invitation to spend the evening with Mr. and Mrs. Wunder. We accepted the invitation with thanks, and worked away packing up our household stuff, with many a sidelong glance into the immediate future, which had for us no ray of light for a horse, nor indeed any prospect of means with which to purchase one. Evening came, and wife and I locked up our house, and wearily went our way to Mr. Wunder's. We found his wife and their bright boy, about eight years old, attentive, and bent on making us feel free and entirely at home. In about an hour, Mr. Wunder appeared in full dress, reminding me of an aldermanic Englishman at home. Indeed, he was a Cincinnati alderman. We were elegantly entertained, and at his well-filled table, which gave signs of all good cheer in variety and abundance, we enjoyed true hospitality. Our hard day's work in packing furniture gave an edge to our appetite, and his cheerful company, and his quiet wife's gentle manners, and their evident good-will to us, enhanced the happiness of the occasion.

After supper I asked him if we should engage in religious service. He responded, "Yes," and laid his large Bible on the stand. I read a chapter, sang a hymn, and led in prayer, and invoked on him and his God's blessing, while we renewed the consecration of ourselves to God. At the close of worship he and she left the room, and wife and I and the beautiful boy had everything our own way. On their return he began conversation by inquiring how and when we would go to our new field of labor. I replied that we would leave Cincinnati, at four P. M. next day on the steamer *Fleetwood*, and reach Ripley the same evening. He said that he knew all about my district, having bought and driven from all parts of it, cattle, sheep, and hogs, and added:

"You will need a first-rate horse to carry you on that large district. I have," he went on, "a first-rate, full blood mare of the Morgan breed, good in harness, and a remarkable animal under the saddle. She is five years old, large, and very active. If you will accept her as a present, I will find great pleasure in presenting her to you, and all the more gratefully in view of your kind attentions as pastor and minister to my wife's deceased sister, for which we feel truly grateful. The horse is in pasture a mile back of Covington. If you will take her I will have her brought to the *Fleetwood*, and you can use her next Saturday to go to your first appointment."

I was perfectly surprised, and entirely relieved by such unexpected good-will. I had not said a word about my perplexities in the matter of a horse, nor did Mr. Wunder know of my necessities. But God knew all, and relieved, and opened an effectual door for my deliverance. I thanked my benefactor, with tears in my eyes. His wife shared his joy, and seemed to enjoy our surprise and gratitude.

For four successive years this animal never missed an appointment. With me she shared all the labors of travel, always on time, always ready, always willing. She endeared herself to me and mine. If there is a future for animals, I shall be glad to meet Nelly there.

CHAPTER IX.

UNIVERSALISM.

"He who of old would rend the oak,
Dreamed not of the rebound."

WHILE I was pastor of Miami Circuit, in
1839, with Levi P. Miller as my colleague,
I resided in Montgomery, O., in the mansion of
Hon. Alexander Duncan, who was absent most
of the year in Washington, being a member of
Congress.

I had many conflicts with the Universalists, of
whom there was a large number on the circuit;
also many debates with the Baptists. One Sabbath I preached, six miles south-west of West
Chester, a sermon which occupied two hours, on
the subjects and mode of baptism. Repairing to
the house of a brother, I requested the family not
to prepare dinner for me, as I should be late for
my appointment at West Chester if I waited for
a regular dinner, but to give me two bowls of the
morning's milk, and to give my horse a gallon of
oats. I was soon through with my dinner and in
saddle, with a lively headway. As I approached
the village I saw a triplet of horsemen bounding
toward me, and we soon met. They proved to be
two brothers Conrey, and another member of the
West Chester society. They reined up their

panting steeds and said: "Brother Moody, there is the utmost excitement in West Chester. The town is all alive, and everybody is astir and anxious for you to come. We were advised to ride and notify you that the notable Robert Smith, the great Universalist preacher, is in town, and preached a powerful Universalist sermon this morning; and at its close he said: 'I learn that Rev. Granville Moody is to preach in this town at half past two o'clock, P. M., to-day. He has much to say throughout this county against Universalism, I am informed. He knows me. He attended a debate I had with a Campbellite preacher in Sharonville, south of here. I will now prophesy that he will not open his mouth against Universalism in any way in my presence; but will, when he sees me in the audience, be "as mild as a sucking dove," and will preach on some theme that will lead him far away from Universalism. He knows me too well to venture one sentence, directly or indirectly, against Universalism. Just meet me this afternoon, and see that he will not attack this faith once delivered to the saints. His craft will be to preach on some biographic or historic subject, and Universalism will not be assailed. He will not touch it with tongue or tongs. I know him well, and Universalism will go scot-free to-day. I shall take a seat directly in front of him, and when he sees me he will be as mum as a mouse. Come to the Methodist Church this afternoon, and see if I am not a prophet.'"

I replied to the brethren that I had preached

over two hours on baptism that morning, and felt too much exhausted to preach at any length, and would just notice him politely and invite him to debate the next Tuesday morning at ten o'clock. They objected that it was harvest-time, and that everybody would be busy during the week, and that what was done must be done that afternoon. I again pleaded my exhaustion after the excessive labors of the morning, and said I would explain all, and that we could have the debate early in the fall. They said that now is the accepted time; and if for any reason I did not then reply, the result would be disastrous. I told them that we preachers must sit together in the pulpit; that Brother Conrey must pray, and that we should see what we should see in the outcome.

We went to the church, and lo! each window was entirely cleared of both sashes, the house was packed full of people, and a crowd surrounded the house from ten to fifteen feet wide, and it was actually with difficulty that we could reach the pulpit. Within six feet of it sat the Universalist preacher, large and portly, and as brave as any man. His morning sermon and personal notice of me as a preacher had excited the two Churches, Methodist and Presbyterian, and had gathered nearly the town and township for the occasion. I had not yet determined to notice him, but knelt down for private prayer and said, "Lord, what wilt thou have me to do?" I received a short, sharp, encouraging response that seemed like three definitive sentences: "I am with you always;

fear not. Open thy mouth ; I will fill it." I responded : "Ebenezer ! Hallelujah !"

I arose with fearless heart and whispered to
Brother Conrey : "You pray. I will attack him."
To the congregation I said : "Let us pray. Brother
Conrey will be our mouth to God." And such an
agonizing prayer as that man uttered ! It was
devout, appropriate, fervent, effectual, and availed
much. I recollect some petitions : "Be with our
youthful pastor this day. May he lay off Saul's
armor, and, with five smooth stones from Siloa's
brook, may he successfully attack this modern
Goliath of Gath. Clear his eye and nerve his
arm, and may the sword of the Lord and of
Gideon do wondrous execution here to-day. Blow
out the false alluring lights of hell, that voyagers
on this rocky reef may keep aloof from the mael-
strom and coast of perdition, and cross the Pacific
Ocean of gospel grace, and land on the far-off,
flowery shore, where the Captain of our salvation
receives believing men to the Eden of love."

The people were carried away from formalism,
and Baptists, Lutherans, and Presbyterians joined
in long and loud amens with Methodists. I then
requested the congregation to unite in sacred song,
and announced an appropriate hymn. I laid the
Bible on the side of the pulpit and remarked
that the subject of the present discourse would
not be found in these lively oracles divine ; but
would be found in the Apocrypha of Robert
Smith, who in this morning's sermon declared
that Mr. Moody would not dare to say one word

against Universalism in his presence. Shades of
the mighty heretics of ancient and modern times,
well may ye stand aghast in such a presence as
Robert Smith! In his peerless presence language
is impotent. But who, and what of this mighty
man of renown? Alas! he is but one of the
fifteen hundred millions of our apostate race.
There were myriads before him, and myriads
beside him, and myriads shall succeed him. Who
is he? But one of the fallen race of Adam,
whose inherited humanity has been degraded by
the man "whose guilty fall corrupts his race, and
taints us all."

The sermon was mainly a presentation of the
statements of Scripture concerning the future life,
with the conclusion that necessarily follows; the
denunciations of God against sin, from that of the
angels which kept not their first estate to that of
the last apostate soul of Adam's race. No words
can be coined more explicit than those of Christ,
when he refers to the awards of the great day:
"These shall go away into everlasting punishment,
but the righteous into life eternal."

O Universalism, how have your abettors ram-
bled ruthlessly away from the truth as it is in
Jesus! It is the new edition of Satan's earliest
lie, uttered to Adam and Eve, for their unbelief,
and by this false statement removed them from
their first estate, and brought death into the world
and all our woe as well. "Ye shall not surely
die," is still the arch-deceiver's lie.

The attention of the audience was unflagging

throughout all the discourse. I felt a consciousness of divine approval, and that I was helped in
presenting the truth as it is in Jesus. A divine
unction was upon me, and I spoke in demonstration of the Spirit and with power from on high.
I believe reverently that God was present, giving
testimony to the words of truth and soberness. I
spoke as a dying man to dying men.

I invited Mr. Smith to reply; but he declined
on account of the lateness of the hour, nor could
he meet me in debate on Tuesday; and having a
ministerial engagement at a distance, he could not
say when he could reply to the discourse he had
just heard.

I served the remaining months till conference,
when I was appointed to Oxford. At this place
I met Mr. Smith, about two months after getting
settled. He drove up to the parsonage door, and
was fastening his horse when I saw and recognized him. I said to my wife: "Lizzie! there is
that Universalist preacher I preached against in
West Chester. I suspect he has come to have a
debate with me here. But it is well; 'let the
hardest fend off.'" I went out to him and shook
hands, walked into the parsonage with him, and
introduced him to my wife. He thanked me for
my kind and faithful treatment of him at the time
I preached against him, and for my successful
attack on Universalism. "Yes, sir," he said,
"that sermon was the most puissant assault that
I had ever met during all the years of my life as
a Universalist preacher. You carried your line

of argument triumphantly over the basal ranges of Universalism as I had never heard it done before, and I met a Waterloo defeat, such as I had never expected to meet. When you concluded I was defeated, horse, foot, and dragoon. I have renounced Universalism, and came to see you to-day to ask you, as a favor, that you give me the outlines of that argument, which I wish to put into a book I am publishing on the grounds of my change of opinions." I told him I had not a single line of all I said that day on Universalism. I had almost concluded not to say one word that afternoon on the subject of Universalism ; but my irresolution vanished on hearing that powerful prayer of Brother Conrey. He said he remembered that prayer, that it was the key-note of success. I added: "Well, I made up my mind to attack Universalism while I was on my knees in private prayer. The whole affair was extemporaneous; your request for a copy is an impossibility, I had not one written line, and it vanished with the breath that gave it birth. I have not a fragment of that sermon to hand you."

He said he had held scores of debates, East and West, but had never had such an attack as that. He united with the followers of Alexander Campbell. I replied to the surprise he manifested on being told that the discourse was extemporaneous:

"If you shall speak or preach extempore,
You may be less correct, but much more free ;
New thoughts will spring up as you pass along,
And honest zeal for many faults atone."

CHAPTER X.

AT OXFORD.

ABOUT the third Thursday in September, 1840, I came to the pastorate of Oxford Station. President George Junkin was elected a few months previously to Miami University, and reached Oxford the same day that I did. He preached his first sermon at the Associate Reformed Church, of which Mr. Claybaugh was pastor, the ensuing Sabbath afternoon. A notice of the service, with invitation to attend Dr. Junkin's initiatory service, was furnished to the Methodist, and, we presume, to all the Churches in Oxford. I gave out the notice with pleasure, and urged all our congregation to go and hear the Doctor's sermon at half-past two P. M.

I went at the hour, finding a densely crowded audience, but succeeded in getting a sitting in the third pew from the door. Dr. Junkin had the unenviable sobriquet of "Heresy Hunter," and he signalized his debut on this occasion by an onslaught on Methodism. "I saw," he said, "diagonally opposite this building a Methodist Episcopal Church, where, I presume, the doctrines of John Wesley are dispensed itinerantly, and you will hear the possibility and danger of a child of God backsliding, and so becoming a child of Satan;

an heir of grace and glory losing both by back-sliding; a child of God and an heir of glory laps-ing into the character and condition and doom of an apostate; a regenerated man liable to final and fatal degeneration! No, my dear friends, we have not so learned Christ nor Christianity. Neither the craft nor malice of Satan and all his hosts is able to pluck a soul away from Christ, nor drive saints to their undoing. But such crudities in logic and theology will have their day. In pass-ing through your noble State I spent a day or two in its capital, and was pleased to notice the ample provision made for the infirm in mind."

I restrained my feelings till the close of the meeting, and just as the terminal words of the benediction were uttered, I stepped out into the aisle and said: "Dr. Junkin, I invite you and this audience to the Methodist Church, in this place, to hear my reply to the attack at this hour on its well-known theological tenets, the possibility and danger of a saint's total apostasy from a state of grace. As Paul saith: 'Take heed, brethren, lest there be in any of you an evil heart of unbelief, in departing from the living God; for we are made partakers of Christ if we hold the beginning of our confidence steadfast to the end.' This Sabbath evening, if you please, Dr. Junkin, and this audience."

I went to my study, having told my wife to ex-cuse me to all callers, and at half-past six P. M. to have a cup of tea and some toast ready for me. What an afternoon was that of devout and confiding prayer for divine direction and illumination and aid! I prayed: "O Lord, give me a text and divine direction. Lay thine hand upon me, so that, speaking, I may speak only as the oracles of God." The text I selected was Colossians i, 19–23: "For it pleased the Father that in him should all fullness dwell; and, having made peace through the blood of his cross, by him to reconcile all things unto himself; by him, I say, whether they be things in earth or things in heaven. And you, that were sometime alienated and enemies in your mind by wicked works, yet now hath he reconciled in the body of his flesh through death, to present you holy and unblamable and unreprovable in his sight: if ye continue in the faith grounded and settled, and be not moved away from the hope of the gospel, which ye have heard, and which was preached to every creature which is under heaven; whereof I Paul am made a minister."

The excitement in the town was intense. It was a bland and moonlit evening. The weather was favorable. The brethren were all alert for the general accommodation. They took all the bottom and top windows out of the frames, so that the people could better see and hear. By preaching-time the house was completely filled, and a multitude outside, double that within, had assembled to hear the young preacher against the old war-horse on the topic of Wesleyan *versus* Calvinistic theology.

The devotional services having been completed,

I proceeded from the foregoing text to present the gospel themes stated:

First. All fullness for saving purposes is found in our Lord Jesus Christ.

Second. Believers are to be presented holy and unblamable in his sight.

Third. The gravamen specified: "If ye continue in the faith, grounded and settled, and be not moved away from the hope of the gospel" as preached by the apostle.

The labor of the evening was bestowed upon the third division of the subject: 1. Continuance in the faith required as the condition of success; 2. Not being moved away from the hope of the gospel enjoined; 3. The possibility of total and final apostasy to perdition; or the danger of total relinquishment of religion by a final departure from the living God.

This last was the case with the apostatizing angels; they departed from the living God by sinning. Jude adduces this apostasy as our warning: "And the angels which kept not their first estate, but left their own habitation, he hath reserved in everlasting chains under darkness, unto the judgment of the great day;" and that judgment is to a ruin complete and eternal. "Depart from me, ye cursed, into everlasting fire prepared for the devil and his angels," is the doom of the condemned of earth. These once holy angels sinned against God during their probationary state, and were cast out of heaven under the abiding and withering curse of a sin-hating

God. Their first estate was a holy one. They, in common with all the angelic hosts, were limited in their locomotion, and by the fiat of Jehovah were confined to their specified apartments as the test of their obedience. The command was, "Thus far shalt thou go, and no farther." God was pleased to put these lofty beings, with astonishing powers of locomotion, on the bounds. "Stay here," he said, "nor cross those lines into the circumjacent regions, till I see fit to give you the bounds of the universe for the range of your curiosity and adventure, as your reward. Your submission to this, my limitation, shall be the test of your submission to my rightful sovereignty." Lucifer, the son of the morning, at length questioned the right of such restriction: "What! must we be cabined, cribbed, confined to these diminutive restrictions, and limited to these domains of restricted commerce? What harm can come from the unlimited use of these bright wings of ours? 'Tis blank and purblind abuse of our rights to interpose with such tyranny, and expect our blind obedience to his fiat. And see afar what shining zones and starry scenes; and see yon bright forms of light and beauty; and list, ay, listen to their songs of rapturous joy, transcending ours afar. I am going." A spirit of wild disregard for God sprang up, and spread along the hosts, till one-third of the number joined in the dread revolt. A mighty multitude against the supremacy of heaven; angels who kept not their first estate, but left their own habitation.

This is the inspired record of that great apostasy; and we have the warrant of the Word of inspiration to cite these backsliding angels as a warning against the crime of high-handed apostates. I but follow the practice of inspiration in adducing this instance of apostasy from God and holiness and heaven. This obedience to God was the ground of the election of that portion of the angels known as "the elect angels," referred to by Paul when he said to Timothy: "I charge thee, before God and the Lord Jesus Christ, and the elect angels, that thou observe these things."

We see this doctrine in 2 Chronicles xv, 2: "The Lord is with you, while ye be with him; and if ye seek him he will be found of you; but if ye forsake him, he will forsake you." We hear David in his adress to Solomon say: "And thou, Solomon my son, know thou the God of thy father, and serve him with a perfect heart and with a willing mind; for the Lord searcheth all hearts, and understandeth all the imaginations of the thoughts; if thou seek him, he will be found of thee; but if thou forsake him, he will cast thee off for ever." In Ezekiel xviii, 24-26: "But when the righteous man turneth away from his righteousness, and committeth iniquity, and doeth according to all the abominations that the wicked man doeth, shall he live? All his righteousness that he hath done shall not be mentioned; in his trespass that he hath trespassed, and in his sin that he hath sinned, in them shall he die. Yet ye say, The way of the Lord is not equal.

Hear now, O house of Israel, Is not my way equal? are not your ways unequal? When a righteous man turneth away from his righteousness, and committeth iniquity, and dieth in them; for his iniquity that he hath done shall he die." In the thirtieth verse: "Therefore will I judge you, O house of Israel, every one according to his ways, saith the Lord God. Repent and turn yourselves from all your transgressions, so iniquity shall not be your ruin." Verse 32: "For I have no pleasure in the death of him that dieth, saith the Lord God; wherefore turn yourselves and live."

In Matthew v, 13, Christ says of his own peculiar people: "Ye are the salt of the earth; but if the salt have lost his savor, wherewith shall it be salted? it is thenceforth good for nothing, but to be cast out, and to be trodden under the foot of men." Thus salt may lose its saltness, and then wherewith shall it be salted again? It is to be cast out. Maundrell, the traveler, speaks of vast beds and ridges and jetties of rock-salt, that had become sharply crystallized; but had lost the last vestige of saline qualities, and were good for nothing but to be cast out on slippery places, in icy times to be trodden under feet of men, to keep them from falling. Christ knew of no means of restoring the saltness. We may say by Christ's authority as Mr. Wesley does in the hymn:

> "Ah! Lord, with trembling I confess,
> A gracious soul may fall from grace;
> The salt may lose its seasoning power,
> And never, never find it more.

> Lest that my fearful state may be,
> Each moment knit my soul to thee;
> And lead me to the mount above,
> Through the low vale of humble love."

In Matthew xviii, we find the instructive histories of the debtor who owed ten thousand talents, but whose compassionate creditor, when the debtor owned the debt, loosed him and forgave him the debt. This same pardoned debtor went out and laid hands on his fellow-servant, who owed him one hundred pence, and took him by the throat, saying: "Pay me that thou owest. And his fellow-servant said, Have patience with me, and I will pay thee all. And he would not; but went and cast him into prison, till he should pay the debt. So when his fellow-servants saw what was done, they were very sorry, and came and told unto their lord all that was done. Then his lord, after that he had called him, said unto him, . . . I forgave thee all that debt, . . . shouldest not thou also have had compassion on thy fellow-servant, even as I had pity on thee? And his lord was wroth, and delivered him to the tormentors, till he should pay all that was due unto him. So likewise shall my heavenly Father do also unto you, if ye from your hearts forgive not every one his brother his trespasses." Our moral debt is legally due, but graciously remitted; but when we act unbecomingly, the rightful claim is justly as well as legally due, and we will be delivered to the tormentors, till we shall pay all. Thus our gracious pardon will be revoked if our subsequent conduct to our debtors be at variance with the forgiving spirit that had released us.

Final apostasy is possible ; for a man forgiven, renewed, and adopted, may fall away, come into condemnation again, and die therein, and thus become a castaway,—1 Corinthians, ix, 27: "But I keep my body under, and bring it into subjection ; lest that by any means, when I have preached to others, I myself should be a castaway." Thus Saint Paul declared the danger of total and final apostasy from Christ in his own case ; and if apostasy was possible to him, surely it is to us also. In 2 Peter ii, 21 : "For it had been better for them not to have known the way of righteousness, than, after they had known it, to turn from the holy commandment delivered unto them."

Thus we find Ezekiel, Paul, and Peter, all agreeing in terms unequivocal and definite to the possibility and danger of total and final apostasy from Christ. "Therefore, let him that thinketh he standeth, take heed lest he fall."

The epistle to the Hebrews is, as a whole, an inspired argument and warning against the lapse of real Christians from their state in grace to an apostasy, complete and final, from Christ and Christianity. The epistle teaches that real Christians may renounce Christ and the hopes of Christianity, and measure back their steps to the broad road that leads to destruction. In chapter vi, 4–6, it is written : "For it is impossible for those who were once enlightened, and have tasted of the heavenly gift, and were made partakers of

the Holy Ghost, and have tasted the good word of
God, and the powers of the world to come, and
have fallen away, to renew them again unto repentance ; seeing they crucify to themselves the
Son of God afresh, and put him to an open shame."
Dr. McKnight, a celebrated Calvinistic commentator, gives this rendering in the sixth verse,
boldly affirming that there is no "if" in the original, and that the English should appear, "and
have fallen away."

"He that despised Moses' law died without
mercy under two or three witnesses ; of how much
sorer punishment, suppose ye, shall he be thought
worthy, who hath trodden under foot the Son of
God, and hath counted the blood of the covenant,
wherewith he was sanctified, an unholy thing, and
hath done despite unto the Spirit of grace? . . .
It is a fearful thing to fall into the hands of the
living God." "Now the just shall live by faith,
but if any man draw back, my soul shall have no
pleasure in him. But we are not of them that
draw back unto perdition, but of them that believe to the saving of the soul." "Looking diligently lest any man fail of the grace of God ;
lest any root of bitterness springing up trouble
you, and thereby many be defiled." " See that ye
refuse not him that speaketh. For if they escaped
not who refused him that spake on earth, much
more shall not we escape, if we turn away from
him that speaketh from heaven : . . . wherefore we receiving a kingdom which can not be
moved, let us have grace, whereby we may serve

God acceptably, with reverence and godly fear; for our God is a consuming fire."

Peter (Second Epistle i, 9) saith: "But he that lacketh these things is blind, and can not see afar off, and hath forgotten that he was purged from his old sins;" and ii, 20, 21: "For if, after they have escaped the pollutions of the world through the knowledge of the Lord and Savior Jesus Christ, they are again entangled therein, and overcome, the latter end is worse with them than the beginning. For it had been better for them not to have known the way of righteousness, than, after they have known it, to turn from the holy commandment delivered unto them." In chapter iii, 17: "Ye therefore, beloved, seeing ye know these things before, beware lest ye also, being led away with the error of the wicked, fall from your own steadfastness." Thus plainly does inspired Peter teach the doctrine and the facts of apostasy from Christ in the most positive manner. In vain does an uninspired man deny the danger of a saint's apostasy from Christ, with these plain declarations of the Bible.

John, in his Second Epistle, eighth verse, saith to the elect lady and her children, whom he loved in the truth: "Look to yourselves, that we lose not those things which we have wrought, but that we receive a full reward." So there was danger of losing the religion they had. In the final utterances of Jesus Christ in Revelation, he declares: "And if any man shall take away from the words of the book of this prophecy, God shall

take away his part out of the book of life, and out
of the holy city, and from the things which are
written in this book. He which justifieth, saith,
Surely I come quickly. Amen. Even so, come,
Lord Jesus."

This sermon, delivered promptly in the evening of the day on which Dr. Junkin made his
ruthless attack on Methodism, had its designed
effect in Oxford, and was followed by successive
sermons from the Methodist pulpit for the ensuing two years. The Calvinists were alarmed and
aroused as never known to be before, and every
pulpit in the town was alive with polemic theology, and the young students shared in the general excitement.

On Saturday forenoon I went to the post-office,
and had to wait for the distribution of a large
mail. Scores of students were assembled there,
and the faculty of the college were generally
present. Mr. William Y. Patton, of Mississippi, a
member of the Methodist Episcopal Church, and
a student in the senior class of the university,
was in the company. Addressing one of the professors of the university, he said: "Professor,
please re-state your argument from the foreknowl-
edge of God, which you used before the class
yesterday morning, to Brother Moody." The professor seemed reluctant, but Mr. Patton insisted ;
and there, in the presence of two hundred or three
hundred persons, a debate commenced, which
lasted till nearly twelve o'clock, noon. He insisted that Calvinism was not rightly presented,

and I quoted: "By the decree of God, for the manifestation of his glory, some men and angels are predestined to everlasting life, and others foreordained to everlasting death. Those angels and men, thus predestinated and foreordained, are particularly and unchangeably designed, and their number is so certain and definite that it can not be either increased or diminished. Those of mankind that are predestinated unto life, God, before the foundation of the world was laid, according to his eternal and immutable purpose, and the secret counsel and good pleasure of his will, hath chosen in Christ unto everlasting glory, out of his own free grace and love, without any foresight of faith or good works, or perseverance in either of them or any other thing in the creature, as conditions or causes moving him thereunto; and all to the praise of his glorious grace. As God hath appointed the elect unto glory, so hath he foreordained all the means thereunto. Wherefore they who are elected, being fallen in Adam, are redeemed by Christ, are effectually called unto faith in Christ, by his Spirit working in due season, are justified, adopted, sanctified, and kept by his power, through faith unto salvation. Neither are any other redeemed by Christ, effectually called, justified, adopted, sanctified, and saved, but the elect only."

The professor affected to be horrified at these quotations, denied that the Confession of Faith contained any such statements, charged it to our ignorance or prejudice that we imputed such doc-

trines to them.   I instantly requested Mr. Patton
to go to President Junkin and get a Confession of
Faith.   Being fleet of foot, he went to the college
and brought from President Junkin the book.   We
selected a committee of reference, composed of
Lawyer Mayo and two others, to whom the Confession of Faith was committed, and, after stating
my quotation, I turned to the well-known article,
and found that my recollection of it was perfect,
and called the attention of the committee to it,
and they fully agreed, and stated that I had exactly quoted said article, word for word, and to the
confusion of Calvinism, and to the triumph of
truth.   My victory was complete and positive, and
the effect was glorious.

The Presbyterians then sent off, and bought a
large box of "Annan's Difficulties of Arminian
Methodism," and circulated them.   I then published an edition of five hundred copies of the
"Dagon of Calvinism," which wrought effectually
in favor of the truth.

In the United States there are about fifty sects
which profess to take the Bible as a sufficient
rule of faith and practice.   Those called Protestants are about equally divided into Calvinists and
Free-willers.   Both systems of doctrine held by
them were formulated and adopted about the
time of the Reformation.   Since that time there has
been but little progress in theological knowledge
except as expressed, from time to time, by numerous secessions from old bodies, and the adoption
of reformed creeds.   These new movements, which

are the foot-prints of progress, have been invariably
denounced by the adherents of old ideas as heretical, dangerous, and soul-destroying, but were, in
fact, the means of preserving and perpetuating the
Christian religion upon the earth.   Luther, born in
1483, Calvin in 1509, Arminius in 1560, debated
these subjects fully.   However, the doctrines bearing the names of Arminianism and Calvinism divided men hundreds of years before Calvin or Arminius existed.

Fatalism and predestination, considered in their
alleged effects on man's will and action, are substantially the same thing.   Aristotle, who died five
hundred years before Christ's incarnation, taught
the doctrine of fatalism.   The Pharisees were
mainly predestinarians.   Mohammed taught his
disciplest he same doctrine ; namely, that whatsoever happens in this life was predestined and
irrevocably fixed by the Supreme Power.   This
doctrine, as applied to the Christian system by
John Calvin, is as follows : " Predestination we call
the eternal decree of God, by which he hath determined, in himself, what he would have become of every individual of mankind.   For they
are not all created with a similar destiny ; but
eternal life is foreordained for some, and eternal
damnation for others.   Every man, therefore,
being created for one or the other of these ends,
we say he is predestined either to life or death."
Again, in speaking of total depravity, inherited
from Adam, and our accountability, he says:
" Nevertheless we derive from Adam not only the

punishment, but also the pollution of sin, to which
punishment is justly due."

Of the five points of Calvinism, as adopted by
the Synod of Dort, an expounder says: "Election
is the immutable purpose of God, by which, before the foundations of the earth were laid, God
chose out of the whole human race a certain number of men, neither better nor worse than others,
to salvation in Christ, whom he had, even from
eternity, constituted head of all the elect." After
paying an eloquent tribute to the sufficiency of
Christ's atonement, to expiate the sin of the whole,
this commentator observes: "God willed that
Christ, through the blood of the cross, should efficiently redeem all those, and those only, who
were from all eternity chosen to salvation;" "God
does not take away his Spirit wholly from his
own elect, even in lamentable falls; nor permits
them to decline from the grace of adoption and
justification."

The foregoing are the peculiar doctrines of
those Christians known as Calvinists, and, no
doubt, they are theoretically and honestly entertained; but, viewed from a practical stand-point,
it is certain nobody believes them, simply because
such ideas are not practical. If the elect fall
into sin, as is admitted, like reprobates or common sinners, no one can possibly tell who those
predestined to eternal life are. Further, men, by
virtue of their natural and moral instincts, generally take a very hopeful view of their own
chances of heaven through the Divine mercy.

All have noticed how hopeful parents are of the salvation of their own families or relatives, even when in death they left no proof of having found Christ. Possibly some might allow that their neighbors or neighbors' children had gone to hell as predestinated reprobates, but they have not the slightest notion of making their own bed in that horrible place, nor of assigning their own families to the pit!

Neither do Calvinists act on that principle in their daily conduct and dealing with their fellow-men. They feel and confess by their acts that they are responsible to God and the laws of society for their voluntary acts of right and wrong. They seldom, if ever, set up the plea in extenuation of their misdoings that God predestinated them from all eternity; therefore, but few ever believed Calvinism in a practical sense.

John Calvin did not believe it. Michael Servetus, the Antitrinitarian, was born in 1500 A. D. His rejection of the doctrine of the Trinity greatly incensed the Papists and Calvinists. He escaped the vengeance of the priests of Rome; but the Calvinists caught him passing through Geneva, and burnt him alive, on the 27th of November, 1553. Calvin was then supreme at Geneva, and his secretary drew up the charges and appeared as the principal witness. Now, if Calvin had believed his own doctrine, he never could have given his consent to the burning of Servetus as a heretic, when it had been predestinated from all eternity that he should be such.

In the Constitution of the Presbyterian Church in the United States of America, containing the "Confession of Faith, the Catechisms, and the Directory for the Worship of God," you may find the following, and you may easily discern the further points of difference between Methodism and Calvinism :

"God, from all eternity, did, by the most wise and holy counsel of his own will, freely and unchangeably ordain whatsoever comes to pass, yet so as thereby neither is God the author of sin, nor is violence offered to the will of the creature, nor is the liberty or contingency of second causes taken away, but rather established. Although God knows whatsoever may or can come to pass upon all supposed conditions, yet he hath not decreed anything, because he foresaw it as future, or as that which could come to pass upon such conditions." Having disposed of the elect, the language proceeds : " The rest of mankind God was pleased, according to the unsearchable counsel of his own will, whereby he extendeth or withholdeth mercy as he pleaseth, for the glory of his soverign power over his creatures, to pass by, and to ordain them to dishonor and wrath for their sin, to the praise of his glorious justice.

Every minister in the Presbyterian Church before being licensed to preach, every ruling elder and every deacon before entering upon the duties of his office, is required to give an affirmative answer to the following, among other questions: " Do you sincerely receive and adopt the Confession of Faith of this Church, as containing the system of doctrine taught in the Holy Scriptures?"

The foregoing statements of distinctive doctrine may be safely set down as the peculiar doctrine of the Presbyterian Church. These are not the doctrines of the Methodist Episcopal Church; this is plain and positive and well known. We preach a free, a full, an increasing and abounding and attested salvation to every son and daughter of fallen Adam, through the second Adam, who is "the way, the truth, and the life."

CHAPTER XI.

INCIDENTS IN ITINERANT LIFE.

IT was the rule at Wesley Chapel, Cincinnati, when I was stationed there, for one of the pastors to be present in the Church office from nine A. M. to eleven A. M., to attend on calls. One morning a shrewd old negro, named Job Dundee, called in and sat awhile. He was a remarkable man, and a power in the Church. I said to him: "Uncle Job, how came you to be a Methodist Christian?" "Well, sar," said he, "I'll tell you. You see I bought a forty-acre lot of land down the river here, and I put up a smart log-cabin, and cleared about thirty acres. I had a ten-acre field left, which I kept for a hog-lot, as it was nearly covered with heavy hickory and oak and beech trees. I kept my hogs there, and in the fall I would cut up my corn in the stalk, and throw it over the fence, and the hogs would eat stalks and all; and they would ravage among the pea-vines; the nuts would fall from the trees, and they would eat up the fallen acorns and nuts; and with this variety of feed, if you ever saw hogs grow, mine did. One beautiful Sabbath morning I went out to see my hogs, and they were busy, and I was counting how much they would average me by killing-time, about Christmas. I averaged them at about two hundred and sixty-five pounds a head. As I sat and watched them, I noticed they never once looked up to the trees to see where their feed came from, but kept their heads and eyes down on the ground; and presently something said to me: 'Job Dundee, ain't you just like them 'ar stupid swine out yander? You have been eating and drinking and roaming and sleeping, and never once looked up to heaven, and to your great and gracious God, to see where your blessings came from. Just like them stupid hogs, you live on God's goodness; but you never look up to your Father in heaven to think where your daily blessings come from. I remember a hymn which says:

'Fools never lift their thoughts so high;
Like brutes they live, like brutes they die.'

"Conviction of sin came, and conviction that I more resembled the stupid, willful, rooting hog than a man made in the image of God. I felt humbled and alarmed, and convinced of sin, and especially of ingratitude. I seemed to hear a voice saying: 'The ox knoweth his owner, and the ass his master's crib; but Israel doth not know, my people doth not consider.' 'By God we live and move and have our being, and it is reasonable and right that we should live to Him by whom we live.'

"My mind condemned me, my conscience accused me. I got down off the fence, and down by the lowest rail I bowed myself before God that blessed Sabbath morning, and felt and acknowledged my badness of heart, and selfish condition, and guiltiness before him in whom we live. I bewailed my stupidity and swinishness, that had made me, like the hog, to go with my eyes on the earth, in search of earthly good, while forgetting God, my Maker. I saw myself as I had never seen myself before. I repented of all my sins, asked forgiveness for Jesus' sake; I looked up, and was forgiven. I became a new creature; old things had passed away; behold! all things had become new. I had a new God; a new hope; a new rule of life; a new class of feelings. I found a new way; and for more than thirty years I have lived on the heavenly manna. I love the ever-living God, in whom and to whom I live."

During this narration his whole body was in motion with his soul. His dark countenance was all aglow with celestial light. Tears of joy mingled with his enraptured speech, and I greatly enjoyed the recital of his transition from his natural state. He went away rejoicing in hope of the glory of God. He has passed away, to join the general assembly and Church of the first-born, whose names are written in heaven.

During my second pastorate in Fulton, in 1844, a strange occurrence took place. My wife's long and severe illness required me to go to several strange places. One of these was a bakery on the corner of Fifth and Sycamore Streets, with a door opening into each street. By direction of our family physician I went to this bakery for Boston crackers. Whilst standing at the counter, Dr.

Strickland was standing in the area of the room. Having made my purchase, as we went to the door he told me that a lady stopped and looked at me intently, then went around to the other door and looked earnestly again, as if she were acquainted and wanted to speak to me. "There she goes up Sycamore Street," said he, pointing to her. "That is she, dressed in black; she has stopped and is looking back at you. She seems to know you. She is coming back."

By this time she approached near enough to speak, and asked me if I was a preacher; and if I preached in a brick church, with an elevated causeway at the end of the church, by which the congregation enter and retire from it. Had the church one center aisle, with large pews on the right and left? Was the pulpit shaped like a half-circle, with a large altar surrounding it? Did you have a great revival meeting last winter, and have many joined your Church? I answered her affirmatively, telling her we had between one hundred and two hundred unite with Church during the meeting.

She then asked me what business I had in that corner bakery, where liquors were sold. I explained that they baked the best bread of that kind in the city, and that, by direction of my family physician, I was there making my purchase. Then she said: "You are the very man I have looked for in every pulpit in this city for three months; but I have sought in vain, till I happened to see you standing at the counter of this coffee-house-bakery, and I could not account for your being in such a place after seeing you stand in the pulpit as a preacher of the gospel, and leading so many into the way of God. O, it is you, sir, that I saw in the long brick church, preaching Christ Jesus the Lord.

"I was asking for the true and right ways of the Lord. I searched the Bible. I went to hear the different preachers preach. I prayed for God to guide me aright, but all was in vain. I took sick and lay for three or four weeks, and then died, and was conveyed to that holy, happy place called heaven, where I saw Christ enthroned in glory unseen on earth. I approached the throne of grace and glory, and God in Christ spoke in peace to me, and said: 'You must stay here a short time, and then return to earth, and tell some of the things you have seen and heard here, and some things you must be silent about, of which you will be warned by the Holy Spirit.' I remained in heaven about two days, seeing and hearing much about Emmanuel and the nature and mysteries of the kingdom, in words unlawful to be uttered upon earth. At this time I asked my angelic conductor: 'Who, in yonder world, called earth, is preaching the truth? for there are so many kinds of preachers and various kinds of gospel; who is right?'

"And the angel said: 'Let us go to Jesus Christ, the Lord, and he will tell us all about it, if it is best and right for you to know.' So we approached the throne, and my conductor stated my wish, and the Lord, with a benignant smile, said : 'Go with her to earth, and let her hear the gospel preached in its purity and fullness, and return here to join the chorus of the skies.'

"The angel guide bowed in reverence, as I also did, and we departed ; and, with speed unknown before, we came into the atmosphere of earth, and approached a lighted city, and went by a stream of water, and came to a place where a great hill spread back from a beautiful river. We sped along the banks of the river, and went down a causeway and along a narrow bridge, and entered the gable end of a house crowded with people, and there in the pulpit, you, sir, stood and preached the gospel of Jesus Christ. You then urged your hearers to come to Jesus, with the prayer of penitence to obtain mercy and find grace to help in every time of need. You then asked the Church to sing, and invited mourners to the altar, and they came by scores—men, women, and children, young and old—and knelt and prayed, and agonized with God in prayer.

"You then declared that the happy gates of gospel grace stand open, free and wide, and urged every one to part with Satan and his sins, and avouch the Lord to be his God. The people rushed forward and joined the Church, and sealed themselves unto the Lord, and were graciously received, and sealed with baptisms of the Holy Ghost.

"It was now late in the evening. The congregation was dismissed, chiefly with solemn, smiling faces. My angel conductor and I returned to heaven to relate what we had seen and heard, and there was joy in heaven over the tidings of souls renewed and sins forgiven. Now, I have told you all that happened at your Church that night; are these things so?"

I replied: "Madam, yes, they are. We have enjoyed multiplied seasons of like precious and abounding grace. I will give you directions how to find our church. I want you to come up next Sabbath, and see if you can recognize the place of worship." I then wrote on a card a description of the way, and invited the woman to come at nine o'clock and attend class-meeting, and then, at half past ten o'clock A. M., hear me preach.

Next Sabbath morning I was watching for her, and went down street to meet her. She met me with a solemn smile, saying: "I was here before. These are the very steps we went down the side-hill. There is the causeway to the gable-end of the church; there is the doorway we passed into the church." When I opened the church-door, the woman stopped, saying: "This is the very place we came to; there is the half-round pulpit, the central aisle; all is exactly as I told you when I saw you in Cincinnati at the bakery with Dr. Strickland."

We went to the parsonage, then to the church, then home to dinner, and talked the whole matter over with wonder, love, and praise. The woman's husband had objected to the burial of her body when she was supposed to be dead, on account of its remaining warmth; and after an apparent absence of her soul from it for two or three days, she came out of her trance, and related the occurrences to me and to Dr. Strickland, who was as much surprised as I was myself at these details.

In September, 1866, I was appointed pastor of the Methodist Episcopal Church in Ripley, Ohio. I arrived, was settled, and began pastoral work by the middle of the month. I at once commenced making pastoral calls, using my class-leaders as guides. One of them, named Campbell Howard, the leader of the class which met at noon on Sundays, was a man eminent for character and practical piety and godliness, a strictly exemplary man. We commenced the pastoral visitation of his large class, the members of which lived in the country within a radius of three miles around Ripley, and the visits employed us nearly three days.

About three o'clock in the afternoon of the second day's visitation, we came to a halt at a large gate, about a mile and a half from town, and Brother Howard said: "We have a member living up this private road on yonder hill-top; but I do not know that it will do any good to visit him, as he has not attended class for six months; and he is out with us, because I dunned him for five dollars due on last year's quarterage. He quit attending Church, and, I fear, does not care much for religion now." I replied: "He is the very man we need to see; let us go. I am sent specially to the lost sheep of the house of Israel." He smiled approval, opened the gate,

and drove into the open field, which extended
back from the turnpike, and commenced ascending
the steep hill. We soon had to fasten our horses
to a tree, and climb the hill afoot. We followed
the margin of a meandering rivulet, that found
its devious course adown the steep declivities of
the farm.

As we were wending our way along, we saw
in the road ahead of us a group made up of a
man, a woman, and three small children, the youngest carried by the mother, while the father, with
wearied steps, carried a bag of potatoes. They
had stopped on our approach, and Brother Howard, in an undertone, told me that the man was
the son of the old gentleman we were going to
visit, that those with him were his wife and children, and that they had just moved in from Indiana. The man had been sick for a long time in
Indiana, and they were in very poor circumstances.
I said that we might do them good in their troubles.
Brother Howard introduced me, and I spoke
kindly to the man and his wife, asking the names
of their children, and said: "I hope you have the
comfort and strength of real Christians in your
hearts to aid you in bearing the ills that flesh is
heir to." They answered that they were not Christians, and the wife added: "I have often thought
it would be better for us both, and for our children
with us, if we were true Christians." "Well,"
said I, "what hinders your becoming Christians
right here and now? God is willing. Christ is a
precious Savior for you. The Holy Spirit waits

to enter in.   Here is the class-leader, Brother
Howard; I am the pastor of the Church in Ripley,
and here is this rippling mountain current, with
its pure and sparkling waters for your baptism,
and equally for your children.   Just here and now
repent, believe, obey, and be at peace with God,
and go down to your house with the gospel's
double blessing, pardon, and holiness—a fivefold
blessing.   Indeed, I can promise you, here and
hereafter, pardon for all the past; a new heart and
a right spirit; an assured sense of God's favor
and blessing; providential guidance, living, and
dying a good hope through grace; and, after
death, the plenitude of heaven.   Now, why not
give yourselves to God right here and now, and
consecrate yourselves, and your children with you,
to be the Lord's forever, and claim and have him
as your God in Christ forever?   Amen."

At the close of this gospel overture the woman
was in tears, and said: "I wish he would do so.   It
is right we should, and I am so glad we may.   We
ought to have done so long before now, and I believe it would be best and the right thing to do."
"What!" said the husband, "out here?   Let us
wait till some Sunday, and join the Church then."
"What!" said I, "when God says: 'To-day, if ye
will hear his voice;' 'Now is the accepted time;
behold, now is the day of salvation?'   To-day,
and here, and now, repent, believe, obey, and be
at peace with God."   The tears rolled down both
their faces, and I continued: "Here is the pure,
rippling water, saying, 'Come, believe, obey, and

be at peace with God.'" He said: "We will."
I directed the mother to give her sleeping babe to
the class-leader, and they came and knelt down
by the glad, laughing waters, and sealed their covenant with God, having the answer of a good conscience, and their bodies washed with pure water.

I recited the service for baptism from memory,
and both parties responded appropriately. Standing beside the rapidly running stream, which
seemed delighted with its part of the service in
supplying the sacramental water, I asked them,
individually and jointly, the questions in the bap-
tismal covenant. I baptized them in the name of
the Holy Trinity, closing with the Lord's Prayer.

They arose with Jehovah's shining seal of bap-
tismal waters upon them, and we gave them the
right hand of Christian fellowship. Then I quoted,
"The promise is unto you and your children;"
and asked them, "Will you present your household to the Lord?" They gladly agreed together
to do so. I knelt down by the running stream,
after having repeated from memory the formula
for infant baptism. I received the children into
my arms, and naming each child after the name
given by the parents, I baptized them in the
name of the Holy Trinity, and added: "The
Lord receive and bless and save and remember
this solemn service in all succeeding years." The
name given to the baby was Ulysses Grant, and
I prayed: "May this child 'fight it out on this
line, if it takes all his summers' and all his
years." I called on Brother Howard to conclude

the service with prayer; and then, pronouncing the apostolic benediction, I dismissed the company.

The baptized family resumed their journey down the hill, and we went up the hill to the house of the father and mother, to whom we reported in detail what the son and his wife had done, and how their children all were baptized into the Church of God. The father was surprised, delighted, and deeply affected at what had occurred. He wept and rejoiced, and repented too; and pledged us to resume his duties in the Church, and start afresh for heaven. He promised, with a full and penitent heart, to co-operate in the good work begun in his son's family. He kept his promise faithfully and persistently to the day of his death, some years afterward.

The next Sabbath the young man was present at the church, and himself and wife united therewith.

In the winter of 1875 I left Ripley one Friday morning to attend the second quarterly meeting for Williamsburg Station. The weather was very inclement, and I was encompassed with blankets, coverlets, and India-rubber clothes in abundance. At a certain point I turned off from the turnpike into a mud road. I soon discovered a mud-hole in the center of the road, and thought I could pass it on the left; but the horse, shying from the left, plunged the right wheel into the hole, which proved to be two feet deep, the wheel sinking up to the hub, and the buggy careened.

The horse became very much excited and

restive, while I was so bound up in wraps that it required great exertion to extricate myself. Fortunately I succeeded in doing this, and leaped out, sinking in the mud to my knees, and then to my hips. I took the horse by the bit, when a man and boy came along. We unloosed the harness and righted up the buggy.

After getting the horse into the shafts, and myself back into the buggy, I asked the man what I should pay him for the assistance he had rendered. His reply was remarkable: "When you find any other man in trouble, help him out as I have helped you, and that will square the account." I commended the Christian sentiment expressed, and thanking him for the sentiment, I also thanked him warmly for the assistance he had just rendered me. I asked him: "Are you a Christian?" "No," he replied, "I am not, and never expect to be." I preached Jesus and his salvation to him so earnestly, that he inquired: "Who are you?" I replied: "I am a Methodist preacher, now presiding elder of this Ripley District, and am on my way to Williamsburg to hold the second quarterly meeting for that station." "What," said he, "are you Granville Moody?" "I am," said I. "Well, I have heard so much about you that I am glad to see you." I hoped that we should both rejoice that we had formed each other's acquaintance.

I then proposed that we join in united prayer at six A. M., and at one P. M. and at six P. M. for a five minutes' prayer till we should meet again three months hence. I urged him to agree to this arrangement. I wept, and he wept, and said: "I will." I said: "Thank God for that promise, and let us now pray before we part." I prayed that this strange interview might result in his speedy conversion. His face was covered with tears when I closed. I pronounced the benediction upon him, and we parted. I learned afterward that this man was the terror of the whole county, a pugilist, and a hard case that everybody was afraid of, and that there was small ground to hope for his conversion. I requested the Church, at the quarterly meeting, to pray to God for the man's awakening, conversion, and salvation. I engaged as many as I could interest in the man that helped me, that God would help him who so timely assisted his servant in in his distress.

Some three months afterward as I was passing through that neighborhood in my buggy, I met the man, and our recognition was mutual. What an experience he had to relate! He said that the next evening he went to a protracted meeting, and related at the close of the meeting, to the congregation, what had happened in the way, and requested an interest in the prayers of that congregation, then and there. He kneeled at the mourners' bench, and in a short time the prayers of all for his salvation were answered. He joined the Church; his wife was converted, and also united with the Church. His daughters shared in the abounding grace, and the revival in the neighborhood spread till scores were converted and added to the Church. He told me of what God

had done for his soul, and insisted that my mishap
in being upset in the road was the means of
setting him up with the people of God. He rejoiced that he had met me in my adversity; it had
proved a means of grace to his soul. Glory be to
the wonder-working God, who brings good out
of evil!

CHAPTER XII.

SABBATH-KEEPING.

A T the close of my second term of service in Fulton, the brethren from all parts of the conference wrote me to charter a light-draught steamer to take them from Cincinnati to Marietta, the place selected for the session of the Ohio Conference. I made a contract with the owners of the *Little Ben* to take one hundred preachers from Cincinnati to Marietta and intermediate points and return, at certain rates; to leave Cincinnati at nine A. M., on Tuesday, the last week in August.

At early dawn of the day on which conference was to open, we were forty or fifty miles below Marietta. I asked the captain when he could land us at our destination. He replied: "Not before half past ten or eleven o'clock." I asked if that was the best he could do, and was told it was, unless we could make some arrangement with the engineer to increase the speed of the boat.

I took the hint, and went to the engineer and asked him if he could increase the speed of the boat so that we might reach Marietta by nine o'clock. He informed me that he could by raising the pressure of steam some ten or twenty pounds, but that it would incur a risk of explosion. It would also require the splitting of wood to feed the furnaces. The additional expense would be about fifty dollars. "Will you put us there by nine o'clock for an additional fifty dollars?" He answered affirmatively, and I went up-stairs to consult with the brethren and raise the amount.

Bishop Soule was among the first to agree to the proposition. As each preacher handed in the fifty cents needed from him, he also made a pledge to pray for safety. I went down and told the engineer the result. Soon a strange elasticity was observed in the movements of our steamer. We raised waves twice the former size on the starboard and port. *Little Ben* seemed instinct with life and rolled ahead. At eight-forty-five we made the landing, and, wending our way to the church, were in time for the opening services.

This was a. stormy conference. The recent action of the General Conference (1844), in requesting, or rather requiring, Bishop Andrew to cease his episcopal services till the embarrassments growing out of his relation to slavery should cease, produced much excitement. The session was prolonged till Friday of the second week.

In returning from conference the steamer got aground, and we were on a bar all Friday night. All hands were up early to get the steamer afloat. After ineffectual efforts, the officers and crew unanimously elected me captain to get the steamboat afloat. I agreed to take charge on condition that there be no profane swearing. I got two scows from the adjacent shore, and unloaded the cargo and about one hundred passengers into them ; planted

spars on her opposite bows, and, by means of the
capstan, lifted the bow, started the wheels, and by
so combining these forces, hove the boat into
deeper water. We reloaded the steamboat, dispensed with the scows, and, going about a mile
below Guyandotte, we made fast to the shore. I
received a vote of thanks from the crew and passengers for my management.

I arose early next morning, the Sabbath, and
was suprised to find steam up, and preparations
being made to get under way. I went to the captain and protested against traveling on the holy
Sabbath-day. He insisted on going, and I resisted,
claiming that I had chartered the steamboat to
and from conference; that we had, by bad steer-
age, lost a day, and that we, as Christian ministers, protested against being compelled to break
the holy day of the Lord by doing ordinary work
therein.

A Jew took sides with the captain, and insisted
on going forward. I remarked to George W.
Walker that this man had not in any way kept or
sought to keep Saturday, his own Jewish Sabbath-
day, and now he wanted us to be compelled to
break the Lord's-day, and, withal, that I saw him
eating slice after slice of ham yesterday as I sat
opposite him at table, and that a hog-eating Jew
was a poor counselor, and a worse example for
Christian ministers to follow. He did not keep
his own Sabbath on yesterday, and now comes
demanding that a steamboat, with one hundred
Christian ministers on her, shall break the Sab-

bath of the Lord our Savior. "No," said I, "let us not yield to this Christ-despising Jew, and break God's law of the Sabbath that was made for man, and to be kept holy in all our dwellings." "No," said the now sainted George W. Walker, "I shall not remain on board this steamboat if its owners persist in breaking the Lord's-day of rest by running it to-day."

Bishop Waugh came to me and said: "What are you going to do if the captain insists on making the trip to-day?" "Do?" said I, "why, I shall insist on being set ashore." "Good!" said the bishop; "I 'll go ashore with you." He got his trunk out of his room into the cabin. Just then Bishop Soule came and took Bishop Waugh into his state-room. Shortly after, Bishop Waugh came to me and said: "Brother Moody, I believe I will not leave the boat this morning; we are providentially detained." "And so you will voluntarily travel on the Sabbath, because a steersman, maybe with a glass too much ahead, detained the steamer till Sabbath morning? Do as you are advised; but as for me, I shall keep the Sabbath of the Lord, and leave this Sabbath-breaking steamboat, captain, and crew."

And so we did. Some ten or twelve ministers asked to be set ashore. The captain, when ten or eleven had gone over the "narrow way," turned the other side of the plank up, which was so greasy from having bacon handled over it that I could not walk the plank without slipping on its greasy surface. While the captain was halloing, I went to the furnace, and holding a silver quarter of a dollar to the black fireman told him to throw a large bucket of ashes on the greasy way. He did it with such precision and swiftness as made walking safe, and trunk in hand I descended the way of holiness, safely reached the shore, and received the congratulations of my comrades who had preceded me. We piled our trunks upon the beach, clambered up the banks, and the steamer rang her bell and went on her way.

We saw a fair country spreading around, a large brick house on a gentle eminence, and wended our way to it. As we approached the spacious house, we saw its owner, a courtly gentleman, approaching us. When he came within hailing distance, he removed his large white hat, and bowed, and said: "Gentlemen, I bid you welcome to the hospitalities of my home. My name is Ladely. You are welcome to my premises." George W. Walker then addressed him, saying: "We are Methodist preachers of the Ohio Conference, which has just closed its session in Marietta. Our steamer met with a mishap, and we were all Saturday regaining the channel, and were laid up here yesterday in the evening. This morning the captain fired up, and, after an early breakfast, insisted on starting; but governed by our principles, which forbid traveling on the Lord's-day, we left the Sabbath-breaking steamboat, and so are here."

Smiles and tears mingled in his countenance. "Welcome! welcome! welcome! Brethren beloved in the Lord, I welcome you each and all to my heart and home. I also am a Methodist, and shall rejoice to shelter you."

After introducing us to his family, he said: "It is but half after eight o'clock, and we shall be delighted to hear you preach. For expediting business, let me preside as bishop, and you will aid me in making the appointments for the day. There will be two places in Guyandotte. I will recommend Walker and Moody to them; to a country appointment in a large church, Brother Gassner; to the academy, William Herr."

Thus we were assigned, and, stepping to the door, he called his colored man, who quickly responded, as "the King's business requires haste." "Dick," he said, "you go to Guyandotte with this appointment to our preacher. Pompey, you go with this appointment to the country church. Abraham, you take this appointment to the academy. Tell in each place that divine worship and preaching by Ohio preachers will begin at half-past ten o'clock this morning. Now hurry, boys, and tell the preachers, if they please, to invite and urge all their people to meet here this evening for a mass-meeting." We were requested to announce meetings at three P. M. and at half-past seven P. M., at Representative Ladely's.

We each had a pleasant day with our stranger friends; but the evening meeting was a huge one. The ample house-lot held hundreds of orderly listeners, and a multitude of Negroes came to hear the Ohio preachers who honored God in keeping his Sabbath holy. After two or three addresses by two or three of us, we turned the service into an experience-meeting, and white and yellow and black people mingled their recitals of what grace had wrought in their souls, and the good hope all entertained through grace. It was indeed good to be there. I have no doubt that God was there, and abundantly blessed the visitors and the visited.

After a night of refreshing sleep we were called up to an early breakfast, so that we could get on the *Dinkey*, a small boat drawing but one foot of water. Congressman Ladely had detailed one of his slaves to go out and watch the arrival of the boat, and had sent our baggage down to the landing. We had a delightful season of family worship, and then, with hearty relish, broke our fast of the night with thankfulness of heart, and went on our way rejoicing.

We were perfectly satisfied with our choice and acts that beautiful September morning; when, *presto*, what is this? Here, out of the channel and fast on a sand-bar, lay our Sabbath-breaking, God-defying, reckless *Little Ben*, her guards crowded with Bishop Soule and about seventy Methodist preachers going home from conference, but now stalled in their Sabbath-breaking *Little Ben*. We passed within a rod of their side, but passed in silence. In their lugubrious countenances they seemed to give utterance to the monitory apothegm, "The way of the transgressor is hard." Bishop Waugh had left the *Little Ben* and taken an open boat to go to Portsmouth and preach in the evening; but he found the sun and its reflection on the waters of the Ohio so severe, that his skin was much scorched, and he appeared before the audience in poor plight for preaching.

Our boat reached Portsmouth in due time to take the regular packet for Cincinnati at six P. M. the same evening; and thus we, Sabbath-keeping Christians, beat the Sabbath-breaking Christians, and got to Cincinnati a long time ahead of them, and found that all is well that ends well. "The end crowns the action."

Religion always ends well. Whatever difficulties may be met with in the way, the end is best. The general truth is abundantly verified that "wisdom's ways are ways of pleasantness, and all her paths are peace." Religion is true wisdom.

CHAPTER XIII.

EXTRACTS FROM EARLY WRITINGS.

PUTTING ON CHRIST.

IN order to put on Christ, we must put off the old man, or nature, which is corrupt by deceitful lusts. Our old habits are like a filthy, tattered garment. Christ will not impart the righteousness which is by faith till, like Bartimeus, we cast away our garment, and come to him for clean garments. If we could put on the new and clean garment over the old and filthy one, how then could we get the old garment off?

Christ will not have concord with Belial. "If any man be in Christ he is a new creature." He is a Christian, and "a Christian is the highest style of man." He has a new God, a new rule of action, a new object of pursuit, a new nature, a new heart, a new name, a new road, a living way, new companions, new desires, hopes, fears, aversions, anxieties, and determinations; and, if faithful, he shall have, as a residence, a mansion in the house of God in the New Jerusalem.—*May 23, 1839.*

NEGATIONS.

Positive terms may be understood in different degrees of latitude. But this is impossible concerning negative terms, inasmuch as a negative admits of no degrees. Thus the exclusion of the impenitent unbeliever is expressed in the strongest negative terms,— "They shall not taste of my supper;" "not enter into my rest;" "hath not life;" "shall not see life;" "their worm dieth not, and their fire is not quenched."

Now annex the positive terms,—"Shall be damned;" "shall be destroyed with everlasting destruction;" "shall be ill with the wicked;" "torment shall ascend up forever and ever;" and you have the whole case strongly stated by Him who can not lie. Future punishment in eternal succession is as plainly revealed as future joy, and in the same way, in endless duration.—*May 24, 1839.*

FUNDAMENTAL DOCTRINES.

Faith in the propitiatory sacrifice of Jesus Christ by all who have heard the gospel, appears from the Word of God to be fundamental, necessary "*causa sine qua non*" in the Christian religion. For if Christ is set forth as a propitiation through faith in his blood, then faith in his blood is fundamental; and, as the text speaks of him as a propitiation, then faith must have reference to him in that character. How can this exist in a person who denies the atonement, and considers the death, the blood of Christ, merely exemplary or as that of a martyr?

We are said to be justified by that faith of which he is the object; and if the conceptions of the Socinians of that object are essentially different from ours, then their faith must be as different, and ours or theirs essentially defective or erroneous. If God's plan of saving sinners requires a cordial acceptance of Christ as the propitiation for the sins of the world; if we have redemption in his blood by faith therein; if looking to Christ as crucified is a condition of cure according to Christ's own teaching when he refers to the brazen serpent,—then they who reject deliberately and habitually every idea of vicarious atonement can not be saved in that way.

Christ is said to be the end of the law for righteousness to every one that believeth. Then justification is the result of faith in Christ as the great antitype of the legal sacrifices and ceremonies. He was our vicar to die for us; not only for our good, but in our place and as our victim. How else could he have fulfilled those types? We are assured from the New Testament, especially by the Epistle to the Hebrews, that the daily and annual sacrifices offered by the Jews were typical of Christ; but if they typified him at all, it must have been in his death; and if they typified anything in his death, it must have been the atonement which he made. They could not typify in him the death of a martyr, sealing his doctrine with his blood, or an example. These are true as far as they go, but they do not go far enough. "He was wounded for our transgressions, bruised for our iniquities; the chastisement of our peace was upon him, and by his stripes we are healed." Thus by him we receive the atonement. How, then, can those be benefited by Christ as the Lamb slain, an offering for sin, who deny the atonement and reject the atoning blooddi vine?

THE TRUTH.

God says: "Buy the truth, and sell it not." Buy it, cost what it may. If it cost thee toil and labor, buy it. If thou must sacrifice ease and emolument, buy it. If thou give the world in exchange, buy it. If it cost thee thy life, still buy the truth; thou wilt be an infinite gainer. Sell it not on any conditions; thou wilt be a loser though a universe were received in exchange; "for what shall it profit a man if he shall gain the whole world, and lose his own soul?" Even a heathen hath said, "No evil man is happy;" and a greater than Cicero has said, "There is no peace to the wicked."

BEREAVEMENTS.

Bereavements are sometimes rendered peculiarly afflictive by the consideration that our sins have been the cause of the decease of those dear to us, and by conscience we are compelled to put that interpretation on the occurrence recorded in 1 Kings xvii, 18; viz., "to bring our sins to remembrance." We look on the beloved dead whom we have pierced and slain, whom we have neglected or treated with cold and indifferent behaviour, and no marvel that we mourn bitterly whilst we exclaim, "What have I done?"

Ofttimes what we call bereavements are investments in heaven, transferred there by our Heavenly Father, who cares for us and evinces his concern for our weal, by storing up treasure for us in heaven, inasmuch as we are so negligent in this important matter. Heaven is richer by those removals which cause us so much pain, and earth is intentionally impoverished in order to displace our affections from its mutable joys, and induce us to look at those things which are above, where Christ sitteth at the right hand of God. Our earthly adhesions are broken or dissolved, so as to wean our hearts from earthly things, and produce in us the spirit of pilgrims and sojourners, declaring plainly that "here we have no continuing city, but we seek one to come that hath foundations, whose builder and maker is God."

Thus are we prepared to say, "What have I here? What do I here? Give me food to eat and raiment to put on, and be with me in the way that I go, so that

I come to my Father's house in peace, and the Lord shall be my God."

> "When Heaven would set our spirits free,
> And earth's enchantments end,
> It takes the most effectual way,
> And robs us of a friend."

Speaking politically, the departure of those who are in Christ is a removal of the deposits from the bank of earth to the safe inclosures of heaven, to be disbursed to us as we shall need when mortality shall be swallowed up of life. They are not lost, but gone before; and could their voices be heard from on high, they would exhort us to follow them up the shining way to see the glories unseen by mortal eyes, and enjoy the felicities of our Father's house. They, in supereminence of beatific vision, enjoy the presence of their Lord, whilst onward, in the dateless and irrevoluble circle of eternity, the river of God's pleasure rolls, supplying immortal pleasures for the honored sons of God. Shall we, then, hang our harps upon the willows, and our heads like bulrushes, and mourn for their decease, when we know that they have died to live? They live above, and have received their golden harps, strung and tuned for endless years, and are pouring forth the full, free, melodious notes, which angels use in honor of their God. Rather let us, by holy aspiration and spiritual musings, enkindle our affections till they burst in songs of praise to enliven our heavenward pilgrimage, and thus make the services of earth a prelude to those holier exercises which shall engage our enlarged capacities when we shall see Him as he is.

Our friends, our relatives, have gone—whither? To their Father and our Father. We remember their love, dear before, but O, how much dearer now!

Could we see them, we should love them more than we did, more than we do. They are freed from all imperfection, and adorned with the splendors of the skies; they, with radiant glories, reflect the luster of the central sun, high in the climes of bliss. My own dear babe is there, my first-born, my lovely Ellen; freed from pain and free from the pollutions of the world; warbling the praises of her father's God; caroling the glories of the satisfying portion of her mother's saintly spirit; waiting, according to the intelligence received from heaven's King, to welcome us into the everlasting habitations. Come, death and some celestial band, to guide us upon high!

Early in my ministerial life I was called to be the stay and support of a widowed mother, who was mourning the loss of the best of husbands, the kindest of fathers. With anguished heart and weeping eyes, and womanly eloquence of grief, she told the tale of woe, but mourned not as those who have no hope. My father, William Moody, lived a life of faith, and to Christian precept added the influence of a holy life. Beloved by his family, respected in the world, honored in the Church, he passed the term of his sojourning here in humble love and filial fear. For him the grave had no terrors, eternity no alarms. With an Abrahamic faith, he resigned his all to God. When asked by my dear mother whether light shone upon his path, he replied with heroic calmness, although in the height of the last conflict with the last enemy, "Harriet, I have trusted Christ; I must trust Christ; I do trust Christ;" and calmly rendered up his life at the command of God.

My brother, Edward Payson Moody, died at the age of nine years, and gave us satisfactory evidence that he sleeps in Jesus. Lately sister Ellen (Mrs.

Holliday) lost her babe, her boy, her only child; Brother William has five babes in glory; many have gone. We are going, like clouds driven by the steady wind. Rapidly we are hastening from horizon to horizon, and soon, away from the gaze of mortals hurried, we shall enter the boundless expanse of eternity, the horizonless range of being, with immutable character, corresponding to the permanent institutions of successive duration. Great God, forbid that any of us, as clouds without water carried about of winds, or wandering stars, should be hurried to the blackness of darkness forever !

> " Then soon or late, o'er life's rough sea
>   By storms and tempests driven,
> O may we meet, no wanderer lost,
>   A family in heaven !"

I have stood by the bedside of the Christian when death was feeling for his heart-strings; when the long-loved scenes of his life were retiring, proclaiming their emptiness when the world, the hollow-hearted world, owned itself to be a bruised, broken reed; and the physician was there, his rigid, set features showing with how much fortitude he had taken his stand against diseases, the van of death, and disputed every inch of territory with the ruthless invader, but all in vain. Baffled, disappointed, conquered, he grounds his arms and yields his patient, though reluctantly. And there were friends and family connections; and there, too, was the frail form of her who, in early life, by the now dying man, was led to the altar, and there promised to love, obey, and keep him in sickness as in health, and forsaking all others to cleave to him till death should them part. Faithfully she kept her plighted vows, and through storm and calm, and joys and sorrows, she has accompanied him; and, like the vine, the

fruitful vine, she embraced him for weal or woe, for
better or for worse. The tendrils of her affections en-
twined themselves around the boughs of his more
rugged nature. The evergreen of her love, alike in
winter and in spring, adorned him most enviably,
clinging to him alike in the spring of life and when
wintry winds prevailed. When others, like neighboring
trees, stretched forth the hand of welcome, and wooed
her thence, she, with unchecked affections, clasped
him closer, still his wife, the light of his eyes, his solace
amid sorrows.

Yes, I have seen her at his dying bed. Her heart,
filled by its trembling fears, o'erflows in lamentations
and mourning and woe. She embraces the loved
form, though the seal of death is there. She lays her
fainting head on the heaving bosom of the dying man,
and holds strange converse with his fluttering spirit.
His eyes would fain kindle into the soft effulgence
of reciprocated love, but they fail. He lays his hand
upon her throbbing head, his tongue faiis to supply
the vehicle of thought or love; but, still as the grave,
as though under its silent solemn influences, whilst
his frame shakes and his limbs tremble with the chills
of death, he embraces her and imprints, with lips quivering in agony, as first in life's fair morn, so now
in life's decline, the pledge of heart-felt love. His blessing, like the dew of heaven, rests upon his children,
whilst his speaking eye and faltering tongue, and
every action, say, Meet me in heaven.

Yes, I have witnessed such scenes. I have, as a
minister of the gospel, administered the stimulating
cordials of God's promises. I have seen death conquered in the conflict, or held at bay by the majesty
of holiness. I have seen the believer walk, not fly
nor run, but walk as though he were in an eastern

spice-grove, through the valley of the shadow of death, devoid of fear.   We have sung the songs of Zion, the songs of deliverance here in the strangest part of the strange land, till all the regions were vocal with the re-echoed notes of triumph.   And between the music of both worlds the holy spirit took its upward flight.

The abundant entrance thus administered into the mansions of glory illuminated, as it were with heaven's own radiance, the favored apartment, and we felt that "God was not far from every one of us."

> "Such the prospects that arise
>   To the dying Christian's eyes;
>   Such the glorious vista faith
>   Opens through the shades of death."
> —*Montgomery, October, 29, 1839.*

THE WORD MADE FLESH.

Should it be asked why Christ is called the "Word," the proper answer seems to be, that as a thought or conception of the understanding is communicated by words, so is the divine will made known by Jesus Christ to man.   He is the offspring and emanation of the eternal mind, a promanation pure and undivided, like that of light, which is the proper issue of the sun, and yet coeval with its parent orb. Since the sun can not be supposed, by the most exact and philosophical imagination, to exist a moment without emitting light,—and if one were eternal, the other, though strictly and properly produced by it, would be as strictly and properly coeternal with it,— so Jesus Christ is styled the only begotten of the Father, the brightness of the Father's glory, the express image of his person; according to a more literal rendering, "the outbeaming of the Father's glory."

As its regards the figurative allusion of the writer of this text, we may observe that, as to the sun, it has an inherent splendor and a proceeding splendor; the latter is not only of, or from, the former, but of the same nature identically; and also was in the inherent splendor as well as now that it hath proceeded from it, it is the proceeding splendor. Had the inherent splendor been eternal, the proceeding splendor would likewise have been eternal. So Jesus is, according to the Nicæan creed adopted in the primitive and purest ages of Christianity, "God of God; very God of very God; begotten, not made; of one substance, power, and glory with the Father; Light of Light." As we can not know the mind of man but by speech, nor see the sun but by his emitted light, so no man knoweth the Father but the Son and he to whom he will reveal Him.—*October, 1839.*

THE BIBLE.

The great Jehovah has spoken to man. He has revealed his will. His word is for a lamp to our feet, a light to our path. It contains the only and sufficient rule of faith and practice. It is able to make us wise unto salvation. How invaluable, then! Its worth is countless. Dark, dreary, and cheerless must be the condition of those who enjoy not its light. It is difficult even to conceive their destitution.

We have contemplated man as a weary, way-worn traveler, without a guide, whose pathway is dark and dismal as the wing of the angel of despair,—surrounded by snares, exposed to dangers, seductive influences breathing around him, no kind guiding hand, no light beaming on his way, and beguiled by the adversary, the deceiver. As a voyager on life's tempestuous sea, he has no pilot, compass, or chart. The sea he navigates is full of dangers; hidden rocks and treacherous whirlpools are on every side. The curtains of midnight envelop his gloom. The storm is up. The wing of the tempest sweeps onward with fury. That bird alone, whose birthplace was the habitation of storms, whose cradle-bed was the bannered clouds of heaven, rides in the wild and universal disorder which prevails.

Such is man's condition without the influences of divine revelation. Thanks be to God for this unspeakable gift, a guide for the Christian to

> "The home of the Father above,
> The palace of angels and God!"

It is at once pilot, chart, and compass, by which we may navigate safely the dangerous sea of life. It is the star which lends its steady light to the darkness of our way. It is the glorious beacon-light, kindled by Jehovah himself, to conduct man's frail and storm-stossed bark to the haven of endless rest. May its light rejoice every habitation and every heart!—*Montgomery, July 22, 1840.*

Experimental knowledge is theoretical knowledge applied and acted upon. For instance, the woman who had been diseased twelve years, said within herself, "If I may but touch;" this was her opinion. She came and touched his garment, and felt in her body that she was healed; this was her experience. So the sinner hears of Christ, forms an opinion of his ability and willingness to save; he lays hold upon the hope set before him, and obtains a knowledge of salvation by the remission of sins.

I would rather suffer for speaking the truth than that the truth should suffer in consequence of my not speaking.

CHAPTER XIV.

REPORTS FROM VARIOUS CHARGES.

Fulton, Feb. 29, 1836.—Gratitude constrains me to announce to the friends of Jesus, that we have been favored with his presence, I may say almost uninterruptedly, since the 20th of September. Since then we have had between ninety and ninety-five applications for a probationary relation to the Church. Many have experienced religion, and the work is progressing. But the best of all is, God is with us as a refiner and purifier. Since last Monday eve, four of our members (one a class-leader) have obtained the blessing of sanctification, and are now the living witnesses of Jesus that sin is all destroyed. Last night between twenty-five and thirty of our members presented themselves at the altar as candidates for this great salvation; and with strong crying, and tears, and groanings which could not be uttered, waited for the descent of the Holy Ghost. It was a glorious time. We felt that God was not far from every one of us; and, glory to his name, he left his bessings behind him. Two found that their hallowing Lord had wrought a perfect cure, and we believe that many are stepping into the pool.

Montgomery, April 2, 1840.—West Chester Circuit has been favored with a gracious outpouring of the Spirit. As the result of a series of protracted meetings, about one hundred and eighty names have been received. The work is advancing steadily. Our congregations have been increasing. Many are counting the cost, whose names we expect soon to enroll as followers of the Lamb. The diversity of sentiment on religious subjects, which exists in this region so extensively, has much retarded the progress of the gospel. Truth has to contend with nearly every grade of error and delusion, from Calvinism down to Universalism; but truth is mighty, and is prevailing.

Lancaster, December 16, 1847.—We have been favored with a revival in this charge. The altar of prayer has been surrounded, night after night, with awakened persons seeking religion. Souls have been converted every evening. Many are seeking the blessing of perfect love.

Zanesville, Feb. 13, 1850.—The Seventh Street charge is in the midst of a glorious revival. This work of grace was decidedly developed about six weeks since, and has steadily progressed in interest; and, I think, the prospect has never been so good for a general work as at present. The membership have been quickened by the spirit of grace, many backsliders have been reclaimed, the deep-seated carelessness of the impenitent has been disturbed, and a general seriousness pervades the overflowing congregations which crowd the spacious church in this charge. Our beloved presiding elder, the venerable Jacob Young, has abounded in labors with us; his solemn sermons, agonizing prayers, fervent expostulations, and faithful exhortations, we believe, will not soon be forgotten. Long may his valuable life be spared! The altar has been crowded, night after night, with penitent persons, as also the pews in front of the altar, while ever and anon the shout of victory ascended from those who found deliverance through the blood of the Lamb. We have received an accession of one hundred and twenty-two to the station—some twelve or fifteen of them by certificate—the rest on trial. These persons are of a class that promise great usefulness to the Church. We think you will hear from us again soon.

March 18, 1850.—About a month ago, we had the pleasure of reporting the progress of a blessed revival of religious interest in this station, at the close of which we said: "We think you will hear from us again soon." Thank God, that expectation has been realized! The meeting has been protracted, nearly without interruption, till the present time. The altar has been surrounded with inquiring souls, and "the hand of the Lord was present to heal." Upward of forty persons have been added to the Church since our last report, making, in all, some one hundred and sixty, with a fair prospect still. As a society, we feel the vast responsibility that rests upon us, and rejoice with trembling. O, that we may be kept from the evil that is in the world!

Zanesville, O., April 30, 1851.—We have just closed the labors of our third quarterly meeting. It was, indeed, a time of interest and profit; and

now that the time of our departure from this station is approaching, we deem it proper, with profound gratitude to God, to report progress, and
state the results of the labors of the Church in
this charge during our pastoral connection with it.
Since last November there have been two hundred and twenty-six applications for membership,
one hundred and ninety-four on trial, and thirty-
two by certificate—most of whom have been
received and classed; which, with the one hundred and eighty-three received during our first
year in this charge make, within the last eighteen
months, the total of four hundred and nine acces-
sions to the Church.

The revival has brought a great number of
young men into our communion, greatly increasing the· strength of this charge, and they still
promise great usefulness in this arm of the army.
I have found the membership emphatically a
working people, gladly co-operating with us in all
the holy enterprises of the Church; and our approaching separation, by the limitation of our
economy, fills our hearts with sorrow. "We have
them in our hearts, to live and die with them;"
for, take them all in all, we fear that "we ne'er
shall look upon their like again." The religious
instruction of children has not been overlooked.
We catechise them on the afternoon of each Saturday; and our Sabbath-school is in full tide of
successful operation—from two hundred and seventy to three hundred children in attendance,
under the care of an efficient corps of thirty-five

teachers, most of whom are truly pious and enthu-
siastically devoted to the work.

We yet look for a large harvest from this fruitful field, although we regret that so few children
have been gathered into the fold of Christ during
the gracious visitation of the Church. In addition to our Sabbath services, we have a general class-meeting on Monday evening, preaching
Wednesday evening, prayer-meeting on Friday
evening of each week, all of which are well attended; and by this steady drill we hope to train
up these volunteers to be intelligent, consistent,
and efficient disciples of the Lord Jesus Christ.
With increasing confidence in the heaven-honored
union of "free grace and free seats," and all the
appliances and means of our beloved Methodism,
as set forth in her admirable Discipline, we remain
your fellow-laborer in the kingdom of God.

DEDICATION AT FULTON.

We had the pleasure of attending the dedication
of the new and beautiful chapel in Fulton, of which
Rev. G. Moody is pastor. The corner-stone was laid
about June 1st. Our expectations were more than
realized; and we had a demonstration of the benevo-
lent enterprise of the Fulton Methodists, than whom
a more united, pious, devoted, and liberal membership can not be found. The chapel occupies a central and commanding position, and is unsurpassed for
neatness and convenience by any church in the city.
Though large, it was filled to overflowing.

The dedication sermon was preached by Rev. G.

W. Walker, from Luke i, 33, which was listened to with great interest; and, as an evidence of its effect upon the hearers, a collection was taken up amounting to one thousand dollars. The sermon was spoken of as one of Brother Walker's happiest efforts. In the afternoon an appropriate and interesting sermon was preached by Rev. J. T. Mitchell, and the sacraments of the Church were administered by the pastor. Rev. W. P. Strickland conducted the evening services, during which the Church received a heavenly baptism. It was, indeed, a time of refreshing from the presence of the Lord.

Every pious heart seemed filled to overflowing, and one general shout of praise and triumph went up to God. A more unequivocal divine approbation we never felt or witnessed. Thirteen persons, seven of whom were young men in the vigor of life, presented themselves for membership. The language of the poet, as it swelled out from the full hearts of Zion's worshipers on that occasion, never appeared more impressive :

> "These temples of thy grace,
> How beautiful they stand,
> The honor of our native place,
> The bulwarks of our land!"

The prospects of this station are highly flattering, and we anticipate great success the ensuing conference year.   VISITOR.

CINCINNATI, 1844.

METHODISM IN COLUMBUS.

In 1845, Granville Moody had a time of prosperity, and at the end of his first year reported six hundred and forty-four members. He led in the effort to or-

ganize a second Church. Mr. William Neil gave an
eligible lot; a church was built, and christened Wesley Chapel. During 1846, Brother Moody arranged for
the division of Town Street membership into two
bands, representing six hundred members to be divided.—*T., in Western Christian Advocate.*

On our arrival at Columbus at eleven o'clock P. M.,
July 29, 1845, we found excellent accommodations at
the Neil House, the mammoth house of the West—
an immense pile of buildings, overshadowing all others
in the capital of our State. Mr. Neil has lately generously donated to the Methodist Episcopal Church a
lot on High Street. on which we notice the foundations of the new church, so much needed in Columbus. We pray that God may bless him and his family.
This is true patriotism. "He loveth our nation and
hath built us a synagogue," was spoken to the credit of
one of old time. Before we had finished the duties of
our morning habiliments (which do not require much
time for us), our old friend Moody roused us by his
importunate rap, rap, rap, at our door, and insisted
that our traveling companion, Brother S. Williams,
Esq., and myself should breakfast at the parsonage.
And very soon we found ourselves comfortably seated
in the parsonage parlor, and greeted so heartily by
Sister Moody that we felt ourself entirely at home,
enjoying a Methodist preacher's welcome. Columbus
contains about ten thousand inhabitants, and is really
a thriving place. . . . Brother Moody's labors
have been greatly blessed during the last year, so that,
through the instrumentality of his labors, the Church
has grown in grace and in numbers.—*Charles Elliott,
Editor W. C. Advocate.*

Springfield, March 4, 1853.—The present conference year in Columbia Street charge, as the
past, has been marked with great interest. The
Word of God, which we have been permitted to
bear to this people, has not returned void, but
has accomplished that whereunto it was sent.
About six weeks since, we noticed special indications of a revival; the faith of the Church waxed
strong, and their supplications were fervent, importunate, and, of course, effectual. We can not
say there was no excitement; this, to minds concerned upon subjects of such solemnity, sublimity,
and paramount importance as religion presents,
were, indeed, impossible. The truths of revelation, applied by the Holy Spirit, stirred the dangerous slumber of careless sinners. There was a
deep moving of the mental waters, a tumultuous
invasion of conscience by the lashing waves of
conviction, exhibiting, in Pentecostal type, the
presence and power of the Spirit. We know that
the work was of God, that, in truth, he was revealed in solemn majesty and matchless grace, and
strong hearts bowed at his presence; the countenances of the people seemed to gather blackness;
sinners in Zion were afraid; fearfulness surprised
them, while their hearts meditated terror, and every
action said: "Who among us shall dwell with the
devouring fire; who among us shall dwell with
everlasting burnings?" The altar of prayer has
been thronged with penitent persons; last Sabbath day more than forty were at the altar, and
in the evening of the same day, thirty-five kneeled

at the favored spot, while the Church, with one accord, surrounded them, as with a wall of warm hearts in unison of prayer, and from that altar scores have arisen to rejoice in boundless Mercy's pardoning love.

One hundred and forty have been added to the Church, and even a larger number have chosen the good part which shall not be taken away from them. The religious influence has extended into our sister Churches, and their labors are being crowned with success. Since the opening of the present week, there are encouraging indications in the High Street charge, under Brother Weakley's labors.

Dayton, December 14, 1854.—For the last six weeks the spirit of grace has descended on Raper Chapel charge, like showers that water the earth. We found that the Church had a mind to work; and to work we went, the Lord working with us mightily, and we are graciously permitted to announce a revival in progress. There has been a general quickening of believers, and an awakening influence upon the unregenerate, with an intense desire to hear the word of life, so much so, that our commodious chapel is filled to overflowing, many being unable to find seats. The altar of prayer has been approached, night after night, by penitent souls, and many have found peace in believing. The cases of conversion have been as strongly marked as any I ever witnessed. Between fifty and sixty persons have been added to the charge since the first of November. The field is indeed "white to the harvest," and we hope for a glorious ingathering to this fold during the winter.

APPOINTMENTS FROM 1833 TO 1882.

1833–34.—Springfield Circuit, Joshua Boucher preacher in charge; William H. Raper, presiding elder.

1834–35.—London Circuit, with the same colleagues. My father, William Moody, died in Baltimore, Md., in September of this year.

1835–36.—Fulton, Leroy Swormstedt, presiding elder. Favored with large revival influences from on high during this year. The Lord was with me day by day. Glory be to his name! January 19, 1836, married Miss Lucretia Elizabeth Harris, eldest daughter of Mr. William Hickman Harris and Elizabeth, his wife, at their home, four miles east of Springfield, Clarke County, Ohio, Joshua Boucher performing the nuptial ceremony.

1836–37.—Wesley Chapel, Cincinnati, as junior preacher; W. H. Raper was preacher in charge. We enjoyed great success in the charge. J. N. Maffitt spent one month with us.

1837–38.—Troy Circuit, J. Boucher in charge; George W. Walker, presiding elder. Had a glorious revival of religion, and large ingatherings in Troy, Palmer Chapel, New Carlisle, and Grafton Chapel. Elizabeth Ellen Moody was born August 17, 1838.

1838–39.—Junior preacher on Franklin Circuit, with George W. Maley, preacher in charge. We had a glorious revival in Franklin—one hundred and twenty added to the Church, and many additions at other points. Elizabeth Ellen Moody died December 56, 1838.

1839-40.—Miami Circuit, Levi P. Miller, preacher in charge. Resided in Montgomery, Hamilton County, in the mansion of Alexander Duncan. Clifford Neff Moody was born in Dr. Duncan's house, April 25, 1840. Had many conflicts with Baptists on immersion, and with Universalists. Glorious meetings in many places on this charge. Zion was built up in troublous times.

1840-42.—Oxford Station, Geo. W. Walker, presiding elder. Here Dr. Junkin attacked Methodism in his inaugural address as president of Miami University. I replied, and a controversy on Calvinism ensued, which proved of benefit to Methodism.

1842-43.—Lebanon Station, Geo. W. Walker, presiding elder. William Hickman Harris Moody was born November 14, 1842. Many worthy members in this Church.

1843-45.—I was appointed preacher in charge of Fulton Station; built a large new church here, which was called McKendree Chapel. We were favored with a glorious revival of religion these two years.

1845-47.—Columbus Station, Robert O. Spencer, presiding elder. Here a large church was built during my pastorate. We had a gracious revival of religion, and many members were added to the Church. Glory be to God.

1847–49.—Lancaster Station, John W. Clark, presiding elder. Harriet Elizabeth Moody born November 5, 1847. We were blessed with a glorious revival, and many joined to the Lord and to the Church.

1849–51.—Zanesville, Jacob Young, presiding elder. Here we had a glorious revival, and multitudes were added to the Church, such as shall be saved. Glory be to God!

1851–53.—Springfield, Michael Marlay, presiding elder. Mary Ellen Moody born March 10, 1852. Delegate to the General Conference held in Boston, May, 1852. Glorious revival both years.

1853–55.—Raper Chapel, Dayton, same presiding elder. Granville Moody, Jr., was born July 2, 1854. Here revival followed revival, and, the Church, walking in the fear of the Lord and the comfort of the Holy Ghost, was edified and multiplied.

1855–57.—Xenia. Here we were again blessed with revival influences, and the Church was increased in numbers and graces. Charles Payson Moody was born May 20, 1857.

1857–59.—Piqua. Greene Street charge. Very pleasant and profitable years. Revivals both winters. Delegate to the General Conference held at Buffalo, N. Y., 1860.

1859–60.—Urbana. Enjoyed a great revival here. Rev. (now Bishop) William Taylor spent a month with me. His presence was a great blessing to us all.

1860–61.—Cincinnati. Morris Chapel.

In 1861 I was transferred into the volunteer army of the United States, and was appointed by the special agency of Governor Dennison to the command of the Seventy-fourth Regiment, Ohio Volunteer Infantry, as colonel, with Lieutenant-Colonel Alexander Von Schrader; and Alexander S. Ballard, Major; with Captains Thomas C. Bell, Stephen A. Bassford, Samuel T. Owens, Austin McDowell, Joseph Fisher, Walter Crook, Albion W. Bostwick, Robert P. Findley, Joseph H. Ballard, Patrick Dwyer; Rev. Samuel Marshall, a Baptist clergyman, as chaplain. Between Chaplain Marshall and myself the purest and strongest Christian friendship sprang up, and grew with our growth and strengthened with our strength; it was like to that of David and Jonathan. Blessed man! His mortal remains repose in the cemetery near Jamestown, Ohio. Peace to his sleeping dust!

In May, 1863, I was reluctantly compelled by severe illness to resign my commission as colonel commanding the Seventy-fourth Regiment. The surgeons informed me that my case was hopeless if I remained in the army.

In 1864 I was appointed presiding elder of the Cincinnati District, as successor of Rev. John T. Mitchell, deceased. Delegate to the General Conference held in Philadelphia in May, 1864.

1865-67.—Piqua. I had a gracious and glorious revival of religion, and rebuilt the church edifice, raising the whole massive structure by screws some six feet; adding a large building on the rear of the church.

Whilst here, my daughter, Clifford Neff, was married to Lieutenant-Commander Joseph Fyffe, of the United States Navy, August 17, 1865.

1867–69.—Ripley.   Had a glorious revival here.   A new church was commenced, which, when finished, cost $32,000.

1869–72.—Stationed in Newport, Ky.   I found the new Church greatly in debt, devised a successful plan for extinguishing the Church debt, and was favored with several distinct revivals of religion.   While in this charge my daughter, Harriet Elizabeth, was married to Mr. O. J. Rowe, of Binghamton, N. Y.

1872–74.—York Street, Cincinnati.   In this charge were many of the excellent of the earth.

1874–78.—I was appointed presiding elder of Ripley District, a most valuable field of ministerial labor.   We were highly favored with times of refreshing from the presence of the Lord and the ingathering of hundreds of souls into the fold of Jesus.   In this broad field of labor, which was one hundred miles in length and forty miles broad, there was not one mile of railway.   Delegate to the General Conference held in Baltimore in May, 1876.

Mary Ellen, our third daughter, was married to Rev. Professor Hugh Boyd, of Cornell College, Mt. Vernon, Ia., August 20, 1874.

Granville Moody, Jr., and Miss Jennie Parkisson, only daughter of Mr. William Kenton Parkisson, of Jasper County, Indiana, were married by me in her father's residence, January 19, 1876.

1873-79.—Middletown. I here found an admirable, intelligent, and united membership, full of faith, hope, and love, and ready for every good work. Peace be to this Church! I love it much.

1879-81.—Hamilton. This charge is very large in membership, and I sincerely endeavored to form a second charge, but without success.

I here formed the acquaintance of Judge Hume and his family. They very frequently attended my ministry, and I entertain the highest respect for them, one and all. He was a decided Democrat, and I was a decided Republican; but our friendship was like unto that which existed between David and Jonathan. At the last conference session held in Hamilton, wife and self were the invited guests of Judge Hume, and a most pleasant week we spent at his mansion. God grant us a happy meeting in the mansions of the skies!

Charles Payson, my youngest son, and Miss Ida Parkisson, daughter of Mr. Addison Parkisson, all of Jasper County, Ind., were married by me at the residence of the bride's father, September, 17, 1879.

1881-83.—Stationed at Jamestown. My health failing in the last third of my second conference year, I deemed it best to ask the conference for a change of relation from that of effective to that of superannuated.

My request was granted, and I removed to Mt. Vernon, Iowa, to reside with my daughter Mary and her husband, Professor Boyd.

CHAPTER XV.

DREAMS, PRESCIENCE, AND THE PRETERNATURAL.

AT the commencement of my second term of pastoral service in Springfield, I related at the breakfast-table a strange dream I had the night before. I dreamed that I had preached a sermon to the Church on early and persistent sympathy with sinful persons—the aged, the middle-aged, the young—with direct and special efforts to induce them to think upon their ways, and make haste and delay not the great task of repentance toward God; and then persistent faith in our Lord Jesus Christ as "the way, the truth, and the life." I asked and urged sinful persons to come to the altar of prayer, saying, with David: "I will go to the altar of God; I will wait and see what he will say to me." When I said, "Shall I not this evening hear some one say, by appropriate action, if not in words:

'I can but perish if I go,
 I am resolved to try;
For if I stay away I know,
 I must forever die?'

lo! a little girl of twelve, neatly but yet poorly dressed, came forward to the altar and knelt down. The membership, generally, took up their overcoats and wraps, and were about to take their departure, leaving the poor little girl at the altar of prayer, with but a small portion of the Church to remain and pray with and for her.

I noticed the movement, and expostulated with them, and reminded them that the minimum might become the maximum if they stayed and prayed with this little girl; and reminded them that they who were faithful in that which is least, would assuredly be faithful in greater things. "Come, brethren and sisters," I said, "stop and turn to God's altar, and mingle your tears with this solitary mourner. Christ is now saying to us: 'He that is faithful over a few things, I will make him ruler over many things.' Come, brethren and sisters, tarry and mingle your sympathies, and pour out your prayers faithfully with this one child, the first to seek our sympathies and ask our prayers. God will bless your labors with an altar crowded with seekers of religion, and the Church shall right speedily be called upon to rejoice over souls renewed and sins forgiven."

In my dream I saw the whole Church return to the altar, and each made the cause of the little girl his own; and speedily the loosened current of salvation came down from above. The little girl was converted, and the whole Church was blessed. A great revival followed; scores and hundreds were added to the Church.

I awaked from my slumbers, and lo! it was but a dream. My family and Miss Sarah Y. Millis noted the dream, as I told it, with interest and queries of mind.

Monday evening came; the meeting was large, and the foregoing scenes were all really enacted with wonderful regularity. The youthful, solitary mourner was at the altar; the Church retired; the pastor halted them, repeating the foregoing expostulation; they returned to duty; the juvenile penitent found acceptance, verifying the promise: "I love them that love me, and they that seek me early shall find me." The next evening there were six at the altar, the third evening nine, the fourth thirteen; and so on till nearly two hundred souls had fled for refuge and laid hold on the hope set before them in the gospel. On returning home that first Monday evening Miss Millis and my wife accosted me on entering the parsonage, saying: "Your dream, related at the breakfast-table, has been fulfilled literally. You told this morning just what we saw and heard at Church this evening."

The secret of the Lord is with them that fear him, and he will show them his covenant. Amen.

While I was the pastor of York Street Church, Cincinnati, in 1872–3, a singular and unaccountable occurrence took place. I dreamed that Mrs. Williams, wife of Professor W. G. Williams, of the Ohio Wesleyan University, Delaware, O., had died the past night in Delaware. At the breakfast-table I told my wife and daughter Mary that I dreamed I was going along the street in front of the residence of Professor Williams, in Delaware, and saw Professors Williams and Whitlock

16

walking with locked arms, and looking very sad. I accosted them with the phrase: "Why, you are out early this morning." "Yes," replied Professor Whitlock, "we are astir early. Professor Williams's wife died this morning, and we are astir early to arrange for the burial." I stood astonished, and asked in reference to her death and disease, and said to Professor Williams: "I sympathize with you, Professor, but we do not sorrow as others who have no hope; for if we believe that Jesus died and rose again, even so also them which sleep in Jesus will God bring with him. The dead in Christ shall rise first; so shall we ever be with the Lord." My daughter said: "I will go around to Mr. Davis's [the brother of Mrs. Williams], and see if they have heard anything from her." She went, and at the door of the brother's house met a messenger with a telegram in his hand, announcing the death as having occurred the past night. Mary returned with the intelligence, and I repaired to the residence of the brother, and narrated my dream as I had to my wife and family.

During my pastorate in 1850, I became acquainted with Squire A. His wife and three daughters were members of my charge. He had been a magistrate of the city for a number of years, and prominent as a politician. Going down Main Street the day after the repeal of the Missouri Compromise, I met the stalwart squire at his office door, and he accosted me with the inquiry, "What do you think of the abrogation of the Missouri Compromise, and the Dred Scott Decision?" I replied, disapproving both, and added: "'Whom the gods intend to destroy they first make mad.' This is the beginning of the end of the huge system of American slavery." "Why, those are my sentiments precisely, parson; give me your hand." I found myself alone with this singular and eminent man of the law and acknowledged leader of his party. He was sixty-eight years old, had chronic asthma and enlargement of the heart. A sudden concern came over me like a divine impression of duty, and I said: "Squire, what about your soul and its safety and preparation for the change of death?" "Well, parson, I do n't know much about those questions; indeed I do n't." "Well, you are the main one to know the things that make for your peace. One of these days your laboring lungs will subside, and if I attend your obsequies what can I say about your soul and your future condition?" "O," said the magistrate, "you will have nothing to do on that occasion; for years before I came to this city I selected Rev. Samuel Cox to attend my obsequies." "Well, I am glad that you have taken forethought about your funeral, and selected your minister. But what will he be warranted to say on that occasion? Let us attend those obsequies; let us attend that not far-off funeral, and see and hear. Behold that gloomy hearse, with nodding plumes, betokening death's victory. See the long, lingering array of carriages, occupying two full squares! Let us go

into the house, not by the front entrance, that is
blocked by the crowd, but by the side avenue
approach. We are in: all the avenues are occupied, all spaces filled. A minute's long lapse of
silence! We look around. There, nearest to the
coffin, sits the lonely widow, and your daughters
and their husbands in line about it. There are
your friends in the legal and medical professions, and civic officers, merchants, bankers, men,
women, and children, all grave-looking and mute
as the obelisk. Parson Cox arises and says: 'Let
us join in singing,

> "Hark! from the tombs, a doleful sound;
> My ears, attend the cry!"'

Then, after prayer, with open Bible in hand, he
reads Eccl. xii, 5. He speaks of: 1. Man's death;
2. The consequences of death; 3. The preparation
needed for a safe and happy departure: then he
follows with personal remarks,—The deceased has
lived to nearly the limit of human existence. He
has lived in our midst, as a citizen, to old age.
He was a public officer of ability and worth. His
family are members of the Methodist Episcopal
Church. He was not in communion with any
branch of Christ's Church. This we deeply regret. We know that he was lovingly called to a
profession of godliness, but he failed to make such
profession; and fidelity compels us to say that he
never gave evidence of his faith in Christ, nor his
hope of heaven, and thus he passed away from
us without making any confession of personal
faith in Christ or hope in God. My friends, let

us imitate all that was praiseworthy in our departed friend, and avoid all that was the opposite in his career, and timely flee for refuge, and lay hold on the hope that is now set before us, by faith in Christ Jesus, our Savior. And so ends the scene at the house.

"Now, suppose Brother Cox should say: 'We are happy to be permitted to say that, so long before his death, he made public profession of " repentance towards God, and faith in our Lord Jesus Christ." On such a date he sought refuge in the Church, by joining it in full sincerity, and continued onward and upward in a course of progressive holiness and hope, till he "passed through glory's morning gate and entered paradise."' How glorious would such a close of life appear!—like the morning-star, which goes not down, but melts away in the light of heaven. Would not that be a glorious consummation, devoutly to be wished?"

He replied: "What Church shall I join?" "Why," said I, "take your choice. There is the Methodist Church." "O, that is too far away from my home; it would tire me out to walk so far." "Well, join the Presbyterian Church." "What! and climb that long flight of steps, and listen to Calvinism, which teaches me that only the elect get religion? They get it because they can't help it. If they get it, they never lose it; if they lose it, they never had it; and if they get it, they do n't know it, for they only hope they have got it. No; it is a bundle of contradictions; I would not be bothered with its absurdities." "Well, there is the Baptist Church." "No, sir, never. I should have all the crudities of Calvinism to swallow, and then have to be ducked down in the river, or in a tank to be baptized. I believe in baptism by aspersion. The true baptism comes down from above." "Well, then, here is the Episcopal Church." "Pshaw! That is only a few removes from popery. I could almost as well take stock in popery at once. I guess I am the first man that has ever heard his own funeral sermon preached to him before his death."

I replied: "The prudent man foreseeth the evil, and hideth himself. Christ received, confessed, and obeyed, will be to you wisdom, righteousness, sanctification, and redemption."

He went down street and told his friends that I had preached his funeral sermon to him that morning. Time rolled away, and brought autumn and winter in their season. One Sabbath morning his married daughter, Mrs. ——, came to town in her carriage, and put up at her father's home as usual, and he went out and took the horse to the stable. After sermon and class-meeting, she returned to dinner, and shortly after dinner asked her father to get her horse and carriage. He did so, and saw her get in the carriage and drive away. He went into the house, and sat down in a large chair, saying: "Daughter must bring some one with her that can harness her horse for her, for I can not do it; it is too much for my feebleness. I can not do it again." Uttering these words he struggled for breath, fell forward, and died.

Great excitement prevailed. A costly preparation for the funeral followed, and on Tuesday the
funeral took place. I went to the front door, but
it was obstructed by the crowd inside. I was admitted at the side entrance. Strangely every
thing looked, as if I had seen and heard all before.
Parson Cox arose, shook his head violently, as
was his wont, read the last chapter of Ecclesiastes,
then gave out the hymn, "Hark! from the tombs a
doleful sound," and announced as his text, "Man
goeth to his long home, and the mourners go
about the streets!" Then he spoke as already described, word for word. Sentence after sentence
were uttered just as I had used them months before in my office-talk with the deceased. It
seemed like an echo of the language used by me;
or, rather, the very words I employed so long
before were spoken by Brother Cox at this funeral
service with singular exactness. I was impressed,
astonished, alarmed at their utter identity, as so
singularly reproduced by Brother Cox, though he
was not present at the office, nor had I in any way
communicated the conversation to him. Brother
Cox called on me to close the service with prayer,
which I did. The procession was formed, and we
deposited the massive coffin in its last resting-
place, with the formula of the Burial Service.

Let us so live that we may depart this life as
the setting sun disappears through a radiant sunset, and pass the portals of immortality full-orbed,
in glorious effulgence.

While I was commandant at Camp Chase, four

miles west of Columbus, O., the following occurrence took place, inexplicable without providential
action. A high officer in the general government
appeared one afternoon at head-quarters, and spent
a pleasant social hour. I had just received by express, in a nice round cheese-box twenty inches
diameter, a fragrant and luscious loaf-cake, thickly
covered over with frosting, and " E Pluribus Unum "
in raised and ornamental letters across the center.
It came from a lady in La Porte, Ind., the wife of
the post-quartermaster of Camp Chase, between
whom and myself an acquaintance had ripened
into warmest friendship, and his wife had sent me
this luxurious pound-cake. I gave General B.
the history of the cake, and said, " We will now
pay our compliments to the kind benefactress, and
try her fine cake ;" and we were soon enjoying it,
when suddenly an urgent impression came upon
my mind in these words, " Go immediately to
Prison No. 3 ; you are needed there." I asked the
general to excuse me, saying : " I must go to prison
No. 3. Please remain in the office ; I will be back
in fifteen minutes. Enjoy the cake. I feel that I
must be there immediately."

I left, and hurried over the walk to the prison,
entered the office, and went into the inner office,
where a door-keeper is always on duty. " How
are you Mr. D. ; is all well here ?" " Yes, sir, all is
well." At that moment a rap was heard on the side
of the prison-door. The officer went to the door,
and hailed, " Who comes there ?" The answer was
given, " John Z., a stationery-peddler, with a pass."

The door was opened, and a fine-looking man, with manners far superior to those which belong to an ordinary stationery-peddler, appeared with a nice suit of entirely new clothes upon him, hair closely cropped, clean-shaved; a new basket on his arm filled with letter-paper, envelopes, stamps, pens, ink, and red blotting-paper, stamped envelopes, a postal almanac, and regular outfit of a small peddling stationer.

I examined all these things hurriedly, and he remarked: "These things are salable to prisoners, you know;" and he thrust forth a pass into prisons in Camp Chase, signed by David Tod, Governor of Ohio. I examined the pass and found, " If approved by Colonel Granville Moody, Commander of U. S. Camp Chase, near Columbus, Ohio." Said I: "Why was not this pass signed by Colonel Moody ?" His reply was so hurried and confused that he betrayed himself. I said : "You are under arrest, sir." I called a guard, and marched him down to head-quarters, where he was incarcerated in a ten by twelve lock-up. I sent the prison's head man, who called the roll of prisoners every morning and evening, to see and examine the man. He soon after came out smiling, and said : "Colonel, that man is General L., the worst man to have gotten out for all the country. It is well you arrested him as you did." My friend, whom I had left in charge of the cake, was delighted with my adventure and success, when he learned the rank of the officer whose escape came so near proving an accomplished fact. I went to the little lock-up, and addressed my prisoner, and re-marked that Burns had said long before:

> "'For care and trouble set your mind,
> Even when your end's attained;
> For all your schemes may come to naught,
> When every nerve is strained.'

There is strategy in war, and I will have to keep you in this small prison till next Thursday, when I will go with you to Johnson's Island, near San-dusky, where you will have the benefit of lake air." He expostulated in a gentlemanly way, and asked me to suppose a change of cases—myself in a South-ern prison, making every effort for life, liberty, and the pursuit of happiness. "Yes, yes," I said; "but there's many a slip between the cup and the lip; and I think it best for yourself, and for us, to keep you quiet till times change for the better for all parties in the premises." "Pray tell me, Colonel," he said, "how you happened to come into Prison No. 3 just at that instant of time?" I could have told him, but declined.

General B., whom I left with the cake, so unceremoniously, deemed the impression on my mind, so immediate and peremptory and definite, a wonder of wonders, an insoluble myth. But "a God admitted, every mystery ends." "To God's presence oft we owe the presence of our mind."

While I was pastor of Morris Chapel, Cin-cinnati, there was a man whom we will call Blank, living in the domestic department of the Baptist Theological Seminary at Fairmount. It was summer, and the students had left college for their vacation, and the premises were in charge of Brother Blank and his wife. There were in the family three children, and the father of Mr. Blank, whose years were marked with the infirmities of an octogenarian, and he was an object of incessant care. It was during the opening months of the War of the Rebellion, when there was great stringency in financial affairs. One Saturday I was specially engaged in completing my sermons for Sabbath, and hastened immediately after dinner to my study, and seized my pen, when I was arrested by an imperative impression, saying to me: "Go to Fairmount and pastorally visit your Brother Blank, as he is in needy circumstances." The "still, small voice" spoke so positively that I was greatly impressed. But as I was so much behind-hand in pulpit preparation, I resumed my sermon, and the words were precisely and emphatically repeated. I became excited, and arose from the desk and looked around inquiringly, when the direction was clearly repeated the third time, and I put on my coat and started to Fairmount. I went up the steep of the hill, where the college stood, with its impracticable task of teaching that *baptizo* invariably means "immerse." I had walked two miles that sultry Saturday afternoon, berating myself for such a wild-goose chase from such an ambiguous oracle. I went into the spacious hall, and knocked at several doors, but with no response till I came to the last door on the right hand, which was opened to my knock. I found Sister Blank and her three children hale and hearty, and, at the further end of the neatly furnished room, sat in repose a white-haired, venerable man, who, rising, addressed me with native civility, and asked me to be seated. Everything was tidy, and nothing in the appearance of the apartment betrayed any symptom of want or emergency. After an hour's conversation, in which there was no expression of need, want, or distress that I could aid, and after prayer with and for them and the absent head of the interesting circle, I arose and bade them good-bye.

Sister Blank followed me into the hall, and out of the south door on to the grassy plat, and beneath the deep shade of the trees, and as we walked along I said: "Sister Blank, has Brother Blank work nowadays, and is he getting along comfortably in these trying times?" She burst into tears and said: "O, Brother Moody, these are the hardest times we ever passed through. Mr. Blank is in great distress. This morning our grocer told him that he must settle his bill, as he could not trust him any longer. Then he went to another grocer and asked for credit for a bill of groceries, and then to a third, and was refused credit in every case. It is so hard. My children need food, and my father-in-law, now eighty years of age, is entirely dependent upon us, and we have not the means to get supper for the family this evening; and what shall we do for all of the Sabbath-day? We have no food in the house. I am so ashamed to speak of these things, but I can not help it. My husband is nearly distracted, and greatly discouraged. I should not have told you these things, but you asked me so plainly, that I could only tell you all as I have." She hardly suppressed her sobbing with the narration of her heart-felt woes.

I felt for my pocket-book, as with weeping, I said: "I see through it all; I do, I do. How much will suffice you till next week?" She said: "O, I do not know."

I emptied my pocket-book, which contained only seven dollars, and gave them to her. She was so relieved and grateful and thankful, that if I had had twenty dollars she would have assuredly got them all. I told her to tell her husband to come to the parsonage at seven o'clock Monday morning, and I would try to get him employment where he would get good wages. I went down the declivity with a glad heart and free, rejoicing that God is so near to us, and that he had so wondrously revealed himself to me in my study, saying audibly to my spiritual ear or my actual hearing, as the reader may choose, giving the knowledge of immediate duty to relieve one of his suffering saints.

The next day the father, mother, and two children attended Morris Chapel, the parents looking very solemn and thoughtful. After the benediction, I went from the pulpit to the pew where they were waiting to speak with me. As I shook hands with them Brother Blank asked how I knew of his embarrassment, and how it was that I came so opportunely to his house the day before. I told him as written above, and he said:

"And is that so, Brother Moody? Does God take such knowledge and care of us as that? I shall never doubt his loving-kindness any more." I responded:

> "Just in the last distressing hour
> The Lord proclaims his saving power;
> The mount of danger is the place
> Where we shall see surprising grace."

Next morning he came to the parsonage. I told him to cheer up and look bright, for God had singularly stirred me up in his behalf, and a good beginning is encouraging to expect a glorious ending. I introduced him to Brother Royer, who said he could not take another hand, as he had dismissed ten last Saturday night, and should dismiss fifteen or twenty more by next Saturday night. We went up-stairs to see his invalid wife. She listened with interest to my recital of the case, and handed me five dollars for Mrs. Blank. When I told her that her husband could not employ my man in his factory, she motioned me to go into the front room. I soon heard a loving and lively controversy about employing Mr. Blank. Presently he came into the front room, saying: "My wife has got her head set on my employing your man in the factory. Come, let us go down and see the foreman, and find out what can be done." He reported a man going into the army the next day, and told me to send Mr. Blank to fill his place. He worked a year in the factory, then joined my regiment, the Seventy-fourth Ohio Infantry, did good service as an aid to the physicians and surgeons, and was then placed in command of a colored regiment as its colonel. He went to the field, did good service for his country, and returned to the peaceful walks of life at the conclusion of the war.

CHAPTER XVI.

FURTHER INCIDENTS OF MINISTERIAL LIFE.

DURING my pastorate in Zanesville a young Frenchman, a Roman Catholic, became interested in a young lady, a member of my charge, attended Church services with her, and at length called on me to perform the marriage ceremony at the parsonage. About six weeks afterward he came to my study and made known that the current of true love had not flowed as it commenced. He said:

"Reverend sir, I want to talk with you a little. If you came to my shop [he was a journeyman bootmaker], and engaged my services to make you a pair of boots, and I made them, and in a few weeks they ripped, the sole from the upper, and you returned them, I would, without delay, take the boots and mend the rent."

"Well, sir," said I, "that would be only fair, as I should have bought the boots for service."

"That is right, as you say," he answered. "Now, you may remember that, six or seven weeks ago, I employed you to marry me and Miss Elizabeth A. I was greatly pleased with her for about three weeks. We took a small but neat house, which I furnished comfortably and well. She soon began to neglect her house and personal appearance. I go home to dinner, and she is at her mother's. I find the house untidy; there will be no fire; and when I have taken a fellow-work-man home with me to dinner, we have found the house unswept, the bed unmade, and her clothes slatternly upon her. I have been mortified by her appearance and the condition of the house; and when I spoke to her about it, she answered me shortly, and threatened to go home— and actually did go to her mother's. Now, sir, what shall I do? I am disappointed very much, I assure you, and come seeking your advice and agency in the case."

I asked him if he loved her, and he said with all his heart, and that if she would do as she did at first, he would be the happiest of men.

"Well, well," said I, "you come here this afternoon at half-past two o'clock. I will see her and have her here to meet you. We will act and hope for the best, and may be we can get your ripped boot mended."

I went right away to her mother's house, and found her in great distress. I told her kindly of his complaints. She, with tears, confessed her fault. Her mother seconded all my remarks, and wondered if he would take her back. I assured her that if she would promise better behavior he would receive her graciously, and be a loving husband to her. This was like good news from a far country, and she promised thorough amendment. I arranged for her to come to the parsonage at two o'clock P. M. She came, and I left her in the parlor with my faithful wife, who counseled her wisely and lovingly. At half-past two o'clock the door-bell rang. I went gladly to the door, and there was my Frenchman, who asked eagerly if his wife was there. I took him into the parlor. He shook hands with his wife, who seemed very glad to meet him. He was as polite as the veriest Frenchman. I said: "Let us pray." We all knelt down, and I led in prayer; and then called on Mrs. Moody to pray for the newly married couple. She prayed, with nicest discrimination and tenderness and hope, for a reunion. We arose to our feet bettered by God's answer to our well-meant endeavors to restore peace to these disturbed hearts. "Now," said I, "Mr. G., you will open the way in this effort at reconciliation by telling us all the ills of these mishaps." He proceeded very carefully, and with tearful tenderness, and she assented to what he said. Then she, with womanly sweetness, confessed her errings, asked his pardon, and promised amendment for the future. I rejoiced at the prospect of a peaceful settlement, and told them to stand up and be married over again. I went through the entire ritual, making them repeat after me: "I, M, take thee, N, to be my wedded wife, to have and to hold from this day, forward; for better, for worse; for richer, for poorer; in sickness and in health, to love and to cherish till death do us part, according to God's holy ordinance; and thereto I pledge thee my troth." "I, N, take thee, M, to be my wedded husband, to have and to hold from this day forward, for better, for worse; for richer, for poorer; in sickness and in health, to love, cherish, and obey till death do us part, according to God's holy ordinance; and thereto I give thee my troth."

Another prayer followed—God's pardon and blessing were implored. They were doubly married, under better auspices. We arose. They mutually kissed each other. I pronounced the apostolic benediction, and they went forth to a newness of life in the holy bands of matrimony—she a better wife, he a better husband. They lived a happier life than either of them had dreamed before.

This bride was a daughter of a widow, who had spoiled her by indulgence in the careless habits of a listless life, which ill qualified her for the grave realities of a wife, and stewardess of family obligations. Truly,

> "The kindest and the happiest pair
> Have oft occasion to forbear,
> And something, every day they live,
> To pity, and perhaps forgive."

We take the following incident concerning the "Cowhiding of a Minister," from the *Columbian and Great West*. We give the story as there written:

"The incident we are about to relate, occurred a few years since, in the northern part of Ohio. Whatever the defects of the sketch, it possesses at least one merit—that of truthfulness. Among the distinguished members of the clergy in the Buckeye State, the Rev.

Dr. Moody, of the Methodist persuasion, justly holds a prominent position. As a man, possessing a generous amount of native talent, aided by untiring industry, enterprise, and boldness, he is celebrated, not only among those of his own faith, but among all denominations of Christians. Among the leading traits of his character, a strong will and a rather diminutive development of what phrenologists call reverence have become so universally known as to be considered mere eccentricities, and often prevent acts of his from attracting notice, while in other members of his peaceful and self-denying profession they would excite universal wonder.

"At the time of which we write he was the pastor of a large and wealthy Church, in a town which shall be nameless. He was almost idolized by the people, and in many respects occupied a most pleasant and enviable position. But there were some drawbacks to his satisfaction, and not the least important of these was the circumstance that some of his Church members differed from him, both theoretically and practically, on a subject of considerable magnitude. This was nothing more or less than the sale and use of ardent spirits.

"But little had been accomplished in the movement for a temperance reform, and the agitation of the subject had only just commenced; but Dr. M. had become thoroughly convinced that intoxicating beverages were unnecessary and hurtful, and the traffic in them a wrong and an injustice. Having come to this conclusion, he was not the man to sit idly down and expect to work a reformation, without making use of the natural means to produce such a result.

"Several members of his own Church were engaged in the traffic, and he immediately turned his attention to them. By reasoning with them in his own earnest and forcible manner, he soon succeeded in persuading them all to renounce the pernicious traffic.

"We said *all;* but the statement is too sweeping, for there was one exception. Brother Jones was a crabbed, self-willed old grocer, who, though he had been a member of that Church for many years, nevertheless had the reputation of being very far from indifferent to the vanities of this world. And now, when the pastor endeavored to persuade him to give up the traffic in spirits, all his efforts proved futile. He defended himself sturdily on the broad principle that it was no worse now than it always had been ; that the laws of the land gave him permission to sell liquor ; that he had done it for years, and would continue to do so as long as he saw fit.

"Dr. M., however, was not a man to be easily balked when his heart was once set on an object ; so when he found all attempts to reason with this black sheep of his flock proving fruitless, he took more decided measures. He presented the case to the other members of his Church, and, in a short time, Brother Jones was given to understand, in very plain terms, that, unless he saw fit to comply with the wishes of the pastor and the body to which he belonged, official notice would be taken of the matter at once. Somewhat alarmed at this, Brother Jones finally relented, and promised faithfully that, for all time to come, he would abstain from his traffic in the liquid fires. And, for a time, he kept his promise, and was looked upon as a reformed man.

"But the love of lucre proved too strong for the Christian grocer, and, in a few months, he had so far

disregarded his promise as to deal out bad brandy and
worse whisky, at three cents a glass, with more gusto
than ever. The Church, after finding all further remon
strance useless, took immediate cognizance of the
matter, and excommunicated him at once. Then, for
the first time, Brother Jones began to be convinced
that he had been a little too hasty for his own good.
Like a great many other men, he had found his
Church connection an excellent thing for covering his
various derelictions from the right path, and when
this cloak was stripped off, and his character was exposed in its native hue, with no such protection, he
soon found his moral credit decidedly below par.
Thereupon he waxed exceeding wroth, and, judging
correctly that Dr. M. had been the direct cause of what
he termed his persecution, he thereupon determined
to visit vengeance upon his reverend and devoted
head.

"His disgrace was universally known, and he determined that his revenge also should be public. He,
therefore, invited a large number of his friends to be
at his grocery on a certain evening, assuring them
that it was his intention, then and there, to bestow
upon the minister a severe bodily chastisement. The
evening came, and so did they, anxious, as the great
public ever is, to be present on all exciting occasions.
When the grocery was pretty well crowded, a messenger was dispatched to Dr. M., soliciting his presence at once on business of the utmost importance.
Five minutes had not elapsed when the messenger returned, and with him the good parson, wondering if
the erring brother had relented once more. The
moment they entered, the indignant Jones locked the
door behind them, drew himself up to his full height
(about four-feet-six), and addressed the minister in

the most imperious tone : 'Dr. Moody, I am an ill-used man, and you know it. I am vilely persecuted, sir, and you are at the bottom of it all. Now, sir, I have brought you here to-night to show you that you can not do this with impunity.'

" 'Brother Jones,' began the parson.

" 'Do n't brother me, sir,' interrupted that fiery in-dividual. 'I say I have brought you here to-night to teach you a lesson, sir ; to rebuke you, sir ; in short, I intend to cowhide you, sir.'

" And, suiting the action to the word, the excited member of the Jones family immediately produced a cowhide, and began to approach nearer to his clerical opponent.

" 'Brother Jones,' said Dr. M., with a good deal of decision, but with the utmost nonchalance.

" ' Sir?'

" 'Did I understand you to speak of cowhiding me?'

" 'Certainly, you did, sir ; and you will soon hear something more than mere words.'

" 'Brother Jones.'

" ' Sir ?'

" ' Do n't do it.'

" ' And why not, sir ?' asked Jones, in a perfect tor-nado of rage.

" 'You know we Methodists believe in the possi-bility of falling from grace.'

" ' Well, sir ?'

" ' Well, Brother Jones, if you strike me with that cowhide, it is very likely that I shall fall from grace ;' and the parson drew up about six-feet-four of as well-made frame as can easily be found, and looked down on his diminutive opponent with the air of a man who meant what he said.

" ' W-h w-h-y, Doctor,' stammered Jones, taken all

aback. 'You surely do n't intend to say that you 'd
fight?'

" ' I say nothing about that,' replied Dr. M., 'but I
do say, Brother Jones, that if you strike me a single
blow, I shall be very likely to fall from grace; and if I
do fall from grace, you will certainly be the worst
whipped man ever seen in the State of Ohio.'

"Jones did n't carry out his threats; he repented
immediately; so the Doctor had no occasion to fall
from grace. Poor Jones! To this day he is ready to
die with shame if you ask him, 'Who whipped the
minister?' "

The next incident is entitled "The Fighting
Parson," and is clipped from the *Dayton Journal*:

"Colonel Allston, John Morgan's chief of staff, has
been paroled, and is wending his way south. The
Columbus *Journal* published a story about him, which
goes to show that he is a repentant rebel. ' He spoke
in desponding terms of the rebel cause,' said our contemporary, but that ' the rebels regard the success of
the peace-men of the Vallandigham school as their
only hope of being victorious. He looked upon Vallandigham as a true friend of the rebels, and would
hail his election as a promising indication of a speedy
termination of the war, by the withdrawal of our
armies from the rebel States.' This rebel, Colonel
Allston, decorated in secesh uniform, cut a large swath
in Columbus before he left on Wednesday, and nobody rebuked him; but on his way to Zanesville, *via*
the Central Ohio Railroad, he fell into the hands of
one of the faithful. The incident was described to us
by an eye-witness.

"Colonel Allston sat with a brawny Copperhead
on one side of the car, vomiting out treason, which his

fellow - traitor meekly accepted. Colonel Granville
Moody, with his daughter, sat opposite him reading
a newspaper. Colonel M. was restive, but restrained
himself for some time. At last the rebel colonel, in
full rebel uniform, who talked loudly and defiantly,
evidently desirous to attract attention, said that it was
'the duty of the peace Democrats to elect Vallandigham. It was necessary to save them from Lincoln's
cursed tyranny. It was the most damnable tyranny on
the face of the earth. Three months hence you people
of the North will appeal to us [rebels], suppliantly, to
come up and rescue you from Lincoln's despotism.'

"Hardly was the sentence concluded, when Colonel
Moody, flaming with indignation, dashed his paper to
the floor, sprang across the car, seized the insolent
rebel by the throat, and thrusting his knuckles into
his face, hissed through his teeth : 'You infamous
scoundrel! how dare you insult my government with
your treason? How dare you pollute this atmosphere
with your insults to my country? Shut your mouth,
or I'll crush every bone in your infernal body.' Then
the colonel seized the rebel with force enough almost
to raise him from his seat, and, with considerable
trepidation, he stammered, 'I'll—I'll stop.'

"'Stop now, or I'll throw you out of the window.
I know your rights as a paroled prisoner ; you are
under the protection of the government. That does
not authorize you to abuse and insult it. You
have abused your privilege. No man in rebel uniform
shall abuse my government in my hearing without
paying the penalty of his insolence.'

"By this time Allston's big copperhead friend attempted to say something. 'Not a word from you!'
cried Colonel M. 'You miserable copperhead, you sat
here and listened to this rebel's treason without

resenting it. If you had a grain of manhood you would
have saved me the necessity of interfering. Not a word
from you, or I'll take you in hand. You are meaner
than this rebel. You have all the instincts of a traitor,
without the courage of a rebel.' That settled the fellow, and he subsided. A third attempted to interpose,
and was summarily disposed of in a similar manner. The rebel colonel sank back into his seat and
endeavored to look composed, but his mind was evidently ill at ease. Colonel Moody was right. He
shed his blood for his country; he knew that a paroled
rebel had no right to insult the government which
protected him, and justly felt it his duty to teach the
villain a lesson he would not forget."

I give in this connection an incident illustra-
tive of muscular Christianity at Camp Chase. During the year 1862 I was in command of the camp,
having under my supervision six thousand rebel
prisoners, composed of generals, colonels, majors,
captains, and privates. There was a large space
of the camp set apart for rebels, surrounded with
a stockade twelve feet high, and sufficiently under
guard to control their Southern feelings.

One beautiful afternoon a splendid carriage,
drawn by a magnificent pair of prancing horses,
driven by a servant in livery, was seen to enter
the camp and approach the rebel stockade. In a
few moments the gates were thrown open, and
the carriage was about to enter, when the movement attracted my attention, and I immediately
ordered a halt, and demanded by what authority
those gates were opened. "By my authority,"

said a richly dressed lady within the carriage. "And who gave you your authority?" "Governor Tod." "Please let me see it," said I. The pass read: "Permit the bearer to enter Camp Chase and visit prisoners, provided it meets with the approbation of the commanding officer." I read the pass, and said: "Governor Tod has no authority whatever to pass you into this camp, because it is a national, and not a State camp. It is true that we respect the authority of Governor Tod, and treat his requests with due courtesy; but he says to admit you if it meets my approbation, and why was not this request sent to head-quarters?" "Because I did not see fit to send it to you," was the reply. "Then," said I to the coachman, "drive out. You will not be permitted to remain." He moved slowly, and pretended he could not turn round, when I ordered the men to drop their guns, and take hold of the bits of the horses and back the carriage out—which was speedily done.

"I will report you to Governor Tod," said the voice of the lady; "for you are not fit for the position you occupy; and I will see that you are removed and properly punished for insulting a lady." I found out that Mrs. Judge T. had, for a month, been visiting rebel prisoners and supplying them with the choicest of luxuries, and on this occasion her carriage was filled with supplies to bless the hearts of those with whom she was in sympathy. I said to her: "Madam, you not only came here, and by your supposed authority risked the escape of all these prisoners, who are but ill-guarded with the small force now in camp, but you have been providing rebels with aid and sympathy, when there are one hundred and fifty sick and dying soldiers in our own hospital who would gladly receive those delicacies in your carriage, and would rise up and call your name blessed." The only reply was: "You are no gentleman, and I will report your conduct;" and, with the speed of the wind, the coachman hurried her away to the capital, maddened with rage. As soon as she left I demanded: "Who ordered these gates to be opened?" The officer in charge replied that he did. I demanded the surrender of his sword, and sent him under charges to head-quarters.

In a very short time a courier arrived in haste from Governor Tod to me, asking me to come at once to the city—to which request I immediately gave heed. I found Governor Tod and General Buckingham, adjutant-general of Ohio, awaiting my coming, and we immediately retired to a private room in the capitol to hold a council of war. The door was closed, and Governor Tod said to me: "We sent for you because there is trouble. Mrs. Judge T. has brought an account of a terrible insult you gave her in commanding her to leave Camp Chase this afternoon; and her husband is very, very angry, and swears that he will shoot you on sight. Now let us hear from you the facts just as they occurred, as we have only heard the statement of Judge T." I, with precision and accuracy, gave every detail, even to the particulars of the conversation, and spoke of

my urging her to give her delicacies to the sick
in the hospital, with such earnestness that, during
the recital of the plea, Governor Tod shed tears.
After hearing my statement, he said with emphasis: "Colonel Moody, you were exactly right, and
I do not see how you could have done otherwise."
General Buckingham said: "If Colonel Moody
had done otherwise, I should have reported him as
derelict in duty, and insisted on his removal."
"But," continued the governor, "T. is exceedingly wroth, and swears that no street or sidewalk
is large enough to hold you both, and that he will
kill you at sight."   I showed him my brace of six-
shooters, and said: "Governor Tod, I keep these
for dogs, and these are dog-days."

The next morning, early, I went into the city
and met a friend, who took me into his carriage.
He said: "Colonel Moody, the whole city is in com-
motion and whirl of excitement at your reported
treatment of Mrs. T. yesterday, and report says
that Judge T. is determined to kill you; while the
Democrats are white with pent-up wrath."   I had
never seen Judge T., and while this conversation
was going on the friend pointed him out to me.
I immediately took the lines out of the hands of
my friend and drove into the presence of Judge
T., who was reading letters in front of the post-
office.   I stood before him, and looked him in the
eye.   As he saw me he turned white, then red in a
moment, so perturbed was his flow of thought;
and, excusing himself to some friends, he immediately started to the State-house, whither I fol-

lowed him at once, and showed myself willing to
be shot at by the man who had shaken the city
of Columbus by his threats of dire vengeance.
Three times he escaped my eye as I followed
after him, and that is all the effort he has ever
made to kill me from that day to this.

The opposition papers and rebel sympathizers
did their best to make political capital out of this
incident; but I had the approving evidence of my
own conscience in the discharge of duty, and my
commanding officer sanctioned all that I did as
just and right.

The large flag of the United States had floated
in apparent safety in the north-east corner of
Camp Chase till the spring of 1861, when a violent,
whirling wind enwrapped it in its unseen folds,
and down it came, hanging and clinging around
the staff, which was broken off fifty or sixty feet
from the ground. This accident called forth the
jubilant hurrahs of the imprisoned rebels, and
they laughed and danced, and prophesied that it
was a type of the destiny of the accursed Republic. "Down with the flag! God is on our side!
The winds, in their courses, fight against this
abhorred flag!" The secesh preachers mouthed
it into a prolepsis of the fall of the Republic—the
ruin of which was hereby foreshadowed. "So let
every banner of Stars and Stripes fall and fade and
perish and pass away. Hurrah for the Stars and
Bars!" Meanwhile, forgetting the limit of nine
feet from the walls of the wooden fencing, their
buoyant, boastful spirit overleaped all boundaries,

and they rejoiced that the whirlwinds of heaven joined them in warring against the Stars and Stripes. "Hurrah for Jeff Davis and the Confederacy!" they shouted.

The tumult was increasing, and some one came into my office, which was just opposite the fallen flag, and called me out. I ran to the flag and called the reserved guards to follow me, which they did promptly; and when I reached the summit of the fence on the guard-route, there were from three to four hundred men within three to five feet of the fence, and every mouth was opened with objurgations on the fallen flag. I cried out: "Go to your limits beyond the fence, and cease your insults to the flag of the free!" They shouted only the more, and heaped their insults on the flag. I ordered silence, and bade them remember they were largely outside their limits. "Retire at once to your limits or take the consequences! March at once!" Not one obeyed the orders, but they heaped derisions on the fallen flag. I shouted: "Guards! ready! aim!" The guards, in almost solid phalanx, leveled their rifles, when the crowd, seeing the possible consequences, started back to their tents, each one shouting to the other: "Run, run! run for your lives, men, run;" and run they did, till not a rebel could be seen in the whole yards. "Guards, recover arms! shoulder arms! order arms! rest!" The carpenters were called out, flag-poles were fitted and bands applied; and, in less than an hour, the flag-staff was repaired and the old "beauty and glory" was bent on it afresh, amid the cheering of hundreds of patriotic voices.

After the battle of Bull Run there was a requisition made on the military at Camp Chase, which left the guard over six thousand prisoners entirely inadequate. This was speedily known among the prisoners, and their expectations and schemes for breaking out were developed to their slaves, who were interested in our cause whilst in the employment of their masters in the prison. We found it to our interest to leave their former slaves in their employment for awhile; for thus it was "a wheel working within a wheel," and working for our good by way of espionage. These slaves knew all the plans of the officers, and we were speedily apprised of their schemes and projects.

The morning the regiments left for the field of active service we were duly informed of their plans for escape. We had not more than sixty soldiers left for guard duty, and many of these were invalids. I called for my horse, and was soon closeted with Governor Tod and staff in consultation. I represented the condition of things in the camp, the expectation of the rebel officers to make an effort to escape that night, and the necessity of re-enforcing the defenses. The result was, the governor wrote to Colonel Carrington, of the Eighteenth Regiment of United States regular troops, who was about sixteen miles distant, to come by forced march to re-enforce the prison camp-guard. Meanwhile volunteer guards were sent from Columbus to serve one night. I also procured over two hundred new lanterns to be suspended as an auxiliary force on the summit of the prison fences, to afford superior illumination. I organized skeleton regiments, with three to five officers to each company, to march into camp at about eight o'clock P. M., in company distance, with colonel, lieutenant-colonel, and major, who were to form regiments and march them into camp under orders, as if whole companies were in line, and to come to head-quarters; and, after salutes of officers, be assigned to quarters near the walls of the prisons.

These orders were carried out to the letter, and the impression that our guard-line was largely re-enforced was made on the minds of the prisoners. Two imaginary re-enforcements of our guard officers and men were effectually made during the dense darkness of that fearful night. Every officer, sutler, and private was put into requisition. About two o'clock A. M., Colonel Carrington arrived with about three hundred regular soldiers, and by four A. M. they were in position on the platforms around the summit of our prison fences; and, when daylight dawned, they were seen by the prisoners, to their discomfiture.

Colonel Carrington kept up the Regular Army regulations and discipline, and thus an outbreak was prevented by prevision. Forewarned, we were forearmed. The good will of the Negroes to the government was shown. They were imprisoned temporarily with their masters, with whom they

were taken and holden. Their good-will served
us many a good turn in times of war. Some persons, who did not understand all things, animad-
verted on the confinement of the slaves of the
captured secessionists with their masters, little
knowing what allies these slaves were to us. In
a short time the government gave to these men
their liberty, and furnished them with good homes.
I sent them east, west, south, and north in
Ohio, free.

At this time, nearly all the students in the
Ohio Wesleyan University, realizing the Nation's
need of all her sons on the battle line, left the
college in Delaware, Ohio, and came to our camp
and volunteered in the National service. Rev.
Frederick Merrick, president of the university,
came to me in Camp Chase to get my influence
for their return to college. But I declined, stating it to be the bounden duty of every student
to take his part in the great struggle, and I advised him to volunteer as chaplain, and go to the
battle-field with his patriotic students. He was a
true patriot, but deemed it *his* duty to take care
of the students officially.

CHAPTER XVII.

VIEWS ON SLAVERY.

THE following extracts, the first relating to the contrabands at Camp Chase, will give the reader my views on the great question of human bondage. They are clipped from the papers of the period, and are inserted in this place because of the interest which has always attached to the subject:

No small measure of indignation was aroused in the public mind, in relation to the *status* of the " colored population " held in confinement at Camp Chase. The committee of the Senate, in their report upon the subject, propounded the inquiry, " Why are those Negroes there at all?" And the question was certainly a most appropriate one. It turned out, upon investigation, however, that they were placed there as prisoners of war—a position as dignified as that enjoyed by their masters. It was shown that the Negroes were taken as participants in the rebel cause, some with arms in their hands against our loyal troops, and against our flag, others aiding their rebel masters in camp duty. This being the case, they were sent by General Halleck to Camp Chase in the same category as their masters were; namely, as prisoners of war taken in battle. General Halleck made no distinction in complexion; but, from " snowy white to sooty," consigned all thus captured to the military prison. The commandant of the post, Colonel Moody, received them, not as servants of the white men whom they accompanied, but as persons consigned to his military charge in the capacity of prisoners, by virtue of the orders of his chief-in-command. When placed together in the camp prison, the haughty Secesh, too shiftless to wait upon themselves, incontinently fell back upon their usual assumption of *otium cum dignitate*, requiring the Negroes to serve them. This it had been their custom to do, several of them having been, indeed, the slaves of some of these officers.

But to this position of affairs Colonel Moody gave no assent. To show this, we need but refer to his orders concerning them ; for, when finding need of an additional force in his hospital for washing, nursing, and caring for the sick generally, he respected the convenience of these prison gentry so little as to issue an order to his post surgeon to detail from the prison all the Negro men he might need for that purpose. This he did, because of their being experienced in such personal service, and without the smallest regard to, or even a thought of, their being under any claim to service upon the insolent Secesh of the prison.

Again, when Colonel Moody received an order from the War Department · to forward some fifty of these Secesh officers to Fort Warren, under the guard of a United States officer sent for that purpose, he made out the list in conformity with the order, and issued the necessary marching orders. And, behold, when these Fort Warren gentry came forth from their prison, Colonel Moody was surprised to find a number of Negroes marching in the rear of their white fellow-prisoners of the Secesh persuasion, and each Negro carrying trunk, valise, carpet-sack, etc., for these top-loftical masters, who seemed to be quite unaware that they were not in Secessia. But Colonel Moody speedily dispelled their delusion on this subject. The line was at halt, and, in a voice of sternest tone, he demanded: " What are those Negro men in the line for?" He was insolently told by the Secesh that the Negroes were their servants, and were to carry their baggage. " No, sir," shouted Colonel Moody. " We recognize no such relations here, nor in this country. You have no such claim to them, nor to their service." Then, turning to the Negroes, he ordered them at once to lay down the baggage, and clear out of the line. The Negroes hesitated, looking alternately at him and at Secesh, as if studying which to obey. Seeing their hesitation, Colonel Moody shouted, in tones that left no doubt as to which had better be obeyed, " Throw down that baggage, and clear the line, every one of you!" and at the same time ordered an officer and a squad of soldiers to see his order executed, and march the Negroes back to prison. This was promptly done, and the Secesh were allowed the high privilege of getting their trunks and other traps to the railroad station in such manner as best they could. Also, when the Negroes were detailed to hospital service, a Secesh, Colonel Hanson, offered to furnish the money for an officer to hire a man for such service, so that his man, " Jim," might be left for waiting on himself; but this Colonel Moody absolutely refused.

The subject received a stormy ventilation in the Ohio House of Representatives—a kind of March wind to usher in the first of April. But whatever may have been the fact about "permitting" slavery to exist at Camp Chase, as the Senate's resolution says, we do not see how it could be charged upon Colonel Moody. He simply received the men, black and white, from his superior officer. He kept them in prison alike.

If he detailed the blacks to serve for the hospital, it
was because they knew better than their masters did
how to make themselves useful; and on every occasion, where such claim arose, he sternly and peremptorily refused all recognition of its validity. We
think the statements, made by the officers of his regiment, published in our legislative column, show all
this abundantly. Mr. Cook, Republican, spoke about
an hour on the question, arguing, at length, that there
was no slavery in Camp Chase, and that injustice was
done Colonel Moody as commandant of the camp, and
not only to him, but the Secretary of War and the
President himself. To sustain his positions, he read the
following communications, furnished him by Colonel
Moody. The colonel himself was present. He was
anxious to establish the fact that he in no way winked
at slavery in the performance of his duties, and the
communications below go far to establish this statement:

CAMP CHASE, March 30, 1862.

Some three weeks since, I was present at an interview
between Colonel Moody, commandant at this post, and one
of the prisoners released on parole. During the conversation
the inquiry was made, whether there would be any distinction
drawn between the Negroes and the other prisoners. Colonel
Moody replied that they were all alike prisoners of war, and
would be so considered by him; that the same influence that
would procure admittance to visit the white occupants of the
prison, would also be necessary to hold communication with
the black. I have also, both before and since the period referred to, heard Colonel Moody, in answer to similar inquiries,
make substantially the same reply.

JAMES RODGERS,
Post Sergeant Major.

CAMP CHASE, March 30, 1862.

Some three weeks ago I removed some sick from the prisons, and had them placed in a temporary hospital under guard.

The orders I received from Colonel Moody were to detail such colored men as might be needed for cooks, nurses, or to attend to any services needed for the health and comfort of the prisoners. Several times I have been told, " That boy belongs to me ; I need him to wait on me ;" but in opposition to all their remonstrances, my details were always carried out ; and they were given to understand that their claim to property in man was not recognized here by Colonel Moody, the commander of the post.　　　　　　　E. W. STEELE,
Assistant Surgeon, 74th Regiment.

CAMP CHASE, March 31, 1862.

Since my connection with the prisoners confined at Camp Chase, I have never recognized, either directly or indirectly, the right of property in man ; all prisoners have been held on equal footing, regardless of color. Colonel Moody has never, to my knowledge, recognized the right of one man to hold another as his slave. Governor Tod ordered me to detail any of the blacks that I chose to attend to any hospital duty, pertaining to their own sick ; and, to my certain knowledge, Colonel Moody has peremptorily refused to give Colonel Hanson, a prisoner sent from here to Fort Warren, the privilege of taking his Negroes with him, as either servants or slaves ; and has constantly and positively ignored the relation at this post.　　　　　　　A. S. BALLARD,
Major 74th Regiment, and Superintendent of Prison.

I consider the above statement a perfectly true one.
ALEX. VON SCHRADER,
Lieutenant-Colonel, 74th Regiment.

CAMP CHASE, March 30, 1862.

Some three weeks since, Colonel G. Moody, commandant of this post, issued to me authority to employ any or all of the colored men, as prisoners of this camp, as nurses or attendants in any of the hospitals, or in any service connected with the sanitary duties of the prisoners of this camp ; and on presenting a proposition from Mr. Hayes (major) to hire a man at his expense, in order that he might retain the services of his own, said proposition was promptly pronounced inadmissible and illegitimate, by the commanding colonel.
GEORGE W. MARIS,
Post Surgeon, Camp Chase.

The following article was contributed by me to the *Western Christian Advocate* in 1854. It is reproduced without abbreviation or material change:

By this time your readers are aware that the Nebraska Bill, involving the repeal of the Missouri Compromise, by which slavery was forever prohibited north of 36° 30' north latitude, has passed the House of Representatives; their amendments have been agreed to by the Senate, and this degrading outrage is consummated, and is now the law of the land. It is, indeed, a most significant coincidence, that this bill of abominations was only completed on Friday, May 26th—the day of the great solar eclipse—and the day, too, when the sun of our Republic was shorn of its glory, and a portentous gloom spread all over the land. Nevertheless, we will find hope in the fact that the obscuration was but partial and temporary; and sure as Jehovah reigns, the sad eclipse of the sun of liberty shall be but temporary; it shall emerge from the darkness, and shine with increased luster.

But the deed is done, and the foes of human freedom are indulging in exultant joy. The heartless slave-dealer calculates the great increase in the price of slaves, now that the barrier is removed, which prevented his soul-traffic on that virgin soil consecrated to freedom. The heavy, reluctant reverberations of one hundred cannons, consecrated to the defense of liberty, are forced to give utterance to this triumph of tyrants; and, fired near the White House, they jar harshly on the nerves of freedom. O, I see the genius of liberty,

> "In grief and sorrow bent,
> As o'er some ruined monument,"

with gloom on her brow, and tears in her eye, with anguished spirit and with anxious mien, mourning over this dire calamity, yet calling imploringly and hopefully to her votaries for help in this time of need. And now, betrayed, derided, insulted, what shall we do? Shall we fulfill the cherished predictions of Stephen Arnold Douglas, that the North shall acquiesce? Shall we bow down, and, spaniel-like, lick the foot that kicks us? No, no; never!

A short time after the passage of the Missouri Compromise Act of 1820, the late John Randolph, of Roanoke, Virginia, used the following language on the floor of Congress: "We, of the South, know what we are doing. We are always united, from the Ohio to Florida, and we can always unite, and you of the North are divided. We have conquered you once—in the recent admission of Missouri with slavery—and we can and will conquer you again. Ay, gentlemen, we have driven you to the wall, and when we have you there, we mean to keep you there, and nail you down like base money." This prediction has been but too fully realized, and the North is driven again to the wall, and, that, too, by the perfidy of Northen men! And will they "keep us there?" Will the Free States submit? If they do, they deserve to be slaves. But this remains to be seen. As yet, the Free States are scarcely aware of the evils involved in this bill of abominations, which maketh desolate the hearts and hopes of millions. It is the modern Pandora's box. Nor is hope found at the bottom.

This bill is so shaped as to apply the principle of Congressional non-intervention, as it respects slavery, not merely to Nebraska and Kansas, but equally to the Territories of Minnesota, Oregon, and Washington, to the States of Iowa and California, both of which now contain a limited number of slaves, and also to the States north-west of the Ohio River, hitherto protected by the Ordinance of 1787.

If it be held that the legislation of 1850 "rendered inoperative" the Missouri Compromise Act, for the same reason these principles must be held to have rendered inoperative the Ordinance of 1787, relative to the territory north-west of the Ohio River. Indeed, the terms in which this new doctrine of Congressional non-intervention is announced, are such as to indicate an unlimited application of it. It sweeps away all former limits to slavery, and proclaims liberty to extend slavery in every direction; and if the Free States submit, as they have submitted to the aggressions of the slave-power, and yield, even seemingly, to the doctrine that has gained the sanction of a Congressional enactment, it will be regarded by the South as an invitation to extend the sway of slavery over the whole North. If we allow them to destroy or possess the outworks, they will consider it a virtual assent to occupy the citadel.

The passage of the Nebraska Bill, says the *Union*, "is necessary to prepare the Northern mind for the thick-coming events of the future—the acquisition of Cuba," and a portion of Mexico at least; and the same flagrant perfidy which has forced this measure through Congress will be relied upon to give success to the warlike measures already intimated and initiated by the President and Senate. Thus we may see the scope and scale of the aggressive slave power.

But the Nebraska Bill is not our only danger. There is an organized and determined effort to have "property in man" placed upon the same basis as any other property. Having gained such a recognition under the Constitution of the United States, they expect to be able to hold slaves in all the Territories, and to be able to carry them with them into any of the States at pleasure, without any forfeiture of property in them.

Hitherto the decisions of the United States courts have been, that property in slaves is dependent on local positive laws, and that the title is invalidated the moment the slave is taken by his master, or permitted to go, beyond the jurisdiction of those laws. But Mr. Calhoun, and all of his school, claimed that what the Constitution of the United States recognized as property in one State was, in law and equity, property in every State and everywhere under the national jurisdiction. This doctrine is becoming common at the South, and is advocated by many at the North.

In the Lemmon case, which is now before the Supreme Court, slaveholders expect to get an indorsement of this doctrine, and there is danger that they will succeed; a majority of the judges are from the slave States, as is usual in the distribution of power; and when they are removed by death, their places are sure to be supplied by the most pro-slavery men that can be found; and, after the astonishing and unparalleled and unjust decision given against the Methodist Episcopal Church, and in favor of the South, by this pro-slavery court, what have we to hope for from them? It is more than probable that a majority of that court will assert the right of the master to hold his slaves in any territory of the nation, and *in transitu* in any State; and when this is decided we shall be powerless to resist except by a civil revolution. There is no appeal from the decision of the United States courts but to arms. The alternative, then, will be abject submission or a resort to arms in defense of justice and liberty.

The passage of the Nebraska Bill amounts to a dissolution of the compact by which, hitherto, slavery and freedom have affected to divide the land. Henceforth there can be no compromise between them as between equals; the one must be as abject and subject as the other will be supreme and dictatorial.

It rests with the North to resist or submit, to sink basely down into the condition and attitude of a conquered province, or to rise in its strength, and by stern and steady demand for the repeal of the Nebraska Bill, or its equivalent, restore the landmarks of freedom which our fathers set up, and thus regain their rights and their rightful portion. The North can do it if they will; they will do it if they can—united they will be invincible.

One thing is certain, the hitherto existing regard for compromise measures in the North will be destroyed by recent movements of the slave party, which has repudiated its own compact with the *quid pro quo* in their possession, and as basely, too, as Mississippi repudiated her State debt; and, though the South has gained the Nebraska Bill, it has lost its honor, and sacrificed its plighted faith most flagrantly; and it is and will be understood that confidence can not longer be reposed in Southern honor and integrity, and thus their gain is an emphatic loss.

Nor let the South, after destroying this first-born of all the measures of conciliation, and having established slavery in all the territory allotted to her by her own measure of 1820, imagine for one moment that the North will adhere to the measures of recent date which recognize that first restriction, now that the South have annulled it for their own benefit. They will erelong find out that the repeal of the Missouri Compromise is the virtual repeal of the whole series of measures, and we are thereby absolved from all further obligations to observe them, on the principle that the failure of one party to a contract to meet its obligations, works an honorable release to the party of the other part from its cognate obligations. This is the end of the existing compromises, and will be the barrier to all future ones.

And now for stern, united, persistent action against this common foe. We must ignore mere party and political interests, which are not of vital importance. The action of the South makes this a question of paramount importance to us, and we must combine and array a party of freemen as terrible to tyrants as an army with banners. We must turn a deaf ear to all the doctors of divinity who teach us to obey the behests of those "who frame iniquity by a law," rather than obey conscience, reason, and the Word of God; we must show Douglas that clergymen are not dolts, nor are they to be gagged or intimidated in the holy cause of human rights. Christians must show their devotion to truth and principle to be supreme; and though another Daniel Webster should appear to compel submission to the Nebraska outrage, as he did to the Fugitive-slave Law, we must say: Avaunt, begone! and show the slave power and the slave-catcher that that odious Fugitive-slave Law is henceforth "inoperative;" that the South has released us from its inhuman provisions, and that the panting fugitive, who implores our aid will find that "we hold these truths to be self-evident, that all men are created equal; that they are endowed by their Creator with certain inalienable rights; that among these are life, liberty, and the pursuit of happiness."

We thank the South for uniting the North at last; and now let us aid the freedom-loving emigrant, empowered as he is to vote, to Nebraska; make it missionary ground; form a Methodist conference there forthwith.   Let all the Churches do likewise; circulate antislavery tracts, and the oppressors will be appalled at the terrible reaction which shall overwhelm them and their schemes in a signal defeat.

CHAPTER XVIII.

TEMPERANCE—EXTRACTS FROM PAPERS.

FROM A SPRINGFIELD PAPER (1851).

THE meeting of the Temperance Alliance on Monday evening, at the Columbia Street Church, was numerously attended. Rev. Granville Moody delivered an able address on the subject of intemperance and its appropriate remedy, the enactment of a law similar in its provisions to the Maine Law, embracing the principles of seizure and confiscation. His blows against this monster vice were given with a stalwart arm and hearty good-will; for whatever Mr. Moody finds to do, he does with all his might. His address embodied a vast amount of statistical facts, showing the destructive effects of intemperance on the individual and society, physically, morally, and pecuniarily; and argued with great force the right of society to abate the traffic in liquor as a beverage, on the same grounds that obscene books and pictures, and the apparatus of the gambler are doomed to destruction; the right to protect itself against all nuisances that endanger its health or corrupt its morals.

By vote of the alliance the address was ordered to be printed, when all will have an opportunity of reading it for themselves.

FROM THE "GAZETTE," DAYTON (1854).

MR. EDITOR,—We were much amused by the silly communication of "J. S.," which appeared in the

Empire of the 7th inst. He seems to be specially disturbed by the speeches made by two of our city clergy
in favor of an effective appliance of the new liquor law.
He says : "The whole tone and tenor of their speeches
were counsel, advice, and persuasion to temperance
men, and to members of their Churches especially, to
do things which, if done, must bring down upon those
who do them the contempt and scorn of all who despise mean and dishonest actions." Again he says :
"They would have their followers degrade themselves
by becoming public informers *for vengeance or from
prejudice.*" And so intent is this unscrupulous writer
in urging this allegation, that he repeats it in the last
paragraph, and says that "he merely wishes to call
attention to the fact that the preachers are inducing
their followers to become public informers *for vengeance or from prejudice.*" He also says : "Since the
formation of government, public informers *for vengeance or prejudice* have occupied the same social
position as hangmen." And he asks, as though his
conscience yet twinged or his prudence supplicated to
be heard : "Could mortal man believe it ?" No, no,
Mr. J. S.; moderate your hopes ; restrain your expectations. We assure you that you can not find mortal or
immortal man to believe your senseless charge that
these naughty preachers instigated their followers
against you or your kith and kin, either *"for vengeance or from prejudice ;"* and your threefold repetition of this charge in one short article, that they urged
them to it *"for vengeance or from prejudice,"* shows
that you were afraid no one would believe it ; and
you seem to have proceeded on the maxim, "Throw
enough mud, some may stick."

And, pray, why are the clergy charged with acting
and with actuating others, from the silliness of preju-

dice or the savagism of revenge? Why this fierce
and slanderous attack on the clergy? Why this attempt to call down public odium upon them? What
have they done under the derangement of prejudice
or the savagism of revenge? What if they did "advise, counsel, and persuade" their fellow-citizens to
the appliance and enforcement of this wholesome and
benevolent law (as far as it goes), enacted by the political friends of J. S. for the suppression of intemperance, that greatest source of social and moral evil
and ruin in our midst?

Could clergymen be the friends of society, in this
matter of vital interest, and remain silent? Are they
not expected to be conservators of public morals?
Has it come to this, that honor, uprightness, and dignity require them, or any others, to take the side of
the makers or venders of the accursed thing? Is it
not sickening, too, to find men, pretending even to a
moiety of common sense or morals, coming up to the
aid of intemperance?

This hasty writer, it seems, could not elevate his
thoughts to the conception of higher and nobler motives, as actuating temperance men, than " revenge or
prejudice !" Has he only studied the influence of motives with which he is most familiar? Does he judge
others by himself? Alas! has the traffic in and use
of intoxicating liquors so stultified his mind, and de-
based his heart already, that "revenge or prejudice "
is the only conceivable alternative to him? Could he
not, by a more determined effort, rise to the conception
of better motives for the conduct of those who are engaged in the benign and philanthropic cause of temperance? According to this sapient correspondent,
temperance men are guilty of " revenge and prejudice"
when engaged in a cause which requires a self-sacrific-

ing spirit of active benevolence in staying an evil
which ever leaves want and wretchedness in the track
of its desolating course. We most promptly and positively disclaim such unworthy motives, and affirm,
and every one present at the time will attest, that no
such sentiment was even hinted at, much less avowed,
and the statements of J. S. concerning them are entirely gratuitous.

By the way, was it the fifth resolution which regards with disapprobation the sale of beer, ale, etc., as
beverages, which has called out J. S.? Does he cry out
"because his craft is in danger?" Ah! Demetrius, thy
speech betrayeth thee. This certainly is an age of
progress! It is amusing to hear a liquor-dealer charging clergymen with being "miserable if peace or happiness prevail in a neighborhood for a month," when
it is notorious that peace and happiness can not exist
for a single day where intemperance prevails. To
such we may say in the language of inspiration:
"What hast thou to do with peace?" "Who hath
woe? Who hath sorrow? Who hath contentions?
Who hath babbling? Who hath wounds without
cause? Who hath redness of eyes? They that tarry
long at the wine; they that go to seek mixed wine."

But perchance J. S. acted on the policy of the pursued thief, who ran in order to divert attention, and
exclaimed as he ran: "Stop thief, stop thief!" But
how are we to understand J. S.? Does he wish to
appear before the public as the advocate and defender
of all the woes and wretchedness and misery and
wickedness of intemperance? Does he indeed riot in
the tears of broken-hearted wives and more than
orphaned children? Has he lost sight of the drunkard
in the gutter? Has he, and have his coadjutors closed
their eyes to the cry of crime? Have oppressive

taxes, and crowded almshouses, and crowded jails, and crowded penitentiaries, and the dark gallows with its swinging victims, all failed to impress his mind and their minds with the inconceivable and unmitigated evils of the wrong he defends? Has petty gain blinded the mind, hardened the heart, seared the conscience, blasted the finer sensibilities and sympathies of the souls of the dealers in this accursed thing, and even brought J. S. out as their voluntary advocate? This charge I do not make against him, but I am at a loss to know how he can be exonerated from the blame of endeavoring to hinder those whose only aim is to remove these evils from society. "Be not partakers of other men's sins."

In conclusion, let me ask, Are these sentiments and feelings avowed by J. S., so nearly allied to the spirit that conceived and consummated the Nebraska outrage, which, despising the solemnities of a national compact and compromise, and disregarding the original design of this government, which was to establish liberty and justice, endeavors to open wide the door under the sanctions of our republican government, for the purpose of flooding this land of liberty with all the horrors and wrongs of slavery? Is J. S. striving to shield and promote intemperance in our midst, and slavery in our land, with such determined zeal, that any efforts made against these pet curses of community wake up his indignation in defense of both? Alas! 'tis said that "the vices go in groups." But it may be that the influence of association and oneness of principle are leading him in the wake of the politicians who decry the efforts of the friends of liberty and morals, and decry clergymen in particular (and some men are constitutionally apish). If so, the conflict will not terminate very soon, and their vainly sought victory will furnish the modern illustration of the work of Sisyphus.

On the subject of the office and work of the pulpit, I recommend to J. S. the consideration of the sentiment uttered by that correct and noble-minded poet, Cowper:

> "The pulpit
> Must stand acknowledged, whilst the world shall stand,
> The most important and effectual guard,
> Support, and ornament of virtue's cause."

We are at a loss to determine whether the bad spirit or the bad spelling, the bad sense or the bad syntax, of the communication of J. S. bears the palm. Either the typographers have done him great injustice, or he ought to sue his school-master for his education. But we must be lenient on this point, as he promises not "to throw open the sacerdotal robes of clerical ignorance."

We confess a little curiosity to know who this J. S. is. Some say he is from Pennsylvania, having imported himself to this city at a heavy expense, to assume the post of head secretary to a bag of malt. Of this, however, we have no certain knowledge, and are left to judge his personality from his initials. For what, then, do the letters J. S., stand? If for a name, it might be John Smith; but we are not disposed to slander that respectable individual by the supposition. We prefer to suppose that the initials J. S. stand for terms merely descriptive of a class, the JUG-SUCKERS. For the present we bid them and their champion adieu.

M.

MR. EDITOR,—We noticed a second communication from J. S. in the *Empire* of the 16th inst., upon which we would make a few remarks, not that we deem his article worthy of attention further than this; in meeting J. S. we virtually meet the whole force of the liquor interest in this city, and are afforded an opportunity of speaking to the public upon the subject of temperance, and because he has been made to occupy the nadir as the medium of the bad logic and worse business of the liquor vend. ers. It is really afflicting to see him writhe under the logic which proves him to be utterly reckless in charging temperance men with "*acting from prejudice or revenge*" whilst endeavoring to bring the arm of the law to bear upon drinking-houses, declared by the political associates of J. S. to be public nuisances, and for the abatement of which they have made legal provision, whilst J. S. appears at the portals as their zealous defender. "The wounded bird will flutter."

But J. S. very promptly leaves this absurd position, and informs us of the existence of brothels and gambling establishments in our ward and city, and seemingly banters us to plant our batteries against those great evils. We think that by planting our battery against intemperance we most effectually destroy all these and many associated vices. Intemperance, as it destroys all the tender sensibilities of the heart, banishes the native modesty of our nature, removes the sense of shame, increases the desire for mere sensual indulgences and selfish gratifications, opens the door for all the vices which drown the world in woe, and changes man into a demon of mischief and a demon of personal misery, should call forth our most vigorous opposition. What, indeed, is left of virtue or happiness to the inebriate? Who can follow him anywhere in society, especially to the associations of domestic life, without being shocked at every step,

and, if the observer is capable of sympathy, without
having his heart oppressed with anguish, where, instead of the affectionate husband and kind father, or
dutiful son or loving brother, he only meets the besotted drunkard, the merciless tyrant, the wreck of
every virtue and of every endearing tie?

But what does J. S. really wish? Does he wish
to come out and directly tell us that he is the advocate of drunkards and intemperance? or that those
who make drunkards should not be brought out of
their retreats, and their efforts prevented, because,
forsooth, they are the friends of society and the
benefactors of mankind? The principle involved in
his anathemas upon those who would apply the
liquor law would prevent the application and execution of all law.

He does not tell us this plainly, but indirectly at
least; and, though it is right to arrest a man who
steals our property, or who has broken into our houses
at night, endangering our lives, or the man who coun-
terfeits the public currency or coin, or the man who,
in our markets, sells unwholesome meat, yet, according to J. S., nothing but "revenge or prejudice"
can possibly induce us to oppose strenuously practices
which produce, directly or indirectly, nearly all those
cases of crime which crowd the criminal docket of
this and every other county in Ohio. And, indeed,
the thief and the burglar and the counterfeiter, and
the butcher who sells diseased meat in our markets, are as thoroughly shielded by the arguments of
J. S. as the man who violates the liquor law. Each
of these offenders might cry out with J. S. against
those who would maintain the law of the State against
them. "O, you are mischief-makers, you are informers 'for prejudice or from revenge,' you belong to the

class of hangmen;" and they would be as likely to do so as J. S. and the men he defends; for

> "No rogue e'er felt the halter draw
> With good opinion of the law;
> Or held the statute orthodox
> With love of justice, in the stocks."

Thus we are shut up to the conclusion that J. S., dissatisfied with the legislation which "provides against the evils arising from the liquor-traffic," hopes to make it inoperative by deterring our citizens from applying it, as also all future legislation and efforts of the kind; and thus does he lend his influence to sustain the cause of intemperance, and his measures, harmless only from their impotency, if completely successful, would convert our great nation into a nation of drunkards. *

But J. S. insists upon our making an attack upon the brothels and gambling-hells which, he informs us, do really exist in our ward and city, and he makes earnest inquiry, Why do we not attend to these? We answer, first: Suppose we should, would not J. S. hurl his anathemas upon us as "informers for prejudice or from revenge," and assail us as "mischief-makers," "disturbers of the peace," and endeavor to make us "odious as spies and hangmen?" For this is the broad position he has taken in his articles, and consistency would require him to do so; and if decency would not allow him to defend brothels and gambling as he has defended grog-shops and drinking-houses, some other staunch defender of these "pet curses" could adopt the language of J. S., and with as much propriety too, as in the cause he advocates.

We answer, secondly: That the removal of the facilities for intemperance is the most effectual, and almost the only, way of reaching those nuisances of which he speaks, and which are directly sustained

by the makers and venders of intoxicating liquors;
nuisances which could not exist under the influence
of temperance; nuisances which live, move, and have
their birth and being in the legally declared nuisance
of intemperance, on whose citadel J. S. stands sen-
tinel.   Hence the outcry of Demetrius and his fellow-
craftsmen, "Great is Diana of the Ephesians," whenever this mercenary and soul-destroying craft is assailed; and, indeed, J. S. unwittingly concedes our
whole argument, for he tells us that gamblers in this
city have posted on the walls of one of their rooms the
following motto: "Let him *drink and forget his poverty*, and remember his misery no more." He also
says that "professional gamblers *do not drink;* they
are too wide awake for that—only their victims drink ;"
and, therefore, the motto was intended for them.   Ah,
murder will out.   J. S. states here that gamblers depend on intemperance for their success—fatal admission, *"only their victims* drink." Well, then, if their
success depends on intemperance, shall we not then
most effectually prevent the success of gamblers?   Out
of thine own mouth, J. S., we find the vindication of
our course in endeavoring to circumvent the prolific
crime of intemperance.   Verily, as gamblers depend
on intemperance for their success, they will, no doubt,
feel much indebted to J. S. for opposing those who
would stay the devastating tide of intemperance by
which their business thrives.

From this concession it does appear that the better
judgment of J. S. has not entirely submitted to the
injurious and destructive claims of the cause he defends; but if he is sincere, why does he endeavor to
hinder those healthful movements against intemperance? "Consistency, thou art a jewel." J. S. very
properly expresses his indignation against the beastly,

loathsome, and debasing vice of prostitution, which furnishes such an exhibition of shamelessness, and we deeply lament that there is to be found in our beautiful city, and especially in the Fifth Ward, a place which answers so exactly to the description given in the Bible of her "whose house is the way to hell, going down to the chambers of death; yea, many strong men have been slain by her, and her guests are in the depths of hell."

It is to be regretted that our laws, which punish such houses, as well as their nurseries, the grog-shops, are not more vigorously executed. Benevolence to society, and true philanthropy, would justify such enforcement. And it is still more to be regretted that every attempt to suppress intemperance, the foster-mother of these hyenas of society, should be ascribed to "revenge or prejudice." Does not J. S. know that intemperance does more to produce debauchery and gambling than any thing else in our land? Do not these vices belong to the family of vices produced or nourished by intemperance? Hence, in opposing intemperance, we but lay the ax at the root of this upas-tree; but J. S. cries out, Hands off, hands off; it is all "prejudice or revenge;" and thus does he become in effect the defender of both prostitution and gambling, and a fearful brood of crimes incubated by intemperance.

J. S. thinks that "the devil can be seen by some only in a glass of rum." Verily we think the man must be under the influence of several glasses of rum, who fails to see the demon there, whose name is legion. But J. S. tells us there is no mystery about this liquor-traffic; it is regulated precisely as every other article in the market, by the law of supply and demand, hence; so long as there is a demand for

liquor of any kind, there will be found men to meet
the demand in spite of the most stringent legal enactments; no power on God's earth can prevent it.

Stop, stop, J. S.; you go too fast. We know now by
what medium your mysteries are cleared up; but in
the liquor-traffic it is obvious that your philosophy is at
fault. The fact is, the supply of liquor creates the demand, and not the demand the supply, for the appetite is an artificial one, and not natural; it is an acquired one. The supply and presence of the article
produce the appetite. It is the nature of every vice
to increase its own demands in proportion to the supply of the means of gratification. Remove the supply,
and the appetite decreases and dies out, for it is not a
natural one. Remove the facilities for procuring
liquor, and men will do without it, to the advance-
ment of every interest.

This is also the case with tobacco and opium. No
one has a natural appetite for them; it is an acquired
one. The presence and use of these articles is the occasion of the appetite, and in proportion to the abundance of the supply will be the use. Now, we propose
to banish intoxicating liquor from society as a beverage; and, if no supply, there will be no demand, as the
appetite for alcohol is artificial and not natural. And
O, how many inebriates would rejoice, as they have
often said, if the accursed thing were placed out of
their way, that they might not be led into temptation !
So with brothels and gaming establishments. Their
presence is the occasion of the ruin of thousands who
would not be wrecked in circumstances, in body, in
soul, and in hope, if these accursed places did not
afford such facilities for debasing bestiality and horrid crimes. And when we consider how intemperance inflames the passions of both soul and body, we

need not wonder that gaming-houses and places of prostitution are patronized as extensively as J. S., who has turned "public informer" in these base crimes, attests, though we charitably hope he has not turned informer "for prejudice and from revenge."

We highly approve of the regard which J. S. professes for the sanctity of the Sabbath, and we will render him all proper aid in maintaining its benign influences. And we rejoice also to know that the entire history of the Revolutionary struggle sheds its luster on the ancient and patriotic New England name so intimately interwoven with its events from A. D. 1632 through all its variant but progressive changes. We are not concerned about the puerile and virulent personalities of this would-be censor. His first and last communications abound in low, ribald personalities, the perpetration of which was manifestly the design of both communications; for no one ever charged "prejudice and revenge" on principles, as they are only predicable of persons. We would remind him of the fable of the viper gnawing the file. Meanwhile, we assure J. S. that we feel no bitterness against him, and we are really sorry that the efforts to promote a cause so important to the welfare of our city should have roused his mind and waked up his wrath and indignation. And we regret to learn that on former occasions he has appeared as the opponent of the cause of temperance. And we further regret that, in entering the arena, he chose the weapon of personalities, so plentifully exhibited in both warp and woof of his loosely woven web.

From the piteous complaints, the contortions of countenance, and abhorrent grimaces which he makes when the cup he mingled for others is returned to his own lips, we infer that he does n't like the mixture;

but we think it will be medicinal; and from the improved tone of his last communication, we have considerable hope for our patient.

To conclude for the present, I thank J. S. for affording the occasion of addressing thousands of my fellow-citizens on the high, mighty, moral principles and social interests connected with the benevolent and philanthropic cause of temperance. With this end in view I can very easily bear the unfounded reproach and toothless personalities of this knight-errant of intemperance. And we read that: "Blessed are ye when men shall revile you and persecute you, and shall say all manner of evil against you falsely for my sake." Meanwhile, this case affords an encouraging illustration of the great truth that even "the wrath of man shall praise the Lord, and the remainder of wrath will he restrain." M.

MR. EDITOR,—I notice a third communication from J. S. in the *Empire* of the 21st, containing the usual quantum of abuse and reiteration of demolished charges; to all of which I wish briefly to reply, that the case being now fairly before the public, I am willing to leave it to their verdict, believing they are competent to determine what has been accomplished. Meanwhile, my own conviction is, if possible, more firmly established than ever, that true benevolence and philanthropy would require us to exterminate the traffic in liquor, not only for the sake of the public in general, but for the sake of the liquor-seller, who himself is very generally the victim of his own wicked and criminal business.

As to the charge that clergymen are sometimes mischief-makers, disturbers of the peace, etc., they must expect to suffer such imputations for the part

they may think it their duty to take in opposing vice.
I rejoice to know that the same charge has been made
against them in proportion to their activity in advocating the right and the true and the good, from time
immemorial. Elijah was charged with being a troubler
of Israel. The apostles were charged with troubling
the city exceedingly; and on another occasion Paul
and Silas were charged with having "turned the world
upside down;" and well was it for the world, for it
had been wrong side up for a long time, and it is not
yet fully righted. Even Jesus was reviled in the
same way; and "if they have called the Master
Beelzebub, how much more them of his household."
We know how it has been with those who have labored
in the cause of moral reform, always and everywhere;
and knowing what to expect, we do not complain.

I am sorry to learn, as I do from an intimation in
the last communication of J. S., that he has received
threatening anonymous letters from some source or
other. Why any one should threaten him I know not;
yet that he has been threatened, anonymously, I can not
doubt, for it would be unkind even to suspect that
he is rehearsing on a small scale the ludicrous farce of
"Payne, the Great Shot At." He says, however, in
regard to these threatening anonymous correspond-
ents, that he is ready "to spit upon them and kick
them like the filthiest poodle" in his path. This is
right. Whether they are Church members or Gentiles,
we think they do deserve a castigation for their im-
proper interference, and we think J. S. has hit upon
the very best way of treating them. Deserving of
punishment as they are, he acts wisely to substitute
kicking for writing; for it is very certain they will be
more likely to get their deserts from his boots than
from his pen.

In taking our leave of J. S. for the present, we assure him that he has our best wishes for his welfare. We should not have troubled him or the public with a single line but for the defense and advocacy of the moral principles, social interests, and civil order involved in the holy cause of temperance. M.

Mr. Editor,—J. S. makes another desperate but ineffectual effort to extricate himself from the difficulties which environ him in his absurd position as the knight-errant of the grog-shops. He admits that if our case were at all analagous to the case of Elijah and others specified by me, all of whom were charged with being mischief-makers, troublers of the people, etc., there would be some force in our plea; but he thinks our case is "as wide from theirs as a good action is from a bad one." Well, then, let us see. Our offense is, that we counseled the forming of a Committee of Vigilance, composed of twenty men, to aid in the enforcement of the law "to provide against the evils resulting from the liquor-traffic;" and we may state that, by a subsequent vote, over five hundred persons added themselves to the committee aforesaid, and not merely or mainly as Church members, but the good and true citizens of Dayton generally. This, then, "is the head and front of our offending" to J S. and the grog-shop keepers; for truly "their craft is in danger."

J. S. says those ancient worthies, as Elijah and others, "were not the means of having men dragged before authority for the vengeance of the law," as he gratuitously designates its penalties. What? Did not Elijah accuse, and publicly too, those wicked men who led the Israelites away from God by their sins; and did not that wicked Ahab, who sold himself to work iniquity, say unto Elijah: "Art thou he who troubleth Israel?" And Elijah answered and said: "I have not troubled Israel; but thou and thy father's house, in that ye have forsaken the commandments of the Lord." And did not Elijah gather to Mount Carmel the nine hundred and fifty prophets of Baal and the groves, and did not Elijah say unto them: "Take the prophets of Baal, let not one of them escape?" And they took them, and Elijah brought them down to the brook Kishon, and slew them there. Verily he dragged them before authority, in a sense and to an extent immeasurably beyond anything that we ever counseled or imagined with regard to liquor-sellers, for our object is simply to terminate their ruinous business by appropriate legal suasion, though drunkenness is as destructive of all human interests as was the base idolatry of Baal. Nor do we wonder that Ahab, whose interests were as intimately identified with the accursed false prophets as the interests and propensities of J. S. are with the liquor-sellers, should cry out to Elijah as J. S. does to us: "O thou clerical meddler, thou mischief-maker, art thou he that troubleth Israel?" Thus we see that the charge of J. S. puts him alongside of Ahab, and is just as untrue as to the friends of temperance as was the charge of that wicked Ahab, who sold himself to work iniquity, as alleged against Elijah; and therefore, as J. S. acknowledges that our plea would have some force if the case was at all analogous to the persons referred to, and as we have shown the strict and striking analogy, as far as our case goes, we have the acknowledgment of J. S. to the justice of our plea. He justifies us and condemns himself.

Did not John the Baptist publicly accuse Herod for his unlawful conduct with Herodias, saying to him, "It is not lawful for thee to have thy brother Philip's wife?" Had J. S. flourished eighteen hundred years sooner he might have enjoyed the honor and emolument of being private secretary to Herodias, and would have astonished the natives with his philippics against John the Baptist, charging him with "bad, un-christian motives," guilty of espionage upon the privacy of his neighbors, a spy on the private doings of his fellow-men, and a public informer for prejudice and revenge. And thus has it ever been that those who are active in arresting the progress of vice have been styled meddlesome persons, mischief-makers, and are charged with the worst motives for their best actions. Now, as we show a strict and striking analogy between our case and theirs, we "make out our plea with force," J. S. being judge, and all his vaporing vanishes.

But J. S. tells us that our benevolence in exterminating the liquor-traffic is to the grog-shop keeper like the benevolence of the vulture to the lamb. What! would J. S. have us believe that grog-shop keepers are *lambs?* Is the meek, innocent, and useful lamb the symbol of their nature and business, and is J. S. their shepherd, kind and vigilant, "whose friendly crook shall give them aid," and drive away the ugly vul-tures, the temperance men, far "from the green pas-tures and the still waters" where they rove or rest? And how absurd to compare temperance men to vultures! It is contemptible and ridiculous in the extreme, equaled only by the ravings of the maniac under the influence of delirium tremens. Rather look the truth in the face, and acknowledge that our benevo-lent and philanthropic design is to save community, and liquor-sellers too, from the dark vultures of intem-perance, whose gloomy shadows dim the light of every earthly joy, and shut out the hope of heaven, whilst they prey upon the vital interests of society in every department. We would save the liquor-seller from a business in which he lives to counteract the benevolence of God and man, and send want and misery and infamy and death into habitations otherwise the abode of comfort and hope. We would save him from an employment in which he barters disease and famine and riot and ruin for money to hoard up, to boast of, and be ruined by. His business debases him; and for paltry pelf he can take the beloved wife, and crucify her husband, and turn her from her home to starve and freeze, and make her children beggars and homeless and fatherless, at a price at which one would hardly cut off the head of a dog.

Surely the greatest earthly curse would be to be condemned to such a business; for the most reliable information shows that the venders of ardent spirits not unfrequently become its most signal victims. "In one street in the city of Albany, N. Y., the history of the keepers of seven grog-shops was ascertained for a period of ten years. Not one had prospered, and most of them had become drunkards. In one house, three successive occupants had died of delirium tremens; in another, the keeper, while laboring under the horrible disease, jumped from an upper window, broke his back, and died in great agony. And it is a significant fact that, in a neighboring State's prison, one hundred and fifty of the prisoners have been liquor-sellers." Alas! he ruins his family to gain pelf, and schools his offspring in his own house, with the tippler, the lewd, and the lost; and his children rise up and call him cursed! And THIS is not all, for his business tends to the undoing of himsef and his family and his customers. It seals them over to the adversary, and con-

firms them as the enemies of righteousness through
all the future periods of their being! O, is it not benevolent to stop a business that so mars and spoils
the works of God? Can it be viewed as a wanton of-
ficiousness that would apply moral and legal suasion
combined, to put this crying evil far from us? We
claim in our favor every law of nature, of God, and of
man—the law of kindness, humanity, self-preserva-
tion and necessity—in our endeavor to dam, divert,
or dry up that flood of intemperance, which is pouring desolation upon society and upon souls for time
and for eternity. And yet J. S. would act over, on a
small scale, the Nero of antiquity, who sewed Christians up in the skins of wild animals, and, thus dis-
figured and disguised, let loose ferocious dogs upon
them.

When J. S. shall succeed in showing that grog-
shops are not what the law declares them, "nuisances;"
when he shall show that the business is not injurious
alike to the highest and the lower interests of society;
then, and only then, will he succeed in his cherished
object of rendering the enforcement of the liquor law
odious. Meanwhile he appears in open hostility to
this act of the Legislature, and is engaged in a crusade
against the good it aims to accomplish. But the people understand him. They know his latitude and his
longitude, his interests and his instincts, and I rejoice
to know that his efforts have but stimulated them
to duty.

We would not reflect on the discernment of the
public so much as to point out the weakness of the
efforts of J. S. by any further argumentation. His
ridiculous reiteration of exploded charges, shows con-
clusively that he has absolutely nothing on which to
depend, to cover his defeat, but misrepresentations

and abuse. And they are as harmless as the feeble yelpings of the poodle at the passing moon. We must be excused from noticing him any further at present, on the principle set forth in the reason assigned by a member of the Legislature, who, after listening to an abusive and empty speech from a young and conceited man in his maiden effort, rose and said: "Mr. Speaker and gentlemen of the House, you will please excuse me from making any reply to the individual who has just addressed you; for I always hated to strike at nothing, it wrenches a body so."

We shall not waste time in reiterating our arguments, by which the ridiculous charges of J. S. have been demolished, and on account of which he is so nettled and sore. We only regret that we have not found in him a more competent and honorable opponent; for we have been deprived of

"The stern joy that warriors feel
In foeman worthy of their steel."

J. S. inquires with credulity and alarm for the five hundred auxiliaries to the Committee of Vigilance. Had he attended the public temperance-meeting in the Fifth Ward, he would have had ocular demonstration of the re-enforcement, when by rising vote they declared their determination to aid the Committee of Vigilance in their duties. These things were not done in a corner; and politically, ecclesiastically, and in the temperance cause, we know nothing of the "Know Nothings;" all we ask is an open field and a fair chance.   M.

REASONS FOR OPPOSITION TO THE SALE AND USE OF LIQUORS.

Does any one ask the reasons for our opposition to the sale or use of intoxicating liquors as a beverage, or a vindication of our principles as a temperance advocate, we reply: First. The Bible, that duly authenticated revelation of the mind and will of God, pronounces against it most emphatically. Note then:

Its utterances in Noah's disgrace and drunkenness.

Lot's incest and injury by intoxication.

Law of the Nazarite. (Num. vi, 1-6.)

Wine forbidden to priests. (Lev. x, 8, 9.)

Nadab and Abihu killed by God for intoxication. (Lev. x, 8, 9.)

Son, a drunkard, stoned to death. (Deut. xxi, 22.)

History of Israel in the wilderness—forty years total abstinence. (Deut. xxix, 6.)

Curse of the law against drunkenness. (Deut. xxix, 19.)

Samson's mother prohibited wine. (Judg. xiii, 4, 14.)

David made Uriah drunk to cover his own crime. (2 Sam. xi, 13.)

Nabal represented by his wife as such a son of Belial, that no one could speak to the pesky toper. (1 Sam. xxv, 36.)

Elah hurled from his throne while drunk. (1 Kings, xvi, 8.)

Ben-hadad drunk and conquered. (1 Kings, xx, 13.)

Who hath woe? Who hath wounds without cause? Who hath redness of eyes? They that tarry long at the wine. (Prov. xxiii, 20.)

Be not with wine-bibbers, or thou shalt come to poverty. Wine is a mocker; strong drink is raging. He that is deceived thereby is not wise. (Prov. xx, 1.)

Not for kings to drink wine lest they forget the law. (Prov. xxxi, 4.)

Solomon gave his heart to wine, vanity, and vexation. (Eccl. ii, 3, 11.)

Woe unto them that rise up early, in the morning, that they may follow strong drink. (Isa. v, 11.)

Woe to him who is mighty to drink mixed wines. (Isa. xxii, 23.)

Strong drink shall be bitter to them that drink it. (Isa. xxiv, 9.)

Woe to the drunkards of Ephraim. (Isa. xxviii, 1-7.

Rechabites, honored of God and total abstinence. (Jer. xxxv, 2-6.)

Daniel and Hebrew children teetotalers. (Dan. i, 8.)

Belshazzar's drunken, impious feast. (Dan. v, 1.)

God praised their sons for Nazarites. (Am. ii, 11.)

Woe to them that are at ease in Zion, and drink wine in bowls. (Am. vi, 6.)

Woe to him that putteth his bottle to his neighbor's lips, and maketh him drunken. (Hab. ii, 15.)

John the Baptist used no wine or strong drink. (Luke i, 15.)

If found with drunkards he shall be cut off. (Matt. xxiv, 49.)

If overcome with drunkenness we shall perish. (Luke xxi, 34.)

The wicked slandered the apostles as if drunk on Pentecost. (Acts ii.)

The wicked slandered Jesus as if he were a winebibber. (Matt. xi, 19.)

Good not to drink wine whereby my brother stumbleth. (Rom. xiv, 21.)

With drunkards, no, not to eat. (1 Cor. v, 11.)

Drunkards shall not inherit the kingdom of God. (1 Cor. vi, 10.)

Works of flesh are drunkenness. (Gal. v, 21.)

Be not drunk with wine wherein is excess. (Eph. v, 18.)

Bishops must not be given to wine. (1 Tim, iii, 3.)

God's judgments are represented as cups of strong drink. (Rev. xiv, 10.)

Thus promptly and kindly would the genius of temperance, speaking to us through the Bible, warn us of evil, and dash from our lips and hands the cup of devils, from whose beaded rim the most deadly exhalations rise. Indeed, on this subject a hyperbole of description would still prove an ellipsis of the mournful results of the practice of intoxication.

Second. What are the facts with respect to the great social vice?—

1. That nine-tenths of the inmates of poor-houses were brought there by intoxication.

2. That three-fourths of all the convicts in our penitentiaries were habitual drinkers before the commission of the crimes for which they were arrested.

3. That ninety one-hundredths of all suicides are the immediate or remote victims of intemperance.

4. That in three-fourths of all insolvencies and bankruptcies rum has been the cause.

5. That seventy-five per cent of dishonest clerks, book-keepers, treasurers, and others in offices of trust, are intemperate men.

6. That sixty per cent of all the troubles among officers and men in the army and navy of the United States are attributed to intemperance.

7. That three-fourths of all political disasters and failures in official stations are traced to the bottle.

8. That three-fourths of all collisions on railroads and explosions of boilers or collisions of steamers are from the bottle.

9. That eighty per cent of divorces and domestic infelicities belong to rum.

10. That in all families where the children are neg-

lected and dirty, half naked and half fed, rooms in disorder and filthy, husbands cross and discontented, wives slatterns, peevish, ill-tempered, pesky, and quarrelsome, one or both parents are intemperate.

11. That those who least frequently attend the house of God, and shock ears polite with profanity and ribaldry, are drinking characters.

12. That seldom does a liquor-dealer have cheek enough to show himself in any church of God.

13. That nearly all the evils afore-stated originate in the saloons and dram-shops of our land, the purlieus of perdition and breathing holes of hell.

14. That many of the troubles in our Churches are traceable to intemperance.

15. That losses of property by fire are traceable to liquor, directly or indirectly.

16. That three-fourths of all our taxes for the prosecution of crime are occasioned by the liquor-traffic.

17. That seven-eighths of all criminal cases in our courts come from rum.

18. More than two-thirds of all rum-sellers fall victims to their own evil business, and a like proportion of their families.

19. Because the vile and poisonous adulterations of wine, beer, ale, and whisky are deleterious to the health of those who use them.

20. That seven-eighths of the victims of cholera are found among drunkards.

21. That more than one hundred thousand victims of intemperance are hurried to the grave annually in the United States.

22. That merchants, mechanics, farmers, doctors, and lawyers find most of the losses which they are compelled to sustain are occasioned by drunkards.

23. That intemperance corrupts our politics, and subjects our voters to the rum-sellers.

24. That rum has been the ruin of the poor Indians, the wards of the nation.

25. That nothing so effectually hinders the coming of Christ's kingdom on earth as intemperance.

26. That nothing so much hinders the increase of the elect as rum.

27. That nothing so rapidly fills up the ranks of the reprobates as rum. Ah !

> "Let thy devotees extol thee,
> And thy vaunted virtues sum;
> But the worst of names I'll call thee,
> O, thou hydra-monster, Rum !"

Shakespeare says :

> "I will combine all ills, all wrongs and woes,
> All miseries and crimes, and call thee,--Rum !"

Are you a member of the Church of God, then let me remind you:

1. That intemperance is a sin plainly and positively condemned in the Holy Scriptures.

2. Total abstinence from all intoxicating drinks, as a beverage, is sustained by precept and example in the Bible.

3. There is no way to have drunkenness cease, only by having the total abstinence principle prevail.

4. The Church of God is reformatory in its character. It should be the salt of the earth.

5. Self-denial is indispensably requisite in order to be a Christian.

6. All objections to our principles are but excuses for indulgence.

Hold on, then, friends of temperance, in this holy cause. Do not relax your efforts to save the drunkard, and to remove the curse of strong drink from the communities in which you reside.

"Truth, though it trouble some minds,
Some wicked minds that are both dark and dangerous,
Yet it preserves itself; comes off pure, innocent;
And, like the sun, though never so beclouded,
Will yet break forth in unveiled glory."

22

CHAPTER XIX.

INCIDENTS OF ARMY LIFE.

WHILE stationed at Franklin, the old capital of Tennessee, we were apprised of a cavalry force in the vicinity, which meditated an attack on the Seventy-fourth Regiment. We guarded against it by putting the regiment under greater surveillance, and posted a guard around the town, early on Sabbath morning. The slaves also warned us that there was going to be an attack on us, and that all the secessionists had received notice to retire into their cellars when the attack came off. The cavalry was Wheeler's.

I posted a double guard, and took every precaution, and awaited the projected attack, in readiness to give them a warm reception. About two o'clock P. M. I heard the report of a rifle on our picket-lines, and soon afterward an officer ran to head-quarters, and reported that one of my soldiers was fatally wounded. I returned with him, and found a crowd around their fallen comrade, who was bleeding freely, and in Irish accents bewailing his bad "luck."

It appeared that Patrick had bought of the sutler a can of cherries, which were preserved in spirits, and had eaten many of them, and drunk the liquor. He was badly intoxicated, and showed that while liquor was in, wit was out, and approached our picket-line, and encountered a young American on the line, who promptly hailed him: "Halt! Who comes there?" The answer was returned: "You spalpeen, don't you halt me!" The "Halt" was repeated twice, and twice disregarded by the besotted Irishman, who attempted to cross the guard-line, when the bayonet was thrust through him, and he lay bleeding of a deadly wound. He was yelling, "Holy Mary! Mother of God! Pray for me now, and at the hour of my death. Amen."

"Patrick," said I, "what is up now?"

"Och, sir, the guard there bayoneted me through and through."

"He attempted to cross the line," said the guard, "disregarding my three hails, and I thrust him on duty, sir."

The regimental surgeons were examining the wound, and I beckoned one of them aside and asked as to the probabilities, and was told that the wound was fatal. I had the man taken to the surgeon's tent, where the surgeons completed their attendance. The tent was crowded with soldiers. Patrick looked up wistfully, and said: "Colonel, please have all the men go out." Looking at them he said: "If ye please, comrades!" The men all readily retired, and I closed the apron doors, tied them securely, and took a camp-stool, and sat down beside the man. I handed him an orange which I happened to have in my pocket. "Thank you, Colonel, and for the clearance of the room.

And now I want to confess to you that I am ashamed of myself. It was the whisky which I got in the can of preserved cherries that befooled me; and forcing my way headlong through the guards, the youngster did his duty, and here I am thrust dead, before I got a shot at the rebels myself; struck down by one of my own men in the discharge of his duty."

"Well, well," I said, "never mind that now; you have the weightest things on hand now, Patrick."

"Yes, Colonel. There is another thing on my mind—my wife and three children in Springfield. You know that we, as a regiment, have not been paid off for three or four months, and my family is in need of my pay, and I want to get you to promise me that you will see to it that my poor wife and children get what is coming to me. Send it to them, with my love to each and all. Bad luck to my foolish conduct!"

"Well," said I, "I will see to it that your family get the last cent of your wages."

"That's the best word you've said, Colonel. Poor creatures! I've left you bad enough off; to be sure I have. I wish I could leave you better off, but I can't."

"Well, now, Patrick, you have higher interests to care for; your soul's welfare. This should now be your supreme concern."

"Well, Colonel, I want to confess all my sins to you—from the first to the last. There is no priest about here now; and if there was, I would prefer to confess to you."

"It will do you no good to put me in the priest's place, and confess to me and seek of me for absolution. 'Who can forgive sins but God only?' against whom we have all sinned. Confess your sins to God, Patrick. The ministers of Christ can charge us with offending God, and enjoin true repentance, which consists in having our hearts broken for and from sin ; and enjoin the duty of our returning to God with confession of our sins, deprecation of God's displeasure, supplication for his mercy, and the presentation of genuine repentance which is unto life, not to be repented of, with faith in our Lord Jesus Christ, by which you approach the Father, by the operation of the Holy Spirit, and secure pardoning mercy, renewing grace, adopting love, and hope of heaven."

"But, Colonel, how will I know whether the Lord accepts me, and blesses me with pardon and hope of heaven, as you say?"

"Every one that believeth," I said, " hath the witness in himself. The Spirit searcheth all things, even the depths of our hearts, and the deep things of God ; and the Spirit of God beareth witness with our spirit that we are the children of God; and if children, then heirs of God, through Jesus Christ our Lord. Now, Patrick, let us pray, and I will confess with you and for you."

As I proceeded, he humbly joined me in confession, deprecation, supplication, and renunciation of sin and Satan, with acceptance of Christ as our Prophet, Priest, and King; our Shepherd, Friend, and Guide; our All in all. We consecrated ourselves to the Father, Son, and Holy Spirit, and promised to serve God, wholly, in newness of life. While thus engaged, I said : "Lord, here is poor Patrick, in sore distress. O Lord, if it be possible and proper, we ask thee to spare his life to Patrick and his distant wife, and his three dependent children! O Lord, thy power is equal to thy will; be pleased to command deliverance for poor, distressed Patrick. Exert thy power, O Lord, and may Patrick be snatched from this impending calamity, and his added days shall show forth thy praise!"

"Good Lord," cried out Patrick, "I'll do all that the colonel says."

I rejoiced in spirit to hear him respond so fully as he did to my prayer for himself, and I was seized with the spirit of responsive praises to God for the pardon of poor Patrick's sins, and for averting the calamity of his death; and my petitions were succeeded by praises to a sin-pardoning God, whose power was equal to sparing poor Patrick from death. I closed with the apostolic benediction; and "Glory to the Three in One and One in Three; as it was, is now, and shall be forever. Amen."

"Patrick," I said, "you shall not die, but live and praise the name of the Lord God Almighty."

"Och, Colonel! Why do you talk so to a man that is cut through and through with a bayonet wound?"

"Well, Patrick, nothing is too hard for God; and he has heard and answered our united prayers,

which have been offered. The prayer of faith
hath prevailed. You shall not die, but live and
praise the name of the Lord."

"If the Lord shall spare my life, my life shall
be given to him for his mercy; it shall, it shall."

He fell into a sweet sleep, which lasted several
hours. His wounds healed up. In a week or ten
days he was about the camp on two crutches; and
in about six weeks was well again, and returned
to duty. Months afterward he went into the battle
of Stone River; fought like a veteran hero; was
taken prisoner; exchanged at Libby Prison; went
to Springfield, and spent a time with his family;
reunited with his regiment, and went South
under McCook, Thomas, and Sherman, to glorious
victories.

Sometime after these events I was on a steamboat on the Ohio, above Cincinnati, and after
supper, as I was listlessly sitting in front of my
state-room, who should come up to me but Archbishop Purcell? Politely recognizing me, he sat
down, and said familiarly: "Colonel, let me hear
something from your lips of your army life?" I
thought awhile, and then recited the foregoing
narration. It was supremely interesting to the
archbishop, and his fine countenance was all astir;
and, with staring eyes and listening ears, weeping
or smiling, he listened with wonder and gratitude, surprise and praise, interlocution and commendations interjected; and at last wiped the
tears from his face, extended me his hand, and
thanked me in earnest and eloquent terms for my

kind attentions to one of his charge in such
perilous conditions. "In behalf of the Catholic
Church, which I represent, I thank you for your
tender sympathies for poor Patrick ; and trust that
the event may prove of perpetual benefit to his
soul. I shall long cherish the memories of this
evening's interview." At about nine o'clock we
parted, he having reached his destination, and I
went on my way.

While Andrew Johnson was military governor
of Tennessee, and I was the colonel of an Ohio
regiment, I was dubbed by the boys "the Fighting Parson." We entered Nashville just at the
time that General Buell had concluded to leave
the city. On hearing this startling news, I hastened to the governor's house, and found him
closeted with two friends in serious consultation.
As I entered the others withdrew. To my inquiry, "How are matters going, Governor?" he
replied: "Going! Moody, we are sold. Buell
has resolved to evacuate the city, and called upon
me this morning, requesting me to leave also.
He has given me three hours in which to decide,
and will be here in an hour for my ultimatum.
I have remonstrated against the act. I still believe we can hold the city against the enemy.
What do you think, Moody? Will you stay with
your command?" I replied: "I will stay with
you, and I have faith in God that he will deliver
us from falling into the hands of the enemy."
Said Governor Johnson: "I am glad to hear you
talk of faith in God. Moody, can you pray for

us?" I advised him to stand by the city to the
last, and to telegraph concerning the situation to
Washington. He said the wires were all cut. I
then suggested that he send by courier to Louisville, and thence communicate by wire with Washington; and added, that the wires were not cut to
heaven. Instinctively, we both fell upon our
knees on the floor, which was covered with mat-
ting. Our backs were opposite each other. Then
I prayed: "O Lord, Director of the universe and
Governor of men, I pray thee look upon this earthly
governor in his agony, and sustain and guide
him. ['Amen,' said Johnson.] He appeals to
thee in this hour for comfort and direction—poor,
weak mortal that he is, a creature of clay, and
uncertain as to what to do. I pray thee that if
he is right, that thou wouldst make him as firm
as adamant. ['Amen! amen! amen!'] But if
he is wrong, O Lord, make him *feel* that he is
wrong. ['Amen.'] Leave him not in uncer-
tainty."

Then I poured out my soul in earnest supplication for the Union, the governor, and all who
were straitened in the present emergency. I was
startled by very unnatural sounds, like scrap-
ing upon the floor, as though some huge monster, with claws, was approaching me, and I became powerfully impressed with the idea that
Satan was about to make a bold effort to drive me
from the throne of grace. I prayed the more fervently, and was presently relieved from my apprehensions by Johnson, who, having walked across

23 .

the room upon his knees, threw his arms around
my neck, ejaculating most vehemently, "Amen!
amen! God hear Colonel Moody's prayer!" From
this point the prayer continued but a short time,
when an indescribable sensation of peacefulness
overwhelmed us, and each of us became as calm
as a little child, while it seemed as though the
room was filled with a supernatural atmosphere
settling down upon us as a soft halo. Being fully
conscious of an answer, I ceased praying. We
both rose from the floor, wiping away the tears,
and paced the floor in opposite directions. Presently, meeting about the center, Johnson said:
"Colonel Moody, I feel better. I believe Almighty
God sent you here, and Nashville will be saved.
That prayer has been answered. I feel it. I
know it. My resolution is taken. All the powers
of earth shall not shake me from it. Buell can
go. No more dallying. I stay right here. Let
them come at me." Continuing his epigrammatic
sentences he walked to the window, where he
caught sight of the Federal flag that floated over
the capital. Excited to frenzy, he exclaimed:
"Shall I order that glorious old flag hauled down
to give place to that of rebels? I'll be d—d if
I do!" I cried out: "O Governor, Governor, do n't
indulge in such language under these solemn circumstances." To this rebuke he replied: "I
know 'tis wrong, 'tis wicked, Moody; but if I
allow that old flag to be hauled down, God Almighty will damn me; this nation will damn me;
I shall damn myself." A short time after, General

Buell arrived.   I withdrew; and, as history reports, Nashville was not surrendered.

At Stone River, during the days when my regiment was standing in double columns massed on the two center companies on the reserve line, waiting orders, a staff officer from General George H. Thomas's head-quarters in the field rode up to me and said, hurriedly: "Colonel, I have orders for you.   The regiment on your front has been nearly annihilated.   Hold your men in hand while I go on the line and clear off what is left; and you watch me, and when ready, I will wave my sword three times for you; and do you come on, advancing on the line of battle firing," and off he went.   I turned to my regiment, and said: "Comrades, we go into action in a few minutes.   Off caps, and say your prayers!"

Whilst we were all praying, I watched as well as prayed.   Presently the sign was given, and I interrupted their devotions with, "Battalion, attention!   Order arms!   shoulder arms!   right shoulder shift!   forward, quick time, march!"   Approaching the battle-line, I gave the order: "Battalion, by right and left companies, outward face; by right and left half wheel, forward into line, advance firing; march!"   And then I added: "Now, men, resume your praying; fight for your God, your country, and your kind; aim low and give them 'Hail Columbia;'" but, unfortunately for Columbia, the two center companies opened fire just as I had uttered the word "hail," and the simultaneous fire of one hundred and twenty rifles drowned the word "Columbia," and all the regiment heard was "give them hail." I suppose that it fell on their ears with a shortened accent. The boys, after the battle, stuck to it that I shouted, "Give them hell!"

On Thursday night, at ten o'clock, myself and regiment were ordered out about two miles south or south-west of Murfreesboro. We made the march through deep darkness, and came to a vacant house of hewed cedar logs, and in the back yard were fifteen or twenty small cabins. I resolved to shelter my men in the mansion-house and in these Negro cabins. We deployed companies A and B on the skirmish-lines. Then all was quiet, and I went up the spacious stairway, and into the front room, and up to the window, and looked out into the dense darkness. A stroke of lightning did its revealing work, and another, and another showed me the premises, with the extensive flower-garden in front, with, say, twenty corpses of soldiers strewn here and there. They were our men, shot down on picket duty. Presently a single shot from our picket-line admonished me of danger near, and in a few minutes a squad of men, bearing a wounded man, came to the house and carried him to the rear, and sent for me.

I found a fine-looking officer of the rebel army, who had been reconnoitering our line, and one of our picket-guard fired on him in the darkness, and the ball went through his loins, and he cried out for help. Two of our soldiers went out, and found the wounded and helpless man, and brought him into our camp. I sent for an ambulance to take him to the hospital. Meanwhile, I talked with him. He was a Southerner, intelligent, but sadly deficient in right views of the North, and said if things were as I told him, he had thrown his life away. I prayed with and for him, for which he was very thankful. He was sent to the hospital, and died in about six hours after reaching there.

The morning dawned, and about ten o'clock we departed. As I lingered awhile, I went up-stairs and beheld where a cannon-ball had passed through one of the cedar-logs of the second story, and left the whole in fine splinters, very fine and dry. One of our soldiers in passing along in my presence, took his pipe from his mouth, and set the splinters on fire, and said: "That will finish it, Colonel; come let us go." I set to work and scattered the kindled and kindling splinters, and fought out the vigorous fire, and saved that building from speedy consumption by the devouring flame, and felt I had saved a spacious, costly house for some rebel.

The following prayer was delivered by the author at Spring Grove, on the occasion of decorating the graves of soldiers on Memorial-day, May 30, 1880:

Almighty God! We venerate and adore thee as the Creator of innumerable worlds, the Father of angels and of men. Thou art the supreme and universal Sovereign; our best, our kindest Friend, and the wise and just disposer of our temporal and eternal interests. The principles of equity, fidelity, gratitude, and prudence alike demand of us an adoring and obedient acknowledgment of thy universal dominion. O, thou blessed and only Potentate, King of kings, Lord of lords, Ruler of rulers, the earth, thy footstool, is full of thy works, and the heavens are resplendent with thy glory. In every thing about us we behold the emanations of thy love. In the living green of the fields and the flower-embroidered expanse, in the stars of the firmament, in the balmy breath of spring, and the scowling storm-cloud, we trace the inscriptions of thy matchless beauty, consummate wisdom, and almighty power. Thy way is in the whirlwind and the storm, and the clouds are the dust of thy feet. There is no spot in the illimitable universe unvisited by thy care, and not a sparrow falleth on the ground, nor an empire riseth into existence and power, without thine everlasting providence.

Thou art the Governor among the nations, and we this day bless thee that the lines have fallen to us in pleasant places; yea, we have a goodly heritage. Indeed, thou hast not dealt so with any people. It is a goodly land which the Lord our God has given to us; a land whose broad domain is washed by the waters of earth's greatest oceans; a land whose mountain ranges, fertile valleys, majestic rivers, salubrious climate, and mineral resources are beyond comparison; a land endeared by the patriot's zeal, baptized with his blood, consecrated by the graves and dust of our forefathers; a land the Lord careth for, and upon which his eye has been from the beginning even to the end of the year; a land where, amid much darkness, a brighter light of evangelical truth is shining; where in the midst of awful vice, there is a higher degree of public and private virtue than in any other; a land whose civil, political, and religious institutions are at once the light and admiration of the civilized world, and to imitate which other nations have made convulsive efforts; a land where justice is a terror to evildoers, and equal law spreads its protection over the roof of the cabin as well as over the prouder dome; a land where conscience is freed from fetters, and the various tribes of the one Israel of God keep their solemn assemblies. The Sabbaths of the land are marked by worshiping assemblies, and the Churches have rest, and, walking in the fear of the Lord and in the comfort of the Holy Ghost, are multiplied.

To-day we especially bless thee that when bold, bad men sought the overthrow of our Government, and the dismemberment of our nationality, and inaugurated open, flagrant war to compel the people to submit to this great wrong, that secessionists might erect on more than half the public domain an empire whose corner-stone should be slavery, whose motto was that God "hath *not* made of one blood all nations of men, and that they are *not* created free and equal; and are *not* by him endowed with inalienable rights to life, liberty, and the pursuit of happiness," and that "black men have no rights which white men are bound to respect;" and when alliance was made with foreign hostile powers for aid and comfort in this wicked project, and they began and prosecuted their cruel war for such unholy ends, thou didst frown on them in thy righteous providence, so that when this enemy came in as a flood, thou didst lift up a standard against him; and along our serried lines gleamed our country's starry flag; and beneath its rainbow stripes thou didst marshal Freedom's warriors true, whose swords and bayonets were an iron barrier strong between the lawless and the weak.

We bless thee, that at the call of their country and

their God, they rushed to the gory battle-field, courted the posts of danger, and shook their martial steel in the grim face of Death, and laid down their lives that the Nation might live. We bless thee, that thou didst set the star of liberty on the brow of our firmament, that glory-beaming star, whose holy light was never dimmed by overflowing clouds; and when, as a Nation, we were ready to do justice as well as demand it, thou didst give us decisive victories and National peace.

And now we have met to honor the memory and adorn the graves of the gallant dead, whom thou didst use as instruments in the accomplishment of these great and glorious results. We bless thee, that they gained the martyr wreath in freedom's holy cause, and gained a fame that shall be enduring as thine own eternal laws; and their countrymen, by thy good providence, come with tender love to deck their honored bed; to scatter immortelles o'er their graves, our banner o'er their turf to spread, and on their monument to shower the pearly tears of patriotism and gratitude.

Let thy blessing be upon the parents, wives, and children of our honored dead. May the children of the soldiers ever find in the Government parental care, and in their country a glorious heritage, and prove themselves worthy descendants of the men, who, under God, saved the great Republic! Let the freedom of this land of freemen last "while earth bears a flower, or ocean rolls a wave." May its character be spotless as the sun; may servile or hostile feet never press our soil; may wasting and destruction be averted from our borders; may our gates be salvation, and our walls praise; may our fields yield their increase!

"No more may hosts, encountering hosts,
Their numerous dead deplore,
But lay the martial trumpet by,
And study war no more!"

And may God, even our God, bless us, and be a wall of fire round about us by thy providential protection, and the glory in our midst by the gospel of thy Son! We ask in Christ's name. Amen.

During the Centennial year of our independence, the Grand Army of the Republic met at Arlington, Va., on Memorial-day, May 30th. There were present both Houses of Congress, the clergy of Washington and vicinity, several of the civic societies of the Capital, and the general public. The oration of the day was delivered by the Hon. Stewart L. Woodford, of New York, and a poem read by B. F. Taylor, of Illinois. The duty of offering prayer was assigned to myself. The following is the prayer:

O Thou who art, and wast, and evermore shalt be, the Supreme Ruler of the universe, the Creator of innumerable worlds, the Father of angels and of men, and the Arbiter of the court of ultimate resort, thy glory no eye can bear, no thought can reach; thy power rideth on the whirlwind; thy wisdom searcheth all things, even the hidden things of darkness; thy goodness poureth on our hearts their gladness. To know and acknowledge thee is life for evermore; to adore thee is solemn joy; to trust thee perfect freedom; to have thee as our portion is the all-comprehending good.

We rejoice in thee as the God who hath made of one blood all nations of men to dwell on the face of the whole earth, and hath appointed them their habitation and the bounds thereof, that they might seek, if haply they may find thee, who art not far from every one of us, seeing that in thee we live and move and have our being, and are all thine offspring.

We desire, above all things, a nearer and purer communion with thyself. We would come into thy presence in these religious services with humility, contrition, and gratitude. It becomes us, creatures of a day and crushed before the moth, to appear before thee clothed with humility as with a garment, and to imitate the angels of thy court, who veil their faces with their wings in thy worship. It becomes us to be contrite in heart as thy sinful creatures, and, deprecating thy displeasure, to lay a broken heart on that diamond altar dimmed with the crimson blood of our Lord Jesus Christ, who was delivered to the cross and to its death for our offenses, and rose again for our justification, and lives above to intercede for us men, and for our salvation. It becomes us also to cherish sentiments of profound gratitude for thy kindly dealings with us, thy dependent creatures. In a world of changes and chances, accidents, disease, and death, thou hast wonderfully preserved and indulged us. Thy providence has been our safeguard, support, and consolation. Thou hast redeemed our lives from destruction, and crowned us with loving-kindness and tender mercies. Especially do we as a Christian nation bless thee for the inestimable gift of Jesus Christ, thine only begotten and mysteriously incarnated Son, whom thou hast sent into the world to teach us heavenly truths; to set us an example of perfect holiness; to offer himself through the eternal Spirit "a propitiation for the sins of the world," and that, as a surety and mediator of the new covenant of grace, wields all power in heaven and on earth for the extirpation of

sin from our world, and for the restoration to thy
favor and image the millions of our race who have
fallen away from their allegiance to thy throne by an
unprovoked rebellion against thy rightful authority
and gracious reign. For the success of his undertaking shall ceaseless prayer be made, in which we gladly
unite to-day; and as thy people, we are willing to take
our part of the effort, the toils, and the sacrifice together with him.

Especially do we bless thee, in this Centennial year
of our history, as a people which stands a wonder and
a marvel to the wide, wide world. We rejoice that
thou didst form and preserve this Occidental hemis-
phere to furnish the most magnificent home for man
to be found on the footstool of God. We praise thee
that thou didst sift the Old World to get the precious
seed with which to sow this fruitful soil. Thou didst
pilot them through the rolling deep, and didst receive
their humble worship at Plymouth Rock, and didst
aid them in accomplishing their high and holy avowal
to "found a Church without a bishop, and a State
without a king."

And when they were a small people and few, even
a few, thou didst suffer no man to wrong them. Yea,
thou didst rebuke kings for their sakes, saying, Touch
not mine anointed, and do my prophets no harm ; and
despite the satellites of altar and throne, they grew to
greatness, and one hundred years ago they made declaration of their rights, their purposed independence
of every power but thine ; and "pledged to each other
their lives, their fortunes, and their sacred honor," to
achieve and maintain their supreme nationality, in
firm and avowed dependence upon thine aid. In those
days that tried men's souls, thou didst raise them
up a savior, and a great one, in thy servant Washing-

ton, and didst set this day-star of freedom on the brow
of the firmament, whilst our patriot sires prosecuted
their enterprise through the seven years' war, and
bore our banner of beauty and glory, storm-rifted and
bullet-torn, along and aloft, till it floated in triumph
from the dome of the Temple of Freedom, the *ori-
flamme* and beacon of hope to the oppressed of the
world.

We bless thee, also, that when the thirteen colonies
found a mere confederacy, held together by the outward pressure of the Revolutionary War, utterly unequal
to the task of governing this vast domain in periods
of peace, thou didst inspire and guide them into the
act by which we became a nation amongst the nations
of the earth, vital in every part, and that can only by
annihilation die. We are indissolubly one in the right
of eminent domain, a government of and for and by
the people—one by the necessities of our condition,
which necessities are but increased by our magnificent
growth; and we rejoice together to-day that thou
didst give wisdom to the Convention of Delegates
from every State to form the Constitution of the United
States, the adoption of which by the people of this
ocean-bound Republic, constituted us a Nation amongst
the nations of the earth, as, according to its utterances,
it declared that "We, the people of these United
States, in order to establish justice, provide for the
common defense, insure domestic tranquillity, and secure the blessings of liberty to ourselves and our posterity, do make and ordain this Constitution to be the
supreme law of the land."

We do render thee thanks, O thou Governor
amongst the nations, for thy wisdom, invoked by the
authorized prayer of the framers of the Constitution,
and which still shines in every line of that palladium

of our National rights, the proud central pillar of the temple of freedom.

The vine which thou didst bring out of the Egypt of the political dissonance of Europe, thou didst plant in this land. Thou preparedst room before it, and didst cause it to take deep root, and it filled the land; the hills were covered with the shadow of it, and the boughs thereof were like the goodly cedars; it sent forth its branches to the Mississippi, and its boughs to the Pacific and to Alaska, and when the boar out of the wood would have wasted it, whetting his tusks upon it, they were broken; and when the wild beast of the field would devour it, he was slain; and the vine and branch which thou hast planted for thyself, thou hast protected by Washington, Jackson, Lincoln, Thomas, and Grant, and their colleagues, whom thou didst gird and guard, with the men whom thou madest strong for thyself, and for our protection as a Nation, whose God is the Lord.

In thy all-comprehending providence, thou hast greatly enlarged our borders by transferring to our sovereignty Florida, Louisiana, Texas, New Mexico, California, and Alaska; so that our Nation extends

"From where our green mountain-tops blend with the sky,
    And the giant St. Lawrence is rolled,
To the waves where the balmy Hesperides lie,
    Like a dream of some prophet of old."

To-day we are specially called upon to bless thee that our land has been delivered from the cruel power of the oppressor, who inaugurated open, flagrant, deadly war to compel our Government to submit to its own dissolution and destruction, to accommodate those who hold that all men are not created equal, and deny that thou, the Creator, hast endowed all men with the inalienable rights of life, liberty, and

the pursuit of happiness; and that governments among
men are not formed to preserve those sacred rights,
but rather echo the decision of the ermine, that men
whose only crime is that God jetted their brows, "have
no rights that white men are bound to respect."

We rejoice that the dissemination of thy Holy
Word had so leavened the minds of statesmen and the
masses, that when the rugged issue came, "slavery or
liberty," our thousands and millions rallied around
the banner of freedom, and rushed to gory battle-
fields to meet the frenzied foe, courted the posts of
danger, and shook their martial steel in the grim face
of death. And now, that our war-drums throb no
longer, and our battle-flags are furled, we gather by
thousands to honor the graves of the brave defenders
and deliverers of the Republic, men who breasted the
iron storm of war, and advanced the line of battle
under the darkening wings of the war-cloud,

> "Beneath whose gloom of dusky smoke,
> Our cannon flamed and bomb-shells broke;
> And the sharp, rattling volleys rang,
> And shrapnell screamed and bullets sang,
> While fierce-eyed men, with panting breath,
> Toiled onward at the work of death,"

that our nationality might be preserved and liberty
proclaimed throughout the land. With this fiery gospel they executed thy holy commands "to loose the
bands of wickedness; to undo the heavy burdens; to
let the oppressed go free, and break every yoke;" and
thou didst join the might with the right, and history repeated itself, because thou art the same God on the
Mississippi as thou wast in Egypt. Wonderfully thou
hast freed this Nation from the ever-beginning and
never-ending curse of African slavery, fastened upon

our fathers and our country by old England's cursed lust for gold.

To-day we stand amid the sad memorials of war and death in this silent city of the heroic dead, who gave up their lives on numerous battle-fields, that our country might live, and its citizens be free. To-day we have met to scatter immortelles, cypress, and laurels on their honored remains, and to keep their memories green, while we lay the first floral offerings of spring on their lonely graves.

> " By fairy hands their knell is rung,
> By forms unseen their dirge is sung.
> Here Honor comes, a pilgrim gray,
> To bless the turf that wraps their clay;
> And Freedom doth awhile repair,
> To dwell a weeping hermit there."

We rejoice that our Republic is not unmindful of the services of her soldiers, the unreturning brave, and the great unknown, whose graves we adorn this day, and whose monuments rescue them from oblivion, whilst

> "On fame's eternal camping ground
> Their silent tents are spread,
> And glory guards with solemn round
> The bivouac of the dead."

Command thy blessings, both in Providence and grace, on the widows and children of the brave defenders who sleep around us in this, and in all the cemeteries of all our battle-fields; and may the blood of these martyrs be the seed of the Union! Let thy care be extended to the freedmen of our land; and though their blood still flows on the soil of freedom, may the cries of the spoiled come before thee, and their mournful prayer be heard!

And now, our Heavenly Father, we ask thy blessing on the entire country and all her citizens, however they may have been dissociated by the recent calamities of war. Give to them who may still be inimical a spirit of reconciliation, and may all sectional feelings be merged in the common glory of a restored brotherhood ; and may the bereaved ones be graciously cared for by thy gracious providence ! With thy servant, David, we pray : "Rid us, and deliver us from the hand of strange children, whose mouth speaketh vanity, and their right hand is a right hand of falsehood ; that our sons may be as olive-plants grown up in their youth ; that our daughters may be as corner-stones, polished after the similitude of a palace ; that our garners may be full, affording all manner of store ; that our sheep may bring forth thousands and tens of thousands in our streets ; that our oxen may be strong to labor ; that there be no breaking in, nor going out ; that there be no complaining in our streets. Happy is that people that is in such a case ; yea, happy is that people whose God is the Lord." And all we ask, for Christ's sake ! Amen !

CHAPTER XX.

ADVOCACY OF REFORM AND LIBERTY.

THE extracts given in this chapter are clipped from papers issued when these matters were current. They serve to show the part which the author took on these questions at that time.

From a Springfield Paper, 1851.

THE KOSSUTH MEETING.

The late gathering of the friends of freedom and humanity, at the City Hall, is generally conceded to have been worthy of the occasion. The subject is one for grave consideration. Perhaps no period will be so favorable for settling this question of intervention or non-intervention. The genius and policy of our institutions have been to form no foreign alliances. An asylum was offered to all; to this extent, no more. The nice tact of the Magyar soon perceived this, and he honestly declared to a friend of ours in Columbus, he expected no governmental aid; material aid was all he asked. Two most important avenues remain open,— the influence of public opinion, backed by material aid. Not a despot in Europe but daily feels the immense power wielded by the former. The voice of the press is shackled, public discussion suppressed; still "there is a power behind the throne greater than the throne itself." It is heard in a thousand mysterious mutterings; it is omnipotent and omnipresent. Every step that Louis Napoleon takes leaves the

24

impress of a dagger. The imperial edicts of Austria and Prussia are but the countersign of their manifest destiny. The man who doubts that the free public expression of England and America on a question of international policy will be heard and felt, can hardly be of sane mind. The two powers that control the commerce of the world will be felt in any way they choose to give utterance to their mandates.

These expressions of the public voice are, therefore, eminently desirable. They are sufficiently posted in Europe to know that this voice can readily reach the national councils, and assume a governmental tone. The free-spoken men that gave utterance to public opinion in the City Hall are the same power precisely that liberated the noble Magyar, and yet speed him on his way rejoicing. The address of Rev. G. Moody is everywhere spoken of as a most able and eloquent expositon and vindication of the claims of Hungary. There was a grand turn-out of ladies and gentlemen. Rev. Joshua Boucher was called to the chair. After appropriate prayer, the chairman called upon Rev. Granville Moody to address the meeting. He responded to the call by a speech of about three hours in length, upon "Hungarian History, Kossuth, Liberty, Popery, and Despotism." His remarks were in the main well received, as was evinced by the frequent plaudits with which he was interrupted. He made some happy hits, and said many good things; but we have not space to give even a sketch of what he said.

At the close of the speech the meeting resolved itself into a "Hungarian Aid Association of Clark County." A committee of six was appointed to sell certificates of loans to the Hungarian Fund. In the short time the committee was about its work the subscriptions swelled up into hundreds of dollars. The work is still in progress, and those having the matter in charge are determined that this warm-hearted city, and the patriotic and liberty-loving citizens of Clark, shall not be behind their neighbors in furnishing that aid which is to be used in regaining liberty and independence in down-trodden Hungary.

From a Dayton Newspaper, 1853.

ANTI-NEBRASKA MEETING IN DAYTON.

A large number of the citizens of Dayton, who are opposed to the Nebraska fraud, assembled, last Tuesday evening, in Beckel's Hall. Joseph Barrett presided. Messrs. Craighead, Parrott, and Moody delivered spirited addresses. The address of Rev. Granville Moody was very interesting and stirring. We were happy to hear from Mr. Moody so plain and forcible a condemnation of slavery and its constant aggressions, aided by the General Government, upon the domain of freedom. The watchmen of Zion can not hold their peace without criminal neglect of the interests, temporal, spiritual, and eternal, of millions of souls. Let them speak out!

The following resolutions were adopted as expressive of the sense of the meeting:

"*Resolved*, That it was the original policy of the Government to provide against the extension of slavery, as evinced by the Ordinance of 1787; and that the Nebraska Bill, now before Congress, covering a design to admit slavery into the heart of the continent, overturns the principles of the past, betrays the interests of future generations, and involves deep national disgrace.

"*Resolved*, That this bill, as it excludes from the polls and from office all inhabitants not citizens of the United States; as it opens the door for the extension

of slavery over an immense territory, which should
be sacred to freedom and to free labor; as it violates
the National faith pledged to the Indians in various
treaties; and, above all, as it violates the faith, solemnly pledged to the North in the Act of 1820, has
our determined and uncompromising opposition."

From " The Gospel Herald."

REV. GRANVILLE MOODY ON ROMANISM.

SPRINGFIELD, O., December 24, 1852.

We have heard the whole of these sermons, so far
as the series has progressed. They have occupied
several successive Sabbaths, and will continue, we
learn, for an indefinite period yet to come. They
have furnished topics of discussion entirely new to
the pulpits of this city. Aside from these, among all
learned dissertations and lectures that have graced our
literary halls, since the era of their introduction
amongst us, there is no field of thought which has
been so ably, so thoroughly, and so successfully ex-
plored, as that which has been occupied by the reverend gentleman, whose name stands at the head of
this article. It might be agreeable to our readers, as
well as to ourself, if we were able to give even a succinct analysis of these discourses; but when it is
recollected that they were delivered at weekly intervals, embracing, as they do, so vast an amplitude of
range in the subject-matter presented, it can hardly be
expected that we would be willing to risk the accuracy of our statements, for the sake of a more
general and extended notice.

In whatever else might be deemed of questionable propriety by the thousands who have lately
crowded upon Mr. Moody's ministry, we think that all
have been willing to accord to him great ingenuous-

ness of character, and honesty of purpose; that no
selfish or sinister motive has been allowed to sway him
from the integrity of his high and sacred functions;
that his efforts, throughout, have been character-
ized by a noble, humanitarian, and philanthropic aim;
by a liberality of feeling and sentiment that is worthy
of the cause he advocates; that while he treats with
unmitigated severity a system of doctrines which he
not only believes to be anti-Christian in their ten-
dency, but subversive of good morals and social
order, he has an ardent desire for the reclamation of
those who have been misdirected by the false lights
of the Papal religion.   According to the Christian
apothegm, he "hates the sin, but loves the sinner."

Before we heard for ourself, we had no conception
of the great necessity and importance of having a
clear and full *eclaircissement* of the leading doctrinal
points now at issue between Roman Catholic and
Protestant Churches.   We believe it is essentially
connected with the cause of civil and religious liberty,
with the rights and duties and interests of American
citizens, that they should be kept duly and regularly
informed of all that constitutes the elements of distinction between these two great sects and parties in
this country.   It is not in the light of patriotism alone
that we should urge this; not only from a laudable
desire to keep our institutions on a basis of permanent
security, but in obeying those generous Christian impulses that would direct all their energies and influences in the dissemination of moral and religious
truth, thereby dissipating the clouds of error that now
envelop so large a portion of the population of this
happy and extended domain.   We speak with great
deference, but we are constrained to believe that the
Protestant pulpit in this country has been heretofore

recreant to itself, faithless in the fulfillment of its sacred trusts, and false to the claims of humanity, in keeping silent on this subject.

We have often been pained at the ill-directed efforts of the press, in matters of controversy between Romanists and Protestants. It has been made the vehicle of the most severe and rigorous denunciations, by either party, instead of that mild and pacific spirit which emanates from the law of charity, and which is the legitimate fruit of Christian principle. We read little else in the periodicals of the day besides empty and silly vaporings, sharp sectarian pasquin-ades, bitter criminations, with rancorous and bluster-ing retorts, all addressed to the excited jealousies and angry passions of men. These publications, it is true, are not designed for the ignorant and illiterate masses; but for the higher class of society, the *il-lustrissimi*, who, by such a course of procedure, must forever bar every avenue that would lead to a final triumph of the Protestant faith. We say again, the pulpit is the appropriate theater for these discussions. The living voice, addressed to the living ear, is the only medium through which we can gain access to the hearts and minds of Catholics.

But to return to Mr. Moody. The course he has pursued thus far in his litigation with the Catholics, has been such as, we think, must meet the unquali-fied approval of the large and intelligent auditories he has repeatedly addressed. He has been generous, just, and magnanimous. In his defense of the Protest-ant rule of faith, he has shown himself equal to the high and sacred responsibilities of his station. His argumentation has been lucid, powerful, and con-vincing; drawn from the uncorrupted sources of the Bible, and the archives of the Church from its earliest records. He has advanced no thesis but what has been severely tested at the bar of Reason and Revelation. It is to these points alone to which he would bring his opponents for a just and equitable decision. In his exhibition of the errors of popery, he has drawn largely on the voluminous writings of the Romish Church, and given copious extracts from the decrees of councils and other accredited works.

We have only further to observe, that if the sermons which yet remain to complete the series should be of equal ability with those that have preceded them, we can not but augur the best results, especially to our Catholic friends, many of whom, we learn, have been in regular attendance, and have listened with that profound attention and decorum which the solemnities of the occasion demanded.

Of Mr. Moody's style and manner of presenting his subjects, it is scarcely necessary to speak. He is known to be a bold, vehement, and eloquent speaker—eloquent in thought, and often beautifully chaste in expression. He has great originality and vigor of conception, and is peculiarly happy in his modes of illustration. He has a strong and massive intellect, that grasps a subject with the power of a Titan; and so forcible and logical are his conclusions that any attempt to escape from their consequences would be fruitless and vain. He seeks no ornament or rhetorical display, yet there is always a sufficient amount of drapery on the canvas to exhibit to advantage the brilliant coruscations of his genius. His delivery is often rapid and impetuous, like a mountain torrent that roars and rends and breaks through every opposing barrier, leaving naught but desolation and ruin behind it. He is exceedingly graphic in his delineations of character.

On one occasion, we remember, after he had stripped
the Catholic religion of its extrinsic coverings, its
gilded trappings and meretricious mummery, he held
up the denuded object to the astonished gaze of his
congregation, who seemed to look for the first time on
the appalling spectacle. He rarely adopts the popular method of writing his sermons, but chooses rather
to rely on the spontaneous resources of his mind,
prompted by the exigencies of the occasion.

We make no apology for this hasty and imperfect
sketch of Mr. Moody, nor for any incidental remarks
we have made in such a connection. Opinions varying
from our own may be honestly entertained, and all we ask
for ourself is the same manly and generous concession.

Extract from the ' Western Christian Advocate," January 19, 1853.

We learn that Brother Moody is discussing the
doctrine of Popery in his Church in Springfield, to
crowded houses, with great ability. Few men can
handle the sword polemical, on any subject, to equal
Mr. Moody. We would consider ourself edified in
having the privilege of hearing him.

My views on Romanism are embodied in a
small book with the title, " Popery and its Aims,"
published in Cincinnati in 1871, at the request of
the Methodist Preachers' Meeting, before whom it
was originally read.

From " The Cincinnati Gazette," September 13, 1869.

THE BIBLE IN THE SCHOOLS.

The Wigwam in Fulton was densely crowded yesterday afternoon, to hear addresses on the subject of
the proposed withdrawal of the Bible from the public
schools ; the principal speaker announced for the occasion being the Reverend (or, as he is equally well-

known, Colonel) Granville Moody. At his request, the audience sang Hymn 81, he remarking that it was composed by a young lady under circumstances precisely like those which brought this meeting together. The lady, fired with the spirit of 1620 and 1776—the same fire he hoped burned brightly down to 1869— wrote these verses:

> " We 'll not give up the Bible,
> God's holy book of truth,
> The blessed staff of hoary age,
> The guide of early youth."

The Rev. Mr. Moody then proceeded to address the meeting. He said it was now attempted to proscribe that blessed Book, through which their liberties had been derived, and this at the behests of a power that had ever been the antagonist of human rights and human liberty. As he was accustomed to speak from a text, he would select Isaiah viii, 20, in which the terms used, " To the law and to the testimony," were descriptive of the revelation which God has af forded us, and " if they speak not according to this word, it is because there is no light in them."

There were those in the days of Isaiah who con sulted wizards and those with familiar spirits, rather than the oracles of the Lord their God ; and, in the language of the Word, God reproved them. Instead of the living appealing to departed spirits, and praying to departed saints, they must go " to the testimony." If now as then, and then as now, they speak not according to this standard, but embrace alleged traditions of the Church, said by Romanists to be of equal authority with the Bible itself, it is because there is no light in them, but darkness, just so much as they ignore the Word of God.

They were called now to meet a question of highest importance, suddenly. They had only just come into the "tented field," when they found the foe of humanity, of liberty, and truth upon them. On the skirmish-line the old powers of Romanism and infidelity are blazing away on their front already, and the cry is, " To arms !" and, in response to that cry, the people are now in battle-line, and, in the words of the hymn just sung, they say, " We will not give up the Bible." They will not give it up in their schools, their seminaries, their Churches, but will protect it as the corner-stone of their Republican institutions. The opposition to the Bible is by men who well know where to put their sappers and miners to work. The woodman had got his ax to the very root of the tree of civil and religious liberty; but the Protestants of America, not merely because they love that tree, and watered its roots with their tears, as their fathers enriched them with their blood, until its branches extended from the Atlantic to the Pacific, and its leaves became the " healing of the nations," say to the popes, archbishops, prelates and priests :

> " Spare that tree,
> Touch not a single bough ;
> Its shade has sheltered us,
> And we 'll protect it now."   (Cheers.)

Two hundred and forty nine-years ago a company of Protestants, who fled from the tyranny of the Old World, came to this continent, determined to found a State without a king, and a Church without a prelate. Seeking freedom to worship God with that blessed Book, the Bible, scarred with its battles of centuries, as their guide, they established those institutions which have made us the wonder, if not the envy, of the world. Just before the constitution of the State was adopted, when everything looked dark and unpropitious, when the interests of the North and South and West looked and seemed irreconcilable, and they were about to break up in despair, the aid of God was invoked by prayer, at the solicitation of Benjamin Franklin, and three hours after that the Constitution of the United States was born. All the voices of the past, from Mount Vernon, from the Hermitage, from all the cemeteries and grave-yards, say, " Do not give up the Bible !"

Mr. Moody then proceeded to draw comparison between the condition of Catholic and Protestant countries, and said he felt warranted in the conclusion, that if the Bible was withdrawn from our schools, we would soon pass into the condition of those people who were governed by priestcraft, and had human tradition substituted for the commandment of God. He said he would here cite an anonymous commentary on the Bible, which was worthy of being printed with every copy of that Book :

"It contains everything necessary to be known within the range of its discoveries. It affords a model for the ruler, and a rule for the subject. It gives counsels to a Senate, and authority and direction to magistrates. It cautions a witness, and requires an impartial verdict from a jury. It furnishes a lawyer with the higher law for his guidance, and dictates the sentence to the judge. It sets the husband as the head of the household, and gives honor to the wife as the weaker vessel. It tells him how to rule, and her how to manage. It demands honor for parents, and enjoins obedience upon children. It commands the subject to honor, and the servant to obey. It bids the monarch to be just, and the master to be merciful. It smiles on the bridal hour, and irradiates the gloom of the final scene. It promises food and raiment to the honest and industrious. It points out a faithful and

eternal guardian to the departing, and tells him with
whom to leave his helpless children, with whom his
widow is to be trusted, and promises a father to the
fatherless, and a husband to the widow. It teaches us
how to set our house in order, how to make our
will, appoints a dowry for the wife, and teaches the
descent of property to our children. It defends the
rights of all, threatens the vengeance of God to the
defrauder, the seducer, and the oppressor. It is the
first book, the oldest book, and the best book in the
world. It is a book of history, a depository of the
most sublime doctrines, the most admirable precepts.
It is a book of song and sentiment and poetry, beyond
all competition. It is a treasury of knowledge, a collection of the wisest proverbs. It is rich in biographic
lore. It is a book of models, a book of glorious remembrance, the book of time and the book of eternity,
and the Christian, with a Bible in his hand, resembles
a man standing on the summit of a sunlit mountain,
where suns surround him and elysian prospects rise."

The reverend speaker then read the opinions of
Washington, Chancellor Kent, and others. Washington said: "Of all dispositions and habits which lead
to political prosperity, religion and morality are
indispensable supports. In vain would that man
claim the tribute of patriotism who should labor to
subvert these great pillars of human happiness, these
firmest props of the duties of men and citizens. The
mere politician, equally with the pious man, ought to
respect and cherish them. A volume could not trace
all their connection with private and public felicity.
Let it be simply asked where is the security for property, for reputation, for life, if this sense of religious
obligations deserts the oaths which are the instruments
of investigations in courts of justice; and let us with

caution indulge the supposition that morality can be maintained without religion. Whatever may be conceded to the influence of refined education on minds of peculiar structure, reason and experience both forbid us to expect that national morality can prevail in exclusion of religious principle."

Chancellor Kent, of New York, said: "The general diffusion of the Bible is the next effectual way to civilize and humanize mankind to purity, and exalt the general system of public morals; to give efficacy to the just precepts of municipal and international law, to enforce the observance of prudence, temperance, virtue, and fortitude, and to improve all the relations of domestic and social life."

Chief-Justice Hornblower, of New Jersey, remarks: "Let this precious volume have its due influence on the hearts of men, and our liberties are safe, our country blessed, and the world happy. There is not a tie that binds us to our families, not a virtue that endears our country to us, or us to our country, not a hope that thrills our bosoms in the prospects of future happiness, that has not its foundation in the Holy Book. It is the charter of nations, the palladium of liberty, the standard of righteousness. Its influence can soften the heart of the tyrant, can break the rod of oppression, and exalt the humblest peasant to the dignified rank of an immortal being, an heir of eternal glory."

Robert C. Winthrop, speaker of the House of Representatives, in 1848, says:

"All communities of man must be governed in some way or other. The less they may have of stringent State government, the more they may have of individual self-government. The less they rely on public law or physical force, the more they may rely on

moral restraint. Men, in a word, must be controlled
either by a power within them, or by a power without
them; either by the power of God, or by the strong
arm of man; either by the Bible, or by the bayonet.
It may do for other countries and other governments
to talk about the State supporting religion. Here,
under our free institutions, it is religion which must
support the State."

Go to Scotland, the land of the Bible (I wish I had
Burns's "Cotter's Saturday Night" here, to read the
lines where the peasant poet of nature describes the
gray-headed sire, before the hour for retiring, reading
the sacred page), and compare that country with Italy,
with Portugal, with the south of Ireland; or compare
Bible-loving Massachusetts with any of the South
American States.

In 1717 a committee of Congress, in consequence
of a scarcity of Bibles in the land, ordered an impor-
tation of twenty thousand copies from Holland, Scotland, and elsewhere, and thus constituted the first
Bible Society in America.

The speaker then proceeded to remark that the
Church of Rome had usurped the authority of mingling up the Word of God with its own traditions, and
even to alter the Decalogue by striking out the Second
Commandment. The pope has issued bulls against
the publication of the Bible in the vulgar tongue, as
destructive and heretical. It might be destructive
to Romanism as Romanism was to the Bible, that
was all.

At the close of his remarks, the reverend gentleman requested signature papers to be handed around,
protesting against the exclusion, on the part of the
School Board, of the Bible from the schools.

CHAPTER XXI.

COMBATING ERROR.   .

EVERY minister of the gospel finds error intrenched in the hearts of men. There is
scarcely any form of doctrine which he does not
meet, and more often the false than the true.
Satan himself has been transformed into an angel
of light; and the preacher does not always possess
the wand of Ithuriel to compel him to appear in
his own hideous deformity. In many systems
of philosophy and theology which we account
heretical, "some truths there are, but dashed and
brewed with lies;" and it is difficult to separate
the genuine from the base, and to attack only the
base. In the following extracts from papers written by the author, some of which have been published, the reader will determine for himself how
successfully this has been done, and how well the
right has been upheld.

From the 'Western Christian Advocate," April, 1854.

SPIRIT-RAPPING.

The Daytonians have recently been visited by the
celebrated Judge Edmonds, one of the table-tippers
in Satan's temple of infidelity. The Judge was accompanied by a Doctor Dexter, of whose dexterity in
doctoring soul or body we have not received any
special revelation, may be for want of a medium.

Judge Edmonds estimates the number of believers in Spiritualism at a million in the United States. We think it would trouble him to find ten thousand. His idea that the doctrine is more readily and generally received in the country than in cities, is the very reverse of what we know to be true in this region. There are numerous believers in the city, many of them intelligent, worthy citizens; but among the rural population it would be nearly as hard to find a Spiritualist as a Mormon.

The judge claims that Spiritualism has converted more infidels in six years than all the pulpits in the land have been able to convert in twenty. Converted them to what? A belief in God and immortality This is no conversion at all; for infidelity, as we understand it, does not deny either the being of God or the immortality of the soul. It disbelieves the inspiration of the Scriptures and the divine origin of Christianity. So does Judge Edmonds, or we very greatly misunderstand him; for he scarcely boasts more over all the infidels whom Spiritualism has convinced of what they believed before than over the twenty-seven professors of religion who lapsed from a single Church. The light of the Bible is being diffused most gloriously, bathing the high and the low places of the earth with its celestial glories, and Satan and his allies can not hinder it. He can not stop the press, the altar of liberty and truth, nor shut up the Bible in convents, nor stop men from hearing, and reading, and thinking, and acting; nor can he cover the Church with sackcloth, or despise her powers; for she cometh forth from the wilderness, "fair as the moon, clear as the sun, beautiful as Tirzah, comely as Jerusalem, and terrible as an army with banners."

But one thing Satan can do; he can lie as fast as

ever; and can use all the modern improvements in arts and sciences and society, and can produce that which is suited to the occasion, times, and circumstances; and his present policy seems to be to mix the ingredients of error and damnable heresies with the soul-saving truths of the Word of God, knowing that error is to the soul what poison is to the body; and what with Romanism, Rationalism, Pantheism, Transcendentalism, Swedenborgianism, Universalism, Materialism, Fatalism, Millerism, Mormonism, Spiritualism, drunkenness, slavery, and war, he is fully armed and equipped, and still in the field; and "some will depart from the faith, giving heed to seducing spirits and doctrines of devils." His favorite policy of deception, deep and dark, is to present

> "A sprinkling of truth and a quantum of error,
> Both mixed in the mass and dealt out together,
> With enough of the former to sweeten the latter,
> And pass all together for genuine matter."

Wise and happy is the man who can say, with Paul: "We are not ignorant of his devices." Let every lover of God's truth and humanity take the whole armor of light, and wield "the sword of the Spirit, which is the Word of God," and we shall be invulnerable and invincible; and despite

> "Our secret, sworn, eternal foes,
> Countless, invisible,"

we shall bear the banner of our faith victorious round the world!

Dayton, O., April 6, 1854.

REASONS FOR NOT BEING A BAPTIST.

1st. Because the Greek verbs *bapto* and *baptizo* do not always and necessarily signify to submerge or immerse. (Isa. xxi, 4; Dan. iv, 33; v, 21; Mark vii, 4; Luke xvi, 24; 1 Cor. x, 2; Heb. ix, 10; 1 Peter iii, 21.)

2d. Because the sacred influences of the Holy Spirit, of which baptism is the appointed sign, are applied to the individual and not the individual to them; and are said to be poured out or sprinkled upon. (Psalm lxxii, 6; Isa. xliv, 3; Ezek. xxxvi, 25; Acts ii, 17.)

3d. Because immersion is opposed to some Scriptural allusions. (1 Cor. x, 2; 1 Peter iii, 20, 21.)

4th. Because, though we have the expressions "going down into" and "coming up out of the water," yet these do not necessarily mean being put under, and can not necessarily be construed to sanction such a practice; while the Greek words are frequently and justly rendered "going to" and "coming from" the water of baptism.

5th. Because the circumstances in which the disciples were placed on the day of Pentecost, when three thousand were baptized and added to the Church, render it highly improbable, if not impossible, for them to have been baptized by immersion. There was no river running through Jerusalem.

6th. Because there is not a single instance to be found in the Word of God in which the ordinance of baptism was administered by immersion.

7th. Because it is evident that the expression "buried with Christ by baptism" has no reference to the mode of baptism, and was only designed to teach the true believer's death to sin and resurrection unto right-eousness in Jesus Christ. (Rom. vi, 3–6; Col. ii, 12.)

8th. Because God included the infant progeny of his people in the covenant of salvation made originally with Abraham, and ratified in Christ; while Baptists unjustly exclude them. (Gen. xvii, 7, 10.)

9th. Because neither Christ nor his apostles laid such stress on a mode of baptism as Baptists now do.

10th. Because, on the theory of Baptists, many a devoted minister of Christ could not, for want of bodily strength and health, administer this rite aright.

11th. Because many in the Church and kingdom of Christ could not, by reason of sickness, infirmity, or age, submit to immersion.

12th. Because the administration of baptism by immersion is often associated with danger to health, and indelicacy.

13th. Because immersion in many cases, and in many minds, destroys devotion of mind, and excites agitation of spirit opposed to the equanimity required in religious ordinances.

14th. Because the proscriptive and uncharitable and proselyting spirit so extensively indulged in by immersionists is so unlike to the religion of Christ and his generous gospel.

15th. Because immersionists, by their exclusiveness and their actual or implied proscriptiveness, rend the body, of which Christ is the head; virtually and practically unchristianizing all who can not agree with Baptists in their exclusive views of a mode of application of water to the person, or the person to the water.

16th. Because the earnest exhortation that such proscriptive and prescriptive sectaries are accustomed to urge on the minds of young converts to follow supposed rites unauthorized by the Word of God, and to follow Christ in a mode he never authorized, nor enjoined, nor practiced himself, is unauthorized by the Holy Scriptures; and division of the one body of which Christ is the glorious head—one Lord, one faith, one baptism. " He saved us by the washing of

regeneration and renewing of the Holy Ghost; which
he shed on us abundantly through Jesus Christ our
Savior; that being justified by his grace, we should be
made heirs according to the hope of eternal life."

17th. Because the baptism of Christ is no example
for us to follow, and was not by immersion either.
(Luke iii, 21–23, and Num. iv, 3, 28, 29, 35, 39, 43, 47;
also, Num. viii, 7.) When Christ was baptized, the
Holy Ghost *descended* in bodily shape like a dove upon
him. (Matt. iii, 3–13, 17.)

18th. This baptism of Christ by John was not Christian baptism, for *it* was not commanded nor instituted
till three years afterward, when Christ first instituted
it on the day he ascended into heaven. (Matt. xxviii,
18, 19, 20; Acts, xix, 1–7; where we learn that John's
baptism was not Christian baptism.) Paul says of
the Israelites that they were all baptized to Moses in
the Red Sea. (1 Cor. x, 1–3.) They were all on dry
land when they passed through the Red Sea. There
was an immersion of the Egyptians who followed the
Israelites; and just as the last of the Israelites went
out of the dry pathway through the sea, which was
then dry land to their footsteps, and all reached the
further shore, baptized by sprinkling or pouring (Psa.
lxxvii, 16–20), the waters rolled down upon the haughty
Egyptian armies then in hot pursuit, and God's and
Israel's foes were all immersed and drowned by thousands.

ON THE USE OF TOBACCO.

Having been appointed pastor of the Church in
——, I became acquainted with a Brother B., a
wealthy, intelligent, and popular member of the Church,
and mayor of the city. I found him a very genial, accomplished, and liberal member. His wife and children were worthy members of the Church, and

I respected them very highly in love. But he was an inveterate chewer and smoker of tobacco, which showed its power upon his person plainly. I called his attention to this evil habit, and exhorted him to abstinence, but all in vain. One day I met him in the bank, and, in the presence of the officers and some eight or ten persons, he said:

"Brother Moody, you have been talking to me about my using tobacco, which I do use freely, both chewing and smoking; and now I want to settle this question with you, by asking you a few questions. First. Who made tobacco—God or the devil?"

I replied: "God; for he only can create."

"Very good answer, sir! Second. When did God create it?"

I answered: "On the third day of the six days of creation, 'and herb yielding seed after his kind.'"

"Third. Now, does not the Bible say, 'And God saw that it was good?'"

"Yes," I replied.

"Aha!" he said; "I have you now. God saw that it was good?"

"Yes," I replied, "tobacco is a good thing as a dye-stuff for coloring matter; it was made for and it furnishes the richest and most valuable dye-stuff for coloring brown, extant; and for that, God, its maker, pronounced it good, and 'very good.' But not good for chewing, smoking, dipping, and snuffing. One-half to three-fifths of the whole crop of tobacco of America is shipped to England, France, Spain, Germany, and Prussia as a dye-stuff, and it is used extensively in America for that purpose, and is found to be 'very good' and indispensable for use in its place. But to reduce it to snuff, to dip it, as women do; to chew as plug, and smoke it as cigars, or use it as pro-

vender for pipes, or grind it up into powder as snuff,
whether Maccaboy, Rappee, or Scotch, is an abuse of
a good creature of God for evil purposes. The Bible
asserts, ' Lo, this only have I found, that God hath
made man upright; but they have sought out many
inventions.' And snuff and cigars, and plug and
twist, and fine-cut and Maccaboy, are some of these
many inventions. And there are other culpable inventions of self-indulgent man, who has made also

> ' Whisky and gin, brandy and rum,
>   And many other things that make drunk come.'

Many things which God made for good purposes, man
has appropriated to other and evil purposes in the
error of his ways; but

> ' No evil can from God proceed;
> 'Tis not permitted nor decreed,
> As darkness is not from the sun,
> Nor mounts the shades till it has gone.'

The right use of a thing is legitimate; the mis-
use is its perversion. Tobacco was made for a dye-
stuff, and by it ' we can do things up brown ;' but we
use it for other purposes; its use is then illegitimate
and injurious and pernicious, and by it we seek death
in the error of our ways. Whilst God made tobacco
as a dye-stuff, man has stuffed his nose and mouth
with it; and though God made man upright, he has
sought out many inventions. They are perversions
from good to ill. When first used, tobacco sometimes
causes vomiting; but the practice of using it in any
form soon conquers the distaste against it, and the
persons who use it acquire a relish for it that is strong
and almost unconquerable. Dr. Reuben D. Mussey,
of Cincinnati, has said; ' When I am called to the
sick-bed, I always ask my patients, " Do you use
tobacco in any form ?" If they do, I can not do good

to more than thirty per cent; if they do not use tobacco, I can save eighty-five per cent.' "

By this speech I gained my case, and all cried out,
" Mr. B., you are beaten, you are beaten !"   But

> " Convince a man against his will,
> He's of the same opinion still."

He continued in this dangerous habit several years,
when, on the side of his mouth where he held his cigar
or pipe, a cancer was formed which proved fatal.
Surely " the way of the transgressor is hard," and the
end of these things is death.

From the "Cincinnati Daily Gazette," October 6, 1861.

DEFERENCE TO MORALS IN POLITICAL ACTION.

Politics is " the science of government; that part
of ethics which consists in the regulation and government of a nation or State, for the preservation of its
safety, peace, and prosperity, comprehending the defense of its existence and rights against foreign control or conquest; the augmentation of its strength
and resources, and the protection of its citizens in
their rights, with the preservation and improvement
of their morals."   Webster defines the word " moral "
as follows: " Relating to the practice, manners, or
conduct of men, as social beings, in relation to each
other, and with reference to right or wrong.   The
word moral is applicable to actions that are good or
evil, virtuous or vicious, and has reference to the
' Law of God ' as the standard by which their character
is to be determined."

It is foreign to my purpose to dwell on "moral
law," " moral science," or "moral sense " as embraced
in the term moral, but simply to call attention to our
moral obligations in our political actions.   The senseless outcry against Christians for " dabbling in the

dirty pool of politics," is rendered ridiculous by a
glance at the authoritative definition of the term
"politics" at the head of this essay. The animus of
the outcry shows the character of the men who make
it! Politics may and should be as pure as the sparkling waters from the rock. Politics "is that part of
ethics which consists in . . . the protection of
citizens in their rights, with the preservation and improvement of their morals." Politics, then, is a part
or branch of ethics; and ethics is defined by Paley to
be "the doctrines of morality, the science of moral
philosophy, which teaches men their duty, and the
reasons of it."

If the pool of politics is dirty, it is because men
of dissolute morals have polluted it, and it is a shame
for them to take advantage of their own wrong; and
if it is the object and interest of these men to keep
our politics polluted by driving away those who would
clean out the cesspool of pot-house politicians, it becomes the imperative duty of the friends of morality
to combine their influence in the maintenance of pure
political action, and thus secure the practice of
"righteousness, which exalts a nation." Universal
history, observation, and experience attest that it is
the nature of immorality to lessen and diminish a
people; to sink and depress the spirits of a people, as
we may see in the history of France; to destroy the
wealth of a people; to deprive them of the blessings and honors of liberty, and sink them in the
privations of slavery; to provoke the displeasure of
Almighty God, and bring down national judgments
to complete national ruin. Immorality and irreligion
as certainly dry up the resources of a nation and
hasten its downfall, as a worm at the root of a
fragrant plant or fruitful tree will cause it to fade,

wither, and die. Hence, every endeavor to suppress
vice, and to promote public virtue, is patriotic; the
execution of the laws against vice and immorality is
patriotic; the support of Churches, Sabbath-schools,
and day-schools is patriotic; the suppression of the
hundred-handed system of intemperance, the fruitful
source of most crimes, is patriotic; the observance
of the Sabbath, which "was made for man," and is
of divine authority and universal obligation, is patriotic; and all these are but parts of politics, truly
defined as "the science of government," etc. Why,
then, should a Christian man be warned away from
the arena of political action, as if it were a defilement
to his professional purity and inconsistent with his
profession? Ah! those who are interested in the im-
moralities of corrupt politics, dread the presence of
these "higher-law" men, who are represented as the
"light of the world" and "the salt of the earth!"
Like the Gadarenes, who were engaged in unlawful
business, and altogether sensual, and requested the im-
maculate Christ to depart out of their coasts, so these
would warn away Christians, or bid them hold their
principles in abject abeyance to the worldly ends of
those who ignore moral obligations in political action.

Yet all men are under natural, moral, and legal
obligations to obey God in all their actions—domestic,
social, civil, and political; because he has made them
rational, moral, accountable, and immortal beings, and
no age, condition, secular concerns, or party influence
can dissolve their obligations.

It is indisputably right that civil government
should exist. Wherever there is a relation of dependence, there is demand for government; and as we are
dependent upon God and upon each other, the constitution of humanity and society demands both divine

and human governments. Civil government is necessary as a means to an end, of paramount importance in the moral rectitude and well-being of mankind. It is only by good government, in its widest sense, that virtue flourishes and general and individual tranquillity is felt. A man would far better have a lodge in some vast wilderness, surrounded with wolves, tigers, and bears, than dwell in a community without law, since "man to man is fiercest, deadliest foe."

Civil government has the sanction of God, and is of divine appointment. In Deuteronomy xix, 18, 19, the God of Abraham, our God, gave these particular directions to his people in the execution of law: "And the judge shall make diligent inquisition: and behold, if the witness be a false witness, then shall ye do unto him as he had thought to have done to his brother: so shall ye put away evil from among you." In Ecclesiastes x, 17, the word of inspiration saith: "Blessed art thou, O land, when thy king is the son of nobles, and their princes eat in due season, for strength and not for drunkenness." The Queen of Sheba said to Solomon (2 Chronicles ix, 8): "Blessed be the Lord that set thee upon his throne; for the Lord loved Israel, to establish them for ever, therefore he made thee ruler over them, to do judgment and justice." In Proverbs viii, 15, the Almighty saith: "By me kings reign and princes decree justice." The Lord, by Isaiah (i, 26), promised Israel: "I will purge away the dross and restore thy judges, as at the first, and thy counselors, as at the beginning; and afterward thou shalt be called the city of righteousness, the faithful city. Zion shall be redeemed with judgment, and her converts with righteousness." In Proverbs xxxi, 4, 5, it is declared: "It is not for kings, O Lemuel, it is not for kings to drink wine, nor for princes strong drink, lest they drink and forget the law, and pervert the judgment of any of the afflicted."

Nor does the Christian dispensation and era supersede the necessity of human legislation. We hear the apostle Paul, himself a Roman citizen, and knowing and claiming his rights as a citizen, saying to his brethren in the city of Rome (Romans xiii, 1-6): "Let every soul be subject to the higher powers; for there is no power but of God. The powers that be are ordained of God. Whosoever, therefore, resisteth the power, resisteth the ordinance of God; and they that resist shall receive to themselves damnation. For rulers are not a terror to good works, but to the evil. Wilt thou then not be afraid of the power? Do that which is good, and thou shalt have praise of the same; for he is the minister of God to thee for good. But if thou do that which is evil, be afraid; for he beareth not the sword in vain; for he is the minister of God, a revenger to execute wrath upon him that doeth evil. Wherefore, ye must needs be subject, not only for wrath, but also for conscience' sake. For, for this cause pay ye tribute also, for they are God's ministers, attending continually upon this very thing." What thing? Why the suppression of vice and the encouragement and defense of virtue. And thus we have God's warrant for politics and political action for the same great ends. Human or civil government is, therefore, demanded by our very humanity, by society itself, and has the direct sanction of Him "who is Governor among the nations, King of kings, and Lord of lords."

Again, human agency is called into action by God's enactment, both in the establishment and maintenance of civil government. Thus Moses (Ex. xviii, 25,) "chose able men, out of all Israel, and made them

heads over the people, rulers over thousands, rulers
over hundreds, rulers over fifties, and rulers over tens.
And they judged the people at all seasons; the hard
causes they brought to Moses, but every small matter
they judged themselves." When Moses could not
bear the burden of these hard causes alone, the Lord
said to Moses (Num. xi, 16), "Gather unto me seventy
men of the elders of Israel, and bring them before me,
and I will take of the spirit that is upon thee, and will
put it upon them, and they shall bear the burden of
the people with thee." God's direction to the " United
States of Israel " was (Deut. xvi, 18), " Judges and
officers shalt thou make thee, in all thy gates, which
the Lord thy God giveth thee, throughout thy tribes,
and they shall judge the people with just judgment."
The precise form of government is not, indeed, specified, and as the Israelites were permitted, in some instances, to choose their own form, and as different
forms did exist, we consider that the precise form,
whether monarchical, aristocratic, republican, or a government like ours, which combines the best elements
of all these forms—viz., the monarchical, in our veto
power; the aristocratic, in our Senate; and the republican in our House of Representatives—is not essential
to the divine warrant of which we speak, as the form
is of less consequence than the end or objects to be
attained; viz., the suppression of vice, and the defense and encouragement of public virtue.

Under the different forms of civil government we
find a varied responsibility resting upon the people,
and the more direct the influence that the people have
in establishing government, the creating of laws, and
election of officers, the greater is their responsibility,
the more sacred their political obligations. Hence, in
a republic, like our own, where every man is a sov-

ereign, responsible for his vote only to God, the highest moral obligation in regard to political action exists.

Our duty, then, is:

First. To pray for divine directions. " Moses spake to the Lord, saying, Let the Lord, the God of the spirit of all flesh, set a man over the congregation." (Num. xxvii, 15.) Christians should ask wisdom "from God, who giveth liberally."

Second. We should select and support men of the right stamp for office. Here is the proclamation made by the chief magistrate, on the eve of an election, to the whole nation of Israel, which we would do well to heed: "Take you wise men, and understanding, and known among your tribes, and I will make them rulers over you;" "Moreover, thou shalt provide out of all the people able men, such as fear God, men of truth, hating covetousness; and place such over them, to be rulers of thousands, and rulers of hundreds, rulers of fifties, and rulers of tens." (Deut. i, 13; Ex. xviii, 21.) Notice, 1. The people were to elect—"Take you;" 2. This election was to be from among the "people," and not of any privileged class; 3. These candidates were to possess specified qualifications—men of wisdom, ability, righteousness, and piety; 4. The inauguration was to be by the chief magistrate, Moses. It is of little use to place men in office who are strong, and without wisdom, integrity, and moral courage to do right.

Third. Our officers should be temperance men. (Prov. xxxi, 4.) The devotees of strong drink should never command the suffrages of good citizens. God vetoes it.

Fourth. They must be just men—men that fear God. David in his last hours said: " The God of

Israel said, the Rock of Israel spake to me, He that ruleth over men must be just, ruling in the fear of God. And he shall be as the light of the morning when the sun riseth, even a morning without clouds; as the tender grass, springing out of the earth by clear shining after the rain. But the sons of Belial shall be all of them as thorns thrust away." (2 Sam. xxiii, 3–6.) God's direction to the judges was: "Defend the fatherless, do justice to the afflicted and needy, deliver the poor out of the hand of the wicked." (Psa. lxxxii, 3); "Remember them that are in bonds as bound with them" (Heb. xiii, 3.) "All things whatsoever ye would that men should do to you, do ye even so to them," said the Teacher from the skies. Hence, we have no right, knowingly, to give our votes or use our influence to elect an ignoramus, a tippler, an unjust man, a public violator of God's law.

Do you ask, How shall we know such persons? I reply: First, by their professions; second, by their practices; third, use due diligence to know their true character, spirit, principles, ends, and pledges of the man whom you choose to act as your agent in political affairs, and cast your vote according to the limitations which God has put on it. God having authorized and required civil government, it is not for you to question its necessity, or neglect your duty for it; for he has thrown upon you the responsibility of forming and molding civil government, with the specific view of suppressing vice and fostering virtue; and you are responsible to God, your country, and posterity for your personal vote in the right direction. Then shall the people no longer "mourn because the wicked bear rule," nor will our legislative halls be disgraced by profanity, drunkenness, bribery, oppression, revelry, or Sabbath desecration; but men will be elected to office who will fill their stations in the fear of God. Sabbath profanation, intemperance, bribery, legal injustice, will be extirpated, and the people will rejoice, because the righteous rule, and "righteousness and judgment shall be the stability of our times, and the strength of our salvation." (Isa. xxxiii, 6.)

The voters of free America occupy an elevated position, indeed, before the civilized world. They are the sovereigns of our land; they will come with their ballot to the ballot-box. In the exercise of this right, the weakest man, by virtue of his recognized manhood and citizenship, is as strong as the mightiest. That ballot is the token of inestimable privileges, and involves the responsibility of a priceless trust. It has passed into his hands as a right reaped from fields of blood, and suffering, and death. As he casts his folded vote into the ballot-box, the grandeur of history is represented in the act. To the ballot has been transmitted the dignity of the scepter and the potency of the sword. That folded vote becomes a tongue of justice, a voice of order, a force of imperial law, securing rights, abolishing abuses, and erecting new institutions of truth and love. It is the exercise of an immeasurable power for good or ill; the medium through which you act upon your country; the nerve which unites you with its life and welfare.

> " There is a weapon surer yet,
>   And stronger than the bayonet;
>   A weapon that comes down as still
>   As snow-flakes fall upon the sod,
>   But executes a freemen's will
>   As lightning does the will of God;
>   A weapon that nor bolts nor locks
>   Can bar—it is the ballot-box!"

Now, shall not those who wield that power be placed under the moral and religious restraints of revealed religion as far as possible? May we not expect that Christians will make voting a matter of conscience, and say concerning this high prerogative, "Lord, what wilt thou have me to do?" and then appeal to and apply the truths of the Bible, the infallible oracle of the living God; not, indeed, as expounded by human authority, Protestant or Papal, but as each one shall answer to God for the use or abuse of this talent in his day and generation? Surely, "this day for the hereafter choose we holiness or sin."

From the "Western Christian Advocate," August, 1879.

CAMP-MEETINGS AND THE SABBATH.

We are divinely warned against "becoming partakers of other men's sins;" and when Camp-meeting Associations go into partnership with railroad manaagers, and not only furnish the occasions and inducements to traveling on the Sabbath-day, but require and receive a stipulated proportion of the fares charged for such Sabbath traveling to and from camp-meeting on the Sabbath, and exact a fee for admittance on the Sabbath-day, and rent out lemonade, ice-cream, cigar and tobacco stands, and eating-houses and hotels, and receive the proceeds of such secular business on the sacred day divinely set apart from a common to a holy use, they stand indicted before "the Lord of the Sabbath" for its violation.

No casuistry can clear such associations from the charge of violating the law of the Sabbath, and they are properly chargeable with the violation of our general rules, as a Church, which forbid "the profaning of the day of the Lord, either by doing ordinary work therein, or by buying or selling." Ministers, too, even those who are preaching constantly on holiness, sanctification, perfection, entire consecration, and the higher life, knowingly receive their stipulated fees or salaries from funds which are accumulated by such barefaced desecration of God's holy day, and, preaching a higher life, condescend to this lower life; and the demoralization of the Church and the community around is the result, since the morality of society can never, and will never, rise higher than the morality of the Church. We fully believe in "Scriptural holiness," and have labored forty-seven years in spreading it over the land.

We are cautioned against the great error of "supposing that gain is godliness." (1 Tim. vi, 5.) And Paul tells us that the "perverse disputings of men of corrupt minds, destitute of the truth," have evoked this ruinous supposition. They suppose that gain is godliness; but Paul contradicts them by immediately asserting that "godliness, with contentment, is great gain." To say that gain is godliness, is to say that utility is virtue; but to say that godliness is great gain, is to say that virtue produces utility. There is an essential difference between these two dogmas. The one supposes that gain is the supreme good; the other supposes that godliness is the supreme good. The one supposes there is an intrinsic value in gain only; the other supposes there is an intrinsic and supreme good in godliness only. The one makes happiness the supreme good; the other makes godliness the supreme object of pursuit. And as gain is more agreeable to the human heart than godliness, there is great danger that men will embrace the fatal error that utility is virtue, and that duty consists in seeking happiness rather than godliness.

Law, Paley, Dr. Brown, Hume, Godwin, and many

English, French, and German philosophers make
virtue to consist in utility; or, in other words, these
loose, and in many cases licentious, writers labor to
prove that "gain is godliness;" or, to use the favorite
phrase of infidels and papists, "the end sanctifies the
means;" and their sophistical reasonings are well calculated to bewilder and corrupt the minds of those
minute philosophers who wish to go out of the common way of thinking, and thus free themselves from
moral and religious obligations by adopting the first
principle of infidelity, which is the most disorganizing
and demoralizing principle in the universe; which not
only strikes at the foundation of all religion and morality, but equally tends to subvert all civil government, as it is impossible to bind men by civil authority
after they have lost all sense of religious and moral
obligation; and this same infidel and communistic
doctrine, that leads a people into infidelity, throws
them into anarchy and confusion, and destroys all
civil order and authority.

When advocates of Sabbath-breaking camp-meetings meet us with the plea that they thus have money
to pay the expense of the camp-meeting, and that
they can get it so easily by placing a committee of
the Church to exact a money-consideration at the gate
of the camp-meeting, and rent out ice-cream and lemonade and cigar and tobacco and provision stands,
and run hotels and eating-houses and barber-shops, to
be operated on the holy Sabbath, and are in partnership with railroad companies in running trains on the
Sabbath-day, and gladly receive the wages of unright-
eousness, are they not acting on the key-stone principle that the end sanctifies, ay, and justifies, the
means? Are they not declaring that utility is virtue?
that gain is godliness? And are they not condemned

by the holy apostle in thunder tones, when he rejects, with abhorrence and utter detestation, the dogma which says, "Let us do evil that good may come;" and asserts with vehemence of those who do or say this, "Their damnation is just?" No person may do the least evil that good may come. To do anything evil for the sake of securing even the greatest good, is detestable and "damnable!" A good intention will never justify a bad action in the sight of God, who will condemn evil-doers, though they do evil that good may come. (See Rom. iii, 7.)

In a recent Sabbath-breaking camp-meeting for the promotion of holiness, etc., the minister prayed for good weather on the following Sabbath, that the crowds might assemble, so that they might get a large amount of money out of them, in fees for admission and otherwise; "for thou knowest, O Lord, that our Church is greatly in debt, and it must be paid; therefore, O Lord, give us good weather on Sabbath." Some ministers and managers have more shrewdness in their public addresses to the Throne of grace, but what this preacher uttered in prayer is held by all who believe that "utility is virtue" and "gain is godliness."

The Sabbath was made for man; it was appointed for his spiritual good. Apart from its beneficial influence upon society and upon every temporal interest, it is an institution of unspeakable importance from its bearing upon eternity. In fact, there is no religion without it. The neighborhood, the family, the individual, that willfully violates the holy Sabbath-day is destitute of religion. Those who disregard this sequestered day, who pervert its holy design by attending to secular concerns, who waste the day in idleness, or spend it in riding or walking, or visiting and feasting, or reading secular papers or novels, or writing letters on worldly or domestic affairs, or go off on Sunday excursions to zoological gardens or picnics, or pious gatherings are running their vehicles and loco-motives pell-mell over the commandment which says: "Remember the Sabbath-day, to keep it holy; in it thou shalt not do any work."

The Sabbath, in its divine origin, in its perpetual obligation, in its holy requirements, in its important designs, in its sacred delights, in its typical represen-tation, is worthy of our highest regards and most scrupulous and conscientious observance. 'T is then that the Christian, engaged in warfare with the world, the flesh, and the devil, like a battle-ship at sea, lies by on the government docks for essential repairs of the damage he has received through the week, and prepares again for action, by an increase of that "faith by which he overcomes the world."

Nor are we foes, or indisposed, to our camp-meetings. Nay, verily, they may be conducted to man's good and to God's glory, and the extension of Christ's kingdom, without breaking the law, which is not made void by faith, but established by the faith of the gospel as our rule of life; for though the moral law—the Decalogue—is good for nothing for our justification, it is holy and just and good as our moral directory, and its observance is indispensable to present or ultimate acceptance with God; for "blessed are they that do his commandments [and remem-bering the Sabbath-day to keep it holy, is one of his commandments], that they may have right to the tree of life, and may enter in through the gates into the city; for without are" the worst kind of people. (See Rev. xxii, 14.) I fear that some of these religious transgressors—excuse the association of the terms—have never read or studied what God has ordered on the subject. For their benefit I will transcribe his veto, found in Isa. lviii, 13, 14: "If thou turn away thy foot from the Sabbath, from doing thy pleasure on my holy day; and call the Sabbath a delight, the holy of the Lord, honorable; and shalt honor him, not doing thine own ways, nor finding thine own pleasure, nor speaking thine own words: then shalt thou delight thyself in the Lord; and I will cause thee to ride upon the high places of the earth, and feed thee with the heritage of Jacob thy father: for the mouth of the Lord hath spoken it."

The rule here given implies that men must not profane the Sabbath by doing their ordinary work therein, nor by inducing or furnishing the occasion for other men to do so, in seeking their secular interests, or by spending it in traveling for pleasure, or for recreation, especially under the specious plea of hearing the gospel, and furnishing the occasion and means of making a holiday of God's holy day, but that they should delight in the Sabbath-day, "the holy of the Lord," and call it honorable, and honor him by saying:

> "In holy duties let the day
> In holy comforts pass away."

They should make it their aim to lay aside all employments, pleasures, or discourse which may direct attention from its sanctity, without any other intermission than is really necessary.

The Sabbath-day is specifically a day of rest for the brute creation; and if they had been endowed with reason, and could speak, they would bless our God, who "takes care for oxen," for the merciful provision of the Sabbath. The Sabbath is a rest for man's body, and softens the rigor of the obligation to labor, as it is a day of refreshing pause and needed relaxation. The Sabbath is a day of rest for the mind. It should be hailed with thankfulness, observed with holy awe, enjoyed with pious resolutions to honor God for it, and to seek to be in the Spirit on the Lord's-day, and regard it as a type and pledge of heaven,

"Where congregations ne'er break up,
And Sabbath never ends."

How utterly inconsistent with the Sabbath is the appearance of many of the camp-meetings of the present day! Go to the railroad depots and see the jostling, hurrying crowds buying their round-trip tickets to camp-meeting; see the crowded omnibuses, express wagons, public and private conveyances; every livery stable emptied within ten miles around. Listen to the signal-bells and wild screeching of the escape-pipes and whistles, as the overladen locomotive winds its way along our valleys, puffing defiance to the God of the Sabbath! See the giddy crowds disembogue at the gates! See the poor, panting mules or jaded horses, covered with dust and sweat, with red, protruding tongues, tumbling and reeling as they drag the creaking omnibus to the "camp-meeting gates."

See the red-eyed, bloated, swearing driver, lashing his exhausted team along! See the eager committee, demanding and exacting entrance-fees at the camp-gates, composed of class-leaders, trustees, stewards, "men of *solid piety*, of good natural and acquired abilities, who both know and love Methodist doctrine and discipline!" See these money changers of the temple on the holy Sabbath! See the motley crowds! Hear the oaths and rude jests, and see the ungentle press when the time for general arrivals culminates! They crowd the grounds, throng the aisles. Part of the

usurping crowd hear part or the whole of a sermon,
and then they march and countermarch in single,
double, treble, or quadruple columns. They file right
and left, change front to the rear, wheel by platoons,
undouble files, and, burdened with partners, and bas-
kets, and satchels, and whips, canes and canteens, they
are as terrible as an army with banners, exhibiting the
commingling of the virtuous and vicious. And now
they crowd the boarding-tents, the stands for refresh-
ments, the ice-cream stand, the gingerbread and pea-
nut booth, the lemonade arcade; the crackers and
cheese, apples and peaches and pears; the general as-
sortment stand attached to the boarding-tent, and vying
with an army sutler's establishment,—each Sabbath-
breaker plying his vocation, for which privilege he
has paid the managers of the camp-meeting what they
expected of him for the privilege of " profaning the
day of the Lord by doing ordinary work therein,
and by buying and selling," though absolutely forbidden in terms by our Discipline so to do.

Of our camp-meetings I would say: " As the new
wine is found in the cluster, and one saith, Destroy
it not for a blessing is in it, so will I do for my servants' sake that I may not destroy them all, saith the
Lord. And I will bring a seed out of Jacob, and out
of Judah an inheritor of my mountains, and they shall
dwell there." (Isa. lxv, 8.)

This vexed question will have its solution. The
enlightened conscience of our Church will rally its
forces around the morals of Christianity, and " the
righteousness of the law shall be fulfilled in us
who walk not after the flesh, but after the Spirit."
This will be done in two ways. 1. We can
open our camp-meetings at two P. M. on Monday,
and close them at two P. M. on Saturday. 2. We

can close the gates on Sabbath, and keep them hermetically sealed, and thus not be chargeable nor guilty of giving this great occasion to the enemies of the Lord to blaspheme, and then wear the jewel of consistency, and the white flower of a spotless and blameless life.

We are glad to learn that the higher moral sense of the Methodist Episcopal Church is checking the associations that, bearing the name of Methodist, are bearing our reputation to the dust. The reaction has taken place, the groundswell of holy devotion to the sanctity of "the Sabbath of the Lord" is setting in; and though those who have invested their money in these enterprises, which furnish the occasion for and inducement to these violations of the law of the Sabbath—the occasion favoring the justification of these carpet-baggers, Sabbath journeying, merry-making Christians—yet they are as powerless as Canute to stay the swelling tide against their continuance.

> "The ocean rolled not back
> When Canute gave command."

Already, all over the land, the occasion and inducement and the justification of Sabbath desecration, in connection with our camp-meetings, have been stopped.

Grand old Chautauqua leads the van, and there all access to the grounds, on the Sabbath is prohibited and effectually prevented. I will close with a paragraph from an article by George Lansing Taylor, D. D., in which he so graphically describes the camp-meeting at the Thousand Islands Park, on the St. Lawrence River: "During the whole season no passenger or freight-craft is permitted to land at the company's docks on Sunday. A conspicuous sign and a vigilant watchman enforce this rule. The result of this fidelity to Christian principle is, that passengers come by the steamboat-loads on Thursday, Friday, and Saturday, and spend Sunday, often Monday also, on the ground, in joyful and reverent worship, undisturbed by the sacrilegious uproar of Sabbath arrivals and departures. In consequence of this, the Sabbath services are especially interesting and profitable; and many, who come with no special religious intent, are found in the inquiry-meetings before the holy day is over. The preaching of the gospel on these high days is always a treat. So closed a peerless summer Sabbath-day."

We rejoice to learn that some of our Western Camp-meeting Associations have this year annulled their covenant with railroads, and declined to receive again any part of the fares collected on the Sabbath, and have withheld from all parties the right to sell anything on the Sabbath beyond the bare necessities of life. This is good—an installment on the debt we owe to the Lord of the Sabbath-day. We hope that ere another summer may return, all our camp-meetings shall imitate Chautauqua, Ocean Grove, Thousand Islands, and others, and hear and heed the voice of God saying: "Ye shall keep my Sabbaths and reverence, my sanctuary; I am the Lord " (Lev. xix, 30); "Verily, my Sabbaths ye shall keep, for it is a *sign* between me and you, throughout your generations. Ye shall keep the Sabbath, for it is holy unto you." (Ex. xxxi, 12–18.) At any rate, the Sabbath-honoring camps will get the patronage. Let us imitate the holy women, who, having provided spices and ointments to embalm the body of Jesus after it was laid in the grave, rested the Sabbabth-day, according to the commandment. (Luke, xxiii, 56.)

CHAPTER XXII.

FRAGMENTS OF CLERICAL LIFE.

IN the spring of 1867 I was laboring in Ripley
as pastor. We saw and felt the necessity of
building a new church, and the membership commenced with great unanimity in the work. We
bought two lots on Main Street, and took up a liberal
subscription of some twelve thousand dollars, and
commenced excavation. We finished the deep
foundations, and were ready for the laying of the
corner-stone. A beautiful day it was, indeed, and
we had a noble program, dividing the services
among Presbyterians, Christians, and Disciples.
The whole area of the church, 112 by 45 feet, was
covered with loose planks, and a rostrum for the
clergy was improvised.

At two o'clock P. M. we convened, and took
about thirty minutes in adjusting the outward convenience of an assembly that numbered from a
thousand to twelve hundred people. But during
this convocation of the good, the powers of the
air were on the alert. The heavens gathered darkness; angry masses of clouds drove up the skies;
lightenings flashed; the warring winds made mel-
ancholy music, and low and deep and growling
thunders gave signs of a coming storm. The
pastor of the Presbyterian Church prayed with

amazement; all faces showed signs of fear, and
general uneasiness prevailed. As he terminated the
opening prayer it seemed like the funeral note to
the enterprise, and many countenances seemed to
take pleasure in our sad catastrophe. As he uttered the word "Amen," I said in a loud voice:
"Let us continue in prayer." I felt called upon
to make a special plea unto the Almighty at this
crisis of the powers of darkness, which seemed to
be led onward by "the prince of the power of the
air, the spirit that now worketh in the children
of disobedience." I rehearsed to the Lord the
designs and desires and enterprise of the Church,
his past goodness to them, his near relations to
them, and the influence that the present enterprise would have on the cause of Christ in that
locality. "And now, Lord," I continued, "this
public meeting of the friends of Jesus is interrupted by the powers of darkness, and the prince
of the power of the air; thine enemy, and ours as
well. He seeks to prevent these services, and
thereby dampen the enterprise of this people, and
thwart the enthusiasm of this hour. O God, our
God that ruleth on high, we pray thee to signalize
this hour by thy delivering grace. O, thou God,
who rulest on high, and art mightier than the
howling winds, for thine own name's sake rebuke
the devourer. Thou whom the winds and whirlwinds obey, drive back this portending storm; rebuke these howling winds; and O, thou Lord God
Almighty, exert thy power and bid a counterblast
to go forth and drive these stormy clouds aback,

by the power of thy word; and give us, O Lord, a
sweet and calm season for these services; and may
thy people rejoice in thee, whom winds and storms
and hurricanes obey, and from whose presence
devils fear and fly! We ask this clearance for the
honor of thy name, through Jesus Christ our Lord.
Amen!"

At the closing of this prayer of agony and desire, the wind veered to the opposite point of the
compass, and from blowing up stream, it swept a
hurricane around, and fairly leaped in its course,
and came howling from up-river with a rising
fury, and in a few minutes hurled the black storm
clouds back, back, back, down the river, and a
clear blue sky appeared, and a smiling sun with
gladness in his smile. The change was so direct,
so glorious, so speedy, so palpable, so divine, that
the Church was radiant with joy, and the people
said one to another: "Did you ever see the like?
It is the Lord's doing, and wondrous in our eyes."

The Lord's ear was open to the cry of his
servant, and the solemnity of a great epoch was
upon the whole assembly. The services went on
with increasing interest, lasting some two hours.
It was regarded as a day of wonder. A subscription was solicited, which amounted to nearly or
quite one thousand dollars. The people rejoiced
as if in the immediate presence of God. I closed
the exercises with the doxology and benediction,
and added: "Now to your tents, O Israel, with
all possible dispatch. Farewell." With indescribable speed the clouds mounted the skies, and such

a rain fell as had never fallen before in the memory of any living man in that whole assembly.

The answer to that prayer was a miracle of God's power, and seemed to put new strength into the hearts of God's people in Ripley, which urged them forward in their great undertaking.

We extract from the Ripley *Bee* of the Thursday preceding the dedication the following notice concerning the laying of the corner-stone: "Those who were there will never forget it.   .   .   .   We see to this day, as plainly as if the living scene itself rose before us, the inky blackness of the sudden storm, and hear the rattling peals of thunder directly overhead, and feel the first drops of rain falling in the midst of the ceremonies.   The crowd began to scatter, the preachers and Church officials looked dismayed, as they hastily took their hats and turned to go.   Suddenly a voice above the crash of the thunder called them back.   There stood Dr. Moody towering above them all, his gray beard streaming in the wind, and his flashing eyes upturned to heaven, as he pleaded with a power and eloquence that can never be pictured for the staying of the storm.   Like Moses of old, he dared to remonstrate with God; and the astonished people looked on with wondering pity that he should make such a fool of himself.   But a strange north wind came up, checking the southern storm.   The battling clouds struggled and rolled with fearful rapidity.   The ceremonies went on, and the crowd stayed to 'see Moody get ducked.'   But not a drop of rain fell until the doxology had been sung and the benediction pronounced. With the sounding of the 'amen' came a flash of lightning and a crash of thunder. The heavens were let loose, and such a rain came down as had never been known in the town before. Whether this was a miracle we are not called upon to say, but that it is a fact, none who were there will ever dispute."

While I was pastor of Morris Chapel, Cincinnati, I was passing up to the Book Concern, corner of Main and Eighth Streets, one morning in January, 1861, and came upon a dense crowd of citizens on Main Street, near Seventh, where, in a disreputable house, two policemen, who had entered at eleven o'clock the night before at the request of a father searching for his erring daughter, had been foully and fatally stabbed. As I came near the door, an aged policemen stepped out and said: "Mr. Moody, do come in and speak to our two comrades, and pray with them, as they are both fatally wounded." I went into the elegantly furnished rooms, and the proprietress begged me, as a minister, to pray with the men. I talked to them as dying men, and prayed with and for them. They understood their condition, and I proposed Christian baptism. They both assented, and I baptized them in the name of the Holy Trinity. They became calm, collected, and confiding.

The woman of the house asked me if I thought they would recover. I told her that the attending physician had pronounced the wounds fatal. She sobbed aloud in agony of spirit, and said: "If God will spare these innocent officers' lives I will abandon this abhorred business. In any event, this loathsome career shall cease. I renounce it all." I approved her avowals, of course, and proposed prayer, in which I asked pardon for her from God for the past, and grace in her behalf. Shortly after this prayer both men died. They were buried from Morris Chapel. Four days afterward the red flag of the auctioneer was floating from the house of death, and another haunt of evil-doers was broken up. The proprietress became an attendant at Morris Chapel, occupying a seat, the second from the door on the left entrance to the church. She was plainly yet elegantly appareled in unalleviated black, and was a devout and attentive listener to the Word of life which I proclaimed from Sabbath to Sabbath.

On a Sabbath morning I preached the annual missionary sermon and took the collection, which was very liberal. The woman in black contributed twenty dollars in gold coin. A few days afterward the *Daily Times*, of September 25, 1861, had a report of what it designated "A Missionary Infernal Machine." It spoke of a "mysterious lady, and how she contributed to the missionary cause," as follows:

"A rather singular affair has come to our knowledge which, perhaps, may be of interest to the public generally, and to the religious population particularly. On Sunday, the 8th inst., the Rev. Granville Moody devoted the services of the morning at Morris Chapel, of which he is pastor, to an advocacy of the claims of the missionary cause. On the Monday following a

very neatly dressed lady called at the coal-office of
Mr. Cochnower, immediately below the residence
of Mr. Moody, and engaged the services of a boy to
carry a small basket to the residence of the reverend
gentleman; but perceiving that he was about to deliver it at the wrong door, she hastened after him and
relieved him of his burden, by taking charge of the
basket herself—after which she departed.

"Mr. Moody was, in the evening, apprised of the
mysterious action of the lady; and, upon questioning
his household, found that there had been no basket
left for him, consequently he thought no more of the
matter. On Tuesday morning, as the family were at
prayers, a small boy presented himself at the door,
and handed to the minister a small but very heavy
parcel, which bore this direction, 'Rev. Granville
Moody, for the Missionary Cause.'

"Ministers are not unaccustomed to receive dona-
tions from their friends, but they are generally of a
character not so weighty as the one in question; and,
as Mr. Moody is a strong advocate of Union principles, on any and all occasions, the idea immediately
flashed upon his brain that it was intended by some
secessionist to make him the victim of an infernal
machine, and blow him all to pieces. This thought,
of course, led him to look at the heavy offering in a
very suspicious light, and to induce him to remove
all the little Moodys to a safe distance before he proceeded to open it, in the hope that if the rebels wished
to destroy him, and succeeded, there would be some
of the stock left to give them trouble in all coming
time. In the presence of a friend he proceeded to
undo the fastenings of the bundle. Cautious as to
this proceeding, and fraught with the idea that every
string might pull some unseen trigger, it was placed

around the angle of the wall, and by an outstretched arm, bent at an angle of forty-five degrees, it was freed from its outer fastenings. The next development was a fig-box, the lid of which was fastened down with copper tacks. The danger here appeared to be increasing, and it became necessary to use redoubled vigilance. To remove the lid might cause the explosion of some vile invention of the enemy, and create havoc and destruction. At this point of the proceedings a lucky thought occurred to the minister. Of course the villains intended that he should open it at the top, and some secret spring to the lid should do the work. He could foil them, and satisfy his curiosity by cutting into the bottom.

"To plan and to execute was the work of several minutes, but, after ruining a good pocket-knife, and expending considerable patience, an aperture was made in the box, and out rolled a twenty-dollar gold piece, and then another, and another, with the prospect that there were still 'a few more left of the same sort.' So it was not an infernal machine at all, but a donation, from some very charitable but unknown lady, to the missionary cause, in the behalf of which the reverend gentleman had so eloquently appealed to his hearers on the previous Sabbath. A more thorough and less cautious method was now adopted to relieve the box of its contents, which were found to be neither powder nor lead, but twelve hundred and eighty dollars in that more weighty mineral, gold, all of which, it was the desire of the donor, should be devoted to the enlightenment of the heathen. The money was transferred to the Missionary Society, but no tidings have as yet been gathered as to the lady who thought fit to adopt so mysterious a method in forwarding so liberal a donation."

I think I know the source of the donation mentioned in the foregoing extract. I think the "woman in black" furnished the gold as a sin-offering to the Lord, in proof to the Lord that she had renounced her evil life. A clearer case of sorrow for sin, with deep abasement for iniquity, I never witnessed. I pray God to receive her repentance unto life ; and

> " 'Stablish with her the covenant new,
> And stamp His image on her heart."

In the year 1858 I spent several days in Jasper County, Indiana, where my real estate is located. One day I went to Rensselaer, the county seat of said county, and called at the Methodist parsonage to see the pastor, Aaron Hays, an old friend of mine. During a somewhat protracted conversation, the name of a young man who was teaching school in the town was mentioned. Some things that were said gave me a desire to see him, and know more about him. When I arose to depart, the pastor invited me to return in the evening, and spend the night under his roof. I accepted the invitation.

On going out of the town to meet some engagements for the afternoon, I met a young man coming from the direction in which I was going. I had an impression that he was the one whose name I had heard mentioned at the parsonage. So strong was the impression that when we came near each other, I stopped and asked him his name ; he replied, "Joyce." I said: "Are you the young man who is teaching school in town ; and are the

Methodist minister's children members of your school?" He answered: "Yes." I asked him a number of questions. I found he was a member of the United Brethren Church; had been converted when sixteen years of age; was at the time twenty-two years old; and was now teaching school in order to pay some debts contracted during his struggle in college to secure his education. His purpose was to enter the Christian ministry. He was then a local preacher in the United Brethren Church; had, however, preached only a few times, and had in a few instances announced a hymn, and offered prayer in the Methodist Church at the close of the pastor's sermon. A few more questions brought out the fact that he was becoming much dissatisfied with the United Brethren Church, because of the opposition he found on the part of some of the ministers of that Church to an educated ministry.

He was quite poor, had struggled hard to secure an education, and was rapidly becoming unwilling to give his life to a Church where so little was, at that time, done for the cause of education. His replies to all my questions convinced me at once of a duty I owed to this young man. He was correct and exact in his responses, and gave evidence of a superior mind. I said to him: "Please meet me at the parsonage to-night, and we will continue this conversation."

I went and met my engagement, and returned to the home of my friend, the pastor. The young man soon after came in, and was cordially greeted

by the family, as well as myself. I said to him:
"Brother, I have been thinking much about our
conversation this afternoon, and I am impressed
that God and the Methodist Episcopal Church
have need of you." I added: "You can better
your condition by a change of your Church relations, which will demand no change in your religious views. Suppose you allow me to move in
this change of your Church relations. Come over
into the Methodist Episcopal Church. We can give
you a larger field of labor in the ministry, without
any material change of sentiment; and employment in preaching the gospel, without burdening
you five days in each week with the dull routine
and anxious cares of a pedagogue, and thus leave
but the dull remains of life for the work of the
ministry. Come, my brother, put your case in my
hands this week. I am going to-morrow through
Lafayette, and I will see Benjamin Winans, presiding elder of that district. I will represent you
and your condition to him, as his next quarterly
meeting in —— will be held three weeks from
Saturday. I will ask him to take your name to
the annual conference, so that you may receive an
appointment, under a presiding elder, as a supply
on some circuit. Then the regular recommenda-
tions from some quarterly conference can be taken
up the next year. I will stop on my way home
and get all ready for you to make the change in
your Church relations, and it will be for God's
glory, for your greater usefulness, and will afford
you a competent support, and a much wider field

of usefulness. Now then, dear brother, just say, 'I will,' and, under God and the presiding elder, I will do the rest."

He was much moved at my proposal. He asked several pointed questions about the doctrines and government of the Methodist Episcopal Church, and wanted to know more fully of the nature of the requirements of its ministry. I found that fears were rising in his manly mind as to his competency to the work in our communion, to which he gave becoming utterances, and to which I gave suitable responses. After struggling exercises of mind, commingled with becoming fears of inadequacy to the work, he at length responded: "I agree with you, sir, in sentiment, and I put my application into your hands, and the presiding elder's." I said: "Amen! and may this auspicious interview be an augury of success, with God's blessing!" He was at once received into the Methodist Episcopal Church by Brother Hays, as a full member, on his credentials as a local preacher among the United Brethren.

The next day I found the presiding elder, represented the matter, and met with heartiest co-operation. All the doors and locks, as in Peter's exodus from prison, opened of themselves. The Reverend Brother Joyce rejoiced in the happy change that had taken place in his Church relations. He has had a succession of the best appointments in an Indiana Conference, where he has made full proof of his ministry during thirteen years of service; and, in 1880, he was transferred and appointed to the best charge in the Cincinnati Annual Conference; and, at the last conference, held in Hamilton, he received his fourth appointment to one of the first-class Churches of Cincinnati, Ohio.* "All is well that ends well."

I was recently invited (Hamilton, O., 1883), to dine with this reverend Indiana brother at the residence of Daniel Webster Fitton. Incidentally his exodus was alluded to, and with much feeling he begged me to recite the events of his introduction to Indiana and Ohio Methodism. The narration of these events beguiled and enlivened an hour replete with interest and enraptured with joy.

> "When Time, who steals our years away,
>   Shall take our pleasures too,
> The memory of the past shall stay,
>   And half those joys renew."

The following statement concerning a prayer over a "Sermonette," is taken from the Dayton *Journal*. I have to confess to the truth of it—in the main! "A few years ago, Dr. Moody was waited upon by a committee of the official board with a request to preach shorter sermons. He consented, and on the next Sabbath read a little fifteen-minute address, and closed with a prayer proportionally short, as follows: "Lord, let thy

---

* Isaac W. Joyce, here referred to, was pastor of St. Paul and Trinity Churches in Cincinnati, serving each of these charges three years. In 1886 he was reappointed to St. Paul, and while pastor of that charge was chosen by the Cincinnati Conference a delegate to the General Conference of 1888. At this General Conference he was elected one of the bishops of the Methodist Episcopal Church.—EDITOR.

blessing rest upon this 'sermonette;' and, if thou canst, use it to thy glory.   Amen."

In 1861, Judge Bellamy Storer, seeing me on Fourth Street, in Cincinnati, approached, shrugging first one shoulder and then the other, and exclaimed as we met: "O, Dr. Moody, I spasmodically shrug my shoulders every time I see you, sir; for you are the *fac-simile* of your honored father, my early preceptor in Portland, Maine, who so seasonably and efficiently administered the master's ferule or rattan to my hand or shoulders for juvenile delinquencies when I was a pupil in his seminary.   I twitch my hand or shrug my shoulders involuntarily, as if I were in danger of another feruling or flagellation for misfeasance or malfeasance.   But he was a grand teacher, a preceptor of the olden time, 'who knew his rights, and knowing, dared maintain' them. He was of a regular Puritanic family, and you may well be proud of your ancestry."

On my entrance into the army, Judge Storer presented me with an elegant outfit as colonel.   I named a fort which I built in Jefferson, Tennessee, "Fort Storer;" and another, located diagonally opposite to it, "Fort Thomas," after Hon. Nicholas W. Thomas, formerly mayor of the city of Cincinnati, who presented me with a grand warhorse, black all over—a good description of which may be read in Job xxxix, 19–25.

CHAPTER XXIII.

AS COLONEL OF A REGIMENT.

WHEN the Civil War in the United States was inaugurated after the election of Abraham Lincoln to the Presidency, it was a question with the author how he could best serve his country. After long pondering the matter and conferring with his friends, he came to the definite and solemn conclusion that the government needed his services as a soldier. Belonging to the Church militant, it was not difficult for him to reconcile the work of the ministry with the duty of a patriot. When his friends proposed to recommend him to the governor of Ohio for a commission as colonel of the Seventy-fourth Regiment, some of the companies of which were composed largely of members of the Methodist Episcopal Church, he gave his consent, and he was appointed. The following letters and extracts contain some additional facts concerning his introduction into and connection with the army:

From a Cincinnati Daily Paper, December, 1861.

After a lengthy consideration of the matter, the Rev. Granville Moody has agreed to accept the colonelcy of the Seventy-fourth Regiment. The command was tendered him about one month since, and the offer has remained open, the officers of the regiment hoping that he would finally be induced to accede to their wishes. The only objection as to the position has been from Mr. Moody himself, and that was based upon what he thought to be want of practical military knowledge; but this, on the part of his friends, was considered as fully made up by his sound judgment and the possession of a heart burning with zeal for the Union cause, and brave as a lion's withal. Mr. Moody has received several letters from Governor Dennison, tendering him the colonelcy of the regiment, if he would serve in that capacity. Mr. Moody agreed to accept the position on condition that Major Alexander Von Schrader would act as lieutenant-colonel of the regiment. The major has served quite a number of years in the Prussian service, and is said to be an accomplished military officer. He consented, on condition that the appointment would not conflict with the wishes of the regiment.

In regard to the colonel, we would add, that several of his friends in this city have already tendered him his complete outfit in the field. . . . Last evening a meeting was held at the Armory, on Plum Street. The crowd in attendance exceeded in numbers and enthusiasm any which we have witnessed since the early days of the war. Speeches were warmly received. Colonel Moody delivered an eloquent address, which was responded to by hearty cheers. He invited volunteers to come forward and engage in the war, the holiest the world ever knew. . . .

December 18, 1861, was a great day in Xenia. For several days it was known that Colonel Moody was to arrive and take command of the Seventy-fourth Regiment. He addressed the soldiers and citizens in words so energetic, impassioned, and patriotic, that it seemed as if every soul was stirred. A great many recruits were sworn in during the day, and circumstances indicate that the regiment will soon be full.

APPROVAL OF THE METHODIST PREACHERS' MEETING OF CINCINNATI.

CINCINNATI, November 26, 1861.

Rev. Granville Moody, of Morris Chapel, Cincinnati, having been advised of his unanimous election as colonel of the Seventy-fourth Ohio Regiment, made a statement of facts. He read communications from several distinguished gentlemen, pertaining to the same, and desired the advice of the Methodist Episcopal Preachers' Association in Cincinnati in regard to the propriety of his accepting such a position, as a minister of the gospel. After a full and able discussion of the subject, the following resolution was unanimously adopted:

Resolved, That as members of the Preachers' Association of the Methodist Episcopal Church in Cincinnati, we are of the opinion that Rev. Granville Moody has a providential call to the position of colonel of the Seventy-fourth Ohio Regiment, and cordially approve of his acceptance.   M. DUSTIN, President.

GEORGE PARROTT, Secretary. .

ADJUTANT-GENERAL'S OFFICE, }
COLUMBUS, OHIO, April 19, 1862. }

SPECIAL ORDER, No. 357.

Colonel Granville Moody, of the Seventy-fourth Regiment, O. V. I., is hereby detached from his regiment, retaining his rank and relation to the regiment, and will remain in command of Camp Chase and the prisons at that post. He may detail from his regiment the following named persons to assist him in the discharge of the duties assigned him : viz., etc.

DAVID TOD, Governor.

THE STATE OF OHIO, EXECUTIVE DEPARTMENT,
COLUMBUS, April 19, 1862.

DEAR COLONEL,—The earnest personal and written appeals which you have made to accompany your regiment to the field embarrass me greatly. The strong personal attachment existing between yourself and the men under your command, the expectation and desire of the relatives and immediate friends of your gallant troops, and the extreme pertinacity with which you demand it as a right, added to the peculiar fitness for the command, all tend strongly to induce me to yield to your request. But when I remember that we have at Camp Chase nearly fifteen hundred prisoners (and the number is daily increasing), most of whom are commissioned officers, with but a slight and temporary prison, and with but a few fragments of undrilled and untried troops to guard them, I am compelled to deny your request.

You have now brought the responsible and delicate duty of safely keeping, and humanely treating these prisoners to a perfect system, which, without your personal presence, may be placed in jeopardy.

In addition to my own convictions upon this subject, I learn, from a dispatch just received from General Buckingham, now at Washington City, that it is the wish of Secretary Stanton that you remain in command at Camp Chase.

For these reasons I feel impelled to issue the inclosed order, detaching you from your regiment, and directing that you send it to the field under command of Lieutenant-Colonel Von Schrader. When in my power, consistent with duty, to permit you to join your regiment in the field, it will afford me infinite pleasure to do so. Very respectfully yours,

DAVID TOD, Governor.

COLONEL GRANVILLE MOODY.

At the close of my services at Camp Chase, I received a testimonial from the rebel prisoners, requesting that I should not be removed, and saying: "Should Colonel Moody, at any time, become a prisoner of our (Confederate) government, we hereby earnestly request for him the highest consideration and treatment, as a proper acknowledgment of his kindness and care of us, as prisoners of war, having given us every comfort, liberty, and indulgence at all consistent with our position and with his obligations as commandant of this military post."

HEAD-QUARTERS OHIO MILITIA,
ADJUTANT-GENERAL'S OFFICE,
COLUMBUS, June 24, 1862.

GENERAL ORDER No. 12.

At his own request, Colonel Granville Moody, of the Seventy-fourth Regiment, O. V. I., is hereby relieved from the command of Camp Chase, on and after twelve o'clock M., of the 25th instant, and ordered to join his regiment.

He will turn over his present command at the time above-mentioned to Colonel Charles W. B. Allison, of the Eighty-fifth Regiment, O. V. I., and on or before the second day of July next, set out to join his regiment for duty in the field. By order,

CHARLES W. HILL, Adjutant-General of Ohio.

THE STATE OF OHIO, EXECUTIVE DEPARTMENT,
COLUMBUS, June 24, 1862.

Colonel GRANVILLE MOODY, Seventy-fourth Regiment, O. V. I.:

MY DEAR SIR,—The time has at last arrived, when I can respond favorably to your repeated requests to be permitted to join your regiment. Inclosed I send you an order to that effect.

For the faithful, energetic, and vigilant manner in which you have discharged the various delicate and responsible duties incident to the command of Camp Chase, you have my most profound thanks. You are now about to proceed to a new field of duty, and let me assure you that you carry with you my most sincere wishes for equal success in the discharge of your new responsibilities.

I can hardly expect to meet you again until after the unholy rebellion is put down; and whether that meeting be in heaven or on earth, may we each be able to claim for himself, before the all-seeing eye of the God of battles, that he has faithfully done his duty.

It is a sweet reflection to me to know, that in the varied official intercourse, our personal relations have ever been kind and confiding.

With my kind regards to Mrs. Moody and your daughter, I am, Very truly yours,

DAVID TOD, Governor.

To show the work of the camp, the busy life of the troops, and their conduct in battle, I give the following letter addressed to my wife and children. It was written from the camp in Murfreesforo, Tennessee, the head-quarters of the Seventy-fourth Regiment of the Ohio Volunteer Infantry, on Monday, January 5, 1863:

By the good hand of our gracious God, I am amongst the living to praise him, as I do this day, in that, in answer to our oft-repeated family prayer, he has "spread his shield's protecting blaze when dangers pressed around my head."

On the 26th of December we left Camp Hamilton, seven miles south of Nashville, and com-

menced the forward movement in the midst of a
most pitiless and drenching rain, which lasted all
day; and we camped at night on Stewart's Creek,
in what we called "Cedar Lodge," a wild and
desolate place, where rocks were piled and lodged
on rocks, and ragged cedars rose between. We soon
raised blazing fires, by which we dried our
drenched clothing, and thanked God for ruddy
flames which ministered to our comfort and illu-
mined the otherwise gloomy surroundings of a dark,
drenching, dreary winter night of the last days
of a stormy December season. We got a well-
cooked supper at a wealthy widow's house, whose
sympathies were with the Secesh. She said to us
that she had no sympathy with us "Northern
Yanks" at all. Her squalid negroes sided with
the outspoken Secesh, and they did not want to do
anything to help us "Crusaders" along. But I
half persuaded this secession woman to furnish
my officers with a comfortable supper, and the other
half by the suasion of stern necessity. We had
barely time to eat our supper, and pay her fifty
cents each for the same, when General Negley ordered me to move my command forward to his
head-quarters at once. We had to start at eleven
o'clock that night, and marched by moonlight
over a dreary road three miles to Nolensville, and
thence two miles beyond, and bivouacked in the
woods, where I had to sleep on the saturated
ground, with my head to a stump, and my command all around me. It soon commenced to rain
in torrents; but I slept away, all unconscious of

the drenching rain and echoing thunder and flashing lightning peals, and rose bedrenched, in the dark and lowering morning of a bloody day.

Our forces had severe engagements during all this ill-omened day at Nolensville; but the rebels were driven out, and all our forces possessed it at eventide. When I and my force passed through the place it was a doleful, shattered-looking locality— worse than Goldsmith's " Deserted Village."

Next day, Saturday after Christmas, we started for the Murfreesboro pike, and marched over a desperately bad road. We formed a line of battle on a commanding eminence, and waited orders from the front, whilst our thundering and flying artillery ahead was pouring .destruction on the rear of the retreating rebel foes. All day Saturday our forces were heralded by our bellowing cannon, and our foes were retreating before our advancing columns. At sundown we encamped on the Nolensville turnpike to keep the Sabbath-day in rest; and again I slept on the unsheltered, wet ground, with a blazing fire of logs at our feet, Indian fashion, with our horses picketed around. Sabbath dawned upon us, bright and cheering, and I was in the Spirit on the Lord's-day; and in the deep recesses of my soul I worshiped the Lord of the Sabbath, singing our familiar hymn:

> "Welcome, sweet day of rest,
> That saw the Lord arise."

Really, I enjoyed the camping on the Sabbath. General Rosecrans is a God-fearing man and a devout Catholic Christian—very exemplary in his conduct. He keeps a priest by him continually—Father ——, as he calls him. At four o'clock every morning he attends high mass. General Rosecrans rested his army on the Sabbath according to the commandment, and bright and early the entire army marched on Monday morning to the grand battle-ground, and encamped within half a mile of the great Southern army of over sixty thousand of the chivalry. Our camp was in the edge of a dense and gloomy forest of heavy cedar, whose deep shade and rocky defiles might claim the distinction of being the valley of the shadow of death. Indeed, it seems to have been the valley of death without the shadow.

I made for myself a bed between two massive rocks, about eight feet long and four feet apart. I cut cedar boughs, and laid them in them in the bottom three feet deep for a bed. I piled up rocks, say four feet high, with cedar rails for a bed-bottom, and then put cedar boughs on the rails, and thus had a nice bed, with a wagon-cover overhead; where I said my prayers, and slept soundly till eleven o'clock P. M. At that hour a staff officer rode up to my regimental guard-line, and my guard halted him. "Halt! Who comes there?" "Friend, with the countersign." "Advance, one, with the countersign." It was given over my guard's extended gun and bayonet. "Where is Colonel Moody?" "He is sleeping in his den there; right in front of you, sir." "Call him; I have orders for him." I sprang up; and as I appeared, the chief of staff said: "I have orders for you, sir, from General Thomas;" which he read to me in a low tone, by the light of his lantern. "You are to take your regiment, sir, to the front immediately, taking the guard-line now held by Colonel ——. General Thomas is afraid of him, as he drinks too much whisky on duty; and the hour is full of peril. Order your regiment quietly and quickly under arms, and I will go ahead and remove Colonel ——, and return, and conduct you to the guard-line. Execute your orders by your orderly in whispers, and order him to do the same." I replied: "Ay, ay, sir." He departed, and in quickest order my regiment was in line. The chief soon returned, and conducted me and my regiment silently to the vacated guard-line. He detailed also to my command two full parks of artillery, and said: "General Thomas expects your utmost vigilance and valor, Colonel. Good-night!"

About one hour later the enemy advanced, and we opened on him with artillery and rifles, and so unexpected was our readiness that the engagement did not last over a half hour, when the rebels withdrew from our front and took to their left, and surprised General McCook's command and routed them completely—and thus Stone River battle commenced.

On Wednesday we were in the front of the rebel lines commanded by General Withers, embracing the Rock City Guards and other rebel regiments, containing the very flower of the Southern chivalry. We did our whole duty during these bloody scenes of war. My pen falters in the portrayal of the awful events which then took place. Fire, blood, carnage, groans, shrieks, agonies, and death in horrid forms followed. By God's all-comprehending providence I was saved amid these exciting and appalling scenes. I was wounded in the calf of my right leg. A ball tore through the clothing of my left leg at the knee.

Being ordered to advance on the foe firing, I changed the position of my pistol from its position at my right shoulder, and suspended it over my right breast, so as to have it handy at my front for use, as we advanced on our foes, and met the wild whirl and storm of bullets that our foes hurled on us in that perilous hour. A bullet or bullets struck me in my right breast with awful force, and nearly unseated me from my saddle. I put my hand to my breast, which was writhing with a stinging sensation, and found that my pistol was shattered by the shots; the ramrod was broken off, and the handle, some five inches to the right, was shattered in fragments. Thus my pistol, which I had just changed from rear to front, received the two bullets from the rebel rifles, and saved my life from swift destruction.

The shattered pistol lies before me while I pen this paragraph, a mute witness of God's protecting providence, God's chosen shield for my imperiled life. Had I not removed that pistol from my shoulder to my breast, I should have been shot through by two rebel bullets.

"God guards my soul, he keeps my breath,
    Where thickest dangers come;
Go and return, secure from death,
    Till God shall call thee home."

My horse was shot under me; three balls entering him at once, which were doubtless aimed at me. One ball struck his lower jaw, just where his bridle-bits work; one ball struck him in the shoulder, about two inches from the bend of my knee. One ball struck him two inches back of the root of his ear. O, what terrible scenes were all around me! The dead and wounded and dying were in every direction. It was, indeed, a storm of death.

In the afternoon's battle I received a severe shot through the breast of my coat, grazing and glancing along my breast. I received an order to lead my Seventy-fourth men on the outer picket-lines within four hundred yards of the lines of the enemy. Out we went, took position, detailed Companies A and B as skirmish, and sent them two hundred yards in advance of us. They took intervals of five paces from man to man, and the other eight companies stacked arms, wrapped themselves in their blankets, and lay down by their rifles. The night passed quietly, only a few guns being fired on both sides. At dawn of day, we opened on the foe, with musketry and artillery for thirty minutes; but they made but little response. Yet the Seventy-fourth O. V. I. opened the great battle. We were relieved by the Thirty-seventh Indiana V. I., and retired to our camp for breakfast. Our baggage-wagons were attacked and driven back, so that we had no tents or cooking-utensils, and with but little or nothing to eat— only hard crackers and middling-meat, called, in army parlance, "Hard-tack and sow-belly."

But the enemy gave way before the steady valor of our troops. Onward rolled the tide of war. We drove them over Stone River, in confusion worse confounded, up the wooded hill, into the field beyond; out of this field into the dense woods beyond. We captured six cannon. The Seventy-fourth men hauled two pieces of artillery by hand off to our camp. General Rosecrans, General Negley, and Colonel John F. Miller passed the highest compliments on me personally. General Rosecrans said to our regiment that he must call the Seventy-fourth Regiment "the fighting regiment."

My baggage is back in Nashville. I have not had a change of garments since Christmas, nor have I had my boots and spurs off since then. A change of linen would prove a luxury indeed. I have lost three horses, and my fine overcoat that cost me sixty dollars. I have lost one of the splendid pair of pistols presented to me by Judge Bellamy Storer, on entering the army, with my costly coverlet and blankets. I have no change of clothing left, and the balls tore my clothing so that the officers at large and the men call me the "Ragged Colonel."

The enemy left the entire field of Stone River last Sunday morning by early daylight, and have left us in possession of every thing.   Thanks be to God!

The following letter from the front was addressed to the Book Agents at Cincinnati.   It contains some more of the author's experience while in the field.   It was dated at Murfreesboro, April 27, 1863:

Yesterday (Sabbath) I was detailed as "Corps Field-officer of the Day" for the Fourteenth Army Corps, under command of Major-General Thomas.   This corps embraces the divisions under command of Generals Negley, Rousseau, and Reynolds, making the three fronts of our picket-lines; namely, the south-east, east, and north-east front.   This line is occupied by some fifteen hundred men on guard and picket duty, in three lines; namely: 1. The stations, or main reserves; 2. The outposts of guards, being three to each station; 3. The sentinels on the outer lines of infantry guard, on their beats.   Beyond these lines we have the videttes, and beyond these a line of cavalry guards and scouts.

My duty yesterday was to visit these lines, inspect, suggest, direct, etc.   Well, I did it, and preached ten sermons during the day—nine at the stations aforesaid, and one at the Grand Reserve on the center, where we have a concealed battery and support of fifty men.

After attending to all my duties of a military character, I said to the officers and men at the stations, as they stood drawn up in line, that I had some orders from the head-quarters of the

King Immortal, Eternal, and Invisible, and proceeded to declare to them the gospel of the grace
of God, "teaching them to observe all things
whatsoever were commanded" by the Captain of
our salvation. In this way I had the opportunity
of preaching to hundreds of my fellow-sinners, citizens, and soldiers, and I assure you I found great
delight in this work of faith and labor of love,
which I pursue with the patience of hope. It
seemed like the old circuit preaching that we were
accustomed to in the olden time. You may ask
Dr. Kingsley* whether any of the preachers in
the range of the *Western Christian Advocate* have
done as much preaching as that in one Sabbath.
Last Sabbath week, I preached twice in the morning to the Pioneer Brigade, and in the evening to
the Pontoniers, and I hope with profit.

You can tell old friends that I am preaching as
much, or more, since I came into the army, as I
did before I entered it, and the flame of love to
God and man burns brightly on the altar of my
heart; and should my life be demanded in the holy
cause of my country, I shall rejoice to fall in so
good a cause, believing that,

"Whether upon the gallows high,
  Or in the battle's van,
The fittest place for man to die
  Is where he dies for man."

---

* Dr. Calvin Kingsley was at this time editor of the *Western Christian Advocate.* In 1864 he was elected and ordained
one of the bishops of the Methodist Episcopal Church, and
died at Beyrout, Syria, April 6, 1870, while on an episcopal
tour round the world.—EDITOR.

I have just promised to preach the Fast-day sermon in this place, Murfreesboro, next Thursday, and I trust that God will accept the sacrifice and hear and answer our prayers.

On Wednesday, during the battle of Stone River, we met with reverses on every side. My regiment was discomfited and scattered. I was endeavoring to rally them. As I went over a vacant field I overtook six of my men with a first lieutenant fleeing toward Nashville. I cried out: "Hello, men, there is your regiment to the left. Rally to your regiment!" But they were intent on escape, and kept right on. I rode past and turned, facing them, and presenting my pistol, cried: "Halt!" I threatened a pistol-ball to the man that took another step toward Nashville. The officer said: "Colonel, we are dazed, and don't know what we are doing. If we will at once return to duty, will you report us?" I instantly lowered my pistol and assured them that no man should hear from me. The lieutenant shouted: "Three cheers for Colonel Moody!" They were given, and the men joined their regiment. I rode on in search of further squads, and as I neared a wooded region, a company of nine or ten "gray-backs" sprang out of the woods and opened fire upon me. Soon six more joined them and commenced firing. My horse was soon crippled, stopped short, and stood still. I applied the spurs, he trembled and shrunk, and fell in agony to the ground, dead. I disentangled myself from him, dislodged my two pistols from the holsters, and began my retreat from the men who were firing at me. But in the morning I had received a bullet wound in my right leg below the knee, and I had to limp away from the firing of ten or twelve men.

Just as the firing became rapid, and the bullets were singing wildly around my head and person, a horseman rushed up between me and those firing upon me, and dismounting from his steed shouted: "Here Colonel, get into the saddle and get away quick." I attempted to mount the horse, but failed. My right leg that was wounded was so stiff that it would not straighten out to the stirrup by about three inches. I said: "Comrade, get into the saddle yourself, and let me take my chances."

"Divil a bit; try again, Colonel. Try again, man, or the divils will get you, sure."

I tried again, and Patrick almost lifted me into the saddle, and amidst the "zipping" bullets, which came thick and fast, I strode the saddle, and without waiting to find the stirrups I started for our lines. Patrick nearly kept pace with my frenzied, flying steed, and as we approached our line of men, they gave vent to their pent-up feelings, and shouted: "Hurrah! Bravo! Colonel, are you hit anywhere?" I said: "No, I am through safe, thank God and Patrick, and a good horse."

"Surely," said Patrick, "the odds were terribly against us, Colonel; and it kept Providence and meself very busy, all the time of the fracas, to save us; it did so, Colonel."

At this apt speech the crowding men shouted out: "Good! good! Three cheers for Providence and Paddy, and three cheers for our colonel!" Poor Patrick was killed that same afternoon in the engagement that followed.

A rebel colonel was shot, and fell from his horse, which ran wildly, with the empty saddle, and Patrick had caught him, and mounting, rode down to me in a gallop, just in time to save me. As Jonathan said to his armor-bearer: "There is no restraint to the Lord, to save by many or by few." The next day I went and got my saddle, bridle, and blanket, from my dead horse. Poor fellow! he had gathered himself up gracefully in death, and died a warrior's death.

My clothes were pierced with holes, though not a ball touched my person on this occasion. My coat-front was torn as if a tiger had clawed me. It was on this account and at this time that my regiment nicknamed me the "Ragged Colonel."

During our occupancy of Nashville we expected an assault from General Bragg. I was directed to have the Seventy-fourth Regiment excavate the road leading into Nashville, to the depth of six or eight feet; then to plant lines of slender posts along the route, on which we were to lay a frail platform, covered with earth, as a kind of "dead-fall" for the enemy. Our regiment was aligned along this causeway of death. One morning I received orders to send out my train of thirteen six-mule wagons, to bring in as many loads of old cedar rails to use in constructing this causeway. Four companies of soldiers, each with forty rounds of ammunition, accompanied the wagon-train as guards. They returned at noon, heavily loaded with rails. They aligned in front of my head-quarters for the dinner hour. I had been very busy all the morning in camp-duties, and was *en dishabille*, sitting in front of my tent, waiting the call to dinner.

A gentleman, of military make-up and soldierly mien, rode up hastily, and reined in a magnificent courser of high blood. He addressed me very politely, saying: "Will you inform me, sir, where the Seventy-fourth Regiment is encamped, and where I will find Colonel Moody? Do you know this officer, my man?"

I saw that my courtly querist never suspected that I was the colonel, and I replied: "The Seventy-fourth Regiment is all around you, sir; and these are Colonel Moody's head-quarters."

"Ah! thank you, my man; where can I find Colonel Moody? Do you know him?"

I said in reply: "I can't say that I *know* Colonel Moody or any other man, but I guess you might as well dismount. You are about as near him as is needful; and, as it is just dinner-hour, please dismount and take dinner with Colonel Moody. You are quite welcome, sir."

"Why, sir, my business is with Colonel Moody."

"Well, sir," I replied, "this man answers to that name. Dismount, sir, dismount."

He was quickly on his feet, and removing his

hat, said: "This is Colonel Moody, then! I, sir, am Major Lewis, private secretary of the late General Andrew Jackson, and his chief of staff in the Seminole War. I am of his school of politics, and identified in spirit and action with the United States of North America against her every foe, and hold myself and all that I have as subservient to her national rights and dignity. I have lived on my farm in this vicinity where the armies of the Union and of the Rebellion have alternated their rights, and I have always vindicated the United States in her supremacy over all these lands; and if I or the last shreds of my property can subserve the United States, I stand ready to cast myself and my means into the scale of the Union, the whole Union, and nothing but the Union of the States in one nationality. And now, sir, having been reduced by the ravages of this Rebellion to the actual possession of but thirty acres of a large domain; and depending on those few acres for quarters for myself, provender for my horse, and a home for a favorite cow, your men, this morning, despoiled my household, dismantled my fencing, and there on your wagons are thousands of my rails, the removal of which has turned me out on the world, helpless, an old man who has served this Republic through lengthened years, and whose last wishes are for the success of the cause of our common nationality."

He assumed silence, exhibited dignity, and avowed patriotism, and awaited my response.

"Well, Major," said I, "you have been badly

used, indeed. My men were ignorant of your history, as I was myself. Let us sit down and eat dinner, and we will both feel better after we get our rations. Here, Orderly, take this horse to quarters, and feed him corn or oats, as Major Lewis prefers."

I had a brief interview with the officer who had charge of the wagon-train, and gave him orders to return the rails, and have the same force of men rebuild the fence under the direction of Major Lewis, and then proceed forthwith and get loads of regular Secesh rails, and return by supper-time.

After dinner I introduced him to the officer, and told the men his story, and they gave three cheers and a tiger for Major Lewis, and three times three for "Old Hickory." I appointed Major Lewis commander-in-chief for that afternoon, and they departed with good-will on this labor of love for a patriot. The result was that the premises were better fenced than ever before, and a lasting friendship established between myself and him.

Some months after this occurrence I was ordered into the neighborhood of Major Lewis with my regiment, to act as a pioneer force. He learned of my proximity, and came and met me most cordially, and said: "Colonel, I have the best camping-ground in this vicinity in front of my residence. You are welcome to it for your regiment." His mansion was situated about eighty rods south of the road, and leading to it was a broad drive sixty feet in width, and lined on either side with a row of majestic trees from twenty inches to three feet in diameter, and four rods apart. On either side was a beautiful, verdant lawn of blue-grass. The major, old soldier that he was, said:

"You see, Colonel, you can place five companies on each side, with your quartermaster's tent on one side and your surgeon's tent on the other, and your head-quarters in the middle of the two lines, facing the front gate. As the ground rises from the gate you will be in ship-shape for drill or for action in the event of attack. You, sir, are my guest during the continuance of this duty."

I saw the advantages of the situation, and accepted the invitation with but one exception, viz., that I must occupy my own tent with the soldiers, so as to be accessible to them, and convenient of communication with them in all emergencies. A commander should always be with his men. This camp was like an oasis in the desert.

Coming in from drill one morning, hungry to breakfast, a tired Seventy-fourth boy asked of another if he believed the colonel was a Christian. "Christian, hell!" said the other. "Do you suppose any man is a Christian that will get a fellow out to drill at four o'clock in the morning?"

While my regiment was encamped on College Hill, Nashville, Tennessee, a lady was driven to my head-quarters in a splendid two-horse carriage, and beckoning me to her side, handed me a letter signed by Major-General Buell, stating that Mrs. ——

had lost her "servant," and learning that he had been seen in the camp of the Seventy-fourth Regiment, she wanted the privilege of searching my camp for his recovery, and "you will render her every facility in searching for the recovery of her servants." As she presented the document, she remarked blandly that it was from Major-General Buell. I answered: " I see it is, madam ! I respect General Buell's authority, but my business here is to aid in putting down this rebellion against the United States Government—a rebellion instigated by slaveholders. I recognize the general's authority, and you are at liberty to search the camp ; but I can not assist you in this enterprise, and I must be excused from aiding in the recovery of fugitives from enslavement. Good morning, madam." " I 'll report you to General Buell," said she, and a thousand furies flashed indignant hate from her black eyes as she ordered her coachman to return to Nashville. Meanwhile, her slave, who was within a few feet of her, secreted himself and escaped discovery; but I was ignorant of his whereabouts.

Within a short time after the above incident had occurred—indeed, it was the next day—I received orders from General Buell to start for Franklin, twenty-three miles south of Nashville. The surgeon-general of Buell's army came over to my camp and introduced himself, and said : " Colonel, I have heard of your being ordered to Franklin, that hot-hole of secessionists, and I came over to bring you a few articles from our

surgeon's office, which I wish you to use promptly
in case of sickness or wounds.   I have among the
articles a bottle of pure brandy, which may come
promptly in demand in dangerous cases where a
reliable stimulant is needed.   Now, not one word
of your temperance vocabulary!   I order you to
put this in your trunk, and use it strictly as a
medicine.   Farewell, and mind my prescription."

As we were passing through Nashville on one
of the principal streets, a lady, the postmaster's
wife, ran out to me as I was riding at the head of
my regiment, and presenting me with a tidy
lunch-basket, covered with a towel, said: "I heard
of your order to go to Franklin, and I have gotten
you up a nice dinner for to-day.   Good-bye."
The day was very sultry; it was a toilsome march.
All day my son William exchanged his saddle with
the weariest of the soldiers, so that he was on
foot nearly all that day, preferring to aid the infirm or older men, rather than ride himself.

By sunset we arrived within sight of Franklin,
and I exhorted officers and men to rally, and let
the rebels see them firm and agile as we marched
through the town to a noted grove, a little toward
the south.   I ordered the band to strike up "Yankee
Doodle," and to repeat it till we reached the grove.

Supper being ready, I called "Willy," and then
changed the call to "Lieutenant Moody," but there
was no voice, nor any that answered.   He was
seen last just as the regiment broke ranks.   On
search, I found him at the foot of a large tree, almost breathless and entirely speechless.   I called

six soldiers who carried him to my tent, and the men began to rub him with their hands. I thought of my bottle of brandy; went to my trunk and pulled out the contents, scattered them hither and yon, till I found it. I administered it repeatedly; his lower jaw, which had hung down, closed up, and he opened his beautiful eyes, and feebly articulated, "Father," and I knew his life was spared. He revived rapidly, and asked for something to eat. I then thought of the untouched basket, and there I found a fine roasted chicken, light rolls, butter and preserves—in short, a dainty meal.

The next morning I went in company with Judge Mills, of Yellow Springs, Ohio, up to Franklin, and we selected the spacious court-house for head-quarters. We had left our two horses near the river, and had, for the time being, forgotten them. As I came out of the gate of the court-house, I saw a man riding a fine black horse in a swift gallop approaching us. A single look convinced me that the horse was my own. The rider was mercilessly striking him on the flanks. I resolved to recover him, and running at right angles to his course, I met the frantic horse at full speed, caught his bridle, and was dragged along for some distance. I reached up and caught the freebooter by the throat, and hurled him to the ground. Judge Mills rushed up and held the horse, while I took after the thief, who ran on his hands and feet faster than I could go as a biped. I pelted him with stones, but with his tremendous exertion he got away; and now my horse was doubly dear.

I found a good boarding-place in the center of town. The oldest lawyer in the place advised the people to treat me kindly, and they would all like me. "Did you see his first military order for Franklin, and note his signature? The first and last letters of his signature mean decision. We had better be quiet; for no man who writes so plainly and definitely ever lacks in decision. Do what is right with him and his, and we will have peace."

When General Buell retreated to Louisville, I returned with the Seventy-fourth Regiment to Nashville. The rebel engineer hauled us from Franklin four miles, and then detached his engine from our train, leaving us in a favorable place for Forrest's cavalry to attack us. But Forrest failed to come to time, though in the vicinity, and by a special messenger I got another engine, and retreated successfully to Nashville. I had, however, to secure the loyalty of the engineer by a pistol, which covered him till we were safe in the city.

Colonel George V. Moody, my brother, was a rebel officer. He was of the same height as myself, and resembled me. We met twice during the war; each time I visited him in prison. He commanded a battery at Gettysburg. He was in charge of the train of wagons when Jeff Davis was captured. He was taken to Ft. McHenry, near Baltimore, and put in a dungeon. While there, he bribed a guard, and got him to draw a bullet from his musket, and placed under it a letter, which he had written to me. The guard was not discovered, and I received the powder-blackened billet while making a political speech in Ohio. It ran thus:

DEAR BROTHER,—I am in the dungeon at Fort McHenry, unjustly imprisoned. See the President, and gain a private interview with me, if possible.

Yours,   G. V. MOODY.

I went to President Johnson, got permission, and went to Baltimore, saw my brother, returned, and laid the case before the President, who ordered the release of my rebel brother, making me his keeper. I persuaded him to take the oath of allegiance, and he went home to Mississippi, where he practiced law. In a law-suit some allusion was made to the war, when he retorted: "If so many of you had n't been afflicted with sore heels when we came home to recruit, the war might have resulted very differently." The opposing attorney took mortal offense at this, and my brother was found shot at his desk, and the murderer remains to this day unhung.

Though military duties took up the greater part of the author's time, they did not suspend his ministerial functions. He assisted the chaplain of the regiment in his services on Sunday, and, as already stated, often preached. While we were encamped near Murfreesboro, Tenn., I received a note from the first section of the Pontoon

Train, Pioneer Brigade, dated April 17, 1868, as follows:

To COLONEL MOODY, Seventy-fourth O. V. I.:

DEAR SIR,—We, the officers and soldiers belonging to the first section, Pontoon Train, desiring as we do religious instruction, and knowing your worth as a soldier and your zeal as a Christian, do respectfully request you, if agreeable and convenient, to address us on next Sabbath evening at seven o'clock, at which time we promise to give you our undivided attention.

With highest respect, I am your obedient servant,

E. GLEASON,

Lieutenant Commanding Section.

It may be readily inferred that this request was complied with, and that those who were present paid " undivided attention."

Before entering upon the duties of a colonel in the army, the author of this Retrospect had no acquaintance whatever with practical military life. He was thus compelled to begin with the beginning of the details connected with camp and field service, and it afforded him a satisfaction to know that he did not discredit his position. The following notice, from the *Ohio State Journal*, gives a hint as to his readiness while at Camp Chase, to join his regiment at the front. The extract is dated June 10, 1862:

Colonel Granville Moody, ever prompt and ready for any emergency, is increasing in his energies in comfortably providing for the wants of the soldier. The troops are clothed, armed, and equipped, according to law, as fast as they arrive at camp. Saturday last was a day long to be remembered at Camp

Chase. On that occasion a long flag-staff was raised, one hundred and five feet high, and from the top floated that standard sheet, the Stars and Stripes, of huge proportions, forty-two feet long and twenty-seven feet wide, which was elevated to its position by the hands of Governor Brough and Ex-Governor Dennison, amidst the shouts of thousands.

After the speaking, Colonel Moody, of the Seventy-fourth, mounted on his fine black charger, marched the battalions out to the parade-ground, and there drilled them through two-thirds of Hardee, like one perfectly familiar with all the military tactics, to the great credit of himself and soldiery. The colonel has greatly improved himself in military knowledge since he came to this post, and might now be considered almost a finished soldier in the military art.

On Sunday Colonel Moody preached to some two thousand attentive soldiers from this text: "Choose ye this day whom ye will serve." There are some fears that we are to lose the services of Colonel Moody, which have been so serviceable at this post. There seems to be a loud and earnest call from his regiment for his· presence there, and, from the signs of the times, I should not be surprised to hear at any time that the colonel is under marching orders. This would be good news for Colonel Moody, as he has ever been anxious to join his regiment.

Exposure in camp and wounds on the battle-field seriously affected my health. In consequence, not only for my own good, but for that of the army as well, I felt compelled to throw up my commission. The details of my leaving the army are told in an extract from one of the newspapers of the time, which is here given.

It will be a surprise to many to hear that the famous fighting Methodist preacher, Colonel Granville Moody, has resigned. This was owing in chief to the effects of exposure in the recent battles here. The regimental, brigade, division, and corps surgeons all combine in certifying to his physical disability for field-service. The colonel has received from Colonel Miller, General Negley, General Thomas, and General Rosecrans, private letters of the most complimentary character, and I understand that they will also recommend to the War Department that he may receive an appointment, such as his physical abilities will enable him to fill, and "such as will be a fitting acknowledgment of his past services to his country." The following is Colonel Moody's letter of resignation:

HEAD-QUARTERS SEVENTY-FOURTH REGIMENT, O. V. I. }
    MURFREESBORO, TENNESSEE, May 14, 1863.   }
COLONEL C. GODDARD, A. A. G. Dep't. of the Cumberland:

SIR,—In consequence of the exposure connected with the battles of Stone River, I contracted a disease which greatly disqualifies me for field-duty, and, at intervals, which return frequently, I am totally unable to perform the active duties of my office, and therefore respectfully tender my resignation of the commission I have the honor to hold as colonel commanding the Seventy-fourth Regiment, O. V. I. Please see surgeon's certificates which accompany this application.

I certify that I am not indebted to the United States; that I have no government property in my possession; that I have not been absent without leave; I was last paid to the 28th day of February, 1863; and that there are no charges against me which can affect my pay.

With entire confidence in the justice of the cause in which I have spent the last seventeen months of my life, with the highest appreciation of the noble volunteer soldiery of our army, and the patriotism, wisdom, and valor of those who have the control of the Army of the Cumberland, whose particular acquaintanceship I am happy to have made; and believing that the Republic will safely and triumphantly pass through the refining ordeal of the present crisis, and come forth to a more glorious future, and wishing for you and your noble band of co-operators the largest measure of success, the full measure of your country's gratitude, and that coming generations may rise up to honor your memory, I have the honor to remain, with the highest personal and official respect,

GRANVILLE MOODY,
Colonel commanding 74th Reg't, O. V. I.

The following is the recommendation referred to in the foregoing extract, which was forwarded to the War Department:

MURFREESBORO, TENN., May 16, 1863.

BRIGADIER-GENERAL L. THOMAS, Adj't-General of the Army:

SIR,—Colonel Granville Moody, Seventy-fourth Regiment, Ohio Volunteers, having resigned on account of physical disability incurred in the service, is respectfully recommended by the undersigned for the position of "Post Chaplain," should a vacancy occur. Colonel Moody was, before entering the service, and still is, a Christian minister, eminent for his ability, energy, and industry. He organized the Seventy-fourth Regiment, Ohio Volunteers, in December, 1861, and has served faithfully ever since, but, owing to physical infirmity, is now disqualified for field service, and has reluctantly resigned. His military experience pre-eminently qualifies him for the position referred to, and his long-continued and faithful services would seem to merit such a recognition.

Very respectfully, your obedient servants,

W. S. ROSECRANS,
Major-General commanding Army of the Cumberland.

GEORGE H. THOMAS,
Major.General U. S. A., commanding 14th Army Corps, Army of the Cumberland.

J. A. GARFIELD,
Brigadier-General, Volunteer Chief of Staff and A. A. G., Staff of General Rosecrans.

JAMES S. NEGLEY,
Major-General commanding 2d Division, 14th Army Corps, Army of the Cumberland.

JOHN F. MILLER,
Colonel 29th Indiana Volunteers, commanding 3d Brigade, 2d Division, 14th Army Corps, Army of the Cumberland.

J. J. REYNOLDS, Maj.-Gen.

D. L. STANLEY, Maj.-Gen.

J. M. NIEBLING,
Colonel commanding 21st O. V. I.

On forwarding the above document to the President, General Rosecrans wrote an additional indorsement, as follows:

Respectfully forwarded to the Adjutant-General of the Army. Reverend Colonel Granville Moody behaved most gallantly at the battle of Stone River, and is a zealous, energetic, and faithful man.

ROSECRANS.

In 1865 I was recommended to the Senate of the United States by the Secretary of War, Hon. Edwin M. Stanton, for the office and rank of "Brigadier-General, by brevet, in the Volunteer Army of the United States of North America, for distin-

guished services in the battles of Stone River,
Tennessee." The recommendation of Secretary
Stanton was honorably approved by the General
Government, and the above rank and title con-
ferred upon me by the Senate of the United
States, March 13, 1865.

CHAPTER XXIV.

IN CIVIL LIFE.

A MINISTER is none the less a citizen because he preaches the gospel. His rights are the same, and his duties the same as those of any other citizen. He may, therefore, take part in all civic celebrations, and even make what are called by the careless, "political speeches." Politics belong to the realm of ethics; and so far as they concern the well-being of society, not as party measures, but as principles of State action, they are proper subjects for discussion by the minister outside the pulpit. The author makes no apology for introducing the following report of a meeting of citizens held on Washington's Birthday, in Springfield, Ohio, 1863. The report is taken from the Springfield *News:*

After an address by General Rodney Mason, Colonel Granville Moody, of the Seventy-fourth Ohio, was called out. The gallant fighting preacher rose up to his full height, and rung out in clarion tones a magnificient speech, as follows:

"I am always sure to be present at any meeting where General Mason speaks. I formed his acquaintance in the fall of 1832. I was always glad to sit at his feet. He is a master Mason, and when he gives the sign of danger he should be heeded. His well-digested remarks have anticipated much that I intended to say. I am satisfied that the utterances of this hour will have the same effect that the words of Demosthenes had upon the Greeks, when the people rose up, with one mind, and exclaimed: ' Let us fight against Philip!' Let us also say: ' Let us fight against Jefferson Davis,' and let us give three cheers for the Union. (Cheers.) There's powder back of that fire. Difficulties show what men or communities are made of. They scatter the temporary illusions of prosperity, and develop hidden resources, and constitute the stern school in which personal and national virtues are trained and perfected. If La Belle France, forgetting Lafayette, wishes to mix in this fight, we say with Patrick Henry, ' Let it come!' and with Thomas Corwin, we assure them that we will 'welcome them with bloody hands to hospitable graves!' Jefferson said: ' I would to God that a sea of fire whose billows tossed against the clouds were between us and Europe!' Their institutions are opposed to ours. They have looked on with green-eyed jealousy at the rising glory of our Republic. Their principles are as different from ours as light from darkness, as heaven from hell, as Christ from Belial. They foster the spirit of aristocracy and despotism, whilst we maintain the rights of man as man, and uphold a pure democracy; and they know that the success of our experiment will be fatal to the old dynasties, and the uprising millions of Europe will follow the light of our starlit flag, and claim and vindicate man's right to self-government.

" It may be the plan of an all-comprehending, bounding, directing, and permissive Providence, judicially to blind France, until she becomes a party with the Rebellion for the monopoly of cotton, and thus arouses the opposition of our Fatherland; and the lion and the unicorn and the American Eagle may throw their proud banners to the battle and the breeze against Napoleon, Jefferson Davis, and the devil; and the descendants of the mighty Queen Bess, under Victoria and Father Abraham, will give them 'Hail Columbia,' and thus, complicating the affairs of Europe, will constitute the turning and overturning predicted by the prophets, and represented by theologians as culminating in the 'good time coming' in 1866. But let this be as it may, our Southern rebels and their allies will find us on hand, and, in the name of the Lord God Almighty, we will give them an almighty thrashing!

"But I was particularly requested to speak to the following resolution:

"'*Resolved*, That cherishing with grateful hearts the memory of the heroic services by our soldiers in the field, we send them greeting, that their declarations of unalloyed patriotism and of firm determination to fight under the old flag, until it shall be acknowledged in every disloyal State, finds a warm response in all loyal hearts, and furnishes abundant assurance that they are prepared for skulking traitors in the rear, as well as open enemies in front.'

"In behalf of the soldiers in the field, I desire, on this occasion, to declare that your appreciation of their services constitutes no small portion of their reward. No tongue or pen has, as yet, been able to portray to those who remain at home the nature and extent of those services you are pleased to style 'heroic,' the memory of which you say you do and will cherish with grateful hearts.

"Self exiled from 'home, sweet home;' sacrificing pecuniary and relative interests; subjected to necessary arbitrary military authority; burdened with weapons of war and martial accouterments, the heavy knapsack and indispensable blanket, the tiresome

march, the ofttimes scanty and irregular ration ; disease lurking in the system or preying upon the
vitals, with hospital or hospitable graves in prospective ; exposure to the pitiless storms of winter; the
frequent bivouac; encamping for the night without
tents or shelter; heavy guard and picket duty; the
perilous reconnoissance; the desperate foraging party;
the midnight march and attack in the surprise of the
foe ; the stern preparation and exhaustive drill which
precedes an engagement; the forced march; the arrival on the field of battle ; the marshaling of heavy
forces for the deadly strife ; the toiling work with pick
and spade and ax in throwing up the long line of
breastworks, rifle-pits, and forts ; and, at length, long
lines of warriors, infantry, artillery, and cavalry, with
their appropriate dispositions for the deadly struggle,
all constituting 'battle's magnificently stern array;'
the hastening aid-de-camp; the careful officers and
generals, on whose shoulders rests a responsibility which
casts its influence on their features; and now, on the
center or wing, or adown the whole line, the fiery foe
opens on the long, dark masses of humanity the infernal storm of round shot, shell, spherical case, grape,
canister or shrapnel, with the more terrific fire of infantry by rank, by battalion, by file, and at will, as
though hell's high carnival was held, and demons
ruled the hour; the painful wound, the life-demand-
ing bayonet-thrust ; the quivering limbs, as life's crimson current flows and fails ; the shattered head ; the
horrid chasm in the manly form through which the
screaming shell has crushed its way; the advance; the
retreat ; the advance again with decimated ranks ; the
confused noise of warriors, and garments rolled in blood;
the shouting of the warriors, and the shock of battle ;
the retreat of the rebel foe; the hearty rejoicing of the

surviving heroes, as they congratulate each other over the success of the day; the solemn burial of the dead; the awful scenes in the hospitals, where kind visits are made by relatives and friends; the frequent burial of comrades; the extreme exhaustion of officers after a decisive battle; a desolated country through which to resume the march, and a repetition of these scenes and series,—make, singly and together, but an imperfect sketch of what is implied in the language of your resolution, when you speak of the 'heroic services of our soldiers in the field.'

"None but real patriots would endure these pains and brave these perils; and they do indeed deserve to live in the memory of those at home, in whose behalf they brave these dangers whilst they stand between your loved homes and the war's desolation."

Here the speaker introduced Sergeant Charles Harrison, the color-bearer of the Seventy-fourth Regiment, who had gallantly borne the National banner through Kentucky and Tennessee, and during the ten days when the regiment chased John Morgan through those States by steam, and only regretted that they could not get within striking distance of the great skedaddler. Old Charlie had served seventeen years in the British army, seven years in Africa, six in St. Helena as guard over the great Napoleon, two years in the Mexican War, in which he followed the old flag at Vera Cruz, Cerro Gordo, Chapultepec, Churubusco, and Molino del Rey, till it floated in triumph over the Halls of the Montezumas; and now, in his old age, has volunteered to defend the flag of his country against its rebel foes. As Old Charlie rose, the very impersonation of the soldier, he was greeted by a perfect storm of applause, and three cheers for Old Charlie, the color-bearer of Colonel Moody's regiment, were

given with a will from the patriotic throng, appreciating the nobility of the rank and file, as well as officers,
in freedom's holy cause. The speaker resuming, said :

"If you could but know half of what 'Old Charlie'
has seen, you would pass the resolution with unanimity
and enthusiasm ; for your sons in the field are worthy
representatives of the warriors of '76, who had

'Souls that could dare, and hands that could strike,
And their sons were not born to be slaves.'

"This resolution also sends to our soldiers in the
field the kindest greetings in view of 'their declarations of unalloyed patriotism, and their determination
to fight on under the old flag, until it shall be acknowledged in every disloyal State.'

"Yes, sir, the utterances of our soldiers in the field
are plain, direct, and they are terribly in earnest, too.
They are the utterances of men who know what they
affirm, and you are right when you characterize them
in this resolution as unalloyed patriotism. The utterances of our soldiers in the field are not as ambiguous
as Delphic oracles, but clear and true as Shiloh's firm
response. Those declarations are as emphatic as the
crack of their rifles, and as unmistakable as the roar
of their cannon, as with brazen, burning lips, they say
with General Jackson : 'The Federal Union, it must
and shall be preserved.'

"Your soldiers in the front, sir, occupy a stand-
point where they can see the Rebellion as you can not
see it ; they can feel the pulse as you can not ; and
after a few weeks' service against rebellion, they are
perfectly united on the sentiment that the Rebellion
can, and only can, be put down by force of arms.
They go there as Republicans or Democrats or Old-
line Whigs, but soon are baptized into one spirit ; and
their short creed is, This affair must be fought out to

the bitter end.   Their 'determination' is parent of their 'declarations,' and, combined, they are but the reverberation of the doctrine of the Farewell Address of him whose birthday we this day gratefully celebrate— 'First in war, first in peace, and first in the hearts of his countrymen.'   I intend, sir, that the audience shall hear those utterances this night.   I shall make thousands and tens of thousands speak to-night through the resolutions passed by our regiments in the field, who, in the language of your resolutions, 'are prepared for skulking traitors in the rear as well as for open enemies in the front.'   Whilst from our inmost souls we abhor, abjure, detest, despise these craven gray-backs, butternuts, Knights of the Golden Circle, who, following Vallandigham, Olds, Voorhees, and other jayhawking sympathizers with rebels, are spouting treason at home, whilst the true friends of the country are speaking in tongues of fire in the front, yet we are glad that they have so early shown their hands, and the virtuous outbursts of patriotism will bury the whole crew as if covered with a mountain avalanche.

"These bold, bad men who are 'rendering aid and comfort to our enemies' by their resolutions and speeches, which are circulated through the South by thousands, constitute the main dependence of the rebels.   Ask a rebel prisoner what is their hope of success, and the invariable reply is, 'A divided North,' 'The Democratic party,' and will flippantly quote Vallandigham, Olds, and other traitors to our holy cause, and say, 'What do you think of that?''   We reply, that they are but the craven cormorants seeking office at the expense of patriotism, and are as contemptible in point of numbers as they are in point of character; that they are but the Shays, Burrs,

Arnolds, and Dorrs of other days by transmigration, and are predoomed, politically, to as quick a death, and to as deep and dark and desperate a damnation, as their infamous prototypes.

"I am glad to know, and soon will show you by the documents, that this is the prevailing sentiment of our soldiers in the front; the men with rifles and bayonets in their hands; the men who, rising above mere party lines, stand warring for the Union against its open and secret foes, led on by the noble General Rosecrans, the idol of the Army of the Cumberland, who will chop right into the center of Cottondom, and plant the flag of the Union in the very heart of the Rebellion.

"Let us now hear from Indiana, the Hoosier State, which wears peerless honors in the grand war for the Constitution." (Cheers.) Here General Milroy's glorious letter to the Democracy of Indiana was read to the audience amid deafening thunders of applause.

Colonel Moody said: "I have known General Milroy for fifteen years—a noble specimen of manhood, a Christian, and 'the highest style of man.' I recollect visiting the Presbyterian Church in Jasper County, Indiana, some years ago, and found Elder Milroy in the Sabbath-school, bending his Herculean form over a class of Hoosier boys, teaching them the Word of God and the way to heaven; and now he is in the field fighting and praying—and fighting all the better for the praying, too.

"Ah yes! the Christian general loves his country, and would join us to-night in saying, practically, 'If any man, Democrat or Republican, loves not the Government, the Constitution, and the Union, let him be Anathema Maranatha;' or, as old Robert Miller, of this county, explained the apostolic execration, 'Let him be damned and double damned'—that is, we say politically, hoping that they may be led by their adversities to the repentance that needeth not to be repented of."

The colonel then referred to the valor of an Irishman in his command who fired sixty rounds of ammunition, and got more from a dead comrade's cartridge-box, firing away until his musket-barrel was so hot he could not hold it. "May God," he said, "inspire you all with such a patriotism as this!" The colonel then spoke of those men who were war men in peace, peace men in war, and but pieces of men at any time.

Colonel Moody's points, and they were without number almost, were received with unbounded enthusiasm. He spoke from his own personal observation, gave the voice of the army as he heard it, and his utterances were responded to unanimously and gloriously by the immense audience.

After the adoption of the resolutions cheers were heartily given as follows: Three for the Ladies' Aid Society, three for Abraham Lincoln, three for the Secretary of the Treasury, three for the Administration, about twelve for General Rosecrans, three for Colonel Moody, three for the loyal editors of Ohio and of the other States, and three dismal groans were given for disloyal editors.

The following speech on the situation of public affairs was delivered by the author at Ripley in the autumn of 1868, just after the State elections:

FELLOW-CITIZENS,—The grand crisis has been passed in safety and triumph. Ten days ago Freedom's battle was fought and won. This Nation and the combined world stood in excited and painful sus-

pense, whilst the heavy columns of our loyal veterans
deployed into the serried line of battle against the
cohorts of oppression and disloyalty, who rallied again
around the banners of the "Lost Cause." The battle-
line stretched westward from the Atlantic coast, over
the craggy ridges of the Alleghanies, and across the
slopes of the Monongahela it rolled its sharp, rattling
volleys throughout Ohio, the grand gate-way to the
mighty West, and the thunder of the right wing was
heard on the advancing line of Indiana's stalwart
sons, and where through frowning mountain-gates
Nebraska's waters roar.

With Cæsar we may say in sharp, short utterances, "*Veni, vidi, vici.*" With an American hero we
may say, " We have met the enemy, and they are ours."
Pennsylvania, Ohio, Indiana, and Nebraska have
followed the victorious career of Vermont and Maine
in these Republican victories over the so-called Democracy. The broken lines and shattered columns of
the foe, and the consternation carried to the very
head-quarters of their camp, attest the completeness of
our victories and give a glorious presage of ultimate
victory for Grant and Colfax on the fast coming 3d
of November. In vain did Seymour, Blair, Vallandigham, Cary, Wade Hampton, Pendleton, Forrest,
Beauregard, Dan Voorhees, and the leaders of the Ku-
Klux Confederate Democracy set a " Barrere" to the
rising flood of patriotism which has swept over the
land. They could not bid this grand ground-swell back.

It may be useful to consider the question, What
is this party which we have sent reeling and howling
back from the battle-line of last Tuesday? which, indeed, was the Gettysburg victory, to be followed by
the Appomattox surrender on the 3d of November.
We have called the party the Ku-Klux Confederate

Democracy, a party that has been false to our National principles, to our National honor, to our Nationality, and to "the holy cause of human liberty and personal rights." It is not the old Democracy that deemed it to be its honor to stand by "our country right or wrong." It is not the party that rallied around General Jackson when he subjugated the nullifiers of South Carolina, and on his death-bed most regretted that he had not hung their traitorous leader, John C. Calhoun, in 1832, who, at that day, held the political ground of the rebels we have just subjugated, and then avowed the nullification doctrine, which constitutes the principal plank in the platform of the so-called Democracy of 1868. It is not the party that first echoed the utterance of "Old Hickory," that "the Federal Union must and shall be preserved." It is not the party that shouted with Stephen A. Douglas, "In this war there are but two parties, patriots and traitors; and whoever does not do all he can to aid the Government in putting down the rebellion is a traitor at heart." It is not the old Democratic party that in Ohio resolved from year to year that "slavery is a moral, social, and political evil that ought to be extirpated." It is not the party that gloried once in the names of Dix, Stanton, Logan, Butler, Morton, Fenton, Burnside, Hooker, Tod, Brough, and hundreds beside, who were formerly lights in the Democracy, before its base apostasy to the lords of slavery, treason, and nullification; but now these patriotic men are found in the Republican ranks, sustaining the true Democracy against the aristocracy of the South and their allies in the North, who endeavored to build an empire of slavery, resting upon the ruins of human rights, and utterly ignoring the principles of '76. But it is the party that abolished the Missouri Compromise

line to admit slavery to the virgin soil of Kansas;
that justified and defended the Border Ruffians; that
removed Governor Reeder; made the accursed pro-
slavery Lecompton Constitution; indorsed the Dred
Scott Decision, "that black men have no rights that
white men are bound to respect;" did all that could
be done to make Kansas a slave State; encouraged the
South to commence and continue open, flagrant,
deadly war to compel our Government to submit to
its own dismemberment; denied our nationality, and
vindicated the South in its claimed right of secession;
opposed the Government calling out troops to defend
our nationality and our sacred rights; defended the
miserable pro-slavery Crittenden Compromise; lauded
the Constitution of the Confederates as vastly superior
to the Constitution of the United States; declared that
Hungary had less cause to complain against Austria
than the Southern States have against the Government
of the United States; and publicly declared sympathy
with secessionists in the Senate and House in the
gloomy winter of 1860-1, and since then in endless
forms. Representative men of this Democracy, high
in place and power, stole the arms of the United
States, and transported them to rebels, and scattered our army and navy, to leave us powerless before
their traitorous allies. Their chosen President, the old
Democratic public functionary, James Buchanan, officially declared the secession of the States, and that
the Government has no right to coerce a sovereign
though refractory State. Governor Pickens, the Democratic Governor of South Carolina, ordered the bom-
bardment of our National fort, Sumter, "to fire the
Southern heart."

This Democratic party, by advocating the Virginia and Kentucky nullification resolutions of 1798,

has been preaching rebellion till it became an accomplished fact. This party has produced all the State sovereignty, nullification conspiracy and civil war, and furnished all the traitors in the United States. This Democracy fought in six hundred battles in the South for the purpose of destroying our Government, whilst the same party rendered aid and comfort to their cause in the North. This Democratic party steadily opposed the war, resisted the draft, denounced President Lincoln for keeping his heaven-recorded oath, and did all they could to embarrass him in the discharge of his bounden duties. This Democracy originated and maintained all the secret, oath-bound societies known as the Sons of Liberty, Order of American Knights, Knights of the Golden Circle, with Vallandigham as commander-in-chief, all pledged to aid rebels in their devilish design to overthrow this glorious Government of ours. This Democracy constantly prophesied the success of our foes and the defeat of our arms, declared that we could never subjugate the chivalry, never rejoiced over the victories of the Union armies, and showed their deep chagrin when rebels were routed, and were all smiles, and said, " Did n't we tell you so?" when our public enemies gained any advantage over our boys in blue. This Democracy assured the rebels that if there was any war on account of their secession, it should all be in the North, and that they would prevent the rebellion from invading the Southern States, should they succeed and break up the Government.

This Democracy nominated for governor of Ohio the thrice-convicted traitor Vallandigham, who met his final defeat last Tuesday. This Democracy used every endeavor to prevent our Government from procuring money to put down the rebellion, by denouncing the issue of bonds and legal-tender notes as unconstitutional; and, by decrying them before our people and the world, endeavored to render them valueless. This Democracy approached Lord Lyons, the representative of Great Britain in Washington, and said to him, that, "beyond a doubt, Southern secession and independence are fixed facts, and they were in favor of its recognition." This Democracy assembled in Chicago in 1864, with Horatio Seymour as their president, and Vallandigham on the Committee on Platform; and on the identical day that General Sherman's shells were crashing through the roofs of the houses in Atlanta, and our "brave boys in blue" were driving the Democracy in gray, under General Hood, out of Atlanta, on that identical day the Copperhead Confederate Democracy passed the resolution that "our effort to sustain our Government by war is a failure, and the public welfare demands that an immediate effort be made for the cessation of hostilities," etc. O, shame on your avowed, recorded cowardice, ye truckling panderers to oppressors and traitors! Well might every loyal lip exclaim,

> "What! hoist a white flag when our triumph is nigh?
> What! crouch before Treason, make Freedom a lie?
> What! spike all our guns when our foe is at bay,
> And the rags of his banner are dropping away?
> Tear down the strong name that our Nation has won,
> And strike our brave bird from his home in the sun?
>
> He's a coward who shrinks from the lift of the sword!
> He's a traitor who mocks at the sacrifice poured!
> Nameless and homeless the doom that should blast
> The knave who stands idly till danger is past!
> But he who submits when the thunders have burst,
> And victory dawns, is of cowards the worst!
>
> By the God of our fathers, this shame we won't share;
> It grows too debasing for freemen to bear;

> And Washington, Jackson, will turn in their graves,
> When our country shall rest on two races of slaves,
> Or, yielding the spirit which bound us of yore,
> And sundered, exist as a Nation no more."

Yet it is the record that this craven, truckling Democracy were thus ready to yield up to negro-drivers the high trust and heritage of our glorious Union, and submit to the parceling out of our National domain to our public enemies. This Democracy denounced our peerless soldiers as " Lincoln's hirelings," " hired Hessians," "outlaws, thieves, and murderers," " hell-hounds," " hired scoundrels." This Democracy, by overt and covert treason, has filled our land with widowhood and orphanage, and made countless homes desolate, and burdened the Nation with an immense public debt and onerous taxation, and now, with Pendleton, would pay it in a depreciated currency. This Democracy, when our arms were triumphant, furnished the Wilkes Booth, who capped the climax of Confederate Ku-Kluxism by the assassination of the wise, the true, the tender, the merciful, the patriotic, the devoted, the peerless Lincoln, whose fame for every virtue fills the world;

> "Whose monument henceforth shall be
> The broken fetters of the slave."

This Democracy of the North, when rebels were conquered and suppliant, rallied about his accidency, Andrew Johnson, with his " my policy," which restored unrepentant rebels to power all over the land, and in the government they sought to destroy; and, had his policy succeeded, repudiation would have been an accomplished fact, and the " lost cause " would have been gained. Ah! he can not mend the numerous breaches he has made. This Democracy resisted the emancipation of the enslaved, the Civil Rights Bill, the .

Fourteenth Constitutional Amendment, the Reconstruction Acts, the formation of free constitutions in
the Southern States, and denied the protection of the
ballot to the men who periled their all for the life of
the Nation. This Democracy filled the graves of three
hundred and fifty thousand patriots by their encouragement to traitors, and their Southern allies starved to
death seventeen thousand patriot soldiers in the prison-
pens of Andersonville, Belle Isle, Libby, and other
hell-holes. This Democracy, having failed to destroy
our Government by force of arms, would destroy its
credit, and, with Judge Thurman, go about the country
making sage arithmetical calculations about the increasing cost of the young Copperhead's shirt with a
circumscribed narrative to it. This Confederate Democracy compelled the Nation to incur this debt to insure our very existence as a Nation; and now that
loyal and disloyal are alike taxed to pay the debt and
its accruing interest, they squirm; they hate the debt,
because by its aid we whipped their friends and saved
the Nation.

This same Democracy assembled, last Fourth of
July, in Tammany Hall, in New York, and, out of one
hundred and eighty-two Southern delegates present,
over one hundred of them were rebel officers; and
there were present more members of the late Congress
of the Confederate States than the same stripe of the
Congress of the United States; and these Secesh dictated the platform of the Democracy, assumed to declare the Reconstruction Laws of the United States
null and void, saying, " We regard the Reconstruction
Acts (so-called) of Congress, as such, usurpations and
unconstitutional, revolutionary and void."

This same Northern Democracy, then and there, as in
the past, affiliated with our public foes—such as Wade

Hamption, Governor Vance, General Preston, General Forrest, of Fort Pillow massacre; General Buckner (for whom General Grant went to Fort Donelson, though Buckner will not go for Grant now); Basil Duke, who burned Augusta and ravaged Ohio, with Morgan; Dykes, who stole and sold the supplies which Northern mothers, wives, and sisters sent to their imprisoned ones in Andersonville; and there, too, was one Joe Williams, a renegade, coal-black Negro delegate from Tennessee,—and there they mingled, mingled, mingled, and Northern Democrats shouted, and readily learned the Southern yell, when Wade Hampton, Butcher Forrest, or General Preston would stride, with plantation manners, into Tammany Hall. In fact, they grinned with delight when their old masters came again. They bowed, and shook hands, and embraced each other, just as they would have done through all the war, had it not been for our line of fighting boys in blue between them.

And now this Democratic Convention select as their representative man, Horatio Seymour, of New York, a man who went into retiracy in Wisconsin when the rebels opened fire on our flag, and refused to speak to a meeting of soldiers there when asked, saying: "No, I don't know how this thing is going to turn out." In 1861, January 30th, in his speech at Tweddle Hall, he said: "Let us see if successful coercion by the North is less revolutionary than successful secession in the South." A few weeks after this, Seymour, in a letter to Judge Ruggles, said "Judge, have you read the Confederate Constitution? I have, and it is preferable to the Federal Constitution. Now, why not avoid all trouble by ourselves adopting the Confederate Constitution?" Shame, O shame on the poor poltroon! In October, 1861, he

33

said: "If it is true that slavery must be abolished to save the Union, the people of the South should be allowed to withdraw themselves from the Government, which can not give them guarantees by its terms." Is it the voice of Jacob or Esau, patriot or traitor?

On the Fourth of July, 1863, Governor Seymour made a speech at Cooper Institute, in ignorance of General Meade's victory at Gettysburg, and evidently in expectation of a successful advance of Lee northward. That speech could not have been better adapted to excite mob violence and a fresh outbreak in aid of the rebels. The whole spirit of the speech was one of hostility to the war, and to President Lincoln's earnest efforts to enforce the laws and save the Nation; and the Wade Hamptons, Vallandighams, and Forrests so understand him to-day! A bloody riot ensued and raged for days, and threatened indiscriminate plunder and murder. Seymour appeared before the rebel mob, got up to hinder the drafting of men to save the country, and, addressing them as "my friends," assured them that he had taken measures to have the draft stopped. He proposed to end this riot by fully acceding to the terms with which the mob commenced its bloody revolt in the interest of Robert Lee's whipped army.

In his letter to President Lincoln, Seymour said: "It is believed by at least one-half the people of the loyal States, that the Conscription Act, which they are called upon to obey because it is on the statute-book, is in itself a violation of the supreme Constitutional law. I do not dwell upon the consequences of a harsh or violent policy before the constitutionality of the law is tested. You can scan the future as well as I. The temper of the people to-day you can readily learn." It was just at the moment when the brilliant successes of Vicksburg and Gettysburg proved that the war was not a failure, that Seymour, on the Fourth, said to the rebel Copperhead, Ku-Klux, bloody, murdering, house-burning mob: "My friends, I am here to show you a test of my friendship. I wish to inform you that I have sent my adjutant-general to Washington to confer with the authorities there, and to have the draft suspended and stopped." (Vociferous cheering.)

Yes, he would have left our army without aid, to be destroyed by rebels. Just at this high juncture, when the Government needed every man it could get to fill up our decimated ranks, so fearfully thinned out by the bloody struggles of Vicksburg and Gettysburg, this Horatio Seymour higgled and haggled with President Lincoln about the exact apportionment of the quotas of the several districts, as a pretext for the vigorous obstructions to the filling up of our army, which he attempted in the obvious interest of the rebel army, now flying before our colors. Lincoln's reply to him, August 7, 1863, was: "I can't consent to suspend the draft in New York, as you request, because, among other reasons, time is important. We are contending with an enemy who drives every able-bodied man he can reach into his ranks, very much as a butcher drives bullocks into a slaughter-pen. No time is wasted, no argument is used, and thus they soon procure an army to turn upon our victorious armies in the field; and if we waste time to obtain a court decision whether a law is Constitutional, which requires a part of those not now in the service to go to the aid of those already in it, and still more, to determine with absolute certainty that we are to get those who are to go in the exact legal proportion to those who are not to go, our cause is lost. My purpose is to be just and Constitutional, and yet practical, in discharging the duty which I am charged to maintain, the unity and free principles of our common country." Thus spoke the patriot President to the traitorous Copperhead who was legging for Jeff Davis and Bob Lee.

A man with half an eye can see the purpose of Seymour. He intended to work into the hands of Jeff Davis and Robert Lee, hinder the filling up of our thinned-out ranks, and give the rebels time to fill up theirs, and conquer us at last. The only part of the country where Seymour's nomination is hailed with satisfaction is in the South, among unrepentant rebels, whose treasonable work he sustained so far as his timid nature dared. They know their man, and they know Frank Blair and his Calhoun Nullification Broadhead letter, and its principles as transformed into the Democratic platform; and they exult over the remote possibility which their eager desire converts into a hope of his election. With the election of Seymour and Blair they boldly boast that the "Lost Cause" would be regained, and every vote cast for Seymour is, ignorantly, designedly, or recklessly, a vote cast for the supremacy of our traitorous, rebellious public enemies.

You may remember that on the 5th of December, 1814, there was a convention that met in the city of Hartford, Connecticut. Among other things they resolved on was "a cessation of hostilities with Great Britain," almost in the same words in which the Democratic Convention in Chicago, with Seymour as its president, resolved upon peace with Southern rebels in arms. Another resolution was, "That the States represented in this convention take measures to protect their citizens from forcible drafts, conscriptions, or imprisonments not authorized by the Constitution of the United States;" and Seymour seems to have plagiarized the very terms in which these white-livered, timid, shivering traitors of the Hartford Convention sought the overthrow of our National rights in that great struggle with our red-coated British enemies and black-hearted Tories in our own land. Ah! he is the true, lineal descendant of the Hartford Convention Tories of 1814, the Rip Van Winkle of that cabal, doomed to eternal infamy, and now risen to be the leader of the Copperheads and Ku-Klux Democracy to their utter destruction on the 3d of November; and let every patriotic heart exclaim, "So mote it be!"

This Seymour, with Vallandigham, the commander-in-chief of the secret, oath-bound, traitorous society, called the Knights of the Golden Circle, and all that kith and kin, are Jacobins of the French school of demagogues. For what, I ask you, was the Jacobin? Let Webster's Unabridged answer: "So named from the place of meeting, which was the monastery of the monks called 'Jacobins.'" The Jacobins of France, during the Revolution of 1798, held secret meetings, in which measures were concocted to direct the proceedings of the National Assembly. Hence, the Jacobin is the member of a club, or other person, who opposes government in a secret and unlawful manner, or by violent means—a turbulent demagogue. "Jacobinism is unreasonable or violent opposition to legitimate government, by secret cabal or irregular means—popular turbulence."

What a picture of the Democracy of our land in 1864-65, headed by Vallandigham and his special defender and apologist, Horatio Seymour, and in closest sympathy with "monks" of every order and name in America, and operating against our Government by means of secret political societies of which Lafayette warned our citizens in his farewell address, saying "Mark my words well; if ever your glorious Government is overthrown, it will be by secret, oath-bound political societies."

Yes, Forrest, of Fort Pillow infamy, said just seven weeks ago, "I can toot my horn and call out four hundred thousand Ku-Klux in a week." These, with the members of the still existing and secretly operating Knights of the Golden Circle in the North, under Vallandigham, threaten the very liberties and life of our Government; and let Seymour and Blair be elected, and Jacobinism become triumphant, and our Government goes down amid the crash of arms in a sea of blood.

This same Seymour, of date of May 10, 1863, wrote a letter about the arrest of the thrice convicted traitor, Vallandigham, in which he says: "It involves a series of offenses against our most sacred rights. If this proceeding is approved by the Goverment, it is not only a step toward revolution, it is revolution. If it is upheld, our liberties are overthrown," etc. Thus did Seymour, whilst governor of New York, side with Vallandigham, and demand his freedom from arrest, to go, like Samson's foxes, spreading the fire of ruin through all our land. No wonder that Vallandigham nominated Seymour for President in the Democratic Convention in New York. He was only paying back the kindness and public sympathy which Seymour showed to him in 1863, as a "true yoke-fellow" in the infamous Jacobinical enterprise of legging for rebels in our life-and-death struggle with them. O shame! shame! to ask patriots to vote for such a man, with such a damning record, to fill the high, yea, the highest post of influence in a Government to which they were so heartlessly false. Did not this Seymour know that after the battle of New Orleans, and whilst it was (unofficially) known that the treaty of peace was concluded, General Jackson still maintained martial law? During that period a Mr. Louillier (almost as ugly a name as Vallandigham) published a denunciatory newspaper article. General Jackson arrested him. A lawyer, by the name of Morel, induced the United States judge, Hall, to order a writ of *habeas corpus* to relieve Mr. Louillier; and General Jackson arrested both the lawyer and the judge. A Mr. Hollander (another Vallandighamer) ventured to say "it was a dirty trick," and General Jackson arrested him. When the officer undertook to serve the writ of *habeas corpus* the general took it from him, and sent him away with a copy. Holding Judge Hall in custody a few days, General Jackson sent him beyond the lines of his encampment, and set him at liberty, with an order to remain out until the ratification of peace was regularly announced. A few days after peace was declared, Judge Hall called General Jackson into his court and fined him one thousand dollars for having arrested him. The general paid the fine, and thirty years afterward the Congress of the United States passed a bill to refund the fine, principal and interest, to General Jackson, and Stephen A. Douglas took a leading part in the Constitutional and judicial questions which were debated, favoring and voting for the bill.

It may be remarked, that we had the same Constitution then as during the late Rebellion. Then there was an invasion. In 1861-5 we had a Rebellion. The rights of the people (for liberty is not license to cripple the Government struggling for its rights and life) suffered no detriment by the conduct of General Jackson, or its subsequent approval by the American Congress. Had Seymour, Vallandigham, Milligan,

Dodd, and Voorhees been there, they would have been denouncing Old Hickory as violently as they denounced President Lincoln, and would have been the chief actors in the Hartford Convention. Ah how history repeats itself! Truly, there is nothing new under the sun.

The policy of sending disloyal persons beyond the lines has high Revolutionary authority. In 1778, the darkest period of the Revolution, when thousands were for making peace with Great Britain, just as the so-called convention of the Democracy at Chicago, with Seymour as president, were for making peace with our Southern rebels, the Legislature of New York (Seymour was not there) passed a bill directed against those who "ungratefully and insidiously, by artful misrepresentations, and a subtle dissemination of doctrines, fears, and apprehensions, false 'in themselves and injurious to the American cause [this would do exactly for an indictment against Vallandigham, Seymour, and the so-called Democracy of 1861–65–68], seduced certain weak-minded persons from the duty they owe to their country; therefore, be it enacted: 1. That all such men be required to take the oath of allegiance as hereinafter prescribed. 2. That if any refuse to take the oath, they shall be removed to within the enemy's lines. 3. That if they afterward return, they shall be adjudged guilty of misprision of treason."

Hundreds of Tories were sent out of the State, their property confiscated, and themselves banished as public enemies to liberty and the Government. So again in our day we see the same kind of men. History repeats itself; but we never learned that the Vallandighams, Voorheeses, and Seymours of that day had the impudence to run for Congress or the Presidency of the United States. That folly and crime was reserved to cap the climax of the Slaveholders' Rebellion.

And now, with Frank Blair's Brodhead letter before us, on which he secured the nomination, we may forecast the immediate future. Blair says: "There is but one way to restore the Government [to rebels] and the Constitution, and that is for the President-elect [Seymour] to declare these Reconstruction Laws of Congress null and void [the Democratic platform also declares this], and compel the army to undo its usurpations at the South, disperse the carpet-bag State governments, etc., and it will not be difficult to compel the Senate to submit once more to the obligations of the Constitution. I repeat that this is the real and only question which we should allow to control us. We must have a President who will execute the will of the people, by trampling into the dust the usurpations of Congress, known as the Reconstruction Acts. I wish to stand before the convention on this issue."

Now, I declare and charge before the great tribunal of American history and law, and before the civilized world, that the above utterances are rank with treason; that John C. Calhoun, the arch traitor of 1832, who shrank abashed before the indignant patriotism of General Jackson, never uttered more treason than is exhibited in this letter of Frank Blair, and fully indorsed by a similar declaration in the platform of the so-called Democracy, as dictated by Wade Hampton in these words: "And we regard the Reconstruction Acts (so-called) of Congress, as such, usurpations and unconstitutional, revolutionary and void."

Ah! this is South Carolina nullification gone to seed. I say this is bald treason, coupled with the threat of violence, on the simple condition that the

Democracy gain power on the fast coming third of
November. This is war to the knife, and the knife
to the hilt! This is the issue. Wade Hampton,
Forrest, Vance, and the Southern delegates to the
New York Convention, went home exultant and
shouting the victory, saying with Vance: "The South
will gain by the election of Seymour and Blair all it
fought for during four long and bloody years." It
was this very Vance who, on the edge of battle, told
his men to "rush on the Yankees, and fill hell so full
of the damned blue-bellies that their feet will stick out
of the windows." Wade Hampton, on his way to the
New York Convention, said at Robert Lee's college
in Virginia: "The cause for which Stonewall Jackson
fought can not be in vain, but will yet triumph in
some form." And they expect its triumph by the
election of Seymour and Blair. But He that sitteth
in the heavens shall laugh at them.

On the occasion of decorating the graves of
soldiers buried in the cemetery at Washington
C. H., Ohio, in 1881, the author delivered the following address:

FELLOW-CITIZENS, LADIES AND GENTLEMEN,—
I thank your committee for affording me this opportunity of addressing you on Decoration-day, with our
heavens all sunshine, and our earth all bloom. My
selected theme for this auspicious hour is, "Patriotism.
the Highest Civic Virtue." Patriotism is love of
one's native or adopted country. It is that passion
which aims to serve one's country; in advancing
its welfare, its honor, its power as a commonwealth,
by maintaining its laws and institutions in vigor
and purity, and by protecting its rights; by defend-

ing it from invasion, and preserving it from overthrow by internal antagonisms, which may threaten
its peace or prosperity. This patriotism is the charac-
teristic of a good citizen. It is the noblest passion
that animates man, in the character or relation of a
citizen; and we may well ask,

> "Breathes there a man with soul so dead,
> Who never to himself hath said,
> This is my own, my native land?"

We candidly confess that we have no sympathy with
that pretended civism or cosmopolitanism which,
under pretense of love to all men, would extinguish
our love for our own country. Such persons ask
superciliously, "Why should I love my cisatlantic
comrades more than my transatlantic fellow-men?"
This hollow question may be answered by propound-
ing a solid question, "Why should I love my own
family more than the family of my neighbor?" The
answer is, Your own family is your own family, and
has special relationships to you and claims upon you,
such as no other family has, or can have, or should
have. God designed it so, and formed our nature for
the reciprocation of such particular affections. They
arise from the very nature of things, and from association of ideas innate in our nature. And the reasons
why one should love his own family more than the
family of his neighbor, are the reasons why he should
love his own nation more than any other nation. And
this particular affection is not inconsistent with the
highest good-will for every other nation, and for the
widest philanthropy as well. With entire confidence,
then, we may affirm that our country is worth our
highest regards. This will appear with prominence
and emphasis when we but glance,—First. At our origin

as citizens. Bancroft, the great historian, says that "God sifted seven great nations of Europe to get the purest seed, with which to sow this great Republic." Second. At their enterprise to "found a Church without a prelate, and a State without a king," thus saving themselves and us from priestcraft and kingcraft at once. Third. At their intelligent appreciation of the rights of man, God-given, inherent and inalienable, and their declaration that governments among men are instituted to preserve these rights, and that it is their duty to change the government when it fails to secure these rights. Fourth. At their bold avowal of their rights, despite the frowns of the most puissant potentate of earth. They did not hesitate to throw down the gauntlet of war at the feet of Great Britain, and pledge their all on the great issue taken. Fifth. At their sacrifices and achievements during the Revolution, the War of 1812, the War with Mexico in 1847–49, and the War of 1861–65 for the suppression of the Slaveholders' Rebellion. Sixth. At their marvelous wisdom in constituting our indissoluble and invincible nationality.

> "These were our patriot sires', and belong
> To them; theirs is the palm-branch and renown.
> Conquerors, and yet the harbingers of peace,—
> Blessings be on their memory and their work!
> We give their names in charge to the sweet lyre;
> The historic Muse, proud of the treasure,
> Marches with it down to latest times.
> And Sculpture, in her turn, gives bonds in stone
> And everlasting brass to guard them well,—
> Ay, and to immortalize her trust!"

Our patriotism gains an inspiration while we consider the grand national domain which Divine Providence has committed to us, in trust, with usufructuary rights. With the greatest propriety we may say with David, whose harp was mightier than his sword, and far outlived his throne, that "the lines have fallen to us in pleasant places, and we have a goodly heritage." De Tocqueville in his book entitled "Views in America as It Is," says: "The territory embraced by the United States of North America furnishes the most magnificent home for man that is to be found on the footstool of Almighty God." Thus we may "see ourselves as others see us." Ours is indeed a goodly land, the glory of all lands, with a national domain stretching from the St. Lawrence on the north, to the Rio Grande upon the south, and from our Atlantic to our Pacific coasts; from the capes of the Chesapeake to the Golden Gates of California; a country equal in size to all of Europe, Russia excepted; extending from the tropics in the south to the great inland seas on the north, and the regions of the highest habitable latitude among the icebergs and volcanoes of Alaska. We may say of our ocean-bound Republic, as classic pen described the renowned shield of Achilles:

"Now the broad shield complete, the artist crowned
With the last band, and poured the ocean round;
In living silver seemed the waves to roll,
And beat the buckler's verge and bound the whole."

We need not the gold of Indus, Ophir, or Africa, nor the spices of Arabia, nor Turkey's fertile soil, nor the mellow skies of Italy, nor the vine-clad hills of France. Nor would we have the population of these countries, with their ignorance and priestcraft, with their superstitions, degradations, and exactions. No, no! We prefer our California, with her inexhaustible mines of gold; our flower-embroidered prairies; our grand old forests, with almost every variety of timber; our towering mountain ranges, with repose written upon their brows;

our fertile valleys, our matchless rivers, our capacious harbors, our rock-bound coasts, our inland seas, our vast coal-beds of every variety of carboniferous deposits, and our subterranean petroleum lakes, by which we become, through the channels of commerce, "the light of the world."

Let an intelligent, candid, and considerate foreigner land in New York, and go in an omnibus, which carries fifty persons, to his hotel, which accommodates six hundred guests, and survey our great maritime metropolis from the Battery or Castle Garden to Harlem River, with its streets ten miles in length, and its population of two millions of citizens. Then let him enter the parlor of a Pullman car, and glide away and away from the rising to the setting sun, and then find himself at Buffalo, still within the boundaries of the State of New York. Let him then stop, and say with Shakespeare, "I will take mine ease at mine inn." Then, at early dawn, let him take steam-cars again, and go thundering along the route of the railway through Ohio and Indiana to Chicago, in Illinois, and find two days employed in the transit of three States. Then, by the matchless Chicago and North-western Railway, let him roll westward over verdant Illinois, whose bending willows, in lengthened lines, seem like the picket-guards of an army with banners. Let him cross the "Father of Waters" at Clinton, and open his eyes in very wonderment as he enters Iowa, with her wide-spread beauties in the leafy month of June, and gaze on your rolling prairies and golden harvests, and wonder if it is a vision of the far-off Glory Land, born in the dreams of night; or if he has, indeed, passed the boundary between terrestrial and celestial climes.

No, my entranced Englishman, this is not heaven; it is only Greene County, Iowa. Sobered down, let him still speed along the Bowyer River, on to Council Bluffs, and over the Missouri River; and passing Omaha westward still to Cheyenne, through Nebraska and Wyoming; and on to Salt Lake City and Tacoma, Nevada Territory; to the Humboldt River; Reno, Summit, Colfax, Lincoln, Sacramento; and by Santa Clara on to San Francisco, at whose Golden Gates he is to stop, as if at the Pillars of Hercules, and see the golden glories of the sun, as he is apparently bathed in Pacific waves, whose glowing smiles seem to welcome him. And now our wearied tourist stops, and sees the ancient motto, "*Ne Plus Ultra*," transferred to the Golden Gates of San Francisco.

It is our rejoicing that over all this vast domain our glorious banner floats to-day, in unquestioned and unquestionable supremacy. Proudly the old Roman said, "I am a Roman citizen;" and with purer pride, and broader warrant for it, every American may say: "I am an American citizen; a citizen of the great Republic."

It was a fable that the waters of Castalia made him who drank of them a poet. But it is a sober truth, that he who catches the spirit of our pioneers, statesmen, heroes, and defenders, is a patriot, and the highest civic honor blushes on his brow. Our patriotism will be augmented when we consider our population in its characteristics and its wondrous increase. A condensed, prophetic representation of the world's history, by Noah, declared that "God shall enlarge Japheth, and he shall dwell in the tents of Shem, and Canaan shall be his servant." How wonderfully has this been fulfilled! The Greeks, the

Macedonians, the Romans, all Europe, Asia Minor, the Gauls, the Germans, and Celts—indeed, nearly all the inhabitants of Europe—are of Japheth, and nearly all the inhabitants of America have descended from Japheth. The American citizen is the representative of nearly all the descendants of Japheth, and we find the mingled peculiarities of Saxon and Norman, German, Scotchman, Irishman, Spaniard, Italian, with probably the survival of the fittest. At the formation of this Government, in 1789, our census showed but three and one-half millions of people. To-day we are largely over fifty millions of souls—a people reared amongst scenes of great natural beauty and sublimity, developing daily an advancing Christian civilization, and gaining in wealth beyond all parallel, having the principles of personal, civil, and religious liberty deeply imbedded in their convictions, desires, determinations, and avowed in our National Constitution. Our agricultural, mechanical and commercial enterprises are making us at once the wonder and marvel and envy of the world, prompting the grateful acknowledgment that David made when he exclaimed concerning the united tribes of Israel: "God hath not dealt so with any nation!" No people in the world have such reasons for patriotism and gratitude to God as we have.

> " Westward the course of Empire takes its way. . . .
> Time's noblest offspring is his last."

The political compact between the thirteen colonies, known as "Articles of Confederation," had accomplished its brief mission; its principal powers respected the operations of the war with Great Britain, and acquired this power only by the outside pressure of the war with England, but became dormant in times of peace, and even its apparent powers were but shadowy and unsubstantial,

> "As is the shade
> By the light quivering aspen made,"

since those "Articles of Confederation" were devoid of all coercive authority.

By this political compact the Continental Congress might make and conclude treaties, but could only recommend the observance of them. They might appoint ambassadors, but they could not pay their board-bills at a third-rate tavern. They might borrow money in their own name, on the faith of the Union, but they could not pay a dollar. They might coin money, but they could not import bullion. They might make war and determine what number of troops were necessary, but they could not raise a single soldier. In short, the Continental Congress, under the Articles of Confederation, might declare everything, but they could do nothing. All such a Congress could do was to recommend their measures to the good-will of the States; but their measures depended solely upon the pleasure of the States; and, in point of fact, many of the most important measures of the Continental Congress were silently or sullenly disregarded by the States, or slowly and reluctantly obeyed. And some of them were openly derided by some of the States, and as openly and boldly refused to be executed. With all that, Congress had no power to punish individuals or States for any breach of their enactments. Their laws were without any penal sanction, and so amounted merely to advice. The citizens obeyed when convenient, and cared but little for persuasions and less for conscientious or patriotic obligations. Moreover, that Congress had no power to imposes taxes, or to collect a revenue for the public services. All that Congress could do, was to make an estimate of the amount needed for the public service, and then to apportion it out to the States to be paid.

After 1783 the States relapsed into utter indifference on this subject, and Congressional requisitions on the States, to pay even the interest on the public debt created to resist England, were openly disregarded. Appeal on appeal was made in vain, and· the Congressional treasury had not one dollar in it. Its credit was gone; public burdens were increasing; public faith was openly violated and prostrated. Withal, Congress had no power to regulate commerce among the States or with foreigners. So that between the States there sprang up jealousies, rivalries, and resentments, which evinced the immediate danger of warfare between contiguous States, and the peace and safety of this Union were made dependent on the measures of the States, over which this emasculate General Government had not the slightest control. Foreign navigation crippled ours, and they monopolized ours as well. Our sailors were out of employment; our mechanics were ruined; our agriculture was profitless; what little money was in the country went abroad to supply our needs, and the state of things was more calamitous than war, and was progressively crowding us to ruin. Weary, doleful years were spent in begging the States to give more power to Congress; but the predominance of State jealousies, and the incompatibility of State interests with each other, prevailed. The Government became imbecile, and tottered to its fall; and the only question was, Shall we stand silently by and see it fall, or rouse, and by true patriotism form a more efficient General Government, before the great interests of the Union should be buried beneath its fall and ruins, as when the lords of the Philistines perished with Samson?

In 1785, Maryland and Virginia sent commissioners to Alexandria, to make arrangements and regulations for the navigation of the Potomac, oyster-beds, fishing, duck-shooting, etc. But feeling the inadequacy of their powers, they recommended enlarged proceedings. In 1786 the Virginia Legislature proposed a convention of commissioners from all the States, to consider all the interests involved and imperiled, and secure common interests and permanent harmony. Pursuant to this, five States sent commissioners to Annapolis. They framed a report to the Continental Congress, advising it to summon a general convention of commissioners from all the States (thirteen), to meet in Philadelphia in May, 1787. Congress agreed, and passed a resolution to call a convention. All the States, except Rhode Island, responded favorably, and elected delegates, and they met in Philadelphia. After protracted discussions and great diversities of opinions, they, after prayer by Rev. Dr. Duche, framed the present Constitution, and recommended it to be laid, by the Congress, before the people of the several States, to be by them considered and ratified in conventions of the representatives of the people, to be called for that purpose. This was effected. Conventions were accordingly called in all the States, except Rhode Island, and after warm discussions, *pro* and *con*, the Constitution was ratified by all of them, except Rhode Island and North Carolina.

The assent of only nine States being required on the passage before the people, Congress took measures for this purpose in September, 1787, as soon as the requisite ratifications were completed. Elections of President and Vice-President were secured, and the necessary elections of senators and representatives being made, the first Congress under the Constitution assembled in New York, then the seat of government, on Wednesday, the fourth day of March, 1789, for commencing proceedings under the new Constitution. A quorum of both Houses, however, did not assemble until the 6th of April, when, the votes of the electors being counted, it was found that George Washington was unanimously elected President, and John Adams was elected Vice-President. On the 30th of April, President Washington was sworn into office, and the new Government immediately went into operation. In the November following, in a new convention, North Carolina adopted the Constitution. In May, 1790, Rhode Island, in her State Convention of the people, also adopted the Constitution. So that all the thirteen States, by the authority of the people thereof, finally became parties of, to, and under the new Government. Thus was achieved another and a still more glorious triumph in the cause of liberty, even greater than that by which we were separated from the odious tyranny of England. The people of the States made the new Government, which constituted them a Nation among the nations of the world.

To those great men, who achieved this victory over State sovereignty, State jealousies, local interests, disunited counsels, and the unwillingness of selfish and narrow-minded politicians to submit to wholesome restraints which the permanent security of liberty demanded, we owe our all as a Nation. New Jersey, Delaware, and Georgia adopted the Constitution unanimously; Connecticut, Pennsylvania, Maryland, and South Carolina, by large majorities; Massachusetts, New York, and Virginia, by bare majorities. Many of the pure and disinterested patriots who stood forth for this change from a mere confederation of sovereign States into an indivisible nationality, did so at the expense of their existing popularity. They had a higher duty to perform than to flatter the prejudice of the people, or to subserve personal, selfish, sectional, or local interests. Many of them went down to their graves without the satisfaction or consolation of knowing that their sacrifices were appreciated. On a close survey of their labors, as developed in the structure of the Constitution, we are compelled to admire their wisdom, sagacity, and forecast, to be impressed with their profound love of liberty, to feel their sense of the value of political responsibility, and to glory in their high resolve to give perpetuity, as well as energy, to the Republican institutions of their country ;

> " To scatter plenty o'er a smiling land,
> And read their history in a nation's eyes."

Truly there were giants in those days, as high above the demagogues of their times as the heavens are above the earth. Compared with their contemporary opponents, or the spawn of those opponents, who by metempsychosis have reappeared in our times, advocating absolute State sovereignty, we may but observe that

> "Pigmies are pigmies still, though perched on Alps,
> And pyramids are pyramids in vales."

For the narrow-minded men with whom they had to contend prated about their pretended sovereignty of States, and would have set up private and local interests at the sacrifice of the general welfare. The demagogues of that day have reappeared in our own day, and of them Goldsmith's criticism is true, that they "to party give up what was meant for mankind."

That the framing and adoption of the Constitution of the United States constituted us one grand nation, is the central pillar of our Nation's glory, and gratefully and proudly we may say of our National motto, "*E Pluribus Unum :*"

> "We are 'many in one' whilst there glitters a star
>   In the blue of the heavens above,
> And tyrants shall quail 'mid their minions afar,
>   When they gaze on that motto of love.
> Though the old Alleghanies may tower to heaven,
>   And the Father of Waters divide,
> The links of our destiny can not be riven
>   Whilst the truth of those words shall abide."

The union of these States in our glorious, supreme, and efficient nationality was an absolute necessity, as seen in contrast with the condition of affairs under the former Articles of Confederation. Our patriot sires so regarded it, and their condition then, and our condition now, alike demand the perpetuity of our glorious, undivided, and indivisible National existence. In the preamble to the Constitution of the United States our fathers say : "We, the people of the United States, in order to form a more perfect union, establish justice, insure domestic tranquillity, provide for the common defense, promote the general welfare, and secure the blessings of liberty to ourselves and our posterity, do ordain and establish this Constitution of the United States of America." This Constitution sets forth the National supremacy in express terms, and in words as strong as Holy Writ.

In Article VI, item second declares : "This Constitution, and the laws of the United States which shall be made in pursuance thereof, and all treaties made, or which shall be made, under the authority of the United States, shall be the supreme law of the land; and the judges in every State shall be bound thereby, anything in the Constitution or in the laws of any State, to the contrary notwithstanding." "The senators and representatives, and the members of the several State Legislatures, and all executive and judicial officers, both of the United States and of the several States, shall be bound by an oath or affirmation to support the Constitution." Here, then, we find no loophole for secession. Our fathers had already had bitter experience of the workings of a mere confederacy of sovereignties, and with the same patriotism that led them onward through the seven long years of bloody strife with England, they felt themselves bound to secure and preserve in perpetuity the priceless boon of a Government of, for, and by the people. The noble men who, under God, had formed this Nation as a Nation, made provision in the Constitution to uphold it by the word of their power and the patriotism of their posterity.

This National Union was the creature of necessities—physical, ancestral, internal, external, geographical, circumstantial, moral, social, political, civil, religious, and prospective, and must endure by virtue of the same necessities; and these necessities are stronger now than when the union of the people of all the States into one grand Nation was formed at first. They are stronger by the vastly greater expanse of domain now covered by its sheltering wings; stronger by the thirteen times multiplied citizens living under its benign influence; stronger by the incalculable increase of the farms, fields, workshops, mines, and ships of the Nation; stronger by increased production of the sea, plow, loom, and anvil; stronger by the grand current of internal and international exchanges; stronger by the long rivers, penetrating regions unknown to our fathers, but now the inher-

itance of their sons; stronger by the artificial roads,
canals, and channels essential to trade and defense;
stronger in steam navigation, peculiarly American,
on our mighty rivers, where the hoarse voice of the
rushing steamers wakes the echoes along our valleys; stronger in steam locomotion on our great land
routes, and in telegraphy, which annihilates space
and binds us all in one; stronger in the freedom of
the seas and the empire of the great waters; stronger
in national honor in all lands; and strongest of all in
the settled purpose and habit of veneration and affection on the part of our people for free institutions so
stupendous and so useful.

The union, then, of these States in one nationality
is not merely because men chose that it shall be, but
because some supreme General Government of this
vast domain must have dominion here, and no other
government than this may, can, might, could, should,
or shall exist on this wide domain which, by right,
belongs to the United States. Every citizen of the
Republic has life, liberty, and the lawful pursuit of happiness, prosperity, precious remembrances, and fondest
hopes for himself, his family, his countrymen, and his
kind on board this old Union ship. It is the property of
each citizen. It is his Government. He is a part of it.
It was made for him, and is maintained by him; and
he knows that it is the only truly wise, beneficent
Government ever devised by freemen. It is his
own Government. As Mr. Lincoln wisely and nobly
phrased it, "It is a Government of, by, and for the
people, and it should not be permitted to perish from
the earth." The severance of this glorious Government was an appalling thought, fearful and ruinous,
as would be the repeal of the law of gravitation in the
physical universe, when orbs would from out their

orbits fly, and collisions, destructions, and death would follow in horrible succession.

Secession is dissolution, and dissolution is death. 'T is the violation of the plighted faith. 'T is the setting up of a private interest against the public good. 'T is an effort to secure a partial advantage by the sacrifice of the general welfare. It is the supreme evil, and affords no remedy for any existing evil. 'T is the ruin against which Washington warned the Republic. 'T is the hydra-monster against which Jackson battled all his life, and, dying, bequeathed the struggles, with his sword, to his nephew, A. J. Donelson, with the injunction to use it for the Union. Secession was Pandora's box; and worse, for despair was in the bottom. Secession was the false mother agreeing to the division of the living child. Secession, as a political right, was a claim for which no Government on earth ever made provision; nor, indeed, could it be done. Secession was studiously avoided and ignored by the rebels themselves in their scheme of self-aggrandizement. Secession was an effort of selfishness, pride, and ambition like that of Satan, which divided heaven, dug hell, and drew earth from its allegiance to the throne of God.

And who would or could reconstruct the fabric of a demolished Government? Who could raise again the Corinthian columns of Constitutional liberty? And if these columns fall, who could again so nicely adjust National Sovereignty and State Rights in local interests and political abeyance? Alas! bitterer tears than ever fell over the fragments of Roman or Grecian art would fall over the fragments of fallen Constitutional liberty. The General Government was not a mere league of sovereign States, dissoluble at will, but a complete National Government. That Consti-

tution made us a Nation, with all the characteristics of
a Nation, and all the prerogatives of a distinct nationality over all the territories and citizens of the thirteen Colonies, and equally so over all the domain we
had acquired, or may yet acquire. Without obliterat-
ing the previous "colonial" divisions, our fathers
bound them round by an all-comprising and permanent nationality. Look calmly at what they did.
They took from the States power to levy armies, to
make war or conclude peace, to enter into treaties
with foreign powers, to coin money, to levy imports.
They interlaced the whole National territory with
ramifications of our vast judicial system, centering
in the city of Washington as the seat of the National
authority. They completed all the branches of a
symmetrical civil authority—legal, executive, and judicial—and without making one syllable of provision
for the withdrawal of any of the parties to the contract; and the arrangement expressly declared that
no State should pass any law conflicting with the laws
of the United States. How puerile the claim of State
sovereignty! Whatever might have been the purpose of the framers and founders of our Government,
as for its Constitution, there can be no doubt as to
what they did. Was there ever an instance in the history of the world in which sovereign and independent
States or powers yielded up such prerogatives and
functions to a mere transient partnership, dissoluble
at the pleasure or caprice of any single one or more
of the parties? The idea is in the last degree preposterous.

Whether they meant it or not, our fathers framed
a Constitution, a Government for a Nation with or-
ganic life, and not a congeries of loosely aggregated
communities. Rebels and traitors talked of the sov-

ereign States of Virginia and South Carolina; and
that, too, under the Constitution of the United States,
by which they were constituted a Nation—a unit,
with its significant motto, "We are many in one"—
one supreme nationality.

What sort of sovereign State was that which could
not build a ship-of-war, nor a fort, nor a mint, nor an
arsenal, nor a custom-house, nor a post-office? which
could neither send nor receive an ambassador? whose
very name, indeed, might be as utterly unknown
to the diplomacy of the world as if it lay in the planet
Neptune, or swung as the tail of the last comet?
Was that a sovereignty to be proud of? Was this
that which the haughty Virginians, the chivalry of the
Old Dominion and the sons of the Huguenots, delighted to vow a permanent allegiance to? No wonder the fanatical and stubborn votary of State sovereignty chafes under a system whose stern and stubborn
fiats stand in contemptuous defiance of his theory.
Nor had the South any pretense for secession on the
ground of wrong done to her by the General Government. Under the shield of the Constitution slavery
reposed as securely as if it had been the one great
fount of every blessing, and the prime object of
National legislation; and the Republican party, on its
accession to power, had no more idea of destroying
that system than it had of

"Untuning the concord of the spheres,
Or shaking the steady pole."

As a party it could not have disturbed the legal
status of slavery in the States if it would, and it
would not if it could.

But secessionists said we would hem them in, and
strangle slavery in its narrow limits. For narrow
South, let them look at the map, and trace the out-

lines of their possession as under the dark rising of
slavery. Glance at Texas and New Mexico, regions
out of which they might have carved half a dozen em-
pires as large as France and England, with their magnificent rivers, their endless varieties of soil and
climate, their stores of agricultural and mineral wealth,
over which nature breathed the softness and lav-
ished the beauties of a perennial spring. Look at
this vast expanse, and talk of being hemmed in!
But, determined on the overthrow of our Government,
the oligarchs of the South made every preparation in
their power to carry out their fell design; and, on
April 12, 1861, they inaugurated open, flagrant, deadly
war to compel our authorities to submit to the dismemberment of our nationality, disrupt the form of
government under which we, as a Nation, had grown
to greatness, that they might establish an oligarchy
whose corner-stone should be human slavery. But
how utterly futile the enterprise! Our best citizens
abandoned the plow, the anvil, and the loom. They
left their shops and stores and factories. They hastened from pew and from pulpit, and from farm and
office and bar. They came from rural districts, and
hamlet, and town, and city. Their cry was,

> "We're coming, Father Abraham,
> A hundred thousand strong."

And they rushed to the fields of danger, and courted
places of peril, and shook their martial steel in the
red eye of war and in the grim face of death. The
goddess of American liberty, with gloom on her brow
and tears in her eye, and with heart wrung with anguish, called upon us imploringly with the voice of
entreaty: "Let not Columbia's glory go down to the
dust." There are times and events paramount to all
others in the history of nations, and of the world as

well. There are eras, epochs, and critical days and hours which engross the causes and interests of centuries foreshortened to a day. Concerning these epochs the bard affirms,

"We are living, we are dwelling,
　In a grand and awful time;
'T is an age on ages telling,
　To be living is sublime."

History records these eventful eras, when all the powers of earth are drawn up in hostile array, and all interests are suspended on a single combat. It is logically and historically true that swords and bayonets think, and war legislates. Such may be regarded to have been the case when the great question was to be decided by a single blow between Greece and Persia, whether freedom or slavery should be the future inheritance of millions. Such was the case when the victory of Constantine determined whether Paganism or Christianity should occupy and hold the iron throne of the Roman Empire. Such was the case when, on the plains of Tours, it was decided whether the Crescent should prevail over the Cross in the West, as it had prevailed in the East. Such was the case when, on the event of the putting to sea of the Spanish Armada, it was to be determined whether Popery or Protestantism should be predominant in Great Britain, and so whether the earth should belong to Christ or Antichrist. Such was the case when, on the plains of Waterloo, the allied armies of Europe decided the doom of the fatalistic Napoleon, who drove the bloody car of war over more than half of Europe; and that victory of the Iron Duke of Wellington and the invincible Blücher checked the man of destiny in his bloody career, and changed the whole current of human affairs. Such was the case when also, at the close of the Revolutionary War, Lord Cornwallis surrendered his sword to our own Washington at Yorktown's closing fight. The great question of man's capability for self-government was put on the passage, and the emphatic act of our heroic fathers was Jehovah's fiat, warranting our existence as a Republican Nation amongst the nations of the earth.

Such, too, was the case when, from Fort Sumter, freedom shrieked her call to freedom's hosts, and on the line of military operations on the Potomac and James Rivers, on the Cumberland and the Mississippi, at Vicksburg and Gettysburg, the question was to be decided by the triumph of the Stars and Stripes over the Stars and Bars. It was the flag of indivisible Union *versus* the flag of Division; the flag of Nationality *versus* the flag of Secession; the flag of Freedom over the flag of Slavery; whether man is capable of self-government or not; whether "we hold these truths," etc., as solemn and divine verities or mere glittering generalities; whether this ocean-bound Republic should be the home and hope of freemen, or of slaves as well. O! this was the crisal hour of America, and of the world as well; and the first gun from Fort Sumter was God's call of the Nation to arms. Wise and patriotic men said and vowed: "God helping me, I never will consent to the destruction or disintegration of this Union formed by our fathers. If we can not live in peace as one Nation, we can not as two; and whenever we acknowledge the Confederacy, we acknowledge the right of secession, and there will be no end to division. New York will come and say: "You have acknowledged the right of the rebel Slave States to secede, and you have let them go and take with them two-thirds of the public domain, three-fourths of the Atlantic coast, and all of the

Gulf coast and States. You yielded the point that the Constitution is the supreme law of the land, and you have agreed that State rights and State sovereignty shall take the place of National sovereignty and supremacy, in violation of the doctrine of Washington and the framers of the Constitution, and Jackson and Clay and Webster. Whenever you recognize one rebellion, and submit to the dismemberment of a part of the States, the door is open wide, and all the other States may set up for themselves, and repudiate your Constitution, Congress, President, Government-debt, and all." New York will insist that she can prosper better alone than in partnership with the rest of the States. Having the port of entry of all nations, the tariff duties would give her unbounded wealth. So Massachusetts would go; and so Maine, with her pine-tree, and "*Dirigo*" on her brow. Thus your Union would be but as a rope of sand, and where would be the Government of the great Republic? Where would be your pensions for your soldiers, who came home maimed, crippled, or diseased in the public defense? Where would be the annual stipend for the widows and orphans, who gave up the husbands and fathers that the country might live? I ask, where are your flag and your nationality? You would have fallen lower than poor pronunciamento Mexico, and been consigned to endless anarchy. With borders to defend against each other's encroachment, border warfare, worse than the border wars of Scotland and England, would follow; and, instead of having peace, you would have interminable war. The Negroes of Kentucky would run away into Ohio; of Virginia and Maryland into Pennsylvania, and their recapture would engender continual strife. It was the striking remark of one of earth's greatest thinkers, that "it is one of the greatest reproaches to human nature that wars are sometimes necessary." The defense of nations, the rights and interests of millions and their posterity as well, sometimes demand resistance against the rapacious injustice of contiguous or of foreign powers. Hence, force must be met with force, and revelation and reason alike declare that

> "War is honorable,
> In those who do their native rights maintain,
> In those whose swords an iron barrier are
> Betwixt the ruthless spoiler and the weak."

It is by pangs and throes that truth is born into the world. It was the birth-throes of war that gave us an existence among the nations of the earth, and made our vast domain a common refuge for the oppressed of all lands, and the late War for the suppression of the Slaveholders' Rebellion has been the efficient means, under the good providence of the God of battles, in preserving to us, and our children after us, the very existence of our Nation. It should ever be borne in mind that Southern traitors, countenanced and aided by Northern confederates, inaugurated the war. Beauregard, with the fiery tongues of eighty pieces of artillery, opened on Fort Sumter, and began the work of blood in order to establish the Confederacy of the slaveholding States, and absolutely legalize, perpetuate, and extend human slavery on two-thirds of the territory to which the Nation had the right of eminent dominion. Their watchword was "Secession and Slavery," two of the most infamous, outrageous, and obnoxious words that were ever mouthed outside of the realms of perdition. The mighty North rose as the tide rises; they moved as billows move navies that are stranded. The Free States arose in their might. The war-drums throbbed forth the pent-up feelings of a citizen soldiery, such as the world had never seen before. Our battle-flags flaunted defiance to the boastful chivalry, who were used to swinging the plantation whip over men, women, and children of the dusky brow, who cringed before their masters in the might of their irresponsible power to exact the unrequited labors and progeny of their poor, down-trodden slaves. Little did these puissant slave-drivers imagine that the God of Moses, who delivered the slaves of Jacob's seed from the bondage of Pharaoh at the passage of the Red Sea, was about to repeat himself on the Potomac, the James, the Cumberland, the Mississippi, and Missouri Rivers, by joining the right with the might in their sanguinary overthrow. Inspiration says (Eccl. v, 8): "If thou seest the oppression of the poor, and violent perverting of judgment and justice in a province, marvel not at the matter; for he that is higher than the highest regardeth, and there be higher than they."

The sublime heroism displayed by our citizen soldiery at Carnifex, Bowling Green, Pea Ridge, Mill Springs, Fort Donelson, Island No. 10, Shiloh, Iuka, Corinth, Pittsburg Landing, Perryville, Stone River, New Orleans, Mobile, Port Gibson, Hilton Head, Grand Gulf, Vicksburg, Port Hudson, Jackson, Tullahoma, Chickamauga, Chattanooga, Lookout Mountain, Kenesaw, Atlanta, Sherman's blazing march to the sea, Rapidan, Chickahominy, James River, Gettysburg, Knoxville, "On to Richmond," Nashville, Franklin, and other fields where our glory was won, presents a solemn pageant, unequaled in all the annals of authentic war. The baptism of blood which inaugurated our repossession of the revolted States has been a sublime and impressive consecration of the Sunny South to the future hopes of the patriot, and the establishment of freedom in that land of oppression.

> "This fratricidal war
>   Grows on the poisonous tree
> That God and men abhor—
>   Accursed slavery!
> And God required that we
>   Shall eat this deadly fruit,
> Till we dig up the tree
>   And burn its every root."

The precious blood poured out on a hundred battle-fields, the heroic lives there laid down, constitute a matchless hecatomb and holocaust offered up through the flames of battle for the preservation of our Nationality, the American Union, and the emancipation of the helpless, shackled millions of our land—the vindication of the declared principles of 1776 in 1861–65.

Against the serried ranks and solid columns of rebel prowess that confronted them, they stood as the ledgy lines of rock amid the foaming, angry billows of the storm-swept ocean; and, when temporarily overwhelmed, they were as unshaken as the continent. Amid confused noise of advancing columns, the shoutings of the captains and the shock of battle, they rallied round the "flag of the free heart's hope and home." No tongue nor pen can describe to those at home the nature and extent of the services of your fathers and brothers and sons. While thus we keep their memory green, and garland all their graves in the beautiful season when spring returns with daisy-slippers on her feet and rose-buds on her brow, let us, in practical gratitude, honor their widows and their children by making them our wards, watching over all their interests, warning them of danger, employing them preferably to others, and thus supply, as far as we may, the loss they have incurred for the National welfare. Let us also conscientiously and religiously, humanely and patriotically, resolve and vow and act and vote and talk so that the legitimate ends for which they volunteered their persons, toil, sufferings, and death shall be secured to the Nation to whose prosperity they consecrated their all.

Alexander H. Stephens, the Vice-President of the Confederacy, said to the South, immediately after the surrender of the Confederate Democracy, of the Slave-ocracy: "Gentlemen, we have lost our all on the field of battle. Our only hope is now to regain in the halls of National legislation what we have so grievously lost in battle." Freemen, do you hear that note of their great fugleman? And are they not busily engaged in this sapping and mining and circumvallating our strongholds of freedom? Have not the "White Liners," the "Night Riders," the "Shot-gun Cavalry," the "Bulldozers," effectually deprived freemen, white and black, of their blood-bought access to the ballot-boxes of the South? Have they not, by tissue ballots, manufactured majorities which devils damned would blush to own? Have they not secured a "solid South" by intimidation and bribery and blood? Have not the Confederate Congress in Washington shown their hand? Are they not endeavoring to break down every legal guard by which a true and pure election can be secured? Are they not trying to banish the unpartisan supervision of the ballot-box as provided for by law? Do they not show their innate hostility to the army of the United States in the most palpable manner? Are they not unwilling that our National authorities shall have within reach the means of securing to every one who has a right to vote that blood-bought right?

We rejoice that Ohio has borne her part so grandly
in the overthrow of the Slaveholders' Rebellion, the
defeat of secession, the vindication of our essential
and historic Nationality and undivided and indivisible Union. Our one hundred and ninety-five regiments returned to Columbus at the close of the
war, and finally handed over their rent and torn and
bullet-riddled battle-flags with honors becoming relics
so venerable, soldiers so true, officers so vigilant and
brave. They recall proud memories of bloody fields;
sweet memories of valor and friendship; sad memories
of fraternal strife; tender memories of our fallen
brothers and sons, whose dying glance was cheered by
their stars; grand memories of heroic virtues; exultant memories of great and decisive victories of our
country, our Union, our Nationality; thankful memories of well-wrought deliverances for ourselves and four
and one-half millions of slaves, now free; immortal
memories mingling with immortality. All these memories twine around the flags, baptized with fire and
blood.

To-day we meet to recount, rehearse, and com-
memorate the deeds of our fallen heroes who died on
the battle-field afar, in the tumult of war, or yielded
up their breath in gloomy hospitals within our military lines, or pined to death in Andersonville prison-
pens, Belle Isle, Castle Thunder, Libby Prison, where
Southern chivalry disgraced humanity in its outrages
on our noble men, not accepting deliverance that they
might obtain a better resurrection. Those heroes who
saved the great Republic live in the cherished memories of millions who, to-day, do scatter earth's choicest
flowers on their honored graves wherever found.

Genius, in its sublimest songs; oratory, in its di-
vinest utterances; history, in its truthful records; and

art, in its costliest monuments, transmit the peerless record of our unreturning braves to distant ages, while youth and worth and blushing beauty shall garland the graves of our country's defenders, in our home cemeteries and on bloody battle-fields, where, before the Slaveholders' Rebellion, there had never before fallen any stain darker than the petals of the peach-bloom or snowy blossom of the welcome strawberry; or on verdant ranges, as of Lookout Mountain or Kenesaw, where daisies, fresh from nature's sleep, stood in smiling beauty, that man might see " the matchless signet of his God." 'T is well that thus we give evidence of our appreciation of the dead who fell in defense of the palladium of the union of our millions in one Nationality. 'T is fitting, sure, that thus we meet by National authority, supreme, to honor the graves of our heroic dead by these floral offerings, whose scented breath speaks with still, small voice as affiants of our patriotic regards.

> "Flowers! When our Savior's calm, benignant eye
> Fell on your gentle beauty, when from you
> That heavenly lesson for our hearts he drew,
> Then in the bosom of your purity
> A voice he set, as in a temple shrine,
> That hasty travelers ne'er might pass you by,
> Unwarned of that sweet oracle divine."

There is a lesson in each of these flowers; there are written words which, if rightly read, will lead the soul from earth's fragrant bosom to hope, to holiness, and to God.

> "Were I, O God! in churchless lands remaining,
> Far from all voice of teachers or divines,
> My soul should find in flowers of thy ordaining,
> Priests, sermons, shrines."

No virtue would here be missing. Whatsoever things are true, honest, pure, just, lovely, of good

report, and virtuous, here you behold them all.   See
Christian faith, turning and clinging to Jesus.   The
passion-flower of endurance mingles with the sun-
flower of faith; from the lily chalice of heavenly-
mindedness rises the fragrance of good deeds.   Behold a rich and ever-blooming garland from God's
garden culled, baptized with sparkling dew-drops, and
bound together with the vine of charity, which is the
bond of perfectness.

Young ladies, I congratulate you on the enviable
position you occupy to-day, as the immediate agents
of a grateful Republic, sent forth in your beauty and
youth and moral loveliness to twine the "Red, White,
and Blue" around the brows of your country's defenders, and garland their lonely graves with peerless
honors.   Your beauteous smiles are, indeed, shaded by
the solemnities of the day, and the graves of the heroic
dead shall be baptized with your crystal tears, while
from the purest depths of your patriotic hearts,
formed for strongest sympathies, you say:

> " The hand that for my country fought,
>   I honor as its daughter ought."

Through your lips of purity and truth the millions
of America say to the shades of the thundering legions:

> "Rest, soldier, rest! Thy country comes,
>   With tender love and true,
>   Freely to deck thine honored bed;
>   Her banner o'er thy turf to spread,
>   And on thy verdant grave to shed
>   Fond memory's pearly dew."

Tread softly, then, amid these honored graves, and
let your footsteps be all aglow with earth's spring
flowers, the signets of our grateful love to our unreturning braves.   Vestals, whose holy duty it is to
keep the fires glowing on the heart and hearthstone,

and on your country's altars, go strew these flowers on the graves of our Nation's defenders—assured that coming generations, your successors in this welcome work will emulate your zeal in similar services, and, with ever-increasing appreciation of the mighty dead, who built themselves into the history of our country, "in the times that tried men's souls," will lay on those graves a beautiful votive offering that shall continue annually,

> "While earth bears a flower,
> Or ocean rolls a wave."

At a reunion of the soldiers belonging to the Seventy-fourth Regiment, Ohio Volunteer Infantry, held at Xenia, Ohio, the author delivered an address, from which the following extracts are made :

And what shall we say to the noble veterans who have returned to grace our homes and halls and groves and churches with their bronzed faces and soldierly bearing? Welcome, welcome, welcome ! We owe you a debt of gratitude and honor and consideration, which we never can liquidate. You have bared your bosoms to the storm of war. You have brought back your shields with "*Vici*" written on them. Again, welcome, welcome, welcome ! And we will share with you the blessings of peace, now that

> "The war-drum throbs no longer,
> And our battle-flags are furled."

Nor will we let this occasion pass without laying our twined garlands of immortelles and forget-me-nots on the graves of our fallen comrades, among whom you will pardon me for mentioning the name of my first-born son, Lieutenant William H. H. Moody, of Company H, of our noble regiment, topographical engineer, and aid on the staff of our grand commander, Major-General James S. Negley. Do I say too much, when I indorse the encomiums pronounced upon him by Generals Negley, Thomas, and Rosecrans? Dear as was the sacrifice, we laid him on the altar of his country, and God took him through the flames of battle to the realms of glory. Truly, I should have deemed my house disgraced if it had stood secure amid the sacrifices of a civil war.

And now let us glance at the grand results achieved by this contest:

1. We have thus proven to the world that we are the worthy descendants of the men who established our Government, and committed it to our trust for generations yet unborn.

2. We have maintained the National life against despots at home, foreign enemies, and domestic sympathizers with rebels.

3. We have struck the monster Secession its death-blow, and laid that malignant spirit in the Hades of perdition.

4. We have extirpated the Upas of slavery from the American soil and made her at once

"The land of the free and the home of the brave."

What our sires avowed in 1776, we achieved in 1865. The sun, as it rolls from east to west does not shine on a single slave. We rejoice to see this curse removed.

5. We have demonstrated the capability of our Republican Government for times of war as well as times of peace.

6. We have challenged the admiration of the world and commanded its respect, while the leading nations

have stood astonished at our patriotism, resources, and prowess.

7. We have shown that no State or combination of States, can rightfully resist a government of, by, and for the people.

8. We have demonstrated man's capability for self-government in his associated capacity.

9. We have shown that the spirit of freedom is the very soul of the Republic, and the genius of liberty still upholds our starry banner as the harbinger of the millennial morning, and the pledge of the latter-day glory of the sodality of humanity.

10. The terrible conflict has developed a purer civilization and the noblest national character the world has ever seen.

11. We have conquered our prejudices as well as our enemies, and acknowledged man's manhood before the law and before our God—a moral triumph, great as those achieved amid confused noise of warriors, and garments rolled in blood. We thank God for the liberation of an oppressed race in our midst, their elevation to their God-given rights of manhood and their enfranchisement. God said: "Give liberty to the blacks or be slaves yourselves." We have reaffirmed by the stern logic of events what our fathers declared in 1776, and now the dusky child of Africa claims his own, and the stars of our flag shed their cheering light on the humble cabin of the dark-browed son of the sun, who now looks up and says: "Am I not a man and a brother?" Yes, the sin of the world has been sacrificed, the crime of ages has been expiated. A slave breathes not on our soil. The sun of liberty melts his chains away wherever his feet press the soil of America.

12. Having put the National rifle and committed the starry flag into the hands of American citizens of African descent, and found them faithful, we will now intrust to them the ballot.

13. We shall bequeath this matchless land and her peerless institutions to our children, better, far better, than we received them from our ancestors, with the fond hope strengthened that they will continue.

14. By the practical assurance that we regard the public debt, contracted to save our National life, to be as sacred as the graves of our soldiers, we exhibit that sterling honesty which alone can exalt a nation; believing that the only debt that we can not pay is the debt of gratitude to God and honor to our most heroic braves.

With this review and prospect, comrades of the gallant Seventy-fourth Ohio Volunteer Infantry, let us close by singing the patriot's and the philanthropist's apostrophe to the glorious country whose synonym is found in our vindicated and perpetuated National motto, *E Pluribus Unum:*

> "My county, 't is of thee,
> Sweet land of liberty,
> Of thee I sing!"

CHAPTER XXV.

MORE FRAGMENTS OF CLERICAL LIFE.

IN 1845, when the obsequies of General Andrew Jackson were being celebrated in Cincinnati by appropriate ceremonies, I was standing on the corner of Fourth and Main Streets, looking at the procession marching in solemn parade to honor his memory. While my attention was diverted, I was robbed of my purse by a pickpocket. I did not seize him in the act, and only caught a glimpse of him as he was escaping. He was soon afterward apprehended. I identified him in open court, under oath, and yet he persisted that I never saw him till that time. His lawyer asked me if I could swear to each bill in the package found on the person of the accused. I told him "no," but that I could swear as to the amount, twenty-five dollars, the same amount as was found in the vest-pocket of the accused when arrested; that there was a one-dollar bill on the Bank of Wooster (the account of the failure of which bank I had read in the morning paper) that I could swear to. He handed me the one-dollar note of the broken bank of Wooster, and kept the rest as his fee for defending the culprit. The thief stole twelve hundred dollars that same day, was convicted of grand larceny, and sentenced to the penitentiary of Ohio for seven years.

After leaving Cincinnati, my next appointment was Columbus, Ohio. James B. Finley was then chaplain of the penitentary. As I stood in the pulpit to preach for him one Sabbath morning, I saw this very robber about eight feet away. After service he solicited an interview with me, which was granted in his cell, and he confessed to me that he was the man who had robbed me, though so persistently denying it in court. He said he belonged to a Christian family, members of the Baptist Church in Pittsburg. "But," continued he, "they do not know where I am. I got into bad company, formed drinking habits, and have gone from bad to worse, till I am here. This prison life is very injurious to me, and my health is failing." I prayed for him. Grace flowed like a stream of mercy upon him, and I fondly hoped that he was restored to divine favor, and renewed in the image of Christ.

I saw Governor Mordecai Bartley the next day about him. The governor heard me patiently; inquired into the case, and on Thanksgiving-day a pardon was put into my hands, which I conveyed to him, and the young man was restored to society, and went on his way rejoicing.

In 1852 I was a delegate to the General Conference, and on May 1st, I reached Boston, Mass., where the sessions were to be held, at two o'clock in the morning. I went to a leading hotel, and, not feeling sleepy, sauntered about the reception-room. Here I found a man speechless from a paroxysm of asthma. I relieved him by warmth and procuring for him potations of strong, hot coffee, till he was so recovered as to give me the key of his trunk, and ask me to take from it some stramonium. A thorough fumigation of it, with a pipe, gave him complete relief.

A port-folio taken from his trunk, as I searched for the dried herb, was plainly marked Rev. J. V. Watson. This was the first of my acquaintance with the Doctor. He insisted upon knowing my name, and when at last I said, "I am Granville Moody, a delegate to the General Conference which meets here to-day," he replied: "You are Granville Moody! Well, sir, you are not the kind of a man I took you to be, at all. I have known you from your opposition to pewed churches, and your constant advocacy of free grace and free sittings."

"Yes, sir," I replied, "that euphonious phrase is my short creed; since faith cometh by hearing, and salvation cometh by faith, I believe that furnishing the freest sittings is befitting a Church that offers salvation on the simple condition of genuine faith in Jesus Christ. The greater the facilities for hearing the gospel message, the greater the likelihood that more will hear and heed, obey and live. There is a philosophical and evangelical fitness in free grace and free sittings—a gospel harmony; and what God hath joined together let no man put asunder."

At the conference of 1863 a petition resulted in my appointment as pastor of Greene Street charge Piqua. I received a warm Methodist welcome, and, as most of the Church were outspoken in their loyalty to the country, I found a hearty welcome to an eminently patriotic and pious people, not least among whom was John Cheever. He was a native of New England, came from Boston, and was in every sense a square Yankee; bright, sharp, keen-visioned, self-reliant, enterprising, sagacious, painstaking, economical, and provident.

After a fall and winter spent amidst the glory of a protracted revival season in the Church, during which multiplied scores were awakened, and converted, and sealed, and saved as heirs of the grace that is in Christ, and all believing men, the spring season dawned with its healing and life-giving power, and I broached the enterprise of rebuilding the old church. It was a Gothic building, eighty by fifty feet. It contained a basement, six feet and a few inches high; an audience-room of seventy feet in length, and galleries on the sides and end. The first story was built of stone, with the walls two and a half or three feet thick. A small sonorous bell was mounted on a wooden building in the rear of the church. The whole contour of this corner building was unique, and marked well the severe manners of the times. A low pitched roof, barn-like in style, suggested that the building was "God's barn," and not inappropriately showed it to be the domicile of a large part of God's favored people; the shelter of the sheep of his pasture, and a home of the flock of his hand.

It had served well its purpose, and the times and needs of this charge indicated change and improvement; I talked to the people pastorally, and preached publicly about the necessity of a change in the Lord's house, and I proposed to raise the upper story nine or ten feet by screws, and build up a wall from the ground to fill the space, and thus furnish an ample basement for Sabbath-school purposes and class-rooms, and to add to the rear a two-story annex, which should contain an infant-class room of twenty by fifty feet, and up-stairs a pastor's study and two class-rooms. Then a bell-tower on the new front of the building would give room for a vestibule. The whole expense was estimated at ten thousand dollars.

Well, this created a division of sentiment, though two-thirds of the Church favored the forward movement. Brother Cheever was in the minority, and he opposed the movement with true Yankee vigor and persistence, arguing against incurring so much expense; and familiar as he was with current prices of every item in building, and the price of every day's labor, he forecast a mighty sum of indebtedness in the projected enterprise. He foretold dismay and disaster and defeat in any movement upon the old and established order of things. I persisted with the majority for advance. At length the third quarterly conference met, every member in his place. Business progressed steadily till the presiding elder called for the report of the trustees. Brother Cheever arose on a question of privilege, and said:

"Brethren, you will be surprised to hear from me this morning, that I am heartily in favor

of Brother Moody's enterprise of rebuilding the
church. Last Sabbath, and the evening of the
Lord's-day, found me in firmest opposition to the
whole enterprise; but the Lord has strangely
turned my mind. I retired to my bedroom and
prayed the Lord to help me to preserve the Greene
Street Charge from going into the wild enterprise
of building a new church in these troublous times.
But there was no voice, nor any that answered. I
then retired to my pillow, and prayed and prayed
again without effect. I then arose and placed the
lamp and the Bible on my large chair, and said:
'Lord, thou seest and knowest the scheme that
Brother Moody has in hand, and thou knowest that
in these times of war it is no fitting time for us to be
planning to build houses or churches. Thou knowest that materials and labor are high. Common
plank and better plank and other kinds of plank
cost about two prices, and paint and glass and putty
and chairs and carpets and lamps are at double ordinary prices. Shingles are so much per thousand,
and hauling costs twice as much as it did. And
now, Lord, I ask thee to show me my duty by
this appeal which I make on my knees to thee.
Thy Word is a light to our feet and a guide to
our steps in every perplexity, and we are in great
perplexity now. I appeal in this way unto thee;
I put this Bible, thy precious Word of truth, before my eyes. Now, Lord, when I open the Book
with my eyes closed, if the place opened upon shall
not refer to building churches, nor indicate anything in regard to building thee a church, then I

shall conclude that I am right and Brother Moody is wrong in urging us to go into building; but if the chapter I open upon speaks of building for thee a church or building for thy worship and service and glory, then, Lord, I shall conclude that it is thy will that we follow Brother Moody's advice, and I will submit my will to thine, and I will do my full share, according to my ability, in this new building cause. Amen.' Then I opened my eyes, and they fell upon this passage, the first chapter of Haggai."

He then read the chapter, and pledged his name to a full *pro rata* of the expense of remodeling that house of worship. The enterprise went on, and the church was remodeled accordingly.

While the author was serving this Church, the news of the victory at Lookout Mountain and Chattanooga was received at Piqua on Thanksgiving morning, November 26, 1863, after the congregation had assembled for worship. The report of what was said and done on that occasion is given in the following extracts from Cincinnati papers. The first is part of the correspondence of the Cincinnati *Gazette*:

The glorious news from Chattanooga this morning cheated the Rev. Colonel Moody out of the opportunity of delivering his Thanksgiving Sermon. The congregation had met at Greene Street Church in accordance with the President's Proclamation, had sung the "President's Hymn," taken up a collection of about sixty dollars for the Sanitary Commission, and our fighting preacher had scarcely got through

his introduction, when the *Gazette* arrived, was brought
into the church, and was handed to him by our
patriotic sexton. The preacher stopped, paused a
moment, and then shouted: "Glorious news!" He read
the headings of the telegraphic news, and said: "The
congregation will all rise. Now three cheers for the old
Stars and Stripes!" They were given with a will, and
the walls of Greene Street rang with the shouts of
sturdy old stewards and leaders. "Now let us sing,
all sing, 'Praise God, from whom all blessings flow.'"

When this was sung, the preacher said: "Now I
have too much good sense to think that you would
rather hear me preach than hear the news." So he
read the dispatches, with your editorial, which was frequently cheered by the congregation. . . . We are
to have a grand wood donation for the families of soldiers on Saturday. Governor Tod, Dr. G. V. Dorsey,
and others will be here. There will be a free dinner
and a flag for the school district bringing the largest
amount of supplies.

And the second extract contains still further
details of the part which the author took on that
memorable day:

After the usual exercises of singing and prayer
had been concluded, the Rev. Colonel Moody came
forward and made one of the most stirring, eloquent, and patriotic addresses ever delivered to an
American audience. Some of the points were so ad-
mirably made, and so fired the audience with patriotism, that they spontaneously gave way to applause,
forgetting, possibly, the decorum due to such a place.
But the colonel did not rebuke them. How could
he? Did he not know that they were enthused by a
pure patriotism, and such a manifestation was the

generous, manly, patriotic expression of loyal hearts? Yes, too well he knew it; and he considered it rather commendable than otherwise, and said it was a Methodist "Amen."

Such bursts of eloquence and patriotism rarely have we had the pleasure of listening to. Everybody was pleased; yes, everybody was completely carried away by the magnetism of his lofty patriotism and his sublime eloquence. It stirred the blood and hearts of the people to such a degree that I think every man, woman, and child present would then and there have willingly made a sacrifice of themselves for our glorious Constitution, Government, and flag. Doubtless Colonel Moody is a good fighter in the field. Such a man would always be brave, it is not in him to be otherwise; but methinks his place is the pulpit and the rostrum. He can serve his country better with his tongue than the sword. Let him then harangue the people, and if they have even a latent particle of patriotism in their composition, he will set it all aglow.

In the address which he made he spoke substantially as follows:

The appointment of a day of National Thanksgiving to Almighty God for the signal victories with which he has been pleased to crown our arms, especially during the last month, has summoned us into his presence, in his temple, at this hour. During the long period of our National prosperity but little attention was paid to the day of Thanksgiving; but that brightness has been suddenly and partially eclipsed. Scenes never before witnessed, and hardly deemed possible, have arisen before us. Hundreds of thousands of our citizens, with all the insignia and munitions of war, have been marshaled, and still the clarion sounds, and mightier hosts are mustering for the championship of this vast continent. On the one hand we find treason and rebellion—reckless, defiant, and rampant; on the other, patriotism and loyalty, with a deep conviction that not only the glory but the very existence of the Nation is at stake. Prompted by patriotism, our young men by thousands have taken the field, and the hoarse war-drum throbs on the National hearts. War is one of the four sure judgments of God which, in his providence, he brings upon a nation to rebuke its wickedness and to make it better and happier, or to destroy it, and leave its wreck a warning to other nations that righteousness "exalteth a nation, and sin is a reproach to any people."

On this day, set apart by the President of the United States as a day of thanksgiving, it becomes us to review the manifold blessings bestowed upon us by God, and cherish sentiments of unbounded gratitude to that benign Providence.

First. Let us this day be thankful to God for our paternity as a Nation. God raised us from pious and excellent ancestors. Almost every other nation rose from a base and degenerate origin.

Second. Let us be thankful that our recent victories have added new glories to the renowned flag of our heroic ancestors. A thousand precious and soul-stirring memories cluster round the old battle-flag,—

> "Our country's flag, with lines of blood,
> Forever telling as it waves
> How, side by side, our fathers stood
> And died, to plant it on their graves."

It is the glory-streaming banner that has so often flaunted defiance to our foes. This is the banner that the sons of South Carolina boast they were the first to dishonor and trail in the dust as eight thousand traitors besieged Fort Sumter.

Third. Let us on this day be thankful that God has recently vouchsafed to the army and navy of the United States those signal victories which warrant our faith in the perpetuity of the Government of the grandest Nationality on earth. With the greatest propriety we may exclaim: "Surely the lines have fallen to us in pleasant places." Our number, intelligence, and resources give us eminent rank among the nations of the earth. Our population exceeds thirty-five millions of souls, and our broad domain is washed by the waters of two oceans. Our census-table shows a duplication of our population in every cycle of twenty-three years; so that, by the time the infant now in the cradle will have reached manhood, our population will amount to seventy millions. One flag floats over the grandest domain on earth.

Fourth. Let us be thankful this day for the success with which God is crowning our efforts to sustain the Union of the States against secession, traitors, and rebels. Our fathers regarded the Union of the States a necessity. Their condition then and our condition now demand it. The Union was the creation of necessities—physical, moral, social, and political. The Union of the States in one Nationality is not merely because men choose that it shall be so, but because some general government must exist here, and no other government than this *can* or *should* or *shall* exist. This Government is the property of every citizen; it is his Government; he is a part of it; it was established for him, and is maintained by him; and he knows, or ought to know, that it is the only true and equal Government that does exist, and that no other government can be as just and equal as our own. By

this glorious Union we have gained all our distinction
and success as a people, and on its maintenance all our
peace and safety depend. Secession is dissolution, and
dissolution is National dishonor—ay, National death.
Secession is the hydra which Jackson battled against.
Secession is a claim that has never been admitted in
any organized government on earth. Secession! It
forgets the thrilling memories of the past. How
utterly unentitled to public confidence is a man or
party that would give the least countenance to those
who, with more than Vandal hands, would rend the
sacred Temple of Liberty from turret to foundation-
stone! Surely such a man or party is as much an
enemy to the Government as Davis or any other
plotter of rebellion.

How deep, beyond the heaviest plummet sounding, must that craven-hearted tool of bogus chivalry
have sunk, who boasts that in the darkest hour
of his country's peril, when men were baring their
brawny breasts to the storm of war, and trembling
women—mothers, wives, and daughters—were praying in secret places for their country's weal, that since
the 4th of July, 1861, he has not voted for an army or
navy appropriation bill; has not voted, and will not
vote, a man or a dollar to aid the Government in its
efforts to conquer those who have inaugurated deadly
war to compel this glorious Government of our fathers
to submit to its own dismemberment and destruction.
How execrable the man who prostitutes his abilities
to the work of prejudicing and poisoning the minds
of the citizens against the Administration which seeks
the maintenance of the Government against rebels
and their domestic and foreign sympathizers; who
speaks of our armies as "invading armies," when
marching on our own soil to maintain our own sover-

eignty against traitors; who counsels the "withdrawing" of that old flag and its heroic defenders from the proud front they occupy at Norfolk, Newbern, Hilton Head, New Orleans, Port Hudson, Helena, Vicksburg, St. Louis, Louisville, Nashville, Murfreesboro, Shelbyville, Manchester, Deckard, Tullahoma, Wheeling, Baltimore, and Annapolis!

Yet he would have them "about face," and meanly march in retreat over the bloody "fields where our glory was won," and ignore the victories of Carnifex Ferry, Laurel Mountain, Mill Springs, Fort Donelson, Island No. 10, Winchester, Pea Ridge, Stone River, and Gettysburg, saying in humiliation and grief,

> "O no, we never mention them,
>   Their names are never heard!"

And thus retreating from the surrendered soil now doubly dear and sacred, and our own by its baptisms of blood of brave and loyal men, we must leave our cherished rights and prized Nationality to the watershed argument of "their kind of a man," and to the decision of the Yanceys, Rhetts, Toombses, Breckenridges, Braggs, Pembertons, Johnstons, Yulees, Benjamins, Wigfalls, Wises, Cobbs, Floyds, Polks, Harrises, Jefferson Davises, and the devil. Leave the lamb with the wolf; leave the goose with the fox; leave gold with a thief; leave helpless innocence with the debauchee, when you leave our Nationality to the tender mercies of traitors and rebels, or elevate such a man to be governor of Ohio. Preposterous, outrageous, contemptible counsel! almost equaling the audacity of Satan himself, when he proposed to Immanuel, the Christ, to fall down and worship him, engaging to give the Savior the whole world, with all its kingdoms, as a consideration, when, poor devil,

he had no more right to the proposed gift than Davis and company have to the territory of the United
States, or the adviser of our National dishonor has to
the suffrage of a true patriot. Surely such a man is as
much an enemy to the unity of the Government as
Davis or any plotter of rebellion anywhere, and infi-
nitely less courageous and magnanimous.

Withdraw our armies from Maryland, Virginia,
North and South Carolina, Florida, Alabama, Mississippi, Texas, Missouri, Kentucky, Tennessee, and
Georgia; withdraw your gun-boats from the Mississippi, and your monitors and line-of-battle ships from
the coasts of the Rebel States, and leave the question of
our Nationality to Davis, Stephens, and Toombs! Was
ever such a proposition cherished in all the records of
sin in all the world? Surely of its author we may
exclaim: "Out ingrate, an hyperbole of meanness
would be an ellipsis for thee!" 'T will be a marvel
and a wonder if any shall be found so mean as to do
him reverence.

"The Negro, all dark in his glen,
    Is nobler and better than thou;
Thou standest a wonder and marvel to men,
    Such perfidy blackens thy brow.
If thou wert my brother by birth,
    At once from thine arms I would sever;
I would own thee nowhere upon earth,
    And quit thee forever and ever,;
And thinking of thee, in my long after years,
Should but kindle my blushes and call forth my tears."

But it is our rejoicing that whilst this would-be
governor of Ohio is counseling the withdrawal of
our armies, as he speaks, *ex cathedra*, from beneath
the folds of the British flag, and from British soil
fulminates his anathemas against our cause, Almighty
God, by the stern logic of events is saying to us, in

the recent victories of Vicksburg, Port Hudson, Tullahoma, Gettysburg, and the extinction of Morgan and his marauding bands, Onward and still onward with Freedom's banners, because of truth and righteousness in the earth. And for these signal tokens of God's approval we should be grateful.

During the session of the General Conference of 1864, which met in Philadelphia, Pennsylvania, I had the honor and pleasure, as a member of a committee of five, consisting of Bishop E. R. Ames, Joseph Cummings, George Peck, Charles Elliott, and myself, to bear the congratulations of the conference to President Lincoln on the general success of our country's cause. Our visit occurred during the battles of the Wilderness. On our trip from Philadelphia on the cars, the question was asked, How shall we proceed in Washington? I stated to the committee that if they would permit, I would take the document to President Lincoln and leave it to him to arrange the hour and detail of our interview. To this they agreed. I went to the White House and told the President's secretary of our presence and mission, and asked him to procure me an interview with the President, which he did with promptness and pleasure.

I was familiar with the President, and showed him the missive of the conference. He said: "Colonel Moody, how came you to do this? It is the very thing I would have asked you to do had I had your ear. I will give you audience at ten o'clock A. M. to-morrow. Just leave the address with me. I will study it to-night, and write my reply. Give my highest respects to the committee."

We were promptly received at the appointed hour and place by the President and his Cabinet. That group furnished a scene for a painter. In the center of the semicircle of his Cabinet, master spirits of the Nation, stood in all the angularity of his person, in all the simplicity, honesty, patriotism, and well-balanced self-will, with unpretending greatness and somber grandeur, ABRAHAM LINCOLN. There stood canny, courtly William H. Seward, Secretary of State; the short, solid, curt, statue-like Edwin M. Stanton, Secretary of War, who, amid all those dark and stormy times, stood like a rugged rock amid ocean surges, with thunders bursting o'er his head; Salmon P. Chase, dark, phlegmatic, significant as an oracle. On the opposite semicircle stood the kingly Bishop Ames; the learned Charles Elliott; the scholarly Joseph Cummings, President of the Wesleyan University at Middletown; the courtly George Peck, of New York, and myself.

Bishop Ames introduced his colleagues of the committee to the President and Cabinet and the distinguished persons present, stated the object of the visit, and requested the secretary of the committee, Dr. Cummings, to read the "Address of the General Conference," which he did, as follows:

To HIS EXCELLENCY, ABRAHAM LINCOLN, PRESIDENT OF THE
    UNITED STATES:

The General Conference of the Methodist Episcopal Church, now in session in Philadelphia, representing nearly seven thousand ministers and nearly a million of members, mindful of their duty as Christian citizens, take the earliest opportunity to express to you the assurance of the loyalty of the Church, her earnest devotion to the interests of the country, and her sympathy with you in the great responsibilities of your high position in this trying hour.

With exultation we point to the record of our Church, as having never been tarnished by disloyalty. She was the first of the Churches to express, by a deputation of her most distinguished ministers, promise of support to the Government in the days of Washington. In her Articles of Religion she has enjoined loyalty as a duty, and has ever given to the Government her most decided support. In this present struggle for the National life, many thousands of her members, and a large number of her ministers have rushed to arms to maintain the cause of God and humanity. They have sealed their devotion to their country with their blood on every battle-field of this terrible war.

We regard this dreadful scourge now desolating our land, and wasting the Nation's life, as the result of a most unnatural, utterly unjustifiable rebellion; involving the crime of treason against the best of human governments, and sin against God. It required our Government to submit to its own dismemberment and destruction, leaving it no alternative but to preserve the National integrity by the use of National resources. If the Government had failed to use its power to preserve the unity of the Nation and maintain its authority, it would have been justly exposed to the wrath of Heaven, and to the reproach and scorn of the civilized world.

Our earnest and constant prayer is that this cruel and

wicked rebellion may be speedily suppressed, and we pledge you our hearty co-operation in all appropriate means to secure this object.

Loyal and hopeful in National adversity, in prosperity thankful, we most heartily congratulate you on the glorious victories recently gained, and rejoice in the belief that our complete triumph is near.

We believe that our National sorrows and calamities have resulted, in a great degree, from our forgetfulness of God and oppression of our fellow-men. Chastened by affliction, may the Nation humbly repent of her sins, lay aside her haughty pride, honor God in all future legislation, and render justice to all who have been wronged! We honor you for your proclamations of liberty, and rejoice in all the acts of the Government designed to secure freedom to the enslaved.

We trust that when military usages and necessities shall justify interference with established institutions, and the removal of wrongs sanctioned by law, the occasion will be improved, not merely to injure our foes and increase the National resources, but also as an opportunity to recognize our obligations to God, and to honor his law. We pray that the time may speedily come when this shall be truly a republican and free country, in no part of which, either State or Territory, shall slavery be known.

The prayers of millions of Christians, with an earnestness never manifested for rulers before, daily ascend to heaven that you may be endued with all needed wisdom and power. Actuated by the sentiments of the loftiest and purest patriotism, our prayer shall be continually for the preservation of our country undivided, for the triumph of our cause, and for a permanent peace, gained by the sacrifice of no moral principles, but founded on the Word of God, and securing righteousness, liberty, and equal rights to all.

Signed in behalf of the General Conference of the Methodist Episcopal Church, Philadelphia, May 14, 1864.

President Lincoln bowed to the committee, and accepted the paper from Dr. Cummings, and pleasantly said: "Gentlemen, by the forethought and kindness of one of your committee, I had the pleasure of reading your noble address; and, as you have addressed me in writing, allow me to respond in like manner." He then opened the drawer of his desk and took out his response, which has thrilled the heart of the Nation, and was, indeed, an amaranthine wreath placed upon the brow of Methodism in that august presence. He said:

Gentlemen,—In response to your address, allow me to attest the accuracy of its historical statements, indorse the sentiments it expresses, and thank you, in the Nation's name, for the sure promise it gives. Nobly sustained, as the Government has been by all the Churches, I would utter nothing which might in the least appear invidious against any. Yet, without this, it may fairly be said that the Methodist Episcopal Church, not less devoted than the best, is by its greater numbers, the most important of all. It is no fault in others that the Methodist Church sends more soldiers to the field, more nurses to the hospitals, and more prayers to heaven than any. God bless the Methodist Church, bless all the Churches, and blessed be God who, in this great trial, giveth us the Churches!

At the instance of Solomon Howard, D. D., and others, and entirely without my knowledge, in 1864 the Indiana University conferred on me the title of Doctor of Divinity. This doctorate was an unexpected honor. I desire to be found worthy of it. The following letter conveyed to me the intelligence:

BLOOMINGTON, IND., July 4, 1864.

REV. G. MOODY, Piqua, Ohio:

DEAR BROTHER,—I have the pleasure of informing you that the degree of D. D., *pro merito*, was conferred upon you by the Indiana State University at the recent Commencement. No diplomas are given for honorary degrees at this intitution, but you will be officially informed by the secretary of the Board of Trustees. Truly and fraternally yours,

C. NUTT,
President of the Indiana State University.

In 1864, in the month of September, I was in Washington City, and met Hon. Samuel Galloway at the White House, and we were heartily welcomed by President Lincoln in his public office. We were invited to meet him that evening at seven o'clock in his private apartments, and we three had a singularly friendly and profitable interview. The President sat in a large easy-chair, and we at his right and left. We discussed in free conversation the times, the President leading the conversation. Among other things he said:

"I tell you, Mr. Galloway, Parson Moody's Church has wielded a controlling influence in these times. Her bishops, presiding elders, and pastors have a wonderful formative influence on the masses of the people. And then their controlling anti-slavery influence has leavened the whole lump. Her weekly papers make her ubiquitous and potential. We never would have gotten through this crusade without the steady influence of the Methodist Episcopal Church, so potential in its philanthropy. The Government is greatly indebted to Methodism in the cause of personal and national freedom. Her question, 'What shall be done for the extirpation of the great evil of slavery?' and her answer, 'We believe that the buying, selling, or holding of human beings, to be used as chattels, is contrary to the laws of God and nature, and inconsistent with the Golden Rule,' as well as her General Rules, discountenance or prohibit slaveholding. Mr. Wesley understood slavery when he said, 'American slavery is the vilest that ever saw the sun,' and when he declared the slave-trade to be the 'sum of all villainies.' The other Christian Churches hold similar views, but the Methodist Church was more outspoken, and unfrocked Bishop Andrew for becoming and remaining a slaveholding bishop; and that became the crucial test, and faithfully the Methodist Church met the issue that was thus episcopally forced upon it.

"But you ask me about emancipation. When Lee undertook to march his pro-slavery columns on the Northern and Free States, I saw a crisis was imminent; and when he headed his army for Antietam I saw that the dread and impending crisis was at our very doors. Gentlemen, I will tell you my experience. I came alone into this room, and knelt down, and with directness I told the Lord that Lee was marching on Washington, and was now on Northern soil, and said : 'Now, Lord, if thou wilt give him a backset, and our forces drive him back, and thus save our National existence, I will assert the inherent right of the National Government to conserve its own interests and preserve its existence by emancipating the slaves in the States in rebellion against the General Government. As slaveholders are actually using slavery to destroy the Nation, it is obviously and indisputably the right and duty of the Executive to destroy that which is and will be used as the means of destroying the National existence. Lord, if thou wilt discomfit, dismay, and defeat Lee in the coming conflict, I will abolish slavery as a military necessity. So help me God! I will. I ask this in the name and for the sake of Jesus Christ, our Lord. Amen.'

"Well, Lee was driven back into Virginia. The vows of God were on me to do as I had said. In this room I wrote the document, and four days after the battle of Antietam I called my Cabinet together to let them know my decision. I read the paper carefully to them, and paused for their opinions. There was ominous silence. At length Mr. Chase said it was premature; Mr. Welles agreed with him; Mr. Seward said it was right, but he thought it premature; Mr. Smith thought it would be ominous of ill; Mr. Blair advised delay; Mr. Bates dreaded its effects upon our armies in the field; only Mr. Stanton heartily agreed with my views, and said: 'Let it go forth and do its work.'

"I said: 'Gentlemen, I did not bring this before you for discussion, but to apprise you of my intention.' I then recounted my prayer and vow, and added: 'Gentlemen, God accepted my tendered pledge, and I hereby fulfill my vow.'"

During the years 1869, 1870, and 1871 the author was stationed at Grace Church, in Newport, Kentucky. His associations with the Kentucky preachers were pleasant, and he was well received by them when transferred to their conference. The following incident must be given in the words of another (Rev. Amon Boreing). O that God's historic people were chosen not only in Abraham but in Christ!

In the spring of 1871 the Kentucky Conference convened in Louisville. Rev. Granville Moody was in attendance, being at that time a member of the Kentucky Conference. The very handsome Jewish synagogue, on the corner of Broadway and Sixth Streets, had just been completed and furnished. Dr. Moody and myself, taking a stroll along the streets, chanced to pass that way, and the door being open Dr. Moody said: "Let's go in." We did so. Just back of the reading-desk, beyond the center of the synagogue, was a wardrobe, the door of which was open. Dr. Moody went up to it, took out the rabbi's turban, put it on, and said: "Now you sit down and I'll preach you a gospel sermon. You will find my text in the Gospel of St. John, first chapter, seventeenth verse: 'For the law was given by Moses, but grace and truth came by Jesus Christ.'" He briefly expounded the text, and then said: "This is the first, and perhaps will be the last, time you will hear Christ preached in a Jewish synagogue. And that is n't all; we had better be getting out of here."

We went to the church where the conference was held, and found a little cluster of preachers standing at the doors. Dr. Moody began to tell that he had on one occasion preached in a Jewish synagogue from John i, 17, repeating the outlines of his sermon just as he had given them to me. They did not believe him, thinking he was joking. He called me, and said: "Here is a man that was present on the occasion, and heard me." Of course I affirmed the truth of his statement. Then, after having as much amusement as he desired, he explained how it was.

Early in September, 1873, I arrived at Ripley, Ohio. At the conference session that year I had been appointed by Bishop Ames presiding elder of the Ripley District. The day after my arrival, whilst I was hard at work in the parsonage of the district, at about three o'clock P. M., a staid and courteous man entered the parlor and introduced himself as D. H. Hamilton, pastor of the Presbyterian Church. After the usual civilities, he said: "I have heard so much about you in this locality as an actor in the Church Militant, and as militant for our country as well, that I have waived all ceremony of introduction and come thus early to bid you welcome, sir, to Ripley, the theater of your former labors; and especially to welcome you to myself as a fellow-laborer in proclaiming the glad tidings of the gospel of our common Savior."

I was delighted with his style, manners, and spirit, and fully reciprocated the cordial greeting, and anticipated the joy and profit, proved in after years, of the society of this genuine Christian, polished gentleman, profound scholar, and original thinker. Strange to relate, within the lapse of ten short minutes we found ourselves enwrapped in the quintuple questions of Arminianism and Calvinistic dogmas. In that improvised disquisition hours rolled by, and still onward rolled, till that September sun went down the western sky, and bequeathed a parting smile on courtly theologic cavaliers, whose keen debate had not a single auditor beside the writer's beloved wife, Lucretia Elizabeth, who was cumbered with the multitudinous cares incident to our intinerant life, as we also were with cumbrous polemic lore. Her half-reproving glances and courtly smiles seemed to say that we were like Milton's fallen angels, who sat apart in discourse more sweet,

> "And reasoned high
> Of providence, foreknowledge, will, and fate,
> Fixed fate, free-will, foreknowledge absolute,
> And found no end, in wandering mazes lost."

At the closing of this singular interview, and with his apology for the interruption of a visit, we parted; and thus began an acquaintance which ripened into the firmest friendship, and bore the fruits of heaven upon earth.

In 1876 the writer was a member of the General Conference, which met that year in Baltimore. On the fourth day of the session the

Address of the Bishops was read. The following extract is made from a paper of the period:

The Episcopal Address read on Thursday morning is a document of more than ordinary force. It was well read by the senior bishop, Janes, who is believed to be the writer. A number of passages were strikingly eloquent, and elicited vehement bursts of applause. Of course it was eminently conservative in tone, giving little support to recent projects of reform. The manner in which the address was received would seem to indicate that the conference is preponderatingly conservative, but probably not so much so as to be unwilling for any modifications.

Brother Granville Moody gave us one of his finest specimens of Western eloquence immediately after the reading of the address. It was really one of the best things of the kind that we have heard for a long time— perfectly spontaneous, and poured forth like a mountain torrent, carrying everything before it. It raised the enthusiasm of the audience to the highest pitch. We give it here:

"Mr. President,—I stand, sir, in this presence, profoundly impressed with the magnificent address of our episcopate. I rejoice in the accuracy of its historic lore. I stand impressed with the profound philosophy of its acute analysis, its heroic grappling with the living issues of the day, and its masterly vindication of the strength of its positions, the justification of its instrumentalities, its grouping of facts, and its clear and keen logic; and I feel that this address belongs to the commonwealth of Methodism in both hemispheres and in all its branches; that it should go to every lonely cabin and every palatial residence; that it should be sent to the officers of our army and navy [laughter]; that it should be sent from center to circumference [laughter and applause]; that the President of the United States should be cheered by its utterances; and that its thunder-tones should fall like the knell of destiny on the ear of the octogenarian usurper of the headship of the Church of God at Rome, which belongs to Christ alone. [Laughter and applause.] I claim, sir, that this glorious address should be spread before the country until Antichrist and Antichristian influences shall be rim-racked and center-shaken [laughter] by its facts and reasonings and prolepsis of the future.

"Why, sir, the spirit that would have led an ancient Roman to say proudly, 'I am a Roman citizen,' leads me, under the same inspiration to say, first, I am an American citizen; and, secondly, I am a member of the Methodist Episcopal Church. [Great applause.] And as there is nothing so successful as success, which blesses everything it touches, let us thank our God for success, as portrayed in the Episcopal Address to which we have listened. And I thank God that this old historic Church, which antedates our Government in its organization, and whose organization in this city distinguishes Baltimore as the Mother of Methodism and the 'Monumental City,' shall continue to gather elements of power around the foundations of our glorious country in the future as in the past, till every citizen thereof shall say, 'May her influence be perpetuated while earth bears a flower or ocean rolls a wave!'

"Profoundly impressed with its paramount and permanent importance, I therefore move that this address be published in every Church paper under our patronage; that it be spread upon the pages of the *Daily Christian Advocate*, and that it be put in pamphlet form, to go where the paper will not go. I want a hundred to send to relatives and friends who are not members of this branch of the Church of Christ, but yet are interested in the spread of Christ's kingdom. I want to send a copy, handsomely gotten up, to my Presbyterian and Congregationalist and Baptist friends, that they may know that we are thoroughly abreast of the age in the furtherance of the gospel mission to the wide, wide world. I therefore move, if I can get a second to my motion, that the address be published as I have indicated."

This motion was seconded by Erastus O. Haven, and adopted. The pamphlet edition was, by vote of the conference, fixed at five thousand copies.

CHAPTER XXVI.

SUPERANNUATION.

HAVING finished his pastorate in Hamilton in 1880, the author was that year appointed to Jamestown, a delightful village in Greene County. While serving the charge during his second year, the fiftieth anniversary of his entering the ministry occurred. His friends in Jamestown and elsewhere took occasion to celebrate the event in a becoming manner, an account of which is here given. It is clipped from the Xenia *Torchlight:*

Last Saturday (March 4, 1882) was made the occasion of a very pleasant surprise to Rev. Dr. Moody, of Jamestown. The date was the completion of fifty years since he preached his first sermon. The occasion, with all its appointments, was truly delightful, and so perfect a surprise to the pastor (his wife was in the secret) that he was able to declare, "I had not even a scintillation of it. Let it never be said again that a woman can not keep a secret." Dr. Moody met the surprise without any undue excitement, but with a cordiality and quiet dignity of demeanor that were simply charming. After dinner Mrs. S. Y. Conwell read a short paper containing reminiscences of the Doctor's pastorate in Zanesville thirty years ago. Then followed speeches (timely, interesting, and beautiful) from several ministers and laymen. To all these Dr. Moody replied, as only he can, bringing smiles to the

lips and tears to the eyes of all present, while he could
not conceal his own emotion. In the course of his
remarks he paid one of the most exquisitely touching
and beautiful tributes to his excellent wife, the companion of forty-six years, which it has ever been our
good fortune to hear. To which Mrs Moody, with
humor, rejoined (truthfully, we suspect): "Pa never
could have got along without me." "Amen!" piously
ejaculated the devoted husband. About five o'clock
P. M., after singing, prayer, and benediction, full of
pathos, as well as devotion, the company dispersed
with many fervent hand-clasps, each declaring that
that day would forever be a green spot in memory,
and adding, "I am so glad it was my privilege to
come."

The following letter from his eldest daughter,
Mrs. Clifford N. Fyffe, was read on the occasion.
It is dated from 34 Washington Street, Norfolk,
Virginia, March 2, 1882, and is here presented, as
it gives an inside view of a pastor's life as it
appeared to a younger member of the family:

MY DEAR FATHER,—Mother writes asking me to
come home to be present on next Saturday, the fiftieth
anniversary of your entrance into the ministry. I
wish very much that I could. do so, but it is quite
impossible; so I write this letter instead, to say
that there is nothing in which I feel so great pride
and satisfaction as in the contemplation of your career.
Its length so unusual, its character so honorable, honored, and useful, surely make reasonable ground for
such feeling.

Having at the threshold of manhood met that wonderful experience, the conversion that so literally
"turned you toward and with" God, it was inevitable

that you should be "separated unto the gospel of
God" and become a "worker together with him."
Your mind being so uplifted by that experience, your
life had to be brought up to a plane where the
weapons of a carnal warfare lose their edge and temper,
and only the panoply of God can fitly arm for the
fight. The spiritual field is the grand arena whereon
can be exercised all knightly virtues, and surely the
opening was a vast one that the young State of Ohio
furnished fifty years ago, in its then almost pioneer
period, to the pioneer preachers of the Methodist
Church. Paul, their great prototype, in his "glorying" could not much outdo their claim. If he could
boast of "labors abundant, of journeyings often, of
perils by water, of perils by his own countrymen, of
perils by the heathen, of perils in the city, of perils
in the wilderness, of perils among false brethren, of
weariness and painfulness, of watchings often, of hun-
ger and thirst, of fastings and cold and nakedness"—
of all these things the early itinerants had also their
share, as well as that daily came upon them, as upon
Paul, the care of the Churches.

If there lacked to them the beatings and stonings,
the stripes and imprisonments, were there not the
"narrow means," the long absences from home on the
circuit, during which children might be born or slip
out of life—anxiety and care upon the points that
touch men most keenly? What would have rendered
such a life bearable but that they also shared Paul's
other and higher glorying, that "in spirit" they "were
caught up to the third heaven, and heard unspeakable
things, so that whether they were in the body or out
of the body they knew not?" Therefore they "took
pleasure in infirmities and distresses and necessities,
and found their weakness strength, and in all patience

39

wrought the work of apostles with signs and wonders and mighty deeds."

But life was not all hardship. There were not only spiritual but material compensations. A fair and fruitful land, dear and close friendships, a growing and broadening culture, and, as life passed and families grew, it could be seen that there were worse lots in life than to be a Methodist preacher's children. Yearly I grow more and more glad that I was one of that class. The Church gave us a steady, if limited, physical provision. We had always the parsonage shelter, food to eat, and raiment to put on ; and these, as well as our social status and educational opportunities, were really always of the best. In the educational matter we had both the Methodist Church and the State of Ohio at our back. Consider the children of any other class of men, and what better has life done for them than for preachers' children? That they are worse than other people's children has been said, but there is no foundation in fact for the statement. Take at random the children of any ten preachers in the Cincinnati Conference, and their careers will disprove the slander.

The itinerants' wives, on whom came their full share of life's hardships, the necessary strict economy, the frequent movings, the unaccustomed duties,— what women they were and are, the pick and flower of the choice Methodist families ! There never failed, at any appointment on the circuit, a " great woman," like her of Shunem, to say to her husband, with that pleasant authority that inheres in a beloved house-mother : " I perceive that this is a holy man of God which passeth by continually. Let us, I pray thee, prepare a little room for him, and set there a bed and a table and a chair and candlestick, and when he cometh he shall turn in thither."

It is the daughters of these women who had the
means and the energy that enabled, and the hospitable
souls that impelled, them to "constrain the servants
of God to eat bread as often as they passed that way,"
who are Methodist preachers' wives. Naturally selected "elect ladies," those of them who live, live to the
Lord and for the Church, as mother, and many others
whose names crowd the mind. Those who rest from
their labors died in the Lord, and their memory
is fragrant of faith and good works. Who that knew
them can forget the spiritual Mrs. Dustin, the gentle
Mrs. Simmons, the seraphic Mrs. Mitchell, the saintly
Mrs. Michael Marlay? Laid aside are the sober and
ofttimes hardly obtained garments of earth, and lo!
"who are these in bright array?" If ever, when
freed from earth, my robes are so washed and made
white that I may be one of the innumerable company
and Church of the First-born, I shall look through all
heaven's hosts for the Methodist preachers' wives, and,
with many I have known from the West and the North,
and some from the East and the South, I hope to sit
under the twelve-fruited tree on the banks of the river
that flows through the "sweet fields beyond the swelling flood." The rest will be very sweet to many, to
all of them, and yet I think none of them would have
chosen a different or easier life as they view it complete.

"A man's life," and a woman's also, "consisteth
not in the abundance of the things that he possesseth,"
but in the abundance of the things that he has done.
Measured thus, your seventy years outrun some centuries of selfish, easy, drifting life. Think of the sermons preached, prayers offered, the white-robed children, some of them now gray-haired men and women,
whom you have held with such always evident fatherly

tenderness in your arms, while "water sealed the covenant" of baptism ; the thousands whose married life began under your benediction ; the tens of thousands to whom your hands have ministered Christ's " broken body and shed blood;" the sick visited and comforted ; the dying to whom you bore " His rod and his staff;" the many graves over which you have read the precious words which rob them of their victory : " I am the resurrection and the life." Add to this the calls for comfort in sorrow and trouble, and perplexities of all sorts, and, besides, work in all departments of human interests, charity, philanthropy, temperance, social life.

Devoted to God and humanity, where was the time for self? Not even time when Willie died to go for one day into the "chamber over the gate," to weep and say, "Would God I had died for thee, my son, O my son !" And in the outset, when the first frail baby-blossom faded, the news brought many miles by a friendly rider, found you persuading men to be reconciled to their Father. And yet how truly the life lost for Christ's sake and the gospel's, has been found in high effort, noble aims, and glorious rewards ! There crowd for utterance many thoughts of that part of your life that lies within my recollection—changes like those of a kaleidoscope. Over some years hung the dim cloud of war, into which, impelled by as strong a "call" as determined you to preach, you went with the Bible in the hand which the sword had left free. Then the breaking of the family circle by death, the gradual dropping away into homes of their own of the rest of the children, the coming up of a little cluster of grandchildren, to whom you are patriarch as well as priest and prophet, and yet so humanly near that perfect love casts out fear.

You and mother stand, now, as alone in your home as when it was first instituted; but that was the cheerful and welcome isolation of youth and hope; this is the pathetic loneliness of age and memory. Even your children are growing gray, and see that the future is not for them as much as for the next generation.

Life has unrolled itself to you, and there is little new experience for you to pass through. Much of usefulness I pray there be yet in store for you, and comfort in the love and society of children and friends. The aftermath of a fertile field is not a small thing, and the closing years of life are its ornament and crown. If by reason of strength your years are fourscore, they will still belong to God and humanity, as all this half-century has done; and by whatever steps, gradual by nature's decline, or by the swift, sudden descent of disease, you come to life's close, those steps will have been ordered by the Lord, whose you are and whom you serve. And when soon or late, we, whom you reared and fitted for life, follow that inevitable path, in the words you have so often said and sung:

> "O may we meet, no wanderer lost,
> A family in heaven!"

At the close of this year the author felt that declining strength demanded his retirement from the active service of the ministry. Accordingly, at the session of the Cincinnati Conference, which met in Dayton, September 6th, he asked for and obtained the relation of superannuate. With regard to his superannuation the following extract is made from the Cincinnati *Commercial*. It is in the report of the conference doings, and is dated September 11, 1882:

Rev. Granville Moody this morning, through his presiding elder, Rev. S. A. Brewster, requested to be removed from an effective to a superannuated relation, and proposes to change his residence to the State of Iowa. The request coming from one so prominent, who had so long served the interests of religion and Methodism, produced a decided sensation among the conference ranks and with outside circles. Before the request was acted upon, Dr. Moody enlisted the absorbed attention of every one in the church in the following address:

"Dear Bishop and Brethren,—In consequence of failing health and diminished strength during the last three years, caused by the recurrence of the disease contracted in the army, from which I have never fully recovered, I deem it proper to ask to be relieved by you from the duties of an effective itinerant Methodist minister, and to be placed on the list of superannuated preachers of the Cincinnati Conference. On the first Saturday of last March my friends celebrated the fiftieth anniversary of my entrance upon the active duties of the ministry; and having served my own generation, and two successive generations as well, according to the will of God and the will of the Church, I deem it best to lay off the harness of an active and efficient ministerial life.

"I feel truly thankful to our bishops for the important trusts committed to my care in the succession of appointments, which I review with gratitude. My record is built into the history of the Methodist Episcopal Church in Ohio, both in the old Ohio Conference and since the organization of the Cincinnati

Conference in 1852; and what is better, my witness is
in heaven, and my record is on high. Their better
part was that which sprang from a loving heart. I
deem it my duty to say that, after fifty-one years of
careful and critical study of the Bible, I consider its
internal, external, and correlative evidences perfectly
conclusive; and I rejoice that I have not spent my
prolonged life in inculcating a system of religion of
doubtful or even questionable veracity, but one that
is demonstrated by prophecies fulfilled and miracles
performed, and is attested by personal experience;
so that,

> 'Tossed on a sea of doubt,
> Here is firm footing, here is solid rock;
> This can sustain us; all is sea beside.'

"I desire to add that in Methodism I have found
Christianity full-orbed, in its own glorious round of rays
complete, and I retire to veteran ranks with profound
sympathy and confidence in Methodism as a revival
of pure and primitive Christianity; and had I another
half-hundred years to live and love and labor, I would
gladly give them all to our Lord and Savior Jesus
Christ, and rejoice in such an economy as Methodism
affords for the utilization of means to its great end
of spreading Christianity over these United States
and all other lands, till our race should hear and heed
the gospel's gladdening sound.

"I have preached Christian doctrine practically,
and Christian practice I have preached doctrinally,
and am receiving 'the end of my faith, even the salvation of my soul.' I now propose to emigrate into
the State of Iowa, which, within a few weeks, carried
the Prohibition platform by a majority of more than
twenty thousand votes—the Massachusetts of the
West, with occidental improvements. I am going to

grow up with that great State, and find there the continuance of the discovered path to the true *Iowa* of heaven, as the Indian word Iowa means 'a home for evermore.'

"Farewell, my beloved and honored brethren in the ministry of reconciliation. Let me assure you of my high appreciation of your general worth, and believe me, that

'If ever fondest prayer
   For others' weal availed on high,
Mine will not all be lost in air,
   But waft your names beyond the sky.'

"Farewell, farewell—adieu! Be with and for God, and be assured that God will be with and for you. In the lovely State of Iowa think of me, and ever believe that I shall endeavor there to represent Ohio Methodism, which is fast coming into line with a prohibition huzza, and coming to stay."

On the conclusion of the author's remarks before the conference, a number of appreciative responses were made, and a special committee, consisting of John F. Marlay, William L. Hypes, John M. Walden, Richard S. Rust, David J. Starr, and William Herr, was appointed to prepare a suitable minute for the conference record. The committee presented the following report, which was adopted by a rising vote:

Rev. Granville Moody, D. D., having, on account of failing health, taken a superannuated relation at the close of fifty years in the active ministry, we, his associates, enter this minute upon the records of our conference:

1. Through all these years Brother Moody has been a faithful Methodist itinerant preacher, loyal to

our beloved Church, earnestly promulgating her doctrines and maintaining her usages; and, when required by circumstances, defending her doctrines and polity with all the force of an intellect remarkable both for natural and acquired powers.

2. His ministry has covered a most eventful period in the history of our Church and our country. He has actively participated in the movements which have resulted in the development of the connectional enterprises and educational institutions of our Church.

3. He bore a distinguished part in the great struggle for the maintenance of the Union, combining in himself the character of a devoted Christian and brave soldier, both in the camp and on the battlefield.

4. We rejoice that through his long career, with a positive character, a burning zeal for the right, and an earnest spirit ever placing him in antagonism to evil, he has maintained an unblemished Christian character.

5. We earnestly pray that, in his retirement from the active ministry, he may be comforted by the gospel he has so efficiently preached, and be sustained by the grace of God.

6. We trust that his valuable life will be spared, and that, in the good providence of God, he may be able to return to our next annual session and deliver his Semi-centennial Sermon, which we hereby request him to preach at that time.

In view of the author's long connection with the work of the ministry in Ohio, and his identification with the history of Methodism during all these years, John M. Walden moved that he be requested to prepare his autobiography for publication. The motion was adopted, and the reader has the answer to this request in the present volume. "If I have done well, and as is fitting the story, it is that which I desired; but if slenderly and meanly, it is that which I could attain unto." So

"What is writ, is writ;
Would it were worthier!"

The foregoing action of the Cincinnati Annual Conference marks the closing hours of my active itinerant life, after fifty years of incessant services in the ministry of the gospel of our Lord Jesus Christ, according to the will of God. That wonderful hour seemed a crisal one to me. It was *the* epoch of my eventful life. It seemed like a solemn pause in time, and I know of no hour which has so impressed me. I was laying off the harness, and yet I could not boast myself then, as I did not when I put the harness on at the age of nineteen years. Yet with tender tearfulness I was grateful to God for the opportunities he had afforded me to "hold forth the word of life," and that "I had not run in vain, nor spent my strength for naught." To God be all the glory; mine the endless bliss!

And now, pleasantly situated with my beloved daughter, Mrs. Mary Moody Boyd, wife of Rev. Hugh Boyd, D. D., Professor of Ancient Languages in Cornell College, Mount Vernon, Linn County, Iowa, in a pleasant apartment for myself and my precious wife, Lucretia Elizabeth Harris Moody, with ample provision for the rest of my life by the good providence of the Lord, who is my shepherd, I can say:

> "O sacred solitude, divine retreat,
>   Choice of the prudent, envy of the great!
>   Here, from the ways of men, laid safe ashore,
>   We smile to hear the distant tempest roar.
>   Here, blessed with ease, with business unperplexed,
>   This life we cherish, and insure the next."

It will be noticed that the conference requested the author to preach a Semi-centennial Sermon at the ensuing session, which was held in Hamilton. Concerning this sermon, the following extract is made from the correspondence of the Cincinnati *Daily Gazette*. It is dated September 4, 1883:

This afternoon Rev. Granville Moody preached his Semi-centennial Sermon. He is probably better known in Ohio than any other minister. His health is failing, and he will retire from the active service of the ministry. The announcement that he would preach his Semi-centennial or Memorial Sermon to-day drew together an immense crowd. The house was packed. The preacher, it was supposed, would give a personal sketch, and relate something of the history of his life, so well known, and yet so new at each rehearsal. But in this they were disappointed. It was a grand sermon, reviewing the life of Christ, his miracles, and the story of his love for fallen man. It was not Moody, but Jesus Christ. The venerable preacher never spoke more loving words of eloquence, or brought tears to the eye oftener than to-day. He was frequently interrupted by his associates in the ministry by cheering words and thanks to God. Said one gentleman, and he tells the whole story: "It was a grand sermon.

People came expecting to hear something of Moody;
but as he began fifty years ago so he ends to-day, always keeping Jesus Christ to the front."

At the next conference (1884) the author was
unable to be present. But his brethren there
kindly remembered him, and sent him the following
token of their regard:

SPRINGFIELD, OHIO, September 11, 1884.

REV. GRANVILLE MOODY, D. D.:

DEAR BROTHER,—The Cincinnati Conference, at
its last session, appointed the undersigned a special committee to convey their profound sympathy with you
as fellow-ministers, and as former fellow-workers in the
Lord's vineyard. We bear a lively remembrance of
your long years of arduous itinerant toil in the ministry
of the Lord Jesus. We gratefully recall your burning
zeal, and your great success in the fields you have occupied. We can never forget our hallowed and blessed
fellowship of toils and sacrifices and sufferings, both
in the conference and in the active itinerant service.

As those of us who are advanced in years recall
all this, we are cheered by your good example of
labor and endurance in former years, and by your
present abundant experience, in your retirement from
the active work of the ministry, of the sustaining and
comforting grace of Christ. Those who are but recently entering the itinerancy, and those who have
wrought in it but few years, are greatly impressed
and inspired by the noble record you have made, and
by the glorious eventide you are enjoying.

We rejoice in your past achievements. We are
glad you are " finishing your course with joy." We
all miss your familiar face and voice at our annual

sessions. We pray that your faith may not fail; that
He "who has begun a good work in you" will complete it fully; and also, and especially, that personally
you may find the promise fulfilled: "At evening time it
shall be light."

We are, dear brother, yours in the kingdom and
patience of Jesus.

THOMAS H. PEARNE, ⎫
WILLIAM YOUNG, ⎬ Committee.
JOHN F. MARLAY, ⎭

Soon after, the following resolutions of the
Ministerial Association of Boone District, Des
Moines Conference, held in Perry, Iowa, Novem-
ber 6, 1884, were sent:

To the REV. GRANVILLE MOODY, D. D., *Greeting :—*

The Ministerial Association of Boone District, Des
Moines Conference, held at Perry, Iowa, November 6,
1884, directed its secretary to forward to you the following expressions of regard:

1. *Resolved*, That we regret the inability of our
venerable brother, Rev. Granville Moody, D. D., to be
present with us in this association.

2. *Resolved*, That we are glad to welcome him as a
resident within the bounds of the Boone District.

3. We desire to express to him our high regard
for one who, for so long a period, has been prominent
and faithful among the Christian workers of our de-
nomination in the West; who, by his abilities and devotion as a Christian minister and patriot has challenged our admiration, and also stimulated multitudes
by his noble example and efficient labors; and we
trust that he may long be spared to bless us with his
wise and pious counsels, and that his declining years

may continue to be brightened with the blessed hope of the "better land."

B. F. W. COZIER, Presiding Elder.
W. W. McGUIRE, Secretary.

These two letters to me were very gratefully received. They showed that I still lived in the lively recollections of the members of the two conferences, and seemed to be a prelude to the Savior's welcome salutation: "Well done, good and faithful servant! Thou hast been faithful over a few things, I will make thee ruler over many things. Enter thou into the joy of thy Lord."

To hear one's commendations from such high source is as cheering, invigorating, and delightful as walking through an Oriental spice-grove, where every prospect pleases, and delicious fragrances vie with each other in exhilarating influences. It is and shall be my daily concern to "finish my course with joy;" and eternity shall then place its unfading stamp upon my name among the followers of the Lamb. *Resurgam!* I shall rise again! Amen! God grant me grace, through the remnant of my days, so to live and act that these welcome utterances may prove resonant of the Savior's final utterance to me—even to me! Truly religion gives part of its reward in hand, the present comfort of having done our duty; and for the rest, it offers us the best security that heaven can give.

"Happy the man," says the *Western Christian - Advocate*, in referring to the foregoing action of the Cincinnati Conference and the Boone District Ministerial Association, "happy the man who thus

enjoys the esteem of those who know him far
and near!"

One night, a few weeks subsequently (December 15, 1884), I had a dream or vision, and
an impression that came upon my mind as vividly
as if it were a divine communication or a revelation
from God. I was asleep to all but divine things.
God appeared to me, saying to my inner spiritual
consciousness, as though it were a communication
direct from God: "Because he hath set his love
upon me, therefore will I deliver him: I will set
him on high, because he hath known my name.
He shall call upon me, and I will answer him:
I will be with him in trouble; I will deliver him,
and honor him. With long life will I satisfy him,
and show him my salvation." Wonderful words
uttered to me personally, as I presume, and making known to me the mind and will of God in
my individual, personal case. I wondered, loved,
adored, and gloried in the Lord who had conde-
scended so low to me—even to me; and my soul
rejoiced in God, my father's God, my mother's
God, my own chosen God, before whom I have
walked amid all the changing scenes of an eventful life since the evening of Thanksgiving-day,
1831, till this fifteenth day of December, 1884—
fifty-three years of a busy life spent in the glad
service of God the Father, Son, and Holy Spirit, the
Three in One, and One in Three, who was, and is,
and is to be. Yes! the sacred, undivided Three
has bivouacked about me in all my walking
through this great wilderness, guiding, guard-

ing, warning, directing, cautioning, encouraging,
strengthening, cheering, and assuring me amid
multitudinous circumstances that have been a
kaleidoscope of wondrous scenes in harmonious
aspects, retrospects, and prospects, and then on this
momentous month, appearing in such an aspect of
tender love, addressing me as erst he addressed
David: "Because he hath set his love upon me!"

And now I do declare and subscribe to this
wondrous communication from God to me, and I
do hereby select those animated words of Holy
Scripture, found in Psalms xci, 14–16, inclusive, as
my funeral text, by whomsoever the sermon may
be preached, as declaring my privileges, prospects, and portion thus singularly revealed to my
mind, and specially pointed out to my perception
by our Lord Jesus Christ, for my comfort and confidence and full assurance of faith unto the end.
My prophet, priest, and king; my shepherd, friend,
and guide!—Jesus, and all in him, is mine.

For several weeks during the winter of 1885–86,
my wife was in failing health, and steadily declined. The following letter describes her condition at the date of its writing:

MOUNT VERNON, LINN COUNTY, IOWA,
January 17, 1886.

MY DEAR DAUGHTER ELIZABETH,—Your precious
mother, Lucretia Elizabeth Moody, for whom you
were named, still lives. She is reduced to a mere
skeleton. Her physician, Dr. Carson, has just left the
house (eight o'clock this morning). He hardly knows
in what befitting terms to express his mind with
regard to your mother's case, but thinks and hopes

that her condition is more hopeful. He is, however, quite reticent and guarded in venturing his opinion. He has been thus reticent for five weeks, last past. He is not sanguine of success in this case, nor has he been so from the incipiency of the disease. He is a faithful and competent and experienced and tender physician; yet he says: "Your wife has a vast power of endurance and vitality." What the *vis medicatrix naturæ*, or healing power of nature, may accomplish is unknown, but her power of endurance has been severely tested, developing great vitality and hold on life. It depends entirely upon the aid which God may send from on high if she weathers this continuous storm.

God's wisdom regulates the bestowment of power, and if he sees best he will say of her suffering: "Thus far shalt thou go and no farther, and here shall thy proud waves be stayed;" or, " It is enough, come up higher; enter thou into the joy of thy Lord." It will all be in mercy and grace to her, however bereaving and sacrificing and irreparable the loss may prove to us.

Precious saint of the Lord Jesus Christ, thy presence was our heaven upon earth, for the Lord was with thee continually. Thy absence will darken earth, thy presence will brighten heaven. On thy departure we shall be warranted in saying:

> "Forever with the Lord!
> Amen: so let it be;
> Life from the dead is in that word,
> 'T is immortality."

She was converted at a Methodist altar, Saturday evening, at Milburn's Chapel, Frederick County, Virginia, and joined the Methodist Church under the labors of the eminent Abolitionist, Rev. Edward Smith, in 1827, when she was ten years of age. She says she never had any trouble after that, but just went along and served God from love. Two weeks after her marriage she sought at God's altar in the Methodist Church, in Fulton, Ohio, the sanctification of her soul, and received that gift of grace in all its power and plenitude, exclaiming in rapturous joy, "I am so happy, so happy!" She has modestly but firmly confessed her complete salvation ever since, bearing a clear testimony to this salvation to the uttermost. Her experience has been continuous and abiding, and occasionally she has testified to this exalting and exalted state of grace spoken of by St. Paul, 1 Thessalonians v, 23-4.

We were married at her father's house (William Hickman Harris) on Buck Creek, four miles northwest of Springfield, Clarke County, Ohio, on Tuesday, January 19, 1836, by Joshua Boucher. We have celebrated our happy marriage days for the last forty-nine years; and if she survives two more days, we will celebrate the fiftieth anniversary of the ever memorable era of our early marriage. She has been better than I took her for, and the worst calamity to me will be her removal by death. But our loss and my loss will prove her immediate, indescribable, and everlasting gain—an exceeding great reward!

We celebrated our happy marriage for fifty years, completed the 19th of January, 1886; and seventeen days afterward my wife was not, for God took her. She died at the residence of our son-in-law, Professor Hugh Boyd, D. D., of Cornell College, Mount Vernon, Iowa. Having shared the vicissitudes and beatitudes of fifty years of itinerant toil in the Methodist Episcopal Church in Ohio, she accompanied me into this western region, and has outstripped me in her militant career, met the king of terrors, and gained her long-sought home, where the weary are at rest.

The following notice of her death is clipped from a Mt. Vernon paper:

At eight o'clock, Friday morning, February 5, 1886, Mrs. Lucretia Elizabeth Moody, wife of General Granville Moody, died in this city, at the residence of her son-in-law, Professor Hugh Boyd, of Cornell College. Mrs. Moody was in her sixty-eighth year, and she and her illustrious husband had just celebrated their golden wedding, they having been married on the 19th of January, 1836.

Her funeral services were held in the Methodist Church, of which her husband was an eminent minister of fifty-four years' standing, on Sunday afternoon, a large congregation being present, and also attending the funeral cortege to the cemetery. The pastor, Rev. F. B. Cherrington, impressively read the ritual as the casket was borne down the aisle to the altar, which was profusely arrayed in flowers and appropriate tokens of affection and of Christian faith. Rev. George Bancroft, of the Troy Conference, an ex-army chaplain, read the Scripture lessons, following with a most impressive and appropriate prayer.

The funeral sermon was preached by Rev. John Hogarth Lozier, of this city, who was an acquaintance of fully a quarter of a century's standing, and was General Moody's comrade and intimate associate during the war, having been by his side in battle, and having been the only chaplain in their brigade during part of that time, and being often assisted in preaching by Colonel (now General) Moody.

His text was John xiv, 4: "Whither I go, ye know." The chaplain graphically referred to Mrs. Moody's hastening from her Ohio home to the side of her husband, who had been four times struck with rebel balls in the battle of Stone River. He spoke of her work for the soldiers who survived that battle, mending both their bullet-torn garments and bodies as best she could. She was not the "good Samaritan" without the oil and the two-pence. He assured the large assembly of saddened hearts present that their numbers would be multiplied by tens of thousands as the tidings of this death should spread eastward among the hearts and homes that had enjoyed the benisons of her earlier life and labors. Such lives become so embalmed in the hearts they have blessed that their memory is forever superior to decay; while such devotion to God, humanity, and country so assimilates the soul to Christ as to render it quite at home with him. When such souls are parted from us, our spiritual vision traces upon the luminous pathway of their ascent the words of the text, "Whither I go, ye know."

General Moody, whose snow-white head has never bowed, save in courtesy, to any but his God, was bowed down with this grief in a manner that touched all hearts; yet he fervently thanked his Maker for so blessed a companionship for so many years.

The four great epochs of my wife's earthly existence are briefly these: Born February 26, 1818; converted to Christ November, 1827; married January 19, 1836; died February 5, 1886. To such as she the words of Longfellow are most applicable:

> "There is no death. What seems so is transition;
>   This life of mortal breath
> Is but the suburb of the life elysian,
>   Whose portal we call death."

When the Cincinnati Conference met the following fall, in Piqua, at the memorial service held in honor of those who had died during the year, William Herr read the following memoir of Mrs. Moody. It was prepared by Mrs. S. J. M. Conwell, who was a long time a faithful and intimate friend of the family:

Lucretia Elizabeth Harris Moody, beloved wife of Rev. Granville Moody, D. D., was born in Virginia, on the present site of Jordan, White Sulphur Springs, February 26, 1818. Her ancestral lineage, on both sides, was of the highest type, not only in social and civil relationships, but better far, in relation to Christianity and the Church of that early day. Mrs. Moody was born to a heritage in the Lord's house. Her sturdy father, William Hickman Harris, secured his noble wife by pledging the godly mother that he would "not hinder, but help Elizabeth to live a Christian life." This same maternal grandmother declared, in a love-feast, that she had been divinely assured that her children's children, to the latest generation, would honor God and love the Savior. Her faith, thus far, has been happily and wonderfully verified. Her name was Elizabeth Kurtz. She came from Germany when ten years old.

In 1831 Mrs. Moody was withdrawn from a ladies' seminary, in Winchester, Va., where she had been a pupil for two or three years, to be brought, as the teachers said protestingly, "to the wilderness of the West." But in this "wilderness," near Springfield, O., Mrs. Moody found her life's work—the labors and duties of which she cheerfully assumed, and performed, without swerving and without regretting, to the end of her earthly pilgrimage. She was keenly sensitive to the beauties of nature, and frequently spoke with enthusiasm of the delights of that westward journey, performed in a gig, accompanied by her oldest brother, while the parents and younger children followed in the family carriage and a six-horse wagon.

In January, 1836, Mrs. Moody was united in marriage to Rev. Granville Moody, her sorrowing survivor, and for half a century Brother and Sister Moody were earnest and pre-eminently successful coworkers in the itinerant ministry. Mrs. Moody was well fitted for her high calling. In a very peculiar sense was she a helpmeet to her companion, and an "ornament in the courts of the Lord's house." Her character, which was unique, impressed itself upon all who came within her influence. She had made excellent use of her early privileges of education; she was progressive, and always a close and correct observer. From an early age she was also endowed with a fine, discriminating sense, and a high quality of courage, which together, kept her invariably calm and self-poised. She possessed, also, a graceful and commanding presence, an intelligent perception of propriety, and a ready power of adaptation to surroundings and to the necessities of practical life. The following beautiful tribute is from the heart and pen of her eldest daughter:

"I need not tell you, my mother's friend, how perennial was the spring of her nature, how alive was every fiber, how acute each pleasure, how natural every emotion, and how unaffected its expression. She was full of all goodly conditions, and of infinite variety. Her tact was perfect, and never at the expense of entire truthfulness, which she gained in part by a wise reticence, both of word and act. She knew to speak, and, far greater knowledge, to keep silence. She knew 'how to be abased and how to abound,' and there was that in her nature that built a home round her, invisibly, intangibly, spiritually, even as she walked in strange places."

Mrs. Moody's Christian character was a rare union of duties and graces. Converted at a camp-meeting in Virginia at the early age of eight years, she was frequently known to say that "never for a moment since that hour had she doubted her justified relation before God and the power of divine grace to keep her faithful to the end." Piety seemed inwrought into the entire web of her life, and, suffusing itself over her whole being, was manifest in the smallest as well as in the great details of faith and duty.

In each of her husband's numerous appointments Mrs. Moody was heartily welcomed as the pastor's wife, and immediately entered, actively and zealously, into every movement to promote the interests of the Redeemer's kingdom. Especially was she interested in, and a happy co-worker with the young, in all their social Church organizations; and in the Sabbath-school, which seldom missed her presence, she was a power, felt and acknowleged by all. It was here that her versatility was most beautifully exemplified, and whether the exercises were of a social, devotional, or literary character, Mrs. Moody was equally at home on the occasion. There was that in her own freshness and sunniness of nature that allied her instinctively to youth, and this amiable disposition, going with her through life, kept her heart still young, as years made their passage over her head. The youngest daughter writes thus:

"Mother never seemed to be more vigorous and enterprising than in the last few years of her life, on

till last March, when I began to see that she was failing. She enjoyed life, too, as well as ever, and made
it such a bright and pleasant thing for all around her,
it was impossible to conceive that she should ever
grow old."

In her earthly, as well as in her divine loves, Mrs.
Moody was eminently practical. Joining industry to
devotion, it was her great aim to be useful, and to con-
duce daily to the comfort and happiness of all around
her. She used to say, pleasantly, "I have no time for
sentimentalities, you see; I love my dear ones with
my hands and feet."

In the memorable year of 1862, Mrs. Moody's
Christian heroism was subjected to the severest test;
but faith and patriotism rose to the occasion, and
nerved her for the sacrifice. Cheerfully, and with
brave heart, she gave up both husband and son to
their country's call, in defense of liberty and righteousness, and not even when the hazards and grim
possibilities of war rose before her as a black wall did
she waver or weep. During their absence from
home, Mrs. Moody disbanded her household in the
parsonage of Morris Chapel, Cincinnati, now "St.
Paul," and went to take care of her aged and feeble
mother, who was at this time living in the loneliness
of widowhood, in the homestead at Springfield. Immediately after the battle of Stone River, learning
from vague and uncertain sources that her husband
was among the wounded, and herself apprehending
the worst, she braved all discomforts and dangers, and
overcame all obstacles to reach him, which she successfully accomplished, traveling, in turn, by railway,
wagon, government ambulance, and finally on horseback, across the field of battle to General Moody's
own head-quarters, in the advance line of the battle-

ground, near Murfreesboro, Tennessee. Mrs. Moody
remarked that "that last stage of the journey, two
miles, might have been performed by stepping
from one dead horse to another, so fierce and fatal
had been the six days' strife of war." Here Mrs.
Moody remained for a fortnight, faithfully and ten-
derly ministering, not only to the needs of her
wounded husband, but to the lesser needs of tattered
and homesick soldiers in his command; and many a
"word, fitly spoken" to them, proved afterwards to be
as "apples of gold in pictures of silver."

The keenest sorrow of Mrs. Moody's married life
came to her in the death of her noble and promising
son, Lieutenant William H. H. Moody, topographical
engineer and staff officer on General Negley's staff,
who, having escaped the deadly weapons of war, yet
fell a victim to the cause, from disease contracted in
the army. He died in the summer of 1864, at the
family residence in Piqua, O., to which station his
father had been appointed by the conference, after
resigning his position in the army, and while himself
was on furlough because of impaired health. Under
the deep affliction of her son's death, Mrs. Moody was
the comfort and strength of all the family, bearing
her own share of sorrow with the Roman mother's
fortitude and the Christian mother's hope. The
sisters have since said : "We thought it impossible that
she felt our brother's death as keenly as we, because
she so controlled her anguish, and let no duty,
however small, pass, even at the very grave's mouth.
But when, later, she told us that 'for years it hurt
her to see the sun shine,' we knew better 'the depth
of her bereavement.'"

This great sorrow, as was apparent to all, brought
her into closer union with the spiritual and unseen.

Her piety wore a deeper and holier tinge. The grace of God, which abounded in her life, was more conspicuous in the spiritual serenity and cheerfulness of soul sustained in the midst of so sad a bereavement. Mother and son are both sleeping the sleep that "God gives to his beloved," in graves widely sundered by areas of earth; but their spirits, doubtless, are sweetly mingling in the celestial communion.

Another sore trial of Mrs. Moody's experience presented itself when her husband's broken health and extremely feeble condition made it necessary for him to ask a superannuated relation to this conference, thus ceasing from the active work of the ministry. But here, again, her supreme good sense and ready acceptance of exigencies, together with an unquestioning submission to the divine will, not only sustained her own spirit, but made her a strength and solace to her husband in the sorrow that well-nigh rent his soul. Lovingly and without fear she went forth with the grand companion and co-laborer of her life, to new scenes, and to smaller spheres of action; and our hearts ejaculated blessings on them as they went, and we knew that they who had been so faithful and successful in that which is much, would neither falter nor fail in that which is less. Their hearts clung ever "to the old friends," and, present or absent, were always loyal to them.

Last winter, about holiday-time, numerous and beautifully wrought cards of invitation were sent forth, bidding friends from every home of the past, to their golden anniversary wedding, which was to be celebrated January 19th, under the commodious roof of their son-in-law, Rev. Professor Hugh Boyd, D. D., of Cornell College, Mt. Vernon, Iowa. The kindly, sympathetic responses to those cards, that poured in upon them for days, by every mail, and reached our sister upon her couch of feebleness, proved a keen pleasure to her—a member of the family said, "one of the rarest delights of her whole life." The single regret was: "O, if I might only see them all!" But, alas! "how swift trod sorrow on the heels of joy!" It proved the last anniversary.

In the first stages of Mrs. Moody's decline, there seemed to be no particular disease, rather only a gradual and gentle exhaustion of strength. But friends were not deceived. Instantly husband and children recognized and reverenced in her that majestic grace of departing days that attends the going out of lofty and virtuous life.

Mrs. Boyd touchingly writes: "Mother came home to us last September, bright and cheerful as ever, but very frail. She continued to grow weaker every day, and by Thanksgiving-time was so feeble that I did not let her rise until after taking her breakfast; and then one day she did not feel like getting up at all, and that was the beginning of the end."

But days of intense suffering were in store for our dear sister, through which she bore herself with sweetness and resignation; though had it been the Heavenly Father's will, she would fain have lingered in life for the sake of the loved one, who, she felt, still needed her presence, and, in his increasing years and feebleness, more than ever. Once, when it seemed to anxious watchers that the death-angel had indeed come, her agonized husband said to her: "Wife, for you to live is Christ, but to die would be your gain." "Yes," she replied, "that is true; but there is work for me yet. You can not spare me; do not talk of my dying." Thus her thought was for others and not herself, even when face to face with the supreme solemnity. A loving watcher by the sick-bed said: "All through her sufferings she was her unselfish self, natural, transparent, clear as crystal, genuine, even in fever and delirium."

At last the messenger came in very truth, and was recognized simultaneously by patient sufferer and waiting friends. With the utmost composure, and with a loving smile for all about her bed, she brokenly articulated, in several attempts, "The Lord is my shepherd!" and stepped trustingly down into the dark valley, through which all who go must journey alone. The date of her death was February 5, 1886.

In connection with the foregoing memoir, Sylvester Weeks read a paper setting forth Mrs. Moody's adaptability to work, in connection with the Woman's Temperance Crusade movement. From that paper the following extract will be in place here:

Mrs. Moody's adaptability shone out most conspicuously in the "Crusade," which, like the "Day of Pentecost," brief in itself, yet put in motion a train of influences which shall move on till He shall reign "whose right it is." Dealing with good men who were conservative, with some impulsive men and women with views bordering on fanaticism, and with wicked men and women whose mercenary profits and sensual indulgences were interfered with, she, as the prompt and efficient leader, conducted the campaign successfully, without alienating a single friend or drawing upon herself the personal malignity of an enemy of the righteous cause. Dr. Moody, presiding elder of the district; Dr. Hamilton, pastor of the Presbyterian Church, and I, were frequently consulted as to methods, and often, after laborious ascent as we reached the summit of a conclusion, we found that her womanly intuition had carried her to the elevation, and she sat serenely waiting with unfatigued energy to carry forward the work. I shall never forget one scene in that ever-memorable movement. I had drawn, in colored crayons, a temperance design on the blackboard, and displaying it in the lecture-room of the Methodist Church in Ripley, whence the ladies started, after prayer and Christian conference, to plead with men as one pleads for his life to abandon their death-dealing business, she stood in her place between the front pew and the communion rail, her queenly form erect, her left hand extended toward the object lesson, of which she said, "The sight of the eye affects the heart;" her right hand, in entreating gesture, extended toward her sister-workers; her head, with its silvery crown of gray and brimming eyes, for a moment cast down as though weighted with its load of intense interest, then upward toward heaven, as though assured of the triumph of the right, received anew her baptism as the consecrated leader of the advance guard of the triumphing temperance and Christian host. Her power of adaptation was not the cunning of nature or the result of culture, but the grace of God to one willing and obedient.

[The author of the foregoing Retrospect did not long survive his wife. He died, as already related in the Preface, June 4, 1887. Many are the anecdotes told of his ministerial and army life, only a few of which he himself repeats, and most of them he gives in the words of others. Had the editor gathered up and included the reminiscences of Dr. Moody's friends and associates in the ministry and laity, this volume might have been extended indefinitely.

No man can paint a good portrait of himself, nor has the author done so here. We see his likeness dimly, and only in profile. But it is that of a master. He himself has departed, but his influence remains. Not more than once or twice in a century does such a man appear. By him the Church is widened, souls are gathered in, and humanity is blessed. The peculiarites and eccentricities of the actor are forgotten with the generation to which he belonged. The labors which he performed and the record of the words which he spoke belong to posterity. By these he still lives. Only when the Lord cometh to make up his jewels can his work be properly estimated.— EDITOR.]

THE END.